"LOOK AT THE EYES," THE CORONER SAID. "THOSE BLOOD VESSELS."

Laura didn't have to look: Cyrus's face in death remained indelible in her memory. "Exophthalmia," she said. "Protrusion of the eyeballs."

Together she and the medical examiner had quickly surmised that Cyrus had died from an acute hyperfunction of his thyroid gland—a condition known as thyrotoxicosis. All the symptoms added up. It was known as a "thyroid storm," and it was a very painful way to die.

"We'd better have a look in here," the M.E. mumbled. He began cutting at the anatomical structures around Cyrus's neck.

"His wife told me that he was apparently healthy one moment, and that he collapsed the next," Laura said. "That's what bothers me about the case. There was no warning and no previous indicators."

The M.E. didn't seem to hear; instead, he pulled the light down even closer, as though his eye had caught something.

"Strange," he muttered.

"What's that?" Laura asked. "What do you have?"

He held the tweezers up close to the light. The object it held was very tiny, perhaps only a centimeter across. "Look at this damned thing."

THE
ETERNITY CURE

HOWARD OLGIN

A Dell Book

**FOR JOSEPH AND MIRIAM OLGIN,
FOR AVIVA AND LANCE,
AND FOR THE PUPSTER**

*ADDITIONAL THANKS TO QUINTON SKINNER
FOR HIS CONTRIBUTIONS TO THE BOOK*

Published by
Dell Publishing
a division of
Bantam Doubleday Dell Publishing Group, Inc.
1540 Broadway
New York, New York 10036

ISBN 0-440-22456-X

Printed in the United States of America

Published simultaneously in Canada

November 1997

10 9 8 7 6 5 4 3 2 1

OPM

Foreword

The technology depicted in this novel was derived from scientific journals and theoretical conversations with individuals working in the fields of engineering and computer science. Many instances depicted have already taken place: the manipulation of single atoms to create a map or symbol; the design of a gear system built out of specially designed molecules; and devices with pincerlike fingers capable of grabbing on to bacteria. There has been much debate and speculation about the future of miniaturized technology; in many cases this ongoing inquiry has inspired concepts that led to this novel.

The sodium-pump mechanism is recognized as essential to the cell's integrity, though its mechanisms are largely unknown. The telomere is another tantalizing discovery from recent medical research with many possible ramifications. Advances in virtual reality are emerging with startling regularity every year; the applications of this technology as depicted in this novel have been extrapolated from real-world research taking place in the private and public sectors. The virtual-reality surgical training simulator, for instance, is being developed for market by a company based in the United States.

It's always vital, when contemplating or depicting advances in technology, to keep a steady eye on the moral implications that will arise for individual subjects. In no other discipline is this more true than in medicine. Every breakthrough brings potential—for good and ill. As one translation of antiquity's Juvenal has it: "All wish to possess knowledge, but few, comparatively speaking, are willing to pay the price."

Howard Olgin, M.D.
Los Angeles, 1997

PART ONE

Prologue

THE HOSPITAL ROOM WAS SILENT AND STILL, SAVE FOR THE flickering images on a television mounted high on the wall, its sound turned down. Light streamed through the windows over the lined and expressionless face of Allie Leonard.

She had suffered from Alzheimer's disease for the past four of her seventy-five years, a span of time in which her husband, William, had died, and in which her mind had steadily deteriorated. Now she could barely speak; only the inches-thick medical chart hanging from the foot of her bed attested to her lengthy and expensive treatment.

Deep within her body something started to go wrong. It was as though she wasn't alone; inside her cells a force floated amid the primitive chemical stew. An isolated sub-set of molecular proteins, designated for coagulation and clotting of the blood, were being produced in radically increased numbers. They poured from the cells, one after another, in a relentless progression.

Clots began to fill Allie's body. Her kidneys failed first, their blood supply cut off. The liver followed quickly, then her spleen. Her lungs began to contract spasmodically.

Her vital-signs monitors began to screech in warning. Allie opened her eyes with a flicker of recognition that something terrible was occurring. Her last thoughts came in a confused jumble as large clots blocked her left pulmonary arteries.

By the time the emergency team reached her room, she was dead.

July 20, 1997. Saudi Arabia.

STEVEN MAXWELL WAITED IN THE UNFORGIVING SUN, HIS hands bound behind his back, the unintelligible jeers and exhortations of the crowd growing louder as the moment of his public execution grew near. He wondered how the hell it had come to this.

The burlap bag covering his head made him feel panicked and claustrophobic; at least he didn't have to look into the eyes of those who shouted at him, and he was spared the sight of the sword that awaited him. In his final moments he had the luxury of reflection.

If he had to pick a moment at which everything had gone wrong for him, he would choose a late afternoon thirteen months before: a rare rainy day in Los Angeles, the clouds low and angry. He had taken the afternoon off from his medical practice and spent it with Angela Mason, a nurse practitioner at his private medical group. Walking Angela out to her car, he saw another vehicle approach. As though in slow motion he saw his wife, Laura Antonelli, rolling down her window.

He had cried out and chased her car down the quiet street where they had lived since their son was a baby.

Laura, a surgeon, had come home on break for a quick lunch. A coincidence, really. The divorce papers had arrived at his new apartment a week later. After all, it hadn't been the first time he was unfaithful.

Laura had cut him off completely, even restricting his visits with the boy, Carlo. Steve had tried to make a new start with Angela, but she was too young for him. He would wake in his apartment every morning, the weight of all that he had thrown away pressing down upon him. It became nearly impossible even to rise for work.

So the International Medical Corps, for other doctors a career dead end, had represented for Steve a new beginning. He was posted with a unit operating in conjunction with the military presence remaining in Saudi Arabia after the Gulf War. It seemed as good a place as any. He lived alone in a small room, dispensing antibiotics and treating heat exhaustion during the day. He spent nights alone, drinking.

He had just begun to feel something resembling peace when he returned home from his duty rotation one evening and found the Saudi police waiting for him. He had laughed when they handcuffed him, thinking they had discovered the bottle of Jack Daniel's in his locker. He thought they intended to put a scare into him in the name of Allah, but he soon understood they weren't playing games. After receiving an anonymous tip they had found nearly two pounds of opium sewn into his mattress.

There was no real jury at his trial, and his lawyer had assumed his guilt and offered little defense. Steve had "confessed" hours after his arrest, following a beating so severe that he feared his spleen had been ruptured. A young woman in her early twenties from Amnesty International had arrived after his conviction, to take notes on his case. She told him what he feared most: that the U.S.

government was taking no action on his behalf. The State Department wasn't willing to expend political capital on behalf of a convicted drug trafficker.

Now the voices screaming in Arabic grew louder; Steve felt the barrel of a rifle press against his back. He walked forward, nearly tripping when he reached a small set of stairs. He began to breathe faster, the acrid smell of his dehydrated breath lingering in the cloth of his cowl.

It was almost humorous. Steve was no saint. His devout Catholic ex–mother-in-law, in a phone call after his divorce from Laura, had coldly listed his failings in a cold voice: he was a drinker, a liar, an adulterer. He had also cheated on his taxes and verged on committing insurance fraud during his final days at his practice. But he was no drug smuggler. He hadn't even known what opium looked like, until they produced the evidence at his trial.

He felt sweat trickle down the back of his neck. When he looked up, he could see the enormous yellow sun diffused through the cloth. A hand pushed him from behind and he fell to his knees.

There had been a lot of time to think. His execution had been delayed by a good piece of timing: a moratorium on beheadings during the *hajj*, or pilgrimage to Mecca, followed by *Eid al Adha*, the Feast of the Sacrifice. He had spent this respite alone in a six-by-eight stone cell, rummaging his memory.

Then he had remembered: the plane. It was unmarked, its engines idling on airstrips designated for military transport. After getting drunk one evening, he had wandered out to the airfield and interrupted a few unfamiliar soldiers unloading cargo from the craft's hold. His arrival had started a small panic, and the moment he had seen a faded hammer and sickle on a steel crate he had wished he had stayed in his quarters.

A deep voice chanted just behind him. Hands pressed his shoulders forward, and he felt hard stone against his chest.

His eyes erupted with light as the cowl was pulled off his head. The sun had never been so bright. His last thought was of Laura and his son. He would never see them again.

January 26, 1998. Tashkent, Uzbekistan.

COLONEL DMITRI BOLKOV LOOKED IMPATIENTLY OUT THE window of his Aeroflot plane, wishing the pilot would hurry up and get the damned thing off the ground. He had never felt comfortable in the Asian republics, even when his position in military intelligence had lent him a special cachet under the Soviet Union. Now that these republics had broken away, he had heard that Russians had been subject to hatred and even violence. These new nations wanted to erase all memory of their time spent under the heel of Moscow.

Bolkov had groaned when he first saw the itinerary that sent him through Tashkent upon his return from Teheran. At least the trip was nearly over. Soon he would be home with Nadia and his daughters. After he had been debriefed, he would take his family to the amusement center at Gorky Park. The children could ride the Ferris wheel and he and Nadia could paddle a boat and be together.

The plane began to taxi onto a free runway. Finally. Bolkov allowed himself a sigh and began to spread his papers on the open seat beside him. Many passengers were packed into the main cabin ahead, but Bolkov had been booked into a cordoned-off rear section assigned to military personnel. Much had changed in Russia, but the power of the army hadn't.

Soon the dusty streets of Tashkent receded below his window, replaced by the rugged stone landscape of Turkmenistan. Bolkov pulled out his notepad. The day before he had had his first contact with the Iranian government; expecting to meet a band of wild-eyed clerics, he met instead with worldly, educated, and highly intelligent men. They had intimidated him.

The meeting had been cordial and polite, a reaffirmation of the tentative goodwill that had been developing between the two nations. Until one minister, a heavily bearded man named Hafez, made a polite suggestion that Moscow find a way to more firmly control its stores of weapons-grade nuclear materials. Bolkov, hiding his surprise, had asked his interpreter to repeat the comment.

The comment had been particularly surprising, because Bolkov had uncovered inventory irregularities among two former-Soviet nuclear stockpiles. He had initiated an investigation just prior to his trip to Iran—an investigation that he had kept secret until he could find concrete evidence.

Bolkov looked across the plane aisle at his aide, Veronski, who was already asleep. They had discussed the issue over caviar the night before in their hotel. Veronski, who knew nothing of Bolkov's investigation, had agreed that the Iranians would never have mentioned such an issue without substantiation. The generals in Moscow would not be happy. As usual, it would be up to Bolkov to find a way to present this information without setting off a reaction against his own staff.

Putting down his pen, Bolkov searched in his bag for the small bottle of vodka he had saved for the long flight home.

As he bent over, the wall of a major blood vessel in his brain gave way with a silent rush of pressure.

Bolkov coughed once, his mind exploding from within, and slumped over. He was thirty-eight years old.

June 20, 1998. Washington, D.C.

THE SPECTATORS IN THE BALCONY, MOSTLY TOURISTS HOPING for a glimpse of democracy at work, stared down in silence at the heated debate taking place on the United States Senate floor. Senator Drexler of Nebraska had just ceded the floor to Senator Patterson of California. Anton Dunleavy, a page in his first week on the job, looked down at the richly ornamented carpet and stifled a yawn. It seemed this day would never end.

On the floor the debate centered around the military budget for the coming year. Patterson, a man in his early seventies with a mane of white hair whose normal speaking voice was an abrasive, accusatory growl, pondered over his notes. He seemed distracted and unfocused.

"What I seem to be hearing from my respected colleagues," he said in a slow voice, "is that we as a nation should sit back and gloat now that we have won the Cold War. They should bear in mind what happens to nations who believe that they no longer have enemies."

Anton sat up straighter in his chair. This job had had promise on the first day, when he was awed by the aura of power in the huge chamber. By lunchtime he had realized that government moved at a glacial pace.

Patterson leaned against his podium and directed his gaze at the majority leader. He rubbed his temples. ''I'll sign off on this budget, but I'd be happier if it were ten percent higher. Ask anyone in the military—they'll tell you the effect these cutbacks will have on morale. Any talk of the alternative plans suggested by . . . You'll have to pardon me. I don't feel well.''

A murmur passed through the room as Patterson suddenly gasped into his microphone. The legislative body, almost as one, turned in their seats to see what had happened. Anton watched Patterson's shoulders quake under his drab brown suit jacket.

''Senator!'' a woman called out, and Anton leapt into the aisle. He took the stairs three at a time. Patterson sank to the floor just before Anton reached him; the old man clung to the podium with an age-spotted hand. A moment later he released his grip with an anguished sigh and fell to the carpet.

A crowd instantly assembled around them. The skin of Patterson's face was flushed a deep mottled crimson. His eyes bulged in their sockets and looked into Anton's without recognition. Anton loosened Patterson's collar, feeling the skin around the senator's neck burning hot above the throbbing veins of his neck.

Around them was an eruption of voices. Anton held Patterson's shoulders tight to the floor as the old man began to spasmodically convulse. Patterson's eyes rolled back into his head, exposing whites darkened with cloudy spots, and then the senator suddenly vomited.

Anton tried to roll Patterson over to keep him from choking, but by then it was over. With a horrible groan Patterson choked and fell limp. His quaking, out of control a moment ago, stopped. Anton closed the senator's eyes, recoiling when he saw the web of spots around his eyes and temples.

Senator Patterson's staff would later say that he had seemed ill all morning—he had suffered from a headache, nausea, and feelings of confusion. He had refused to see a doctor, because he had felt it was vital he speak to the Senate that afternoon.

Coroner's reports would indicate that Patterson's death was caused by an adrenal crisis: an acute hormonal imbalance creating a flood of adrenaline into his central nervous system. It was an agonizing way to die. The condition typically comes about from meningococcal infection, and is known as Waterhouse-Friderichsen syndrome. In this case, however, doctors found no sign of bacterial infection. They surmised that the hemorrhage was a result of old age or an undetectable birth defect.

Within days Robert Chapman, a wealthy Los Angeles entrepreneur, flew to Washington to assume Patterson's Senate seat. Though he had been considered Patterson's successor as a candidate in the next elections, he now assumed the job two years early.

1

DR. LAURA ANTONELLI SCRUBBED HER HANDS WITH DISIN-
fectant soap in the surgical wing of Los Angeles's Valley Memorial Hospital. She caught her reflection in the
mirror: a woman in her mid-thirties, her figure obscured by
drab blue surgical scrubs. Her unruly curls of black hair
were tucked into a paper cap. She had the characteristic
dark eyes and fine nose of her Sicilian family, with a full
mouth that now curled into a smile beneath her paper
mask.

"Looking good for a single mother," she said.

Another surgeon bustled abruptly to the sink next to her,
turning on the tap and pushing out a handful of orange
soap. "Talking to yourself is the first sign of madness,
Antonelli," Mike Peters said as he carefully scrubbed his
fingertips. "Not that I'd mind. Maybe then you'd have
dinner with me."

Laura carefully dried her hands with a sterilized towel,
trying not to blush at having been caught examining her
appearance. "Very funny," she said. "Why are you in here
so early? I thought you never worked before noon."

Peters shrugged. "Hip replacement. Seventy-year-old female. Slip and fall. What about you?"

"Laparoscopic adrenalectomy," Laura said.

"That's a fine way to start your day," Peters said, now meticulously cleansing the backs of his hands. "Will it be your first?"

"There's nothing like the first time," Laura said.

"Nervous?" Peters asked, checking himself in the mirror.

"Of course not," Laura said with mock indignation.

Peters laughed. "Way to be."

Of course she was nervous. The procedure was extremely delicate; removing the tumor perched on Roberto Delgado's adrenal gland entailed deadly risks. It was unlike an ordinary cancer: if she touched or squeezed the tumor too hard, she would send countless adrenaline molecules into the patient's bloodstream. Delgado's blood pressure would shoot up rapidly, potentially blowing out the blood vessels in his brain or heart. Successful removal of the tumor wouldn't mean she could relax either; a sudden fall in adrenaline levels could send the patient into irreversible shock, leading to death through kidney and liver failure.

"No problem," she said to herself as she approached the operating room. She added a silent prayer for a successful operation.

Inside the OR the surgical team was in place. Laura extended her arms before her, feeling a tug as Nurse Benson wrapped her in a surgical gown and fastened it behind her. Laura held out her hands for sterile surgical gloves, working them around her fingers until they were a second skin.

On the steel table Roberto Delgado lay draped in blue cloth, his abdomen exposed and covered with orange antiseptic jelly that the nurses referred to as "slime." At his feet were two trays of surgical instruments and a sizable mound of gauze pads. Laura let her gaze drift the length of the patient's body to his face. His features were slack with the deep slumber of anesthetic. His eyes were covered with cotton wads and taped shut. His autonomic body functions paralyzed by the anesthetic, Delgado's breathing was entirely dependent on a hissing, rhythmic respirator.

"Good morning, Doctor," Gerald Stokes said. The anesthesiologist, a tall man with thick glasses, made a notation in his logbook. "We're prepped and ready."

"Thanks, Jerry," Laura said. "How are the kids?"

"Back in school, out of my hair," Stokes said, glancing away from his life-support monitors. "And how's your boy?"

"Oh, Carlo's fine," Laura said. "This week he wants to be a pro basketball player. I keep waiting for him to say he wants to be a doctor."

Stokes chuckled quietly. Dennis Martinez, the assisting surgeon, took his place on the other side of the table from Laura.

"Well," she said, willing her voice to remain steady, "let's get started. Nurse, I'll start with a scalpel."

"A fine choice," Martinez said, his eyes creased ironically above his mask. Martinez knew that she would be nervous, trying a delicate surgery for the first time. The day before, he had reminded her that he had assisted on five laparoscopic adrenalectomies.

"See one, do one, teach one," Laura said. "Right, Dennis?"

She made a one-inch incision on the patient's abdomen and pushed a gas nozzle through the opening. Soon Delgado's belly began to slowly expand.

"Everything steady over there, Jerry?" Laura asked.

Martinez met her eyes from across the table, and between them passed a tacit understanding. Gerald Stokes was not among the best anesthesiologists at the hospital, and they both knew it. His presence for her created a sense of anxiety that Laura certainly didn't need.

She tried not to dwell on the fact that she had requested a different anesthesiologist—it was a train of thought that would only distract her. It was just another example of the cost-cutting, budget-conscious mentality of Ellington-Faber, the HMO that ran Valley Memorial. Stokes lacked the level of experience she needed for this procedure, but his fees were lower than the two anesthesiologists' she had suggested.

"Looking good, Doctor," Stokes said, making another notation.

The patient's abdomen was soon fully distended into a rounded dome. Laura removed the gas nozzle and pushed a cylinder through the incision. With the flick of a switch she activated the laparoscopic camera and light housed on the end of the device. She turned to the video monitor placed at eye level beside her; there was a precise view of Delgado's abdominal cavity.

"No sign of spreading to the liver," she said, moving the camera slightly. "Let's see—stomach, duodenum, intestine, gallbladder—it all looks good." Scanning into the pelvis, she saw no distal recurrent metastasis—spread of the tumor from the adrenal gland.

Laura handed off the laparoscope to Martinez and made a quick series of ten incisions across the patient's midsection in a boxlike pattern. "Trocars," she ordered. Nurse Benson handed over the ten trocars—elongated plastic tubes that tapered to a point at the bottom—and Laura shoved them through the incisions one at a time.

Still focused on the video monitor, Laura pushed a

grasping tool through a trocar into the patient's belly, used it to isolate the area around the cancerous gland, then passed the device to the second assisting nurse.

"Hot scissors, please," Laura said, and pushed the instrument through the trocar. She thought of the Delgado family: Roberto's wife, his three children, his mother, his aunt—they were all waiting in a lounge outside to hear if the operation was a success. They reminded her of her own close-knit extended family.

"Tilt the patient left-side up," she ordered.

Stokes wheeled his chair away from the monitors to the patient's side. "Got it, Doctor," he murmured. "But let's be careful here. His blood pressure is very fragile, as you know."

"I know it," Laura said a little too harshly. "But it's good to be reminded."

Martinez gave Laura a pointed look as he moved the laparoscope into better position. There were two ways to approach the left adrenal: directly through the abdominal cavity, pushing the intestine aside; or from behind, the retroperitoneal approach she would attempt this morning. She had been successful in trials on laboratory pigs, but now she could afford no errors. A wave of realization passed through her, a sense of her power and responsibility.

Laura watched her instrument on the video monitor, magnified twenty times, as she dissected tissue away from the structures surrounding the patient's kidney. The room fell silent, save for the rhythmic hiss of the respirator and life-support monitors, when Laura attained a clear view of the kidney and, atop it, the smooth violet adrenal gland. On the corner of the gland was a hard, nodular tumor, just as indicated on a preop CAT scan and X-ray.

She could see in her mind's eye the adrenaline pouring

into the patient's system as a result of the tumor. Delgado had come to her office complaining of high blood pressure, facial swelling and discoloration, and persistent blinding headaches. Blood tests subsequently revealed catechol-amines. The diagnosis became pheochromocytoma, a dangerous tumor pouring adrenaline and other precursor hormones into his system. Now that she saw the object itself, manifested on the screen, Laura inhaled deeply. How the tumor had come into being, and why it had grown as quickly as it had, were twin mysteries.

"Careful," Stokes said. "Blood pressure 140/80 . . . 180 now."

Laura moved her instrument closer to the tumor. "Lower the IV fluids. We're about to take the tumor out."

She shifted into a state of complete concentration as she dissected the three arteries entering the gland from behind the kidney.

"Damn it," she hissed. "Got a bleeder." A red streak of blood slashed across the screen. The assisting nurse jerked with shock, jiggling the grasper she held. "Steady, now," Laura said in a calm voice. She inserted two clips and stanched the blood vessel.

"Irrigation," Laura ordered. "Let's stay sharp here. This is the critical phase." Nurse Benson inserted an irrigation tube through a trocar and cleared away a small pool of blood gathered near the kidney.

Laura clipped and ligated the remaining vessels; now she was ready to remove the gland and tumor. "We might have some pressure on the tumor here, Jerry," she said to the anesthesiologist. "The patient's blood pressure might go up. Be ready with the Regitine."

"You're doing good," Martinez whispered.

Her elbows cocked out to either side of her body, Laura squeezed the adrenal gland with a grasper and used hot scissors to cut the final strands of tissue connecting it to the upper pole of the kidney.

Stokes called out, "Blood pressure 180/60 . . . 240 . . . 310."

"The Regitine. Now!" Laura shouted. She cut away the remaining tissue fragments, then pulled the severed gland out of Delgado's body through a trocar and handed it to the scrub nurse.

"Okay, we got it," she said. Martinez sighed deeply and adjusted his hold on the camera. "Now we have to watch out for dropping blood pressure."

"Oh, shit!" Stokes cried an instant later, fumbling his logbook. "Pressure's at 20/0. Now there's no pressure. I can't get him back!"

"Fluids and adrenaline, Jerry. Now!" Laura said, looking at the monitors. Delgado had slipped away in mere seconds.

Stokes knocked a vial of chemicals off his anesthetic cart; it fell to the floor and shattered. "Hold on!" he said, almost pleading. "I have to find another one—"

Laura turned to the scrub nurse. "Adrenaline. Now." In an instant she was passed a long, thick syringe. Laura pressed her hand on Delgado's chest and felt for the proper spot on his breastbone. Tensing her arm, she shoved hard and pierced Delgado's diaphragm, injecting the adrenaline directly into his heart.

Stokes spoke after a long pause, "Blood pressure's at 130 . . . 140 . . . 150. It's steadier now. The pulse is at 80."

"He's going to be okay," Martinez said, glaring at Stokes. "But that was a sorry display. You make your living dealing with crucial situations just like that one."

Laura ignored them, trying to calm the hard pounding of her heart. She paged the pathologist over the hospital intercom and peered at the pheochromocytoma lying under bright surgical lights. The tumor was hard and irregular, almost defiant in its deadly mass.

"I'll close on this one," Martinez said when she returned to the table. His intensity of a moment ago had vanished. "This guy's going to make it, thanks to you. Good work."

"Thanks, Dennis," she said, snapping off her gloves. She knew that Dennis had been under financial stress lately; she had even heard that he had resorted to gambling in an attempt to stay afloat, taking desperate weekend flights to Las Vegas and betting on sports.

Stokes sat before his life-support monitors, staring at his log. Laura thanked the rest of the team, including Stokes. His mistake hadn't caused any serious trouble, mainly because the scrub nurse had possessed the foresight to keep a backup syringe of adrenaline on hand. The total loss of time had only been seconds.

Still, Laura felt stinging anger. The anesthesiologists she had requested wouldn't have made that error; they were experienced, and cool under pressure. Unfortunately, no one at Ellington-Faber cared about such intangible qualities—as long as the numbers added up. It seemed as though every day now featured a new hassle with the HMO bureaucracy.

Laura decided to try to forget about it. She stepped through the automatic doors leading out of the surgical suite toward the waiting room. She would have the pleasure of telling the Delgado family that Roberto would survive. Sometimes she felt as though she lived for such moments.

2

THE DRIVE HOME, IN TYPICAL L.A. FASHION, WAS HELLISH. Laura figured that the five o'clock rush would be impassable, so after she made it over the crest of hills leading out of the San Fernando Valley, she got off the freeway and decided to take surface streets to her mother's house.

She had outsmarted herself. The cars on Bundy Drive were lined up for miles, their drivers waiting impatiently for the complicated four-way traffic lights to finally allow them to push farther into the gridlock. Laura gripped the steering wheel and tried to maintain her cool.

She had filed a complaint immediately after the adrenalectomy. While she had tried to word it so that undue blame wouldn't be placed upon Jerry Stokes, she wanted to make sure that Ellington-Faber knew she was unhappy. She was certain her complaint would end up with all the others she had filed—in a trash can, or in a filing cabinet that no one ever opened.

Ellington-Faber had bought Valley Memorial six months before; everything had changed almost from that day. Laura's patient base and referrals had switched over to the new system. Valley Memorial's specialists and general physicians soon began to air the same litany of complaints in staff meetings: they were losing their autonomy, some were losing work, and their incomes were all shrinking. Within weeks every physician was on his or her own, making do within the new bureaucracy as best they could.

Some physicians hadn't cooperated with Ellington-Faber—particularly when they learned the HMO expected them to lower their fees by as much as ninety percent. A number of doctors had already left the hospital to seek work in an uncertain job market. Others kept their heads down and tried to stay afloat. Their office staffs were dwindling, and whispers of bankruptcy replaced more mundane gossip in the staff rooms and cafeteria.

It seemed she heard a new sad story nearly every week. One doctor, Julius Teiter, a gynecologist Laura had known for years, had closed his local practice and headed for Louisiana. The last Laura had heard, Dr. Teiter had waited more than a year for his Louisiana license. Other physicians had begun to spread themselves thin with multiple commitments, trying to generate income. Some had begun gambling, as Dr. Martinez was rumored to have; Laura had been astonished recently to hear hushed phone calls in the surgical lounge. A new vocabulary was emerging, with talk of beating the spread, and markers and margins.

Laura reached into her briefcase at yet another interminable red light and found the blue rubber ball she kept there for emergencies. Engines and car horns blared all around. She squeezed the ball, trying to work out her stress through repetitive motion.

Laura had always had troubles with authority. The nuns at her parochial school had pegged her as a troublemaker when she was only thirteen. They hadn't understood that she had no problem with the powers that be, as long as they were just and fair.

Which Ellington-Faber wasn't. They had instituted a pricing structure on surgeries—as well as a system of bidding that encouraged undercutting fellow surgeons—that had resulted in Laura's receiving as little as one fifth the amount she used to charge for her work. She had decided she would have to work harder, increasing her caseload in order to keep her and Carlo fed and sheltered without dipping into the money she had saved to send him to college. She had lobbied for more patients and played by Ellington-Faber's rules, thinking she would make the best of a bad situation.

Two weeks before, she had seen a document that had nearly crushed her. While looking through a surgical roster she had examined the patient sheets for that day. She found a black mark on two forms. Looking closer, she saw that someone had crossed her name from the box reserved for surgical referral; in its place another doctor's name was handwritten. Ellington-Faber was utilizing its total control to cut her out, farming out procedures to surgeons they preferred. She had realized that she was now subject to the whims of a faceless system that could wear her down without ever giving a reason why. They were trying to take away her very livelihood.

The blue ball lay on Laura's car seat when she finally turned onto a familiar Santa Monica side street. She parked at the end of the narrow driveway adjoining the Antonelli family's small two-story home.

A warm smell of garlic bread engulfed her as she stepped through the front door into the living room. For a second she allowed the little parlor to transport her into the past—the matching red upholstered chairs and sofa, the faded paneling, the framed photographs of long-dead Old World relatives. Laura, in her blue suit with leather handbag, remembered being the girl that grew up within these walls. She felt continuity, love, and a sense that everything would somehow be all right.

Bounding from the kitchen came her son, Carlo, a short, thin boy with his mother's dark, curly hair and glinting eyes. She knelt to embrace him and give him a kiss.

"Oh, God, Mom," he said. "Cut it out."

"No way," she said. "For a ride home you have to pay the toll."

A clatter of cookware resounded from the kitchen. Laura gently put Carlo down on the floor, where he fussily adjusted his uniform dress shirt and slacks. "Grandma let me have some wine," he proclaimed.

"Is that right?"

"Listen to the little man telling stories," Maria Antonelli said, appearing in the kitchen doorway, drying her hands on a dish towel. "Don't worry, *cara,* he had one sip. And it was watered down."

Laura kissed her mother's warm, dry cheek. "How are you, Mom?"

Maria led her daughter into the kitchen with a wave. *"Bene, bene.* I walked a half mile today, just like you told me to."

Laura accepted a cup of coffee from her mother. Maria opened the oven and looked inside, releasing the smell of fragrant bread. Laura realized she was starving. "Tony and Louise should be home from work soon. You should stay and see them," Maria said distractedly.

Before Laura could remember, the Antonellis had moved from Brooklyn to Los Angeles, where her father worked as a family doctor until his death in the mid-eighties. Vincent Antonelli grew up in New York, but he met Maria on a trip to Italy, which was her home for her first twenty-two years. Maria still lived in the same house her husband had paid off in the sixties, sharing the place with her son, his wife, and their two children.

"What are you dreaming about?" Maria asked. "You're a million miles away."

Carlo came in from the front room, holding Maria's old gray cat and looking bored. "When are we going?" he asked.

"Soon," Laura said. "How was school?"

"Boring," Carlo said, rolling his eyes.

"Tell your momma what I taught you," Maria said, taking a sip of wine and setting a cooking timer.

"Mi madre," he recited, *"è molto carina."*

"Very pretty?" Laura said teasingly. *"Non bellissima?"*

Carlo squirmed uncomfortably; Maria laughed. "Well, go look in my briefcase," Laura said. "I brought you some magazines from my office to help you with that report on Bosnia."

The boy turned on his heels and skipped toward the living room. The old cat came along with a whine of protest.

Maria smiled. "He's a smart boy. He came here after school and did all his homework without me making him."

"He wants to watch baseball on TV tonight," Laura said. "He knows the rules."

It was remarkable, Laura thought, how quickly she had regained her equilibrium through routine, overcoming tragedies and setbacks as though they had never happened. It had been just six months before, about the same time that Ellington-Faber had announced their takeover of Valley Memorial, that Laura had learned that her ex-husband had been executed in the Middle East.

"You're thinking of Steve, aren't you?" Maria said.

She set a foil-covered tray on the table; leftovers for Laura and Carlo to take home.

"How did you know?"

"I just do." Maria craned her neck and looked through the doorway to make sure Carlo wasn't listening. "You used to have the same look when he was out running around on you."

Laura knew her mother didn't mean to be hurtful. Steve had been irresponsible, a drinker who wasted his aptitude for being a physician. He had been unfaithful probably more times than she knew. When he left for the Middle East, Laura had experienced a premonition that she would never see him again.

"You know I never liked him, I told you that enough times," Maria said. "But I'm sorry, especially for Carlo. A boy needs a father."

Throughout her bad marriage—the inattentiveness, the infidelities—Laura had tried to stay strong. Only once had she slipped. Like all doctors, she had access to a wide variety of medications. A year before she finally divorced Steve, she realized that the pills she took in order to sleep had evolved into an array of sedatives and alcohol that she required to get through the day. Steve had been good about it, taking care of Carlo while she endured a ten-day rehab program. In a sense Laura's brush with her own weakness had made her stronger, perhaps lending her the fortitude she needed to finally divorce her husband.

"I'm sorry, let's talk about something else," Maria said. "Why don't you stay here tonight? Tony wants to see you. He and Carlo can watch the football game on my television."

"Baseball, Mom," Laura said, smiling. "And thanks, but I want to get home. It was a hard day."

"You need a bath and some peace and quiet," Maria said. She kissed her daughter's forehead. "I understand."

"I just remembered something," Laura said. "I have to go out of town two days from now. Is it all right if Carlo stays with you? It'll be just for one night."

Carlo appeared in the doorway, his attention divided between *Time* magazine and their conversation. "Well, let me see," Maria said with a wink. "Do I have room for one little boy for a night? I don't know."

"That's all right," Laura said brightly. "I could just have him sleep in the zoo, with the lions and bears."

"Cool!" Carlo exclaimed. He ran across the linoleum floor.

"Looks like it's time to take someone home," Laura said.

"It will be fine," said Maria. "Tony can take him to school."

"Thanks. I'll be in San Diego. I'll leave a number."

"San Diego!" Carlo cried out, wrapping his arms around Laura's waist. "Sandy Eggo!"

"I'm delivering a paper at a conference there," Laura told her mother. "I'll be driving down with Ferry Tafreshi."

"I hope she leaves that husband of hers at home," Maria said.

"Cyrus is coming along. He's giving a talk to drum up business for their new surgical simulator." Laura sensed she was losing her mother's attention; the older woman preferred to remain blissfully unaware of any advance in technology beyond the digital clock. "Anyway, Cyrus is a good man. You'd like him if you gave him a chance."

"I know about people," Maria said. "Your friend Ferry is a very good girl, but that husband of hers is trouble."

Dropping the subject, Laura kissed her mother good-bye. The drive home was relatively easy; Laura hummed along with the radio while Carlo read news articles for his report.

She promised herself that she would spend more time with him in the coming weeks. To hell with Ellington-Faber and memories of Steve. Carlo was her life, and she was the only parent he had. She pledged that she would never allow any harm to come to him, even if it meant giving up her own life.

3

"EMILY, WHERE THE HELL ARE MY CONGRESSIONAL COMMIT-tee rosters? Of all the damned things to lose."

Bob Chapman waited in the doorway of his new office in the U.S. Capitol with a pile of files in his hand. His tie was coming undone, and he felt the first stirrings of caffeine withdrawal; his coffeepot, along with a number of vital documents and files, were still lost in unpacked boxes following his hasty move from Sacramento to Washington.

His assistant, Emily—a woman in her early thirties dressed in a sharp green suit with white hose—looked up from a half-full crate in the reception area. "They're around somewhere, Bob," she said. "We had to pack and move the entire office in two days. You can't expect everything to get back to normal on the first day."

Chapman took a deep breath. Emily was right. And from her tone he knew she understood the true source of his anxiety: he had been thrust into the U.S. Senate with no warning. He worried that he might not be ready for the daunting responsibility facing him.

"Well, try to find the coffeepot first," he said. "Or go down the hall and find some. I'm going crazy here."

Emily was about to respond in her typical long-suffering fashion, when the outer office door opened. A man in a medal-spattered deep blue military uniform walked in carrying, miraculously, a box whose label proclaimed that it contained a brand-new drip coffeemaker.

He stepped over a pile of cardboard boxes and extended his hand to Chapman. "Colonel Neil Reynolds, U.S. Army," he said in a deep, formal voice. "I want to welcome you to Washington."

"Thank you," Chapman replied. When Reynolds drew near, he stood a full head taller than the tyro senator. The colonel's hair was cropped close, military style, over his broad forehead and expressive green eyes. Chapman noted Reynolds's broomstick-straight posture and, almost unconsciously, corrected his own.

Reynolds stared at him expectantly. "Perhaps we can go into your office," he said. "Perhaps I could have a few minutes of your time."

Emily stood up from her work and pressed the wrinkles out of her skirt with her hand, staring at the Colonel. "Emily, would you hold my calls for twenty minutes or so?" Chapman said.

Once inside his office Chapman closed the door firmly and motioned toward a chair across from his desk. "Sorry about the mess," he said.

"I understand," Reynolds said. "You had to move on short notice. It must have been difficult getting organized."

Reynolds placed the coffeemaker on Chapman's desk. Chapman waited for Reynolds to break off eye contact; being the focus of the colonel's gaze was somehow intimidating.

"I'm with the Army Medical Research Center," Reynolds said in a flat voice. "I'm also a medical doctor, specializing in high-technology solutions to surgical problems."

Chapman sighed. "Neil, why are we pretending that we don't know each other?" he asked.

A flash of dismay crossed Reynolds's features; then he smiled, a slight curve distorting his thin lips. "Practice," he said.

"Practice for what?"

"Use your imagination," Reynolds said. As if speaking to a child he continued, "Lesson one in Washington: Appearances are reality. Not many people know of our association. Now that we have you in a prime position to exert some influence, we have to be very careful."

Chapman felt—as he often did with Reynolds—as though he didn't comprehend an essential subtext to their conversation. Reflexively, he chewed on his knuckle.

"Relax, Bob, it's your first day," Reynolds said amiably. "How about hooking up that coffeepot? I could use a cup. Look inside the box, there's a pound of ground coffee inside."

This wasn't how the day should have started, Chapman thought. This was his first afternoon as a United States senator. He now was one of a hundred men who would set policy for the entire nation. He was inexperienced, but he could educate himself as he went along.

Already Bob Chapman felt a familiar sensation—that things were slipping away from his grasp, and that he hadn't anticipated the costs of his compromises. He had grown up in a solid family, with convictions of patriotism and faith. He had endured a tour of duty in Vietnam, believing that his country's actions were just and good. He had entered politics cognizant of the public trust, concentrating on how he could contribute to a nation founded on ideals and justice. At times it worked that way; most of the time it didn't. It filled him with an anger that gnawed at him during fitful nights.

Chapman stopped unpacking the coffeemaker. "What did you just say?" he asked. "That 'we' have me in a prime position? What the hell was that supposed to mean?"

Through the closed door Chapman could hear his office phone ringing continuously. "Keep working on that coffee," Reynolds ordered. Despite himself Chapman found himself obeying. "As for what I said, Bob, I'm sure you understand. Our enterprise is dependent on three factors: cash, connections and know-how abroad, and domestic influence. Your recent appointment makes us much stronger in the latter category."

Chapman stared into the colonel's eyes, trying to discern what Reynolds might be thinking. It was impossible. The man was too sharp, too impermeable. He realized that he truly despised Reynolds, with a depth of emotion that transcended all of his previous dislike for the man. He hated Reynolds's officiousness, his arrogance, even his starched, spotless uniform. Most of all, he hated finding himself already utterly and completely beholden.

"Well, I guess it was a lucky break for us," Chapman said weakly.

"Senator," Reynolds said, crossing his legs, "there's no such thing as luck. Remember that."

Outside the window a jet plane banked in the distance, far from the restricted airspace over Washington. When he realized Reynolds didn't plan to elaborate on his cryptic comment, Chapman plugged in the coffee machine. He was hating Reynolds more by the moment and, he realized, he had good reason.

"How's your family?" Reynolds asked. "And your other business interests?"

Watching coffee pour in a stream into the pristine new pot, Chapman said, "My family is none of your concern. And as for my business ventures, I've placed them with a holding company while I'm here in the Senate. I won't have time to oversee my portfolio, and I need to avoid any appearance of conflict of interest."

"Good," Reynolds said. "You're thinking about your image. That's the first intelligent thing I've heard you say all morning."

Reynolds accepted a cup of coffee and walked to the window, staring out with a stiff, imperious bearing. "I wanted to tell you," he said. "I'm going to southern California this evening, for a medical conference in San Diego. While I'm there, I plan to drop in on Jefferson Faber."

"What business do you have with Faber?" Chapman asked. "Has anything changed regarding our arrangement?"

Reynolds smiled. "If I didn't know better, I'd say you sounded suspicious just now," he said. "Don't worry, Bob. The three of us are partners. You may hate me, but you need me. And I need you."

"I don't hate you," Chapman said, looking away.

"We were on the verge of being honest, you and I," Reynolds said, seeming sincerely crestfallen. "Well, I plan to speak to Jefferson about information I've received that might jeopardize our enterprise in the future. His role is crucial, and probably the most prone to failure."

"That's all you're going to tell me?" Chapman felt his heart leap. "Our futures are locked together, and you're just going to hint around that something might be wrong?"

"I'm sorry, Bob," Reynolds said. "It's an old habit. The military is accustomed to being vague with the legislative branch."

"Don't be funny," Chapman snarled. He felt as though

whatever control he had exerted over his own life (and when was the last time he had truly been in control? A year ago? Two?) had completely vanished. Reynolds was like a sorcerer, holding up mirrors until Chapman couldn't be sure if what he saw was real.

"That's flattering. People always told me I lack a sense of humor." Reynolds began to pace the floor. "Bob, it's no great secret. We had minor trouble during our first operation, and now we're initiating a second. We can't expect to repeat the same plan over and over, never changing, without eventually attracting notice. We had a close call in Saudi Arabia last year, and we have to be extremely cautious regarding our new route of transport. We have to stay very sharp. Do you follow me?"

"Of course," Chapman said, though he didn't, not entirely. All he understood was that Reynolds had arrived twenty minutes ago and stolen from him his dignity and his conviction that his Senate seat represented a new beginning.

"I'm glad," Reynolds said, condescension creeping into his voice. "We should count our blessings. First the meddling Russian, then the American doctor. Now Senator Patterson has stepped aside. The cold hand of death seems to work on our behalf."

Scanning his memory, Chapman's mind raced. The Russian colonel: Reynolds had said, six months before, that an officer in the former Soviet Union might present an obstacle to them. The subject was never brought up again. As for the American doctor, he had heard only fragments from Faber and Reynolds about what had happened. And as for Patterson, the old man had died of natural causes. What in the world was Reynolds going on about?

"There's no such thing as luck," Chapman said blankly, not really sure what he meant.

"There you go," Reynolds said. He stood and clapped Chapman on the shoulder. "I think we're making some progress with you."

"Stop talking to me like that," Chapman said. He roughly pushed Reynolds's hand away. "I *don't* know what you're talking about, and I don't want to know. As a matter of fact, I regret ever meeting you. I'm a United States senator. I don't have to listen to this shit."

Reynolds adjusted one of his medals an imperceptible centimeter. "I'm glad you got that off your chest, Bob," he said. "It's always constructive to make your feelings known."

"Fuck off, Neil," Chapman said. "This conversation is over."

"I'm sure it's comforting for you to feel that you could walk away, Bob. Of course you know it's impossible." Reynolds stared at him, motionless. Only a slight twitch of his nose betrayed his irritation.

Chapman heard Emily's voice outside, speaking to a visitor. He would have to go out there and pretend that everything was normal and right. It was his only choice.

"You're not God, Neil," he said quietly. "You're always a step ahead, but you're just one man. If you try to hurt me, I'll destroy you."

Reynolds's eyes sparkled, with what Chapman interpreted as excitement. The sight chilled him.

"I won't harm you, Bob, you know that," he said. "And, no. I'm not God. But it would serve you well to remember that each man carries a piece of the absolute within him. The inspired among us make it their vocation to hunt down this quality."

Before Chapman could respond, Reynolds suddenly burst out in deep throaty laughter. He opened the office door and said in a loud voice, "All right, Senator. You're on. One-on-one basketball, the loser buys dinner. I'll have my secretary call your assistant.''

Chapman, seated at his desk, felt forced to comply with the act. "A lobster dinner," he barked with forced levity.

Reynolds looked back inside and winked. "Senator, it was a pleasure to meet you. Best of luck for the remainder of your term.''

The colonel left without a backward glance. When his assistant appeared in the doorway, Chapman realized his hands were shaking. "What is it, Emily?"

Emily looked at him strangely. "Representative Lofton from Indiana wants to meet you," she said. "Is anything the matter?"

"Of course not," he said quickly, straightening his tie and standing up. "It's a great day. What could possibly be wrong?"

4

LAURA STIFLED A YAWN AS THE LIGHTS CAME UP IN THE hotel ballroom. She had endured seven presentations at the U.S. Surgical Alliance conference already that morning, and it was only a quarter after ten.

"Stay awake, Laura," Ferry Tafreshi said. "Cyrus is up next. We'll never forgive you if you sleep through it."

Ferry and Laura had become instant friends four years before, when they met at an L.A. day-care center. Each had immediately recognized a kindred spirit: they were both harried, overworked women trying to balance their careers and their children. Both women had been married then—Ferry to Cyrus, a dark, intense man who spent nearly every waking moment working on their family business, Emergent Technologies. To Laura, Ferry represented warmth to Cyrus's curtness, openness to his taciturn impatience. She was eight years younger than Cyrus, and she looked it, with lustrous dark hair and fine Persian features. She and Cyrus had known each other as children in prerevolutionary Teheran.

"I'll perk up," Laura said. "I've been waiting all morning to hear about something besides new endoscopes and laparoscopic Nissens.''

''But you're talking about Nissens later this afternoon,'' Ferry said.

''My point exactly. I can't wait until this is all over with.''

Laura peered around the room at the crowd, which was composed mostly of white male faces. Surgeons from all around the country routinely attended these meetings, where they gave and listened to talks on the most recent developments in surgical technology. The air was casual, but there also was a mood of apprehension. Each new development brought a dark fear for surgeons that they might become out of touch, the medical world might leave them behind. Laura wondered what these physicians' patients would think if they saw their staid, respectable doctors anxiously straining to understand technology they would have to put into practice in a matter of months.

The break between presentations was brief, no more than three minutes. Each spot in the program had been reserved months in advance, with a good deal of political jostling influencing the selections. Cyrus represented a small company pitted against representatives from the giant corporations. His slot, just before lunch and following a long series of speakers, guaranteed a less-than-attentive audience.

Cyrus walked past a long table on the stage, at which were seated several leading medical luminaries. They looked up from their papers and pitchers of water; Cyrus looked behind him at the three large video screens that would transmit his slide show.

''Good morning, ladies and gentlemen,'' he said in a low, accented voice. ''Thank you for your attention. In the next ten minutes I will inform you of developments at

Emergent Technologies, where we have developed a surgical educational system that we are very proud of."

In his natty brown suit, carefully combed hair, and black-framed glasses, Cyrus looked more like a schoolteacher than the technological visionary Laura knew him to be. "He looks nervous," she said to Ferry.

"I know," Ferry whispered. "See how hard he's holding that slide clicker? He looks like he's going to break it."

"Our product is known as the Real-Time Surgical Clinic," Cyrus said. A slide appeared, depicting a young woman wearing a wraparound eyepiece hooked by wires into a computer. She held in her hand a long penlike device.

"Ours is the best virtual-reality surgical simulator on the market," Cyrus continued, clearing his throat. "We provide spatially accurate anatomical structures, visual and tactile feedback, the ability to simulate many common surgical procedures, and moment-to-moment verbal instruction."

Laura looked around, trying to gauge the audience's reaction. Some appeared interested, others seemed bored. This worried her. Emergent Technologies was one of the few small businesses operating in the field of surgical implements; the company was under the constant pressure of their competitors' deep pockets. Cyrus had built the business from nothing, along with Ferry and a few relatives, after Cyrus had received his engineering doctorate from UCLA.

Laura heard Ferry nervously tapping her foot on the floor. Though Ferry and Cyrus rarely talked about it, Laura understood that their company had recently been on the verge of bankruptcy. This presentation could translate into sales—and it might be the difference between success and ruin for the Tafreshi family.

"Don't worry," Laura said, putting her hand on Ferry's shoulder. "You have one of the best products around."

Ferry smiled for an instant before her expression resumed its typical stoic impassivity. "There's something you should know," she said. "I should have told you sooner."

Cyrus's voice echoed from the stage, outlining the benefits of the Real-Time Surgical Clinic for training medical students, and how the system decreased the need for using laboratory animals.

Laura leaned close to Ferry. "What are you talking about? What's the matter?"

"We . . . we might lose the company," Ferry said, looking up at the stage. "We've known for the last nine months that companies were examining our corporate structure, and last week we found out that someone wants to make a hostile takeover. The way we structured the stock, we probably won't have any choice."

Laura grimaced. She knew this would hurt Ferry more than anything short of losing her children. The company was everything to her and Cyrus. It was their greatest pride, as well as the project that drove them both and kept them together. "Who's buying you out?" she asked.

"That's part of the reason I haven't said anything. The offer came from the Ellington-Faber Corporation, the company that owns the HMO you've had so many problems with."

Laura would have preferred a slap in the face. It seemed as though everything in medicine was being eroded by the conglomerates: the spirit of innovation, the confidence and good faith of physicians, even the quality of medical care itself.

"What about those new semiconducting substances Cyrus has been working on?'' Laura asked. ''He's been saying they're going to be worth a fortune.''

''They probably will,'' said Ferry. ''But we won't have time to get them to market. We just don't have the money right now to keep the company.''

''Damn it,'' Laura said. ''What the hell is happening to this country?''

''Don't talk that way,'' Ferry said. Cyrus's voice had become a drone, as though the burdens that weighed upon him had sapped the vitality from his sales pitch. ''This is a great country. We can start over. This isn't the end for us.''

Cyrus finished his presentation and fielded a few questions. Their simulator was an exciting project, a technological innovation that had been unimaginable just a decade before. And, apparently, it was too good a product for a small company with limited clout to hold on to.

The crowd applauded with perhaps a bit more gusto than the previous, more academic, speakers had earned. Ferry and Laura stood up together and clapped heartily. Cyrus walked off without acknowledging the praise, gingerly putting down the slide control and portable microphone for the next presenter to use. He appeared to be a man who didn't care what the future held for him.

5

LAURA SIPPED HER PAPER CUPFUL OF COFFEE AND NERVOUSLY cradled the notes in her hand. There were now three presentations to go before her time arrived. Public speaking was, to her, somewhere on a continuum between a prolonged root canal and the medieval rack. The lights dimmed again, and onstage the conference's faculty took their places at the long wooden table. She recognized two of them—Warren Hayes, a Miami cardiologist, and Cindy Blackman, a laparoscopic surgeon based in Manhattan. The others were unfamiliar, though she knew Will Arlington, a long-haired flamboyant Australian surgeon, by his reputation.

Laura took a deep breath. Situations such as this one were inherently intimidating for her. It was at times such as these, when she could feel anxiety chewing away at her, that Laura felt a very slight glimmer of the weakness that had led her to pills and alcohol. Though the thought of returning to those vices was abhorrent to her, she carried the memory of how those substances had once been able to erase her tension and replace it with heedless oblivion. It was a frightening memory.

Beside Laura, Ferry and Cyrus maintained a grim silence. Laura chided herself for focusing on her own problems. She had spent lunch with the couple, enduring Ferry's charged silence as Cyrus sullenly munched a sandwich, speaking only in clipped grunts. Laura saw that they were resigned to losing their company.

Laura barely noticed when a slide appeared on the middle screen announcing the next presentation. A tall, stiff man in a military uniform stepped onstage from the audience, shielding his eyes from the spotlight's glare.

"Our next speaker is Colonel Neil Reynolds, M.D., from the U.S. Army Medical Research Center," the conference monitor intoned. "His discussion is entitled, 'The New Revolution May Be Too Small for the Human Eye to See.' "

The audience gently applauded. Laura looked up intently at Reynolds, trying to forget that she would stand in his place within the hour.

"Thank you," Reynolds said. He looked out over the audience with an expression that, to Laura, seemed aloof and almost arrogant. "This afternoon I'll run through a few recent developments from the lab that I oversee under the authority of the Department of Defense. Instead of presenting data from hundreds of routine surgeries, I will instead introduce concepts to you that you have never considered. You will be challenged by what I have to say; that is my intent."

Laura felt slightly stung by this; her own lecture, like the preponderance of presentations at any medical conference, focused on long clinical trials and practical applications of a specific surgical technique. In a manner of speaking Reynolds had implied that this was beneath him.

A slide appeared on the screen depicting a dot-pixel map of the globe, the continents in relief against black oceans. "This is the world we live in, graphically illustrated," Reynolds said. "But this map is ten trillion times smaller than our Earth. It consists of atom clusters. It was assembled in my lab."

Low murmuring emerged from the audience. It seemed impossible that atoms could be manipulated in this way. Laura found herself forgetting her impending talk and straining her eyes to see.

"My current work is in a nascent field known as nanotechnology," Reynolds continued. "My unit of measure is the nanometer—which is approximately three atoms long."

The next slide showed a thin, tweezerslike instrument holding a thin square above a larger, flat structure.

"You'll hear about these soon," Reynolds said. "The square object you see is a microscopic blood-pressure sensor being pulled from a single silicon wafer. This device is completely functional and ready for production. We expect it to be commonplace in American hospitals within two to three years."

A rapid succession of slides followed, featuring small machines, lever devices, motors, and sensors. All were magnified for view, and most were too small in their actual dimensions to be viewed by the unaided human eye.

"We have been able to run trials on nanodevices based on silicon and other classified materials," Reynolds said. "The gears and control mechanisms within them are of a microscopic scale."

"My God," Laura whispered to Ferry. "I had heard about advances in miniaturization, but I had no idea they were so far along."

Ferry nodded absently. She looked up at the stage as though seeing more evidence that the world of medical technology, in which she had placed her life's hopes, had betrayed her and passed her by. Cyrus turned away from the stage, staring at the carpet in the open aisle.

"If you have any sense of history," Reynolds said, as though he expected his audience didn't, "you might recall the state of computers and electronics research ten to twenty years ago."

With this Reynolds clicked another slide, which showed a huge machine in a long tiled room. A titter of laughter came from the audience when the familiarity of the sight set in: it was an old-style computer, run on punch cards and occupying huge amounts of space.

"Whoever masters this technology will control the immediate future of the human race." Reynolds's stark pronouncement stunned most of the audience into silence. "What I am talking about today is literally another dimension of space, a new way of understanding physical relationships in the world. As surgeons we are used to dealing with minute blood vessels and delicate nerve clusters. To a micromachine these are enormous tunnels and thick cables."

Laura thought she detected something new in Reynolds's voice. Gone was his cold superiority, replaced by a seemingly honest craving to be understood. He brushed his close-cropped hair from his forehead, and she detected a vulnerability in the man that she hadn't expected.

The next slide showed Reynolds himself, standing in a sterile white medical lab. His features were obsured by a virtual-reality helmet; in his hand he held a joystick device. "We have cameras the size of a pinhead," he said. "With the aid of virtual reality, I have . . . I expect to be able to control a robot implanted within a human body. With a cutting arm, a cautery, and a small bundle of silk, I expect to have the capacity to perform any surgical procedure as though I were actually inside the patient, seeing and feeling everything my nanorobot feels and sees.''

This claim was too much for a large segment of the audience. Next to Laura an older man snorted with derision.

''My time is almost over,'' Reynolds said. ''Allow me to leave you with a few parting thoughts. First, the Japanese government has allocated nearly two hundred million dollars for research in nanotechnology. The United States has devoted a pitifully small amount, but I have set aside nearly all of my unit's funding for this research.''

Reynolds put his hands on the podium and stared out at the audience. ''Very, very soon I expect to provide the medical community with devices that will make the experience of surgery something you have never imagined. You will insert a robot with a needle, put on virtual-reality gear to control the device, and move with impunity through your patient's internal anatomy. The questions you must ask yourself: Will you be ready? Can your skills adapt?''

With this Laura sensed that Reynolds had nearly lost control of the audience. From the back came a man's nervous laughter. In her entire career she had never heard such a revolutionary set of ideas. Reynolds's claims were extraordinary. Laura almost believed him.

''My final statement is in the form of another series of questions.'' Reynolds's demeanor turned cold and stiff again, as though he felt rebuffed by his audience. ''Given that we have taken an oath to cure and to aid, what is our greatest nemesis? Illness and disease, to be sure, but there is a greater specter, one that haunts us all. Could it be that death is no longer grander than the human mind? Could we not find ways to outstrip the designs of our Maker, and throw off the limits of cognition and mortality like a slave's chains?''

Reynolds suddenly became silent; he backed away from the podium slightly, as if he had surprised himself. The conference faculty watched him with expressions of unease.

"Good questions to ponder," Reynolds said, clearing his throat and smiling awkwardly. "I am confident that my work will be of benefit to our professional community. I see I have run over, so there will be no time for questions. Thank you very much."

Several audience members leapt to microphones stationed in the audience. As Reynolds gathered his notes, four voices eagerly spoke at once. "You've given us no idea how close you are to—" said a tall woman near the stage.

"What did you mean by—" said a man from behind Laura, interrupting.

"Are you implying that a genetic solution—" said another voice.

"Please, please," the conference moderator said, taking the clip-on microphone from Reynolds. "Colonel Reynolds's presentation surely merits a moment or so of extra time. If you could ask your questions one by one, in an orderly manner . . ."

But Reynolds shook his head and walked away from the podium. Staring forward, his gaze focused intently on the conference hall's back door, he walked straight down the middle aisle and out. In his wake he left stunned silence.

"Perhaps later," the moderator said, staring at the closed door in disbelief.

Laura shared the general sense of incredulity that permeated the room. Ferry and Cyrus seemed to barely have noticed what had occurred, so immersed were they in their mutual troubles, but Laura had to fight off the urge to bolt for the back door. She wanted to ask Reynolds what he had meant to say next, but the moment had passed.

It was easy for doctors to become jaded. Dozens of cases became hundreds, then thousands. Patients threatened to become a faceless mass, distinguished only by the particular manifestations of their illnesses. The technological innovations of the previous decade kept Laura's work fresh to her. Advances in laparoscopy, virtual reality, and pharmaceuticals provided an unending challenge for the dedicated surgeon—one that could be met only through diligent continuing study and the maintenance of an open mind.

But this. This was incredible. She had to talk to this man, burrow beneath his arrogance (which concealed a greater insecurity, she was sure of it now), and force him to provide answers.

Then a thought occurred to her. She had hoped her discussion of laparoscopic Nissen fundoplication would be somewhat of a hit, even fantasizing that it might be a high point of the conference—or at least something that the doctors would talk about after they left. Now it seemed apparent that particular honor had been bestowed before she ever took the stage.

6

11:53 p.m. Russia.

THE FORMER SOVIET SECRET "CITY" WAS, IN TRUTH, LITTLE more than an overgrown military compound: a series of low-lying dormitories and work facilities set in the shadow of snow-crested hills. The workplaces and the dormitories hunched together behind a perimeter of guard posts and wire fences. The penitentiary air of the place lent irony to the fact that most of those who had lived there had, under the USSR, been considered an elite. Many scientists and technicians were gone now, but some had stayed behind in an atmosphere of stifled anticipation, wondering what Moscow might decide to do with the nuclear materials stored there since the end of the Cold War.

As warheads were dismantled, under compliance with treaties signed with the U.S., the amount of deadly radioactive substances stored there increased. The U.S. and Russia possessed about 650 tons of enriched uranium between them, a not-inconsiderable amount considering that a nuclear bomb could be created with between 3 and 25 kilograms of the substance.

Alongside a barred gate was a corrugated aluminum guard post; there, amid rifles and radio gear, were five young men. They were charged with protecting a relatively small store of weapons-grade uranium that, assembled, coupled with detonators, and delivered to their targets, would have been capable of destroying more than fifty cities.

They were also atrociously drunk. The night was dry, and the wind blew unimpeded from across the hills. Together they huddled around a radio, their young faces red with intoxication, their hands held over a small electric heater. At this hour of the night, and at this stage of their nightly vodka consumption, their conversation had dwindled to stupefied silence.

It was barely noticed when Sergei left the guardhouse; his exit elicited only a muttered complaint when he opened the door and allowed the wind inside. Sergei apologized and stepped outside.

Sergei had been raised in the fertile farmlands south of Moscow, a beautiful place compared to this uninviting setting. But he had blessed his fortune when the army first posted him to the secret city, because his dramatically increased salary had enabled him to send money home to his parents. He knew little and cared less about the politics of nuclear deterrence, or of payloads and first-strike capabilities. What he cared about now was that his salary had been swallowed by inflation. He could have made twenty times what he did—it still wouldn't be enough to rent a two-room apartment in Moscow.

He adjusted his cotton scarf as he jogged across the compound toward the facility's shipping area, glancing back to make sure no one had followed him. Weather had never bothered him in the past but now, curiously, it did. The icy chill seemed to reach some hidden recess of his soul, a place abraded by the uncertainties and loss of meaning of the last few years.

When he slipped inside the warehouse, skirting the piled cartons of canned food, Sergei felt a stab of conscience; what he was about to do might have terrible consequences. So why didn't he care? He cared only that there would be vodka left for him when he returned to the guard post. It was a curious feeling, to be so dead inside.

The package remained where he had left it: it was a small, heavy metal canister that he had stolen earlier in the week from a storage compartment secured only with a padlock. Sergei had left it under a pile of building materials that he knew would probably never be touched. He had disguised it within a burlap sack that obscured the international symbol of deadly radiation affixed to its side.

Moving faster now, afraid of being caught, Sergei stepped into the large hangar that housed the jeeps that the entire city depended on for transportation and patrols. He found the vehicle that would leave the next morning for the south, bound for a supply depot, and left his deadly package within its cargo hold.

The driver had been bribed; he would not ask what the parcel contained. Sergei had parted with a minute fraction of his payment for this assurance.

It was over. Sergei stepped out into the night again, shocked anew by the merciless chill. The refined nuclear material would be taken south the next day and picked up; by whom, Sergei neither knew nor cared. For within the soldier's mattress was cash, a bundle of paper currency that would be doubled when the parcel was successfully delivered.

The soldier suspected he wasn't the only one who had perpetrated this sort of betrayal. In a nuclear inventory taken the previous month, it had been found that the facility housed five percent *more* material than anticipated. Though he wasn't prone to such thoughts, the soldier understood what this implied: that no one truly knew how much fissionable material was stored in the former Soviet Union. Or what might happen to it.

When he reached the guardhouse, his arrival heralded by laconic greetings and slurred protestations about the open door, Sergei was elated to see that one of his comrades had opened a new bottle of vodka. He would need it that night.

7

"THE ULTIMATE GOAL OF THIS SURGICAL PROCEDURE IS TO bring the greater curvature of the patient's stomach to a position behind the esophagus. There it is anchored with sutures into a 360-degree wrap, creating a valve that prevents acid and bile from emerging up into the patient's esophagus. In addition to easing discomfort from reflux and heartburn, this new condition will allow the patient's esophagus to heal from irritation caused by the acids."

Laura paused and took a deep breath. The audience was completely silent. With bright lights trained on her she gratefully could only see a handful of faces in the front row, but that was bad enough. Her peers from around the country stared up expectantly, waiting to hear the results of her extensive work in laparoscopic Nissen surgeries—a procedure that, while practiced more and more, was still at the vanguard of medicine.

Though she didn't consider herself a particularly shy person, public speaking inevitably made her feel like a deer caught in headlights. Two years past, she would have taken a sedative to get her through the presentation. Now she had to conquer her fears alone.

"Next slide," she announced. On the screen appeared a chart listing which patients were candidates for this radical surgery.

"As you can see," she began, "an upper GI series will reveal reflux of acid, along with bile. In many cases this constant irritation will have caused a small ulceration on the esophagus itself. While medication and acid blockers work in a percentage of these cases, for some surgery is the only valid option and, truthfully, their last hope."

Laura wasn't feeling quite as worried as before; in fact, she thought she could discern a change in the audience, a focusing of their attention toward her. To her surprise she began to speak more easily, narrating a slide sequence depicting the touchstones of Nissen surgery: careful dissection of the esophagus viewed through the laparoscope, with special care not to pierce the heart, aorta, or diaphragm; dissection of blood vessels from the stomach's greater curvature to allow movement of the organ; then swinging the stomach around the esophagus and carefully clipping it.

"Here are my final findings," Laura said with a new air of confidence. She displayed a slide showing statistical analysis of her more than three hundred Nissen surgeries. Though Laura in many ways considered herself a family doctor and not much of a high-tech hotshot, she knew the sheer weight of her surgical trials was impressive. She glanced back at the moderator's table and saw the panel staring rapt at her statistics and jotting notes.

It was finally over. Laura put down the slide control and unclipped her microphone. To her amazement a low titter of applause began from the back of the hall. Within seconds the remainder of the audience joined in. Laura had received one of the most enthusiastic responses of the day.

"Maybe this public speaking thing isn't so hard after

all,'' she said to the next speaker, who patiently waited for her to leave the stage. He was a gruff, gray-bearded man, and he pretended not to hear her.

It didn't matter. Trying to hide a beaming smile that tugged at the corners of her mouth, and failing, Laura stepped back into the audience. She felt as though she could conquer the world.

THE AFTERNOON SESSION ENDED AT FOUR O'CLOCK, ALlowing time for coffee and conversation before the evening meal. Laura didn't much relish the idea of dining with her colleagues—nearly all of them were men—in a crowded hotel dining room. Since her portion of the conference was finished, and since she had been given handouts that outlined the following day's talks, she decided to go home a day early. She could be back in L.A. for a late dinner, maybe even early enough to rent a movie with Carlo.

It was tempting to leave right away, but Laura knew that would mean driving through rush-hour traffic. And she wanted to find Ferry and Cyrus, who had disappeared. The mood between the couple had grown progressively grimmer, and Laura wanted at least to try to comfort Ferry before going home.

Biding her time and scanning the unfamiliar faces around her, Laura poured a cup of coffee from a silver urn placed in the sunny open area outside the main hall. Ferry, she decided, had probably gone back to their hotel.

Outside a row of glass doors was a pristine white balcony; Laura walked out, blowing on her coffee and realizing she'd forgotten in which hotel her friends had booked a room. She walked through a cloud of cigarette smoke—it was amazing that some doctors still smoked tobacco, given what they knew about its effects—and made her way for a railing overlooking a small marina.

If nothing else, she could relax for a moment. The water below glistened in the late-afternoon sun. In the distance the brown hills were speckled with sprawling homes. Laura closed her eyes and breathed the cool, salty air. Then she felt a hand on her shoulder and turned, too quickly, spilling her coffee.

Colonel Neil Reynolds calmly examined the damage Laura's coffee had done to his previously spotless blue dress uniform. There were several dark splotches on his jacket, and his medals were dripping. He delicately reached up to wipe away a streak that ran from his nose down to his neck.

"Oh, my God. Shit," Laura stammered, backing away. Her accident had attracted attention, and she found herself the object of glances and stares. "Here, let me help you get that."

"Please, it was my fault," Reynolds said. He produced a handkerchief from his pants pocket and began cleaning himself.

"No, it's my fault. I'm too high strung. I—" Laura paused as Reynolds looked into her eyes. She suppressed a laugh. "You have a big drop of coffee right on the end of your nose," she said.

Reynolds, with a slight grin, dabbed his nose with the handkerchief. Laura saw that his motions were precise and measured, and that he seemed very uncomfortable. She realized that the military medical genius, who had captivated the conference with his hauteur and his breakthroughs, felt shy and awkward.

"That's better," she said. "I'm really sorry. I don't usually throw a drink in a man's face until he gets out of line with me."

Reynolds's eyes creased with a bashful smile. He had rich green eyes, infused with an aura of intelligence that she had underestimated when he was on the stage.

"I'll remember that." He extended his hand. "Dr. Antonelli, I wanted to tell you that your presentation was very impressive. You are probably one of the five most experienced Nissen practitioners here, and you did a good job of outlining trouble spots that come up during the procedure. We don't want these guys rushing home to do the operation without comprehending the risks."

"Exactly," Laura said. "I'm glad you picked up on that."

Reynolds put his hands behind his back, standing stiff, and gazed out at the mountains. He had a forthrightness and dignity that to Laura set him apart from the dozens of men around him. But he seemed to have run out of things to say, and she felt that he was about to leave. It surprised her to realize that she wanted him to stay.

"Your presentation was very impressive, too, Colonel," she said. "I'm sure you've heard that a lot today. I had no idea such progress was being made in nanotechnology."

Reynolds blinked; and it seemed as though something opened up from within him. "Call me Neil," he said. "And thank you. I see my role here as a catalyst for opening doctors' minds—which are notoriously closed to anything new. My work will change the face of medicine within a generation. It's a fact that people are going to have to get used to."

He paused, watching her. She felt she was in the presence of an acutely analytical mind, his gaze taking in information about her that she herself was unaware of. It was a mildly disconcerting sensation, but she had to admit the attention was flattering.

"I'm jealous of you," she found herself saying. "It

must be great to work with a big military research budget. It was a minor miracle that I was able to perform those three hundred Nissens. If the HMO had its way—which it does, more and more—they would send the patients home with a bottle of antacid, no matter how sick they were. And who cares if they developed cancer later from constant acid irritation?''

"I see your point," Reynolds said. He cradled his chin in his hand, as though pondering every ramification of what she had said.

"Well, I don't want to bore you," she said. "I'm sure you know what those of us in the private sector are going through."

"I don't think about it much," he said. At first she thought his manner was dismissive but she realized he was merely being honest.

"I've reached the point where I'm not even sure if my practice can sustain itself," she added. "I'm getting closed out of the HMO bureaucracy, and even when I get the work I'm paid less than half my former fee. It's hard raising a child, when you don't know if you're going to be able to afford to send him to college."

"What about your husband?" Reynolds asked. He motioned to the small diamond ring she wore on her left hand.

"Oh, that." Laura felt herself blushing. "I always wear this to conferences. It keeps guys from hitting on me— some of them, at least. I was married, but now I'm not. I— it's a long story."

"I don't mean to intrude," Reynolds said.

"Don't worry, I'll tell you when you're intruding," she said.

He seemed not to hear. "You have a child?" he asked.

"A son, Carlo. Do you have any children?"

"I'm not married," he said.

A high-masted sailboat crossed the waters below, heading for the marina. Laura heard a pair of doctors behind her arguing about its make and model.

"What HMO are you dealing with?" Reynolds said.

"My hospital was bought out by Ellington-Faber," she answered.

Reynolds's eyes widened a fraction. "I've heard of them," he said. "Basically, my understanding of your situation is as follows: You have to deal with Ellington-Faber in order to continue practicing at your hospital. Second, this managed-care organization is making it impossible for you to pursue your profession, by restricting access to work."

Laura smiled. Reynolds was transparent and supremely self-assured in the same moment. He was also a bit of a schoolboy, trying to impress her with his logic.

"That describes my situation," she said.

"Fine. Then hire a lawyer."

"To do what?" Laura asked. For the first time she suspected she was being condescended to.

"Threaten a restraint-of-trade lawsuit. It hasn't been done much, but it's a growing trend. You have about a ninety-percent chance that your lawsuit will never go to court. They will want to settle with you to keep you quiet, and so they will offer you a very favorable contract."

Laura pondered this. It hadn't occurred to her to take the offensive, to make Ellington-Faber accountable for their policies.

"I'll check it out," she said. Reynolds folded his arms, pleased with himself. "How do you know about this?" she asked.

"I do a lot of reading." He tapped his forehead. "I have a very, very good memory."

The crowd on the deck had begun to disperse, and the

doctors headed back to their hotels to change for dinner. Colonel Reynolds held the glass door open for Laura.

"I have an idea," he said as they walked through the carpeted lobby. "Why don't you sit with me at dinner tonight? I can tell you about my research and you can tell me about your son. It's always been one of my greatest regrets that I never started a family."

"Why didn't you?" Laura asked, genuinely curious.

"Oh, things got in the way." Reynolds fussed with his uniform. "When I returned from Vietnam I immersed myself completely in my work. I didn't know how much I would regret it in the future."

"It's never too late, Neil."

"Perhaps." He checked his watch. "So, how about dinner? I have one of the tables near the speaker's podium. If I flex a little muscle, I can get someone moved."

"They're having speakers during dinner?" Laura asked. "Don't these people ever shut up?"

Reynolds laughed heartily.

She thought for a moment, then said, "Thanks, but I can't. I'm heading home early to spend some time with my son."

Reynolds's face fell when she rejected his invitation. "I live in L.A.," she added. "Just down the road."

"I know," he replied. "I read your biography in the program."

"Well, you have my permission to stay in touch," she said.

That sort of permission would have earned a leer from most men she had known; instead, Reynolds politely nodded his assent. "Then I will," he said. "If you promise not to throw hot coffee on me the next time we meet."

"It's a deal." She shook his hand. "I'm in the book. Don't be shy."

"I'll try not to," he said, still grinning, as though a little dazed. She walked toward the exit, leaving him in the middle of the hotel lobby.

"I live in Virginia," he called out to her. "And work in Washington. Look me up if you're ever around."

"I know where you live," she called out over her shoulder. "I didn't think the Army Medical Research labs were in North Dakota."

Laura stepped out into the afternoon shadows, crossing the street and heading back to her hotel. She would be on the road within a half hour.

She realized she was smiling. Whatever had happened back there, she thought, wasn't bad for a single mother. She could still be pretty damned cool from time to time.

8

6:31 p.m., August 5, near Mashhad, Northeastern Iran.

THE BLEACHED-BLUE SKY ABOVE KUH-E-HAZAR MASJED was a sprawling canopy that seemed to descend impossibly close to the mountains. The rugged peaks resembled fingers reaching toward the heavens. The roads here, south of the Turkmenistan border, were old trading paths and military routes, ridden with holes and jagged breaks in the concrete. A brown truck, its cargo bed covered with green canvas flapping in the wind, snaked determinedly south.

In the truck the driver talked loudly in Farsi with another man, who periodically craned his head out the open window to scan the harsh terrain. They both carried pistols in leather holsters. Between them was a pair of Soviet-issue automatic machine guns.

Dust rose up from the road and made its way into the back of the truck, where three American men were huddled. The dust went into their eyes, down their collars, into their water canteen when they opened it. They held their weapons with nervous anticipation. Through a flap in the tarpaulin they monitored the hills and the road behind them.

"Give me some more of that dried fruit," demanded Ron Jameson from his perch behind the driver. He peered through the dirty windshield at the road ahead.

"Don't hog it," Don Werner said, handing him a United States military-ration plastic packet. His sandy hair was long and uncombed. "After the drop-off we won't get any new supplies for eighteen hours."

"It's so fucking delicious, I don't know if I can help myself," Jameson growled. He shifted uncomfortably, sweating under heavy military fatigues.

Andy Hall watched silently, rocking with the truck's motion. He was younger than his companions, his pale face ringed with freckles. "Jameson," he said in a thick southern accent, "you left your name on that old army jacket. You know we aren't supposed to be carrying any kind of ID."

"He's right," Werner said, looking at Jameson's lapel. "Someone at the drop-off might see it."

Jameson pulled a long serrated blade from a leather pouch strapped to his boot. "I'll cut it off, if it'll make you two old ladies happy." He pressed the blade to his chest and cut off the name tag. When it was loose, he ignited it with a cigarette lighter.

From the front of the truck came angry voices. The driver stared into his mirror, watching the flame as the cloth was consumed.

"Don't worry, Ahab," Jameson called out. "The fire's out."

"They don't understand a word of English," Hall said.

"They're probably worried because they think we're carrying explosives," said Werner.

"Well, they're right," Jameson said. He looked out the windshield. "Just not the kind you can light with a match."

His comment cast a pall of silence over the three Americans. Between them was a wooden crate, nailed shut. Hall and Werner stared at it, contemplating its horrible contents.

Jameson crab-stepped to the rear of the truck, training his binoculars on the hills. "Enjoy the ride, boys," he said. "According to Madison this might be the last time we'll be taking this route."

"What does that mean?" Werner asked, his voice full of suspicion.

"It means, Werner, that Madison got some news through our government connections."

Werner brushed his hair out of his eyes. "News? Why didn't I hear about it?"

"It was a last-minute thing," Jameson replied. "Right before we left, Madison said U.S. satellite surveillance has been focused on these mountains lately. They must be looking for something."

"Looking for something?" Werner asked, his voice rising in pitch. "What could they be looking for besides us?"

Jameson gave Hall a wink of reassurance. "Don't get paranoid, Werner. We're connected, remember? After this drop-off we draw up a new route. We'll stay one step ahead."

"It sounds to me like someone is taking chances with us," Werner said. He reflexively looked down at his gun. "I don't want to get set up."

"It's not like we're moving a shipment of bananas," said Hall. His voice was blasé. "This is important cargo, and it's worth a hell of a lot of money. We have people looking out for us, Werner."

Jameson fished a cigarette out of his jacket and lit it. He smiled through the thick cloud of bluish smoke. "Listen to the kid, Werner," he said. "We're dealing with professionals."

9

OUTSIDE THE CLOSED WINDOW GUNFIRE IMPACTED INTO stuffed targets with a staccato smacking sound; guttural male yells applauded every well-aimed volley, derided every miss.

Inside the compound most of the shades were drawn against the intense afternoon sun, and the sand and dust that blew across the arid valley. Jeanette Madison stood before the only window open to the glare, staring at her reflection imposed upon the desert in the thick Plexiglas.

No one called her Jeanette anymore, or Jeannie, as she used to prefer; they hadn't in years. She was just Madison now, a hard name that suited who she had become. The braids she had worn in her twenties were gone, her hair now shaved close to her scalp. Her body was lean and hard from years of exercise and paramilitary training, her brown skin rough from countless maneuvers in the parched desert.

Bobby probably wouldn't recognize her now. But if he did—if he saw through the diamond hardness to the woman who had once been his wife—he would understand. In a way this notion had kept her going since he died.

When she was alone with her thoughts, she liked to hone her autobiography, seeking meaning in bare facts: She had been born and raised in San Francisco, the only child of neglectful, distant parents. She had been a gifted student, and had won a scholarship to attend the University of California. There she met Professor Robert Madison, a young political science teacher whose academic career had become a constant fight with peer review boards and endless censures for his radical political activities and "inciting his students."

They had married within a year after they met in one of his classes. By then a small mountain of grievances had accumulated against him: unorthodox teaching strategies, lenient grading, and inappropriate relations with students (conducting radical libertarian meetings at the apartment he shared with Jeanette). He had resigned before they could fire him, and the new couple began a long odyssey from university to university. Bobby would teach until he wore out his welcome, while Jeanette gradually finished her own doctorate. Bobby grew more embittered, and after a time he stopped telling her about all of his affiliations, and he refused to identify the voices who phoned their home late into the night. When he died in police custody, felled by a cerebral hemorrhage at forty, he had left for her only questions—mysteries surrounding his final end, conundrums that bled into the political legacy he had left for her, a flaming powder mix of ideas and convictions.

Madison rubbed a smear from the Plexiglas and smiled at her reflection. Thinking of her own story, she had ended up telling Bobby's more than her own. She watched the men outside, still shooting, the recoil of their weapons slinging their arms back with each clipped volley.

Bobby's death had become a radical cause for some time—he had been arrested on the property of a telecommunications company, along with two other men and a tackle box full of explosives. Madison then started to receive calls from all sorts of strange people, who at first offered condolences, then more. They knew of her education in history and politics, and they knew she had absorbed the radical philosophies that had cost Bobby his life. She soon realized that, in his final years, Bobby had protected her from these edgy, disenfranchised men, sparing her from the dangerous strain of radicalism that had infected him.

That was five years before. Within a year of Bobby's death she had joined Patriot's Path, a paramilitary group based near Las Vegas. Antigovernment sentiment fomented there in the West, and eventually she had been able to consolidate two smaller groups under the Patriot's Path umbrella, as well as to recruit new men who were loyal to her. It was in this way that Madison, an African-American woman, became the leader of an antigovernment militia that welcomed libertarians, free-landers, tax refugees, white supremacists, and disaffected veterans. They all answered to her, recognizing her knowledge, intelligence, and her overpowering will. It was through her that they had made bigger plans than any other group of their kind: the sort of plans that brought in cash, which was convertible to weapons, then real power.

Madison closed the blinds, noting with satisfaction that her men had adapted well to the new laser sights she had bought for them. She seated herself at her desk, a huge piece of steel littered with books, pamphlets, scraps of paper, and weaponry.

It was one minute until eleven in the morning. She pulled a dull gray box toward her and made sure it was plugged in. Then she waited, her hands in her lap, breathing softly.

The box rang, piercing the quiet with a shrill electronic noise. Madison punched a button on the console.

"Madison," a deep voice said with fondness. An image resolved itself on the matte black video screen.

Onscreen was Jefferson Faber in his office; behind him was the original Dutch master's canvas he had paid seven million dollars for at a European auction. His suit was of fine fabric, his features lined with middle age but with a fire and energy in his eyes. His hair was combed back from his forehead in aristocratic swirls.

"Hello, Jefferson," she said. "I adore your punctuality."

"I hope that's not all you adore." Faber raised a china cup to his lips; tea, she knew. His face, sharp and angular, with a fine bone structure and the smallest hint of decadence, flashed a reserved grin.

"I assume you're alone," she said.

"As always. But, you know"—he gesticulated toward the ceiling—"the walls have ears. The usual sort of thing."

"That's always a safe assumption," she said. "How is Willard?"

Now the code was in place. The element that had brought them together was Jefferson Faber's own son. After Bobby's death, before the militia pull was too great to refuse, Madison had taught for two semesters at a small college in Washington State. Two semesters—that was how long it had taken for the college administration to learn about her past and about her new political associations. But it had been long enough for her to meet Jefferson Faber; the man looking bored and regal at a parents' weekend. His eyes had met Madison's on a campus lawn, and each had paused with the recognition of a kindred spirit.

"Willard is still away," Faber said, staring at her from the screen. "His trip is going well."

This, too, was code. Madison paused, running her thoughts through mental filters before speaking. "Is that right?" she asked. "I heard there had been problems getting flights. Or that there could be."

"I've been told he may have to find another connection next time, but for now everything's fine."

"I wasn't so sure, after the way you talked last week," she said.

"I told you there was nothing to worry about."

Madison gripped the edge of her desk. She had warned her men about the State Department's increased surveillance, revealed to her in an encoded E-mail transmission from Washington. The contacts in Iran were Faber's, but the men doing the dirty work were hers. They were on their second mission, and more were planned.

"Planes, trains," she mused, straining to maintain the illusion that their conversation was personal. "It's hard enough to travel without having unforeseen problems cropping up."

Faber leaned back in his chair. As always he seemed detached, perhaps even amused. The trustworthiness of others was something Madison regarded as a foolish, damaging ideal. Faber, she knew, was completely self-motivated. In a perverse sense he was the most trustworthy person she dealt with.

"I hate to see you so worried," Faber said. "There's no reason for it. But then, when have I seen you not preoccupied with something .or other? You have to be the most serious woman I've ever met."

"The most serious woman?" Madison asked. "Now, why does that sound like a backhanded insult?"

"Because you want it to," Faber said. He smiled again, more naturally. "All, right, you're also just as grim and deadly as every man I've ever known."

"That's better." She allowed herself to smile.

"It's at this point that I would reach out and touch you, if we were together," Faber said. Madison watched him draw closer to the screen. "It's been far too long."

A low, growling undertone in his voice sent her hand to the screen. "I wouldn't try to stop you," she said.

"I should hope not," said Faber. "I hate it when I have to physically subdue you."

"As if you'd ever be able to," Madison replied.

They stared into each other's eyes, into the pixilated images beamed through fiberoptic wire between Los Angeles and the Nevada desert. The feelings Madison entertained could have been a weakness, she realized, if not for one considerable fact: she was in control. And she knew he wasn't—not with her.

"I'll send you a letter soon," Faber said.

This meant a wire transfer. Patriot's Path's share of money for the latest operation in Iran.

"I love your letters," she said. "They're always so personal."

"And I'll make sure I find a better flight plan for Willard's next vacation," he added. "I'll have my best people look into it."

"Keep an eye on them," she said. "People can get lazy. Or worse. You shouldn't gamble. I know how much your good name means to you."

Faber backed away from the screen, almost imperceptibly, his jaw locked and tense, as though he had just seen something that he had never noticed before but should have. Then his smile returned.

"Stay in touch," Madison said. She turned off the video phone and pushed it to its place at the back of her desk.

When she opened the blinds again the scrubby land outside her window was bare save for riddled targets and dried, sere bushes lining the hills rising to the south. The sun was out, full and punishing; her men had gone inside for shelter.

She didn't believe that there was nothing to worry about. It always took nerve, and a willingness to accept huge risks, to reach an important objective. With that inevitably came the possibility of ruin.

But she had an advantage Faber couldn't claim; she had nothing to lose but her own life. In her most private moments she knew that this gambling stake was one that she could surrender without fear or forethought. In some ways life had ended for her a long time ago.

Madison sat at her desk, among her maps and plans, with things secreted behind the walls that could land her in the same jail system that had killed Bobby. Strange, she thought, that her mind had recently been of a reflective bent. Bobby had occupied her imagination lately more than her other dreams, such as the chaos she wanted to impose on the federal government, or the Holy Grail of the secessionary libertarian republic she envisioned.

"I have everything under control," she said. The room was silent, her words passing without reply.

PART TWO

PART TWO

10

LAURA SIGHED AND WIPED HER PERSPIRING HANDS ON HER black cotton skirt, trying not to be intimidated by the five attorneys, all men, who huddled together at the opposite side of the long mahogany conference table. They could all have emerged from the same mold, with their fine tailored suits, their neat knotted ties, and faces full of the same bland, calm confidence.

"They look like they're going to have me for lunch," Laura whispered.

"Don't say that," Laura's lawyer, Karen Anderson, said. "They might hear you. They act like they smell blood, it's a put-on. We have a good case here."

Karen was a petite, small-boned woman, next to whom Laura felt large and ungainly. She was a junior associate at Brown and Whitfield, a small downtown law firm referred to Laura by an associate in orthopedics. It had been nearly a month since Laura returned from San Diego, fresh from meeting Colonel Neil Reynolds and armed with his off-the-cuff legal advice. To her surprise the law firm had thought her case was interesting and took it at a reduced fee.

Laura had subsequently received a condensed legal education. A case such as hers rarely went to court; if it did, she would walk a tightrope between winning a large settlement and being bankrupted by legal fees. A consequence of victory might be blackballing; HMOs were reluctant to hire a surgeon with a litigious history. What she wanted, she was told by Brown and Whitfield, was a mediation hearing—the chance to make her case quickly, relatively informally, with the best possibility of restitution and the least potential for negative consequences.

One of the Ellington-Faber attorneys, a man in his early thirties with swept-back hair and sleek eyeglasses, looked up from the huddle across the table. "So, Karen," he said to Laura's lawyer, his voice clear and bold. "How are things down there on ground level?"

Next to Laura, Karen stiffened. There was a familiarity in the young man's voice that lent a caustic edge to his dig. "Sleeping well at night, Larry?" Karen asked.

Larry returned the smile with one of his own and gave a smug laugh. Laura dried her hands again, under the table.

A small, hunched man of about sixty entered the room, his gaze fixed on the thick shag carpeting, an ungainly pile of folders tucked under his thin arm. He walked around Laura and the lawyers without a word and took the empty seat at the head of the table. He made a great ceremony out of arranging the files in front of him, carefully unbuttoning his single-breasted suit jacket, and producing a leather glasses case from his inner pocket.

"We'll begin," he said in a husky voice. Only now did he look up at the group. "This is the mediation in the matter of Laura Antonelli versus the Ellington-Faber Corporation. I have reviewed the files and claims, and declare this mediation ready to proceed. My name is Randolph Bowdoin, Esquire, and I have been charged with hearing this matter. My decision is nonbinding but will carry the authority of impartial reason and fairness."

The Ellington-Faber lawyers listened like schoolboys, all save for the oldest among them: Juan Esposito, a sharp-looking man in his fifties who leveled his eyes at Bowdoin as though impatient for him to finish. Laura wasn't sure how to interpret Bowdoin's grave, ceremonious tone. She had been told by Karen that the proceedings would be informal and loose—and that Laura would likely receive solid assurances that her pre-HMO referrals and patient base would be permanently restored. Already it seemed that this strange legal hearing was overly formal, the sort of atmosphere in which Laura imagined she wouldn't fare as well.

Bowdoin squinted at a sheet of paper. "Miss Anderson," he said, "you are representing Miss Antonelli?"

Karen was silent for a long moment; Laura intuitively knew that Bowdoin's old-fashioned terms of address were intentional.

"I am," Karen finally said.

"Please begin."

Karen took a deep breath. To Laura it seemed the young woman was nervous. "My client, Dr. Antonelli," she began, "is a surgeon at Valley Memorial Hospital, where she has practiced for seven years. Eighteen months ago the Ellington-Faber Corporation—specifically, its managed-care division—bought the hospital and instituted its own health plan. During this time Dr. Antonelli's workload and patient base have decreased dramatically. As you can see from the documents filed for this mediation, cases meant for her have been sent, for political reasons, to other doctors. We feel that this represents an unfair restraint of Dr. Antonelli's right to practice medicine and to do business within the medical field—particularly because she is, ostensibly, a member of the Ellington-Faber HMO, with all rights and privileges.''

Karen delivered her speech in a measured monotone. Laura watched the HMOs; they looked, alternately, bored and condescendingly skeptical.

When Karen had finished, Bowdoin peered over his glasses at her with, Laura believed, a hint of disapproval. ''This isn't a court of law, Miss Anderson,'' he said. ''But what you're suggesting implies a degree of conspiracy on the part of Ellington-Faber to limit your client's access to fair commerce. The materials you provided to me don't necessarily prove that this occurred.''

Juan Esposito cleared his throat. ''If I could,'' he said.

Bowdoin still looked at Karen, awaiting her response. She stayed silent. ''Very well, go ahead,'' Bowdoin said, nodding to Esposito.

''Your observations regarding the materials presented by Ms. Antonelli are precisely why we feel her legal action is groundless,'' Esposito said. He looked across the table at Laura and Karen.

''What do we have here?'' Esposito asked, rapping his fountain pen on his copy of the files. ''Dr. Antonelli has obtained some referral sheets, on which she claims her name was taken off and replaced with another. For all we know, this was clerical error. We're to believe that doctors favored by the HMO are given more and better work, but for what reason? Ellington-Faber exists to turn a profit while remaining a good corporate citizen. The managed-care aspect of the company is committed to quality health care at affordable prices. Ms. Antonelli seems to stand for little else than her own material gain, and she seems to want to blame us for its deterioration.''

Esposito halted, as though sensing that he had gone too far. Bowdoin leaned back a little in his chair and lowered his eyes. "You aren't in court, Mr. Esposito," he said. "You should remember that. You don't have to defame anyone's character to make your point. We're here to find an agreement we can all live with."

"I would also like to mention another matter," Esposito said. He glanced at Laura. "Twice in the preceding year, patients who had recently undergone surgery performed by Ms. Antonelli subsequently died. Dr. Antonelli has not been censured because of these untimely deaths—"

"Because they weren't her fault," Karen interrupted. "My client disclosed that information to me in preparation for this mediation. Those deaths had nothing to do with any misconduct on her part."

"Mr. Esposito," Bowdoin said, "I have asked you not to indulge in character assassination."

Laura was stunned by what she had heard. The deaths of those two patients had been upsetting to her, but she had been certain they weren't her fault. And the removal of her name from referral sheets was no clerical error, she knew—she had confirmed it with the clerks in administration. But she hadn't thought to have their statements brought into this arbitration. Ellington-Faber obviously intended to smear her, and why not? They were bigger, stronger. A tightness gripped her chest; she had been foolish to think she could defy big money. Other doctors had been driven out of practice and out of town because of HMO politics. Why should she be any different?

"Part of our packet includes recommendations and reviews from Dr. Antonelli's time at Valley Hospital," Karen said. Her voice lacked the strength with which she had begun.

"Oh, I know," Bowdoin said. "She appears to be an exemplary surgeon. Truly excellent."

"We never said she wasn't," Esposito said. Perhaps

sensing victory, he had softened his tone. "That's why she enjoys membership in our HMO."

Bowdoin nodded, as though in response to something he himself had said. He jotted something down on a piece of paper.

Laura sipped her water and tried not to look across the table. It was impossible not to. What she saw frightened her—the opposing lawyers had all turned away from her, looking out the window or at Bowdoin. It was as though she was no longer formidable enough to spare a glace at. She thought of what Karen had told her earlier—the arbitration was nonbinding, Laura could still press the case in court. But was she willing to drain her entire savings, probably even take out a loan, to fight against deep corporate pockets? What savings did she even have left, save for Carlo's untouchable college fund?

Laura barely noticed when a door opened softly behind her, and she only dimly perceived soft steps on the thick rug circling the table. She did register, though, the shocked expressions of the attorneys across the table. As one they sat up straight in their chairs, looking for all the world as though they had been caught loafing at their jobs.

A tall, thin man in an elegant suit bent over the surprised Bowdoin and spoke to him in a low, deep voice. Karen started to interrupt, but Bowdoin held up a hand for silence.

"Who is that?" Laura whispered. "What's going on?"

Karen didn't answer. The man straightened to his full height and sat with the attorneys. Esposito vacated his own seat and took an empty one at the end of the row, beyond even the young lawyer who had earlier baited Karen.

"Pardon my interruption," the man said. He surveyed the room with ease and a look of entitlement. "My name is Jefferson Faber. I was made aware of this case and I wanted to join you this morning. I apologize for my tardiness, but I ran late at the airport.''

Bowdoin stared expectantly at Karen; obviously, this change required that she respond. ''It's quite all right, Mr. Faber,'' she said, regaining her composure. ''You're welcome to join us, of course.''

Laura felt like a small boat cast about by forces larger than herself. She had never met Faber, but she knew of him from the newspapers—mainly that his corporation's holdings were vast and immeasurable in value. She couldn't imagine what had compelled him to come to this arbitration. Perhaps, she thought, he had come to personally bar her from Valley Memorial.

''I haven't really had a chance to say anything today,'' Laura said. ''Before this is all over I'd like to speak on my own behalf.''

''Of course, Dr. Antonelli,'' Bowdoin said. Faber, folding his hands on the table, inclined almost imperceptibly toward her, his eyes wide with expectation.

''The reason I agreed to this arbitration is because I can't afford to fight Ellington-Faber in court,'' Laura began. She felt Karen's arm on hers, and shook it away. ''No, it's all right. They know it as well as we do, so why hide it?''

The hint of a smile played at the corners of Faber's narrow lips.

''I also agreed to it because I didn't bring an all-or-nothing attitude to this disagreement,'' Laura added. ''I don't want to sue you for a large financial settlement, and I don't want to play games. What I want is fair treatment from your corporation. I want a case load appropriate to my experience and expertise, and at a reasonable fee scale. If I receive assurances from you, in writing, that this will be the case, then I'm willing to drop the whole thing.''

Laura heard Karen exhale deeply. Her lawyer would be disappointed with her, but she didn't care. She even harbored the dawning suspicion that Karen and her firm might have preferred to take this case to court, to try for a large settlement.

Esposito started to speak, then checked himself. He craned his neck and looked to the far end of his row of attorneys, seeking to take his cue from his boss.

"That's very reasonable," Faber said. He pushed back from the table a bit and crossed his long legs. "I'm glad to hear you agree with my own feelings—that we don't need to have a messy confrontation over this matter—"

"Then what do you propose?" Karen interrupted.

Faber ignored her and directly addressed Laura. "You see, there is no changing the fact that Ellington-Faber is now in control of Valley Memorial Hospital. Whether you like it or not, we've cut costs and brought in twenty thousand new client lives to the system."

"I don't care one way or the other," Laura said. "I have patients, not clients. I'm a doctor, that's my entire life. I'm not a businessperson."

Smiling, Faber said, "Fine. I'll tell you, then, that I came here today because of a memorandum sent to me by my legal department. It very eloquently stated the possible ramifications of your case, should it go to trial. I concluded that the best possible solution would be to take care of our differences in a civilized way, and avoid . . . *negative* fallout should we find ourselves in a position from which neither side could back away."

At the mention of his legal department Faber's four lawyers glanced furtively at one another, each seeming to wonder who might receive credit for having brought this matter to Faber's attention—and who might pay for not having done so.

Laura's mind raced. It was clear to her, just from these few moments in his company, that Faber was intelligent and self-protective. He wanted to avoid a trial. Why? Because it might expose corruption in his HMO: the sort of favoritism and price fixing that Laura found herself up against. But even if she won her case, Laura might find herself undesired, to say the least, when she looked for work at another hospital.

"What are you suggesting, Mr. Faber?" she asked.

"Precisely what you have asked for," Faber replied without pause. "I'll have my legal team draw up an agreement. Within it we will stipulate that you will receive a workload commensurate with what you enjoyed prior to the Ellington-Faber takeover."

"In other words," Laura said, "you're offering to put me on your 'A list,' the doctors you prefer to send referrals to."

Faber frowned. "I don't know that there is any such thing."

"Then you don't know what's going on at your own hospital," Laura shot back. "The reason we're here today is that an exclusionary policy exists."

Everyone went silent, with Laura and Faber looking across the table at one another. Though it made her feel slightly childish, Laura struggled not to blink.

"Mr. Faber has registered an offer," Bowdoin said loudly, as though offended that he had been excluded for so long. "Dr. Antonelli, would you like to confer with your lawyer?"

Karen and Laura pulled back from the table, their heads close together. "He's trying to buy you cheap," Karen whispered. "He knows you have a case."

"But he's basically offering me everything I want," Laura said. "The only reason I started all this was because my referrals were being unfairly taken away from me. He's offering to give them back.''

''This could be bigger than just you,'' Karen said. Laura saw a zealous sparkle in the young attorney's expression. ''You have a chance to strike back for all the doctors who are suffering unfairly under HMO corporate politics. We don't even know if Faber's even telling the truth or not. He might find some way to cheat you, or even get you fired.''

''I don't think so,'' Laura replied, glancing across the table. ''We have it on record that he was here—the owner and president of the corporation. I think he's telling the truth.''

Karen sighed, almost angrily. Laura closed her eyes. A chance to strike on behalf of her entire profession, to fight the corporations that had compromised medicine and the quality of patients' health care—it was tempting. But the cost was too high. Perhaps if she were younger, if she didn't have Carlo to support. Her boy had no one else in the world to rely upon. This couldn't be her fight.

Laura turned away from Karen. ''Two things, Mr. Faber,'' she said. ''We need to find a middle ground between the fee structure under the old system and your program. I can't lower my fees every week to keep up. I'm not a corner grocery store.''

For an instant Faber's face flashed with displeasure. ''Granted.''

''Second, I want it written into our agreement that I'll have a more liberal hand in ordering tests for my patients. I'm tired of getting an angry call every time I order an upper GI series to determine what course of action would be safest.''

''We'll work that in,'' Faber said. Esposito grimaced.

''And also,'' Laura continued, ''I'm going into this in

good faith. I expect the same from you. As long as I continue to perform professionally, I don't want any antagonism from Ellington-Faber.''

''That's three things,'' Faber said.

''You're right,'' Laura replied.

With this Faber leaned back in his chair. Esposito passed him a note, which he glanced at and pushed aside. ''You have a deal, Dr. Antonelli,'' he said. ''It's a pleasure to keep a surgeon of your caliber on the Ellington-Faber team.''

Karen slapped shut her file folder and tossed it into her briefcase.

Bowdoin, taking his feet with a groan, said, ''Well, I suppose that's another successful arbitration. I'll be charging my regular fee.''

AFTERWARD KAREN LEFT QUICKLY, OBVIOUSLY DISAPpointed by Laura's quick capitulation. She departed with a promise to call Laura in a day or two. Bowdoin left with his head bowed as upon his entrance, as though his capacity for human interaction began and ended within the official confines of the arbitration session.

Laura paused in the hall, still pondering what had just happened. On one hand she harbored guilt, thinking that some of what Karen had said was true. She had done what she had to do; she was in no position to become a crusader.

Faber walked out of the conference room with brisk strides, his lawyers behind him like royal attendants. When he saw Laura he turned and whispered something to Esposito. As one the lawyers made for the elevators, leaving Faber alone with Laura.

''I'm glad we were able to work things out,'' Faber said as he approached. His hand was cold when Laura shook it.

''So am I,'' Laura said. Faber was taller than she had

thought; she found herself straightening her posture. "My lawyer wanted me to press on, I think. To strike a blow for doctors everywhere."

While she spoke, Laura saw Faber's gaze drifting to her ring finger. He paused there, as though contemplating the wedding band she had decided to wear that day.

"Well, I appreciate your willingness to be straightforward in addressing our differences," Faber said. His eyes were deep blue, flecked with darker strains. "There's no need for business and medicine to be always at odds."

There was something in the way he talked to her, something idle and casual, that made Laura uncomfortable. He seemed a living embodiment of wealth and power with his pristine attire and perfect hair. His easy confidence and cultivated manner barely masked a deeply aggressive nature. Suddenly she wanted to get away from him.

He seemed to sense her turn in mood. "I'll walk you to the elevators," he said. "I'm at Valley Memorial at least once a month. Perhaps I'll drop in on you there. You might allow me to buy you lunch."

"That won't be necessary," she said. "Thanks for coming here and for extending your offer. You said you would produce everything in writing quickly. I'll look forward to it—let's say, in the next day or so."

Faber stiffened and adjusted the knot of his tie, rebuffed. Something angry flashed in his eyes, some hidden part of him lying beneath his civilized veneer.

"I'll be going, then," he said. "Shall I hold the elevator for you?"

"No, thanks," she said. "I have to make a call before I leave."

Laura watched Faber's pinstriped back recede quickly down the hall. She didn't care if he was angry, he deserved it.

Laura found a courtesy phone, punched in her calling-card code, and dialed a long-distance number. It was picked up on the first ring.

"Could I speak to Colonel Neil Reynolds, please?" she asked, smiling.

Laura extended the phone line to the window, where she could see the downtown skyscrapers and a fine brown tint of smog hovering over the city. She heard the sound of her call being transferred.

"This is Neil Reynolds," Neil said.

"Neil, this is Laura Antonelli. Remember me?"

She heard him fumbling with the phone. "Laura, of course," he said nervously. "It's so good to hear from you. You know, I never answer the phone here. I happen to pick one up, and it's you on the line. Maybe I should reconsider my philosophy."

Laura laughed. "Maybe you should," she said. "Look, I called to tell you: We won!"

Neil was silent for a moment. "We won what?"

"Oh, I'm sorry. I'm incoherent. I'm so happy because I just received major concessions from Ellington-Faber as a result of my arbitration hearing. I have you to thank for it, Neil. I'd never have done it if you didn't give me the idea."

"I'm proud of you," Neil said. "That's fantastic—"

"And guess what," Laura interrupted. "Jefferson Faber himself showed up to grant the concessions."

"Jefferson Faber?" Neil asked. "You mean the owner of the HMO?"

"None other."

Outside the window a helicopter buzzed past. Laura, feeling like a schoolgirl, turned away for privacy as a young secretary walked past.

"Well, we're going to have to share a toast over this one," Neil said. "I'm so happy you're going to be free to practice surgery with a minimum of interference again. You know, I was very impressed by your presentation in San Diego.''

"Flatterer," Laura said. "You merely blew away the whole place with your talk."

"Well, I can get passionate about my work."

"You should, from what I saw of it," Laura said. "Look, I have to get to the hospital, but call me, all right? Maybe I'll take you up on that toast."

"I'd truly like that," Neil said.

They hung up. Laura walked to the elevators, feeling a surprising bounce in her step. She didn't know what pleased her more—winning the arbitration, or having a chat with Neil Reynolds.

11

6:50 p.m.

"CARLO, COME ON," LAURA SAID. SHE PUT HER HANDS ON her son's narrow shoulders and squeezed. "Be a good sport. We won't stay late."

Carlo folded his arms. "Mom, I don't want to play with them. They're little kids."

"Big kids played with you when you were little," Laura explained. "Now it's your turn. Life is like that."

"Oh, Mom, don't give me that crap." Carlo glanced at the breakfast nook at the rear of the Tafreshis' kitchen. There Davood and Mina, Ferry and Cyrus Tafreshi's son and daughter, were setting up an elaborate board game with solemn intensity.

Every day Carlo seemed to look more like Steve, in the creases of his brow, in his eyes, in the careless lock of dark hair that fell across his forehead. Laura saw the resemblance all the more when Carlo was being obstinate with her.

"Well, I certainly didn't mean to give you any *crap*," Laura said. "Tell you what. If you don't want to play with Mina and Davood, you can come out to the living room. I'm going to talk about my arbitration hearing, and Ferry and Cyrus are going to tell me what's happening with the buyout of their company.''

Carlo tried to feign a flicker of interest. He was on the cusp between early boyhood and the age at which he would want to be treated like a grown-up. It gave her a deep pleasure when he gazed again at the smaller children's board game, this time with receptive eyes.

''I'll stay in here,'' he said. ''Davood and Mina are nice kids.''

Laura bent down and kissed her son on the forehead. ''They look up to you,'' she whispered. ''It'll make their day if you play with them.''

Carlo walked through the kitchen with a renewed swagger. Laura told the kids to have a good time and pushed through the swivel door leading into the Tafreshis' living room.

''Is everything all right in there?'' Ferry asked, rising from the sofa.

''Fine,'' Laura said. ''I gave Carlo a choice: play with the 'little' kids, or sit through a bunch of boring adults talking about their business.''

From the stuffed leather chair in the corner Cyrus gave a low, humorless laugh. He wore wool slacks, a finely striped shirt open at the collar, and a necktie, as though he had just come from a meeting. Laura knew he never wore a jacket or tie to work.

''Maybe it's not too late for me to go in there,'' he said. ''I'd much prefer a game of Chutes and Ladders to talking about what happened to my career.''

Ferry glanced nervously back and forth between her husband and Laura. ''We don't have to talk about anything,'' she said crossly. ''I invited Laura over because of her good fortune today.''

Laura stood by a row of floor-to-ceiling bookcases lining one wall. Always mesmerized by photographs, she gazed at the framed pictures that represented the Tafreshi family history: aged uncles in Teheran, Cyrus and Ferry at their wedding in Los Angeles, the family home in northern Iran, Davood and Mina.

Ferry and Cyrus's living room, like the rest of their house, was pristine, ordered, and stubbornly modern. They had bought the Santa Monica town house three years before, when Emergent Technologies had been thriving. They had torn down the wallpaper and gutted the fixtures, remaking the place with cool whites and browns meshing with expensive, understated furniture.

Laura heard a loud pop from behind her that made her jump. Cyrus continued to morosely stare at the silent television flickering at the far end of the room.

"I bought champagne," Ferry said. She produced three glasses and showed Laura the bottle. "Nonalcoholic, of course. To celebrate."

It wasn't much of a celebration. When Laura had first met Ferry and Cyrus, they had been happy and obviously still in love. Cyrus had a tendency to be sullen and tense, but when the business began to thrive he could be expansive and gregarious. He and Ferry made an ideal team, with her talent for organization and marketing complementing his technological innovations. They took vacations to the Caribbean together, and visited Iran three times in two years.

Ferry handed Laura a glass, then passed one to Cyrus. "To Laura," she said, "and her victory today."

Laura smiled at her friend, but inside she felt a stirring of anger. Ferry was trying too hard to please; her good cheer seemed forced. It made Laura resent Cyrus's juvenile brooding. Laura knew, from Ferry, that the buyout of

Emergent Technologies was about to make him and his family millionaires several times over.

"And to Cyrus," Laura said, stopping Ferry before they could clink glasses. "And to you, Ferry. I can't wait to hear how you will use your new capital to start a new project—one that I know will revolutionize medical technology."

From his chair Cyrus looked up from the television. Seeing that it would be in bad manners to ignore this flattery, he got up and joined the women. They tapped their glasses together and sipped the champagne.

"Thank you, Laura," Cyrus said. "That was a very nice toast."

Seemingly encouraged by her husband's tone, Ferry motioned for Laura to sit down. As always, Ferry wore a long skirt, today with a white linen blouse. "Tell me all about what happened today," Ferry said. "You only told me you won. I want all the details."

Ferry always loved to gossip about business, the ins and outs of a particular political situation or strategy. She was always learning.

"This I *would* like to hear about," Cyrus said. "Tell me all about how you beat the great Ellington-Faber. Give me something happy to think about when I lay my head on the pillow tonight."

On the silent television troops in some faraway place ran across the camera's lens, a cloud of smoke building and obscuring the image.

"Can you turn that off?" Ferry said, flashing annoyance. "We have a guest, Cyrus."

"Laura's an old friend," Cyrus said, staring at the screen. "She knows how rude I am."

Laura had to laugh. Cyrus's mouth formed a thin half-smile, and he winked at his wife.

"Besides," he continued, "I want to see about this. The Russians are trying to hold down another breakaway region, and as usual it's not working. Don't worry, Laura, I'm listening to you."

"There's not a lot to say about this afternoon," Laura began. Which wasn't true, but she knew the state Cyrus was in. She had seen it in her father, in her husband, in her son from time to time. He was a man who felt he had lost; he hadn't merely failed, he had been bested by an enemy. Laura wondered why it was primarily men who suffered from this overpersonalized view of their setbacks.

"I suppose the most interesting part of the arbitration was when Jefferson Faber showed up," she added.

From the kitchen Davood's voice rang out with a squeal of pleasure. At least someone was having a good time.

Cyrus sat up in his chair and turned off the television with his remote control. "Jefferson Faber?" he asked, his eyes wide. "For a small-time arbitration hearing?"

"Cyrus!" Ferry scolded.

"No, he's right." Laura poured herself a second glass of champagne. "I didn't think I was that much of a threat to the HMO. His team of lawyers were as surprised as me when he walked through the door."

Cyrus pressed his glass against his cheek. "Now, why would the bastard have done that?" he asked, his voice contemplative.

"I suppose my lawsuit was more threatening to the HMO than my lawyer thought," Laura said. "In fact, she didn't want me to settle. She thought Faber had tipped his hand and that I could have pressed for a big settlement."

"Why didn't you?" Cyrus asked.

"Because I'm not a crusader," Laura said, hearing in her voice the hint of a rise to a challenge. "I got what I wanted—a fair chance to practice surgery and make a living. I earn money through my work, not by filing lawsuits.''

''I think you did the right thing,'' Ferry said. ''Your legal costs would have been terrible. We looked into fighting Ellington-Faber's takeover of our company. It could have cost us hundreds of thousands of dollars to fight against them, and we still might have lost.''

Cyrus cast a quick, angry glance at his wife, as though he didn't want Laura to know the details of their losing the company. He recovered himself and returned to his previous pensiveness.

''So what is he like?'' he asked.

''Faber?'' Laura asked, suddenly confused. ''You mean you never met him?''

''The Great Man never sank so low as to meet me,'' Cyrus said bitterly. He shifted in his chair, crossing his legs. ''I am, however, on a first-name basis with a number of his lawyers and representatives.''

''Faber seemed . . .'' Laura paused. ''He walked into the room like a king, listened to what I had to say, and made me a reasonable offer. He was polite, but he acted like he was doing me a favor. As though he had decided to be generous—just this once.''

''In other words,'' Cyrus said, ''a real son of a bitch.''

A crash came from the kitchen, followed by Mina's high-pitched cry. Laura heard Carlo talking in a soothing tone, then in a harsher voice to Davood. Ferry started to get up, but Cyrus held out his hand. ''Stay here,'' he said wearily. ''Talk to your friend. I'll try to restore order.''

''Thank you, Cyrus,'' Ferry said.

On his way to the kitchen Cyrus stopped next to Laura. In an uncharacteristic gesture he fondly patted her on the back.

''I'm sorry to be so sour tonight,'' he said. ''Forgive

me. I'm very glad you were able to take care of the problems with your practice. I think you did the proper thing."

Somewhat stunned, because Cyrus at his most outgoing had never been so complimentary or sensitive, Laura thanked him.

Cyrus opened the swinging door to the kitchen with a monster's roar, and called out, "Where are the little children for the horrible dinosaur to eat? I hope they are tender and young!" The kids, even Carlo, stopped squabbling and shrieked with delight.

Laura joined Ferry on the sofa. Ferry ran her hand through her curly black hair and smiled. "He can be a bear sometimes," she said. "But he'll come through. I'm glad you and Carlo came over tonight. It puts everyone in a better mood."

"You know, Ferry, I hope you don't mind my saying this," Laura began, "but sometimes you're too worried about everyone else. Let's talk about you for a change."

"Oh, well, the money will certainly help us," Ferry said. She was always loath to speak about her own feelings, preferring to talk about her family. "We can set aside enough for Davood and Mina to go to college. Then we'll try to start over."

"Why do you make that sound so impossible?" Laura asked.

Ferry stared down at the floor, as though gathering her thoughts and filtering out those she found undesirable. "In some ways Cyrus has good reason to feel discouraged," she said quietly.

"I know it's hard to lose the company," Laura said. "It breaks my heart, because I know how much work you both put into it. But you're talented people, and I know your staff will join you the minute you start up something new."

"I know," Ferry said, her voice low, obviously not

wanting her husband to hear. "But these new semiconductors Cyrus invented might have been a once-in-a-lifetime breakthrough. We would have made a hundred times the buyout money, if we could have just held on and marketed them ourselves. Cyrus's invention will change things, Laura. I'm convinced of it. I just wish he still owned them."

Laura stayed silent. It was pointless to argue, and she cared too much for Ferry to lie to her. Cyrus was a man of science, and he worked in a field in which a man or woman might expect one great discovery in a lifetime, if that. He had lost more than a building, a staff, and laboratory equipment; he had in fact lost the product of his own intellect and imagination.

"It might not matter, anyway," Ferry said. Her mouth was somewhere between a smile and a frown. "We were naive. We published papers and talked at conferences. Other people have already duplicated Cyrus's work. Cyrus even thinks Faber instigated industrial espionage and distributed his research, so that we would lack the clout to keep the company. It's certainly true that other scientists are producing similar semiconductors already. We might not have even been able to secure a patent."

Laura had never heard this tone of defeat from Ferry in all the time that she had known her.

"You have to move on," Laura said. "What happened is wrong, but you can't give up."

"That's not all," Ferry said. She clasped her hands over her mouth, as though fighting off an impulse to stay quiet. "Something else is bothering Cyrus. I know him too well for him to hide it."

"Cyrus has a lot on his mind—"

"He always has a lot on his mind, his brain is always working. I'm used to that," Ferry said. "Laura, it's something else. I don't know what, but he's hiding something from me.''

''But what?''

''I think he's protecting me from something.'' When Ferry turned to Laura, her eyes were glossy with tears.

''Beware the warrior king who rides the dinosaur's back!'' Both women started when Cyrus burst through the swinging door, the beaming Carlo on his back. Davood and Mina followed, fresh from their scrape and giggling incoherently.

''What's wrong with you two stick-in-the-muds?'' Cyrus asked Laura and Ferry. ''We're having a party in the kitchen. Come join us!''

With that he again smashed through the swinging door, Carlo now roaring as though he were the dinosaur.

Laura wanted to ask Ferry more, but by then Ferry had stood up, ready to join her family, a smile on her face and her eyes devoid of tears.

12

THE UNITED STATES ARMY MEDICAL RESEARCH CENTER lay amid high trees, its grounds encircled by an electrified fence, its entrances guarded by expressionless young men toting rifles. The majority of its laboratories were secured underground; the Center was a place commuters drove past every morning and afternoon without noticing. Its featureless exterior discouraged speculation about what went on inside its walls.

Colonel Neil Reynolds arrived there before eight every morning after driving in from his small house in northeastern Virginia, in which he lived alone. He showed his identification and security clearance at the gate, then used an encoded pass-key to move through the reception area. This same key granted him access to an unmarked restricted elevator that serviced only one building's underground levels. Three stories into the earth his pass was required yet again, to open the thick glass door shielding the most heavily secured labs. Once inside this nest of scientists, fluorescent light, and unimaginably expensive equipment, he reached a door housing a numeric punch pad. Here the code was changed three times a week, committed to memory, and available to no more than three or four technicians and security guards at any one time. Here was Reynolds's private research area.

In Reynolds's outer office two young men sat quietly at their desks, typing rapidly on computer keyboards. Their faces flickered in the screens' illumination. Like everyone who worked for Reynolds, they shared a pinched, harried look. Reynolds demanded a degree of dedication from those around him that bordered on fanaticism. David Bailey, his sandy hair a mess, analyzed a numeric string that was essential to a microrobot's movements. Philip Kang, the head of his class at Carnegie Mellon University, was perfecting the integration of a new, highly miniaturized microcircuitry into a nanomachine's power source. Their finished work was expected at the end of the day.

Reynolds emerged from his inner lab in what, for him, passed for casual wear—pressed military slacks, shirt with epaulets, and a black tie unknotted just a fraction. "Philip," he called out.

Kang closed his eyes, rubbed them with his fingertips, and listened.

"You're paying extra attention to the band-gap voltage, right?" Reynolds asked. "I don't want any fluctuations in the power supply. We should be beyond that already."

Philip Kang had been working for Colonel Reynolds for three months. Six months before, he had been handed his doctoral diploma. "Yes, Colonel," Kang said, his voice a monotone.

Reynolds walked to Kang's desk and grabbed a sheaf of haphazardly stacked printouts. He flipped rapidly from one sheet to the next, humming to himself, already onto the next almost before his eyes had passed over the previous list of numeric data.

"No, no," Reynolds said.

Kang tensed, swiveling his chair around to face Reynolds. "Is there something wrong, sir?"

Reynolds shook his head. "I can see already that you're putting together a code sequence that's nearly two percent short of what we could be achieving. You're losing efficiency in the transfer."

Kang resisted the urge to laugh; he was exhausted, having worked seventy hours or more a week since starting this job. Now Reynolds, after glancing at a sheet of printouts, was claiming he could calculate their veracity to within a percent or two.

"Sir, with all due respect," Kang said, "this circuitry is new. Integrating conduction into a nanosystem is hard enough without having to learn as I go. You have to expect some power loss or fluctuation until we get better at this."

Reynolds's face was tight with concentration, his eyes scanning the last few sheets. Kang had never worked for anyone like Reynolds before. He was almost unknowable. His eyes, recessed into his high cheekbones like twin lamps in a dark field, seemed continually hungry, always consuming information, always seeking. To Kang, at times Neil Reynolds seemed less like a man than a device for processing information.

"Philip, I hear what you're telling me," Reynolds said, stacking the papers and replacing them on Kang's desk. Kang felt his shoulders relax. "And it's unacceptable," Reynolds added, almost as an afterthought.

"But, sir—"

"Learn something now: It is a waste of energy to state the obvious." Reynolds folded his arms and stared at Kang's computer screen. "I know this circuitry is new. I know you have to learn as you go. I know that my nanosystems are the most intricate devices you have ever seen. If you strip away all the rhetoric, what you have told me is that you find your job difficult and, to you, not doing your job well is acceptable. But it isn't. Trim that two percent, Philip, and have everything ready for me before you go home.''

Reynolds started walking back to his lab. In a more gracious tone he added, ''You can stay as late as you need to.''

Reynolds closed the door behind him. It sealed with a hydraulic hiss. Philip Kang sat staring at his computer, his mouth open.

WHEN HE WAS ALONE IN HIS LAB, REYNOLDS LEANED BACK against the closed door and sighed deeply. His interaction with Philip Kang could have gone better. He had to remember to practice psychology—sympathy, comradeship—with his workers. It was the best way in which he could hope to get more and better work from his assistants.

Reynolds dimmed the ambient light in the room with a dial built into the wall. For his current work he needed as little visual or auditory distraction as possible. For this reason he had sabotaged the phone line into this inner sanctum weeks ago, and he had kept the repairmen locked out with various excuses every time they arrived to repair it. He needed solitude, quiet, and, most of all, secrecy. It had always given him solace to be the only keeper of his own secrets—and his latest discoveries constituted the greatest secrets any man had ever known.

In the lowered light the room and the equipment within it took on an amorphous, shadowy quality. The dimmed computer monitors, eleven in all, lit the black computer processors. As if the electronic gear had come to life, all the equipment seemed to be growing wires, with multicolored strips running into and out of the stacks of powerful processors.

On a ridged rubber pad sat Reynolds's workstation, the key to everything: a modular set of metal handles and control devices mounted on a stand, along with a heavy set of wraparound goggles. These devices glowed under an overhead light, its beam tinted crimson by a special bulb. This red appeared to stain the gear black, the mounted lens and intricate eyepiece indistinct and dark. Reynolds prepared to commune with these machines, feeling as though he had waited his entire life for the events of the past month.

He walked onto the rubber pad and donned the goggles, adjusting the elastic strap for tightness. All he saw now was darkness. Reaching out in front of him, he felt the coolness of the control console. He pressed a button that initialized the computer system. Glowing words appeared suspended in the void:

NANOSYSTEM/REYNOLDS IS ACTIVE. CHOOSE OPTION.

An electrical thrill moved up his spine. Finding a plastic mouse with his free hand, he edged an electronic marker through a list of command options. When he reached the one he wanted, he clicked.

ACTIVE DEVICE CONFIRMED. PRESET SEQUENCE, DEMONSTRATION, OR REAL-TIME CONTROL?

The nanorobot was active and responding. Perfect. Reynolds's eyes paused for an instant on the "demonstration" option. He had installed it into the system at a time when he had imagined he might show his progress to others. Now it was a relic of another age.

With another click Reynolds ordered the system to allow him to control the robot's movements and actions with his hand devices. In a moment he would, for all practical purposes, change into a different order of being. He would see what his robot saw. When he moved, it would move.

Then it happened. Without warning the blackness and the letters disintegrated, replaced by a momentary jumble of static. The picture began to resolve itself.

He now viewed what no other man in the history of the world had ever seen. He witnessed the impossible. The imagery was strange and alien, but it was real. Before him was a long tunnel, hazy. Ahead, far in the distance, was a bend. Around him was a surface ridged with small, curved outcroppings, minute irregularities that were foreign to any human engineering. The colors were muted, shades of gray and red, variations in hue such as Reynolds had never imagined. It was akin to seeing through the eyes of a new species.

Reynolds stared raptly ahead. With a slight flick of the hand controls he began to move forward. At the periphery of his vision he saw a pencil-thin leg, that of the robot.

"Beautiful," he whispered.

The robot itself was one tenth of a millimeter in length. It was equipped with two grasping arms and a multitool prosthesis, and was powered by .15 volts of electricity supplied by the new semiconductors obtained for him by Jefferson Faber.

"Don't think of Faber," Reynolds growled to himself. "Don't think of anything. Just concentrate."

With a minute power charge the robot could move, take commands, and transmit data back to Reynolds. It sent back what it saw through a sonar scanning beam, which the computer processors converted to three-dimensional stereoscopic images beamed through Reynolds's virtual-reality goggles. The device was a life-form, albeit one composed of silicon, semiconductors, and microscopic wires.

And now it was in the hypothalamic vessel of a living man, deep under the skin, moving in increments of micrometers toward the hypothalamus of the brain.

"Concentrate," Reynolds commanded himself.

Yesterday the robot had entered the systems surrounding the subject's pituitary gland, subtly changing patterns of blood flow and hormone discharge. And it had worked. The process could be deadly, or beneficial—depending upon Reynolds's desires.

Personality, inclination, the soul: these things were not immutable. They could be changed for the better. People could become more than hidebound systems of reflex and response. He wondered if anyone else would understand what he had found.

"Laura," Reynolds said. He squeezed his eyes shut for a second, then opened them again. His concentration was, at best, half of what it had been the day before.

He thought of her. In the hotel lobby, smiling at him, looking into his eyes. Her hair curled around her ears. Her face animated by an intangible spark that had drawn him to her. She was knowing, caring, engaged in the world in a way that he wasn't. When she talked to him, he felt fondness and a sense of challenge.

It was a hell of a time to become infatuated. Reynolds was honest enough with himself to admit that this was what he felt. A new universe had enveloped his mind—and yet so many of his thoughts centered around this woman he barely knew.

She had called him the day before, delighted with him for giving her a strategy to use against Jefferson Faber. They had talked like old friends, Reynolds ignoring the knocking at his door in his seldom-visited office. When he hung up, he didn't begrudge an instant of the time that she had cost him from his work.

The hypothalamus was nearly reached. Reynolds urged forward the robotic device that acted as his proxy. It didn't move.

"What the hell?" Reynolds muttered.

The image before him shuddered. The great mass of connections that was the hypothalamus flickered within a cloud of shifting purples and grays. Again Reynolds tried to move his device, and couldn't. Then he remembered.

Of course. Here was evidence of how distracted he had become. Feeling for a switch on the console, Reynolds activated a routine that listed options in bold letters superimposed in space. He chose:

AUTOMATIC DISENCUMBERING SEQUENCE.

The images he saw through the goggles grew distorted. The brain structures vibrated, the flow of fluid all around became a viscous haze that obscured his vision.

The nanorobot had become covered with white blood cells sent by the body to combat foreign objects. They were far too small to injure the device, but their combined weight was too much for the robot to bear. To be rid of them the robot shook, at the same time scraping itself with a tiny shaving arm.

"Like a dog shaking off fleas," Reynolds said. He felt himself shake, from his shoulders to his knees, and noted that he had begun to emulate some of his robot's movements. Objectively speaking, it was only natural.

Within a minute the cells were dispersed into a small cloud, which the device passed through as though it were harmless fog. Now nothing stood in the way. Feeling for the controls, Neil Reynolds beheld his own hypothalamus.

Here it was: command central, the home for the integration of sympathetic and parasympathetic functions. Here was the tiny universe that controlled water balance, body temperature, and vital hormones. Through the sonar image Reynolds observed the sloping plain of the ventricular floor, the soft curve of one mamillary body, the branching limbs of the paraventricular nucleus.

It was nothing short of looking into his own soul.

His movements quicker now, Reynolds accomplished what he had come to do. He grasped the tiny implant in his brain and directed it to increase its stimulating charge. Numbers paraded through his consciousness, ratios and equations. His ideas were like tangible objects, existing beyond words.

Then he felt it. The pituitary adjustments he had performed on himself the day before had prepared his brain for this current series of adjustments. It was working.

Reynolds felt his back stiffen. A DNA helix appeared in his mind's eye, dancing, rotating. Details sprang out at him, beckoning for attention. He saw numerals that exploded into brilliant colors. Metabolic power, the body's electricity: why had it ever seemed like a mystery?

His ears filled with a roar, and Reynolds reached out for the workstation's cool metal to hold himself upright. In a flash of almost unbearable intensity he comprehended how limited he once had been.

Laura. Her smile in the hotel lobby, her voice, the way he felt about her. Her presence in his mind disappeared; the double helix returned. The sequence . . . the sequence. He understood it all.

Neil Reynolds gasped. "Discipline," he hissed through clenched teeth. "Focus."

Every step had felt like this, at first, before he had learned to control his new capabilities. It would pass. It would pass.

A flood of images exploded: his life, others' lives,

space, distance, mathematics, and the balance of the body's forces interweaving like a pattern on a rug. From somewhere deep within him, some part that stubbornly refused to be touched, a voice shouted within the soundless ether, terrified.

13

LAURA WALKED DOWN THE STAIRS, GLANCING UP ONCE TO make sure the green glowing night-light was turned on in the hall. If he woke in the night needing to use the bathroom, Carlo would invariably wake her for help negotiating the dark corridor. Parenting, at times, was a proactive science.

She was in the kitchen pouring a cup of rose-hip tea when the phone rang. Dressed in pajamas and slippers, Laura moved quickly into the living room to answer it.

"Laura, you sound breathless. I hope I didn't catch you at a bad time."

"Neil!" she said. "No, it's not a problem at all. I just put Carlo to bed an hour ago. I ran to catch the phone before it woke him up."

"Because then he'd never get back to sleep again?"

"Neil, he's not an infant—he's seven years old," Laura teased. "It's just common courtesy, the same as you'd extend to an adult."

Neil chuckled. "Shows you what I know."

She put her tea on the coffee table and stretched out on

the couch. "Well, you're excused. Even men who have children can be pretty clueless sometimes."

"You're very kind," Neil said.

"Neil, you sound so *sincere*!" Laura said.

She heard an electronic beep in the background. Neil apologized for it. "Where are you?" she asked. "Still at work? It must be after one o'clock there."

"I tend to work late when I'm at a vital stage of my research."

"Well, you're one up on me," Laura said. "After my residency I called a moratorium on late nights, unless it's an absolute emergency."

Neil laughed softly. "Well, I suppose I really got used to burning the candle in Vietnam. We were on call for up to a week at a time."

"Really?" she asked. "All right, Neil. It's time for you to tell me your story. Don't edit out the racy parts."

After some extended cajoling Neil acquiesced. He recited, as though he were a boy doing a book report: "I was born in Baltimore, where my father was a doctor. I attended the University of Virginia, all the way until I received my M.D. Right after that I was drafted into Vietnam, where I spent two years as an army surgeon."

"Two years," Laura marveled. "Was it hard for you?"

"Not as hard as it was on the soldiers. I just stitched them up," Neil said. "I stayed on with the army after that. Other than my father nearly all the men in my family were in the service. It was just the natural thing for me to do."

"You sound defensive about it," Laura commented.

"Well, I don't want people to get the wrong idea about me," he said. "There's a stereotype that people in the military are rigid and hardheaded—"

"Whereas you're a party animal who's into meditation and personal encounter groups."

A moment of silence. "Hardly," he finally said, laughing.

"Hey, we're making progress," Laura said. "I made a silly joke and you didn't think I was giving you a hard time."

They laughed together. "Come on, tell me more," she said. "I'll just drink my tea and listen."

"Oh, well, I don't know," he said. "What else have I done that's interesting? I worked in Russia."

"No kidding?" she asked. "Before or after the fall of the Soviet Union?"

"After," he said. "U.S. officers weren't exactly welcome there under the old regime."

"That makes sense."

"It was three years ago," he added. "I went as part of a team touring medical facilities on military bases, offering suggestions and comparing notes. It was really edifying. I made a lot of connections."

"Connections?" she asked.

"Well, you know," he stammered. "I made the acquaintance of other doctors and military men. And women. Well, by women I mean, not, you know, just—"

Laura erupted with laughter. "You know," she said, "we really have to reach the point where I don't make you so shy. Because you're a very interesting man, Neil. I enjoy talking to you."

"I enjoy it too," he said. "I have to be honest, I don't have a lot of friends. I tend to spend all my time at work or at home. After I met you in San Diego, I felt really lucky. It isn't often I come across someone who I want to know. Or who, I guess, is willing to approach me. People have said that I act like I don't want any contact with the human race. It really isn't true, you know."

Laura didn't answer. His impromptu confession was touching, if a bit sad.

"Who are you talking to?"

Laura jumped with shock and sat upright. Carlo was in the doorway, rubbing his eyes and rocking on his heels.

"What are you doing up, Carlo?" she asked. Neil remained quiet on the line, obviously having figured out what was going on.

"I had a bad dream," he said.

"Oh, poor baby," Laura said in a reassuring tone. "Tell you what. I'm talking to a friend. Go on back to your room, and I'll be there in two minutes."

Carlo held up two fingers. "Two minutes? Promise?" he demanded.

"Promise."

Carlo walked slowly upstairs. "Sounds like I should let you go," Neil said.

"Looks that way," she replied. "But thanks for calling. It was really nice."

"I didn't want to intrude—"

"Please," she said. "You're not the only one who's always either at work or at home. It's nice to have someone to talk to."

"Then you don't mind if I call again?" he said hopefully.

"Do I mind? You'll be in trouble if you don't."

They hung up with a promise to speak again soon. Laura found Carlo already almost asleep.

"What did you dream about?" she asked. She rearranged his tangled blankets.

"Daddy," Carlo said. "I dreamed he was coming to see me, and it was scary."

Laura stayed with Carlo until after he sank into a deep slumber. In her heart was the remainder of the easy pleasure she had experienced talking to Neil, combined with a deep sadness for her son. She hoped that his nightmares would end someday.

14

UPON WAKING LAURA WAS PLUNGED INTO A DOMESTIC nightmare. She had overslept by a half hour, and she was due in surgery at eight. Carlo was sure to miss his bus, which meant she would have to drop him off at school on the way to the hospital.

She threw open the door to his room; under the blankets his little form was inert. "Wake up!" she yelled. "We're late!"

Carlo, unlike his mother, never had trouble rising in the morning. So when she saw him stir, Laura grabbed her robe and headed for the shower. She ran the water, hopped into the tub, and listened to the traffic report on her water-proof radio.

"The San Diego Freeway is a *major* mess," the announcer said with forced levity. Laura hurriedly rinsed her hair. "This is a good day to call in sick, listeners."

With a groan Laura dried off and headed back to her room to get dressed. She listened for the usual sound of Carlo's morning: drawers slamming, a rap tape playing, his high voice singing along. But there was nothing.

"Carlo!" she yelled into his room. He hadn't budged.

Federico, their fat tabby, lay sprawled in the nook of Carlo's leg.

"Carlo, we're running late." Laura nudged the boy, sending the startled Federico sprinting into the hall. Carlo mumbled incoherently. "Come on, get up. I have to drive you to school, and I have an important surgery this morning."

Carlo rolled over to face away from her. Without thinking Laura grabbed the pile of blankets and pulled them off Carlo like a magician with a tablecloth. Carlo lay curled in his pajamas on the bare bed, his head covered by his hands.

"I'm not going to tell you again," she threatened.

Carlo sat bolt upright in bed, his eyes glassy with sleep. "*God,* Mom. I'm getting up. Why don't you leave me the hell alone, anyway?"

Laura gritted her teeth; when she was a little girl, if she had spoken that way to her mother, she would have received a hard slap. Laura tried to be more tolerant. Instead of punishing him she tightened the sash of her robe and started for the door.

"I'm going to be dressed in fifteen minutes," she said icily. "Just be ready. We'll have to eat breakfast in the car."

In her room she put on a slip and a skirt, her pulse racing as she searched for a matching blouse and jacket. Even with the door closed she heard Carlo slamming around in his room; that morning's rap selection blared at an unusually obnoxious volume. She pulled her hair into a ponytail, the curls messily falling out around her face.

"I look like shit," she said. The bathroom door slammed. Federico meowed in the hallway, hungry for his morning meal.

* * *

THEY RODE TOGETHER TO CARLO'S SCHOOL LIKE TWO ENE-
mies. Carlo complained that his bagel was stale and
dropped it, smearing butter all over the seat. Laura cursed
under her breath at the traffic. By the time they reached the
school, her back was coated with a film of sweat. The air
seemed dirtier than usual that morning, the drivers more
selfish and aggressive. Another fight broke out between
them over lunch money—Carlo asked for extra change that
she knew he would spend on soda and junk food. After a
grudging kiss on the cheek he slammed the car door and
jogged away, not looking back.

On the way to the hospital she was stuck in a torrent of
stop-and-go traffic all the way into the San Fernando Valley. She wished she could live the entire morning over
again, this time doing everything right; she also wondered
how much his foul mood had been connected to his dream
of Steve the night before.

She and Carlo had been at odds too often lately: two
days of harmony would be followed by a fight about his
bedtime, or how much TV he could watch. At times such
as these they acted like two cell-mates. Carlo had learned
to test the bounds of his mother's authority, catching her
when she was weak or tired or preoccupied. If only his
father had lived. If only Steve had been a good husband.
Carlo needed a man in his life, another authority figure, an
example of how to grow up.

That's it, Laura thought to herself as she pulled into the
doctors' parking lot at Valley Memorial. *Stop it with the if-
only's and start giving yourself some credit. You can make
it, you can raise him by yourself.*

In the surgical lounge she tossed ice cubes into a cup of
steaming coffee and drank it while staring at the television.
Several surgeons, all men, were sprawled in couches and
chairs, some reading the newspaper, one talking on a cellu-

lar phone. There were Russian troops on the news again, marching into a town in the Caucasus. A Russian diplomat appeared on the screen and said everything was under control.

"Under control, my ass. They've got it under control— and I'm a millionaire movie star."

Dennis Martinez stood behind Laura, drinking a bottle of carrot juice. "Good morning," he said, shaking his head at the television.

Martinez was scheduled to assist Laura in surgery that morning. She was glad: he was skilled, with good hands, and she had learned that she could count on him.

Laura noted that she stood at least three inches taller than him. Despite his short stature he possessed a cool dignity that had made him the subject of much romantic speculation before he married a woman from his native Guatemala. "You have carrot juice in your mustache," she said.

He smiled shyly and wiped his sleeve across his upper lip. "I'm a little nervous this morning," he said.

"Your first laparoscopic Nissen," Laura said. "Don't worry. I can do them in my sleep."

"I'd prefer you stay awake," Martinez said.

"It's a deal." She checked her watch. "I'll meet you in the OR in fifteen minutes. I have to run over to my office to check my messages."

Even before she was out the door Laura sensed the mood shift in the lounge. Surgery was still a boys' club, its members prone to creating a fraternity-house atmosphere. Early in her career Laura had tried to be one of the boys, swearing and betting on sports. She had long since given up. Some chasms were never meant to be bridged.

Laura's office was a short sprint across an enclosed walkway from the surgical suites. The walkway was enclosed by glass and lined with ficus trees—a recent addition, since the Ellington-Faber takeover.

Laura found Terri, her assistant, on the phone. Young and pretty, with a cropped strawberry-blond hairdo, Terri controlled the details of Laura's practice with uncommon sharpness and attention to detail. She silently waved hello and passed Laura a stack of mail and messages.

Laura closed her office door and opened the blinds. Among the messages were three new referrals for surgical cases. Since signing Jefferson Faber's papers a week before, Laura had already seen ample evidence that the businessman planned to keep his word. Though she didn't trust him, she had started to feel a measure of security about her job.

She had ten minutes left until surgery. Laura flipped through the messages, barely registering names, until she saw that Ferry had called only fifteen minutes before. That was odd; Ferry never called Laura at work. Punching Ferry's home number, Laura checked her watch. Eight minutes. Ferry answered on the second ring.

"I just got your message," Laura told her friend. She paused. "Ferry, is something the matter? Your voice sounds strange."

"I just needed to talk. Cyrus is at our old office now, making sure he got all of the disks and files he kept as part of the deal."

Ferry sounded as though she had been crying. "Something is happening to him, Laura. He's been taking the phone into our bedroom and locking the door. Last night I heard him in there yelling. When he comes out, he won't talk to anyone. Not even Davood and Mina."

Laura ran through a list of possibilities. An affair? Gambling? A drinking problem? None of these was likely; Cyrus was a devout Muslim and, despite his foul moods, completely dedicated to his family.

"Do you think it has to do with the buyout?" Laura asked.

Ferry sighed. "Cyrus never cared about paperwork, all he wanted was to be alone in his lab," she said. "I reviewed all the papers and signed them myself. He couldn't have hidden anything from me."

Laura recalled what Ferry had said a few nights ago: she suspected Cyrus was protecting her from something. But what? She glanced at her watch. Three minutes.

"Ferry, I'm really sorry, but I have to go to surgery. Maybe it's nothing. You know how Cyrus feels about selling the company—he's probably blowing some minor detail out of proportion. Give him time."

"You're probably right," Ferry said.

"Do something nice for yourself," Laura said. "You're a wealthy lady now. Buy yourself a dress, go to a spa, and order the works. Let everyone else fret for a while."

"Maybe I'll do just that," Ferry said.

"I'll call you soon," Laura said. "I promise."

She hung up and sprinted out of the office, shouting a hurried good-bye to Terri. When she reached the surgical suites—nearly bowling over a slow-moving orderly in her haste—Laura's thoughts drifted back to Cyrus and Ferry.

Ferry was no fool. If she was suspicious of Cyrus, it was almost a sure bet that he was up to something. Laura spent the two minutes it took her to change into scrubs and a mask trying to imagine what Cyrus had gotten himself into. She came up empty.

15

8:15 a.m.

LAURA ASKED FOR A WIPE AS SHE PEERED AT THE TELEVISION monitor positioned above the patient's head. From her side a nurse pressed a sponge to Laura's brow.

"Thank you," Laura said. Screens at either end of the operating table displayed the same image: that of the electrocautery and dissecting scissors inside the patient, sparks of electricity spitting from their tips. Laura manipulated the instruments through trocars—plastic tubes inserted through small incisions in the patient's inflated abdomen. From the top of the esophagus she first moved laterally, then deeper down.

Across the table Dennis Martinez retracted the esophagus, his eyes fixed in rapt concentration over his powder-blue mask.

Laura had performed Nissen surgery more than three hundred times, but each operation always contained an element of the new and dangerous. Beneath her sharp titanium scissors lay the aorta. If she nicked it, blood would spurt as if from a geyser, blotting out the camera and forcing her to make a wide, damaging cut in the patient's belly.

Millimeters away was the delicate diaphragm. If she

made a single errant move, air from the lung cavity would sweep into the body, shifting the heart and strangulating its blood flow from the vena cava. The patient would die instantly. And less than an inch behind her scissors was the heart itself. After a direct puncture the patient would bleed out in minutes.

"Good work, Dennis," she said. "Keep up that retraction."

Martinez responded with a subtle nod. Laura glanced to one side, resting her eyes for a few precious seconds. Behind the surgical draping the anesthetist sat sentinel over the patient. The man on the table was named Charles Netter, an African-American man in his early fifties who had appeared in Laura's office with a history of excruciating reflux pain. An upper GI series had revealed a small ulceration at the end of his esophagus, caused by acids and bile from his stomach. Antacids and blockers hadn't helped, and the ulcer had increased in size. A final biopsy revealed what might have been a premalignant lesion.

Laura dissected one fiber at a time as she began to expose the esophagus, all the while sensitive to the heart beating just above her instrument. Finally she found the window she sought—the clearance behind the esophagus and in front of the diaphragm and aorta.

"Got it," she said, staring up at the video screen. Martinez grunted in assent. "Pressure?"

Albert Gold, a thirtyish anesthesiologist known in the hospital for his meticulous record-keeping and attention to detail, responded instantly. "Blood pressure 132/20," he said in his deep baritone. "130/40, 130 . . . 110/30."

"Not so much pressure on the goose," Laura said.

Laura knew Martinez's traction on the esophagus could potentially cause a nerve reflex in the area, dropping Netter's blood pressure.

"Got it," Martinez said. "Sorry."

"Pressure rising," Gold said. "Back to 130/40."

"Relax, Dennis," Laura said, looking into Martinez's eyes across the table. "We're doing fine."

The room was hushed as Laura worked deeper into her dissection. She felt total control over her movements, as well as the sense of almost preternatural ease she always felt when reaching the most difficult stages of an operation. Then, without warning, a jet of blood shot across the screen.

"Oh, no," she said. "I nicked a damned vessel."

The nurse standing by Laura's side gave out an involuntary gasp; crimson blood spilled into the abdominal cavity. For a brief second the nurse holding the camera in place shuddered, making the image dance. An errant jet of blood shot onto the camera lens, obscuring the view.

"Suction!" Laura said. "Pull that camera out of there."

She wiped clean the camera lens with alcohol and put it back into the trocar, handing it off to the nurse. The inside of Netter's body swam on the screen until the nurse was able to again locate the proper angle.

"Point the camera at the bleeder," Laura said. She tried to exude calm, knowing from experience that panic was contagious in the OR. "Show me the bleeder. I need an endoclip."

The device was handed to Laura; she shoved it through an open trocar, found the point of bleeding, and quickly clipped it shut. After suction and irrigation she could see that the bleeding had stopped.

"Good, it was minor," Martinez said. Laura could tell from his tone that he was trying to be reassuring. It was nice of him, but she didn't need it. She had long since learned that stepping into a surgical gown means accepting minor mistakes. The good surgeon corrects problems, then forgets about them.

The major phase of the surgery still lay ahead—swinging the flap, bringing the greater curvature of the stomach behind the esophagus, and anchoring it with sutures into a 360-degree wrap through the stomach's other anterior surface. Netter's esophagus would be spared the bombardment of acids from the stomach and duodenum it had suffered from, and hopefully his lesion would abate before it became cancerous.

She began dissecting blood vessels from the stomach's greater curvature, the gastroepiploics. "Tilt the patient upward," she ordered.

Gold quickly responded, cranking a level beneath the heavy surgical table to tilt the patient. Feeling herself in a rhythm, Laura attacked the blood vessels between the stomach and spleen, careful not to spark any more bleeding.

Despite herself her mind wandered. Laura imagined Carlo at school. She thought about Ferry and Cyrus. And she thought about Neil Reynolds and how fond of him she had become after meeting him once and speaking on the phone a few times. She wondered if she would see him again, and was amazed to realize how strongly she hoped she would. It had been a very long time since she had developed such feelings for a man.

"Could someone turn on some music?" she asked the room at large. "Anything. I need help concentrating."

The scrub nurse flipped on the portable radio perched on a ledge next to the supply cabinet; Rolling Stones music filled the room, Mick Jagger proclaiming that he was coming to someone's emotional rescue.

"Not the oldies station," Martinez groaned.

"I like the oldies station," Laura said, looking up. "You sound like my son."

"Hey, I'm a couple of years older than you." She saw Martinez smile through his mask. "I just like something more current."

"The patient's lightening up," Laura said to Gold. She had noticed a twitch in Netter's musculature. "Get him under, Al."

"I'm on it," Gold's swivel chair scraped across the OR floor. Within seconds he had injected additional muscle relaxant into the intravenous tubing. "Sorry about that."

With Martinez's help Laura completed wrapping Netter's stomach around his esophagus. "2–0 silk," she requested. Inserting the needle and thread through a trocar, careful not to catch a valve and release the gases that kept Netter's abdomen inflated, Laura placed three stitches on the stomach, then the esophagus. This completed the wrap.

"Perfect," she said. "Not too tight."

Martinez sighed. "Just right."

Laura stepped away from the table. "Well, Dennis, you've assisted on your first laparoscopic Nissen," she said. "Do you mind closing up?"

"My first—and my last one here," he replied.

"What do you mean?" Laura asked.

"I took a job in Alabama," Martinez said. He started to apply stitches to the patient. "I can't afford to stay here— not with my mortgage and debts. I took a beating selling off the house, but at least I'll be getting a fresh start."

Laura was shocked. Dennis hadn't given any sign that he was considering another job. Perhaps, she thought, he had been playing it safe. He might have found himself on even fewer referral sheets if he had made it known that he was considering a move.

"Hey, don't look so sad," Dennis said. "I'll send you a

postcard. If you and the kid are ever in the South, look us up.''

''When are you leaving?'' Laura asked.

''The day after tomorrow.''

''I'm really sorry to see you go, Dennis,'' she said. ''I hope things work out better for you there.''

''Thanks,'' Dennis said. ''We'll see.''

Laura began peeling off her surgical gloves. Martinez was bent over the patient, ready to stitch closed the tiny series of incisions through which they had rearranged Netter's anatomy. She liked Dennis, and she trusted him in the OR. He would be missed. It seemed that not everyone had been as lucky as she in winning concessions against Ellington-Faber; she guiltily wondered if she could have made things better by continuing her fight in court.

When she returned to her office carrying a salad and soda from the cafeteria, Laura opened the door to the sound of Terri loudly cursing. It was such a surprise that she stood in the doorway for a moment, listening. Then she heard banging, as though a fight had broken out.

Behind the partition shielding the reception area from the inner office, Laura found Terri standing over the office fax machine. The device was in three separate pieces, and a long roll of paper had unfurled across the floor. Terri was a mess, her forehead sweaty, the sleeves of her blouse rolled up and wrinkled.

''Anything I can help with?'' Laura asked.

Terri looked up, her eyes bulging with surprise and frustration. ''I thought I was alone,'' she said. ''Sorry. I wouldn't have been screaming like that if there were any patients out there.''

''It's all right,'' Laura said. She eyed the fax machine. It was more than six years old, and notoriously finicky. ''Looks like it's time for some new equipment.''

Terri grabbed one of the amputated machine pieces. "I didn't take it apart," she said. "It just sort of collapsed. Maybe I can fix it."

Terri had been steadfastly supportive through the hard times of the previous months. At times Laura hadn't even been sure she could afford to keep a full-time assistant, much less order expensive supplies. Terri, knowing this, had responded by cutting corners everywhere she could.

"Enough is enough," Laura said. "Order a new one. A better one."

Terri had seen the papers sent by Ellington-Faber and knew that the practice's fortunes had ostensibly changed. Before the younger woman could reply, the phone began to ring.

"I'll get that in my office," Laura said. "Try to give that thing a dignified burial."

By the time Laura put down her salad and soda, the phone had rung eight times. She hoped the caller had stayed on the line. "Hello?" she said, wiping spilled salad dressing off of her surgical scrubs.

"Laura? You're answering your own phone now?"

She recognized the voice immediately. "Neil? What are you up to? Aren't they keeping you busy enough out there in Washington?"

A pause. "Uh—maybe I called at a bad time."

"Come on," Laura said, laughing. "I'm just giving you a hard way to go. I'm really glad to hear from you."

Reynolds's chuckle sounded forced. *God,* Laura thought, *he's really nervous.*

"Well, I was just thinking—" he began.

"That sounds dangerous."

This time his laugh was genuine. "Maybe you're right," he said. "But I was thinking how much I've enjoyed talking with you recently. I may be . . . well, I may be shy, but I wanted you to know that I look forward to our talks. They've been the high point of my days.''

Laura discovered herself unconsciously running her hand through her hair. She saw her face reflected in her office window; she was beaming. It had been a long time since she had been charmed by the strong, awkward type.

"Well, Colonel," she said with deliberate slowness, "I've enjoyed it too. I was afraid you might think I was only being so friendly because you helped me with your legal suggestion."

"Oh, of course not," Reynolds said, his voice formal and stuffy.

Laura laughed out loud. "You're for real, aren't you, Neil?" she asked, half serious. "This isn't just an act, is it?"

"I . . . what do you mean?"

"Never mind. You're not acting." She opened the lid of her salad, spilling more dressing on a stack of case files.

"Well, I called for a reason." He sounded as if he was gathering his courage, like a schoolboy about to ask her for a date. "Did I tell you I have a friend who is a part owner of the professional basketball team there in Los Angeles?"

"No, you didn't," Laura said. "Which team?"

"Well, my friend tells me one team tends to win, and the other doesn't. He owns part of the team that tends to win."

Laura laughed. "To tell you the truth, that doesn't help. I don't know the first thing about sports."

"Neither do I," Reynolds said. "But what about your son?"

"He's crazy about basketball," she said. "Posters, trading cards, the works."

"Then it's settled." Reynolds's voice reflected renewed confidence. "I'll fly to L.A. on Friday, pick up you and your son, and take you to the game. We'll be able to sit in the owners' section. I assume those are good seats."

"Friday?" Laura asked. She had thought she would like to see Neil again, but now some part of her wanted to run away. Did she really want to complicate her life like this?

"Friday," Reynolds repeated. "Unless you have other plans."

Other plans? She might watch TV with Carlo, they might visit her mother, or Ferry and Cyrus. This was how they spent nearly every weekend. She would be a coward to refuse—and Carlo would never forgive her for turning down the chance to sit in luxury seats at a professional basketball game.

"All right, Friday," she said.

"Good. I'll be in at around five, allowing for the time difference. I'll get a hotel room and call you from there."

They hung up after exchanging good-byes. "That's that," Laura said to the empty office.

"Did you say something?" Terri asked, appearing in the doorway.

Since she had started working for Laura, Terri had persistently tried to set her boss up for dates with various friends and relatives. Laura realized that her side of her conversation with Neil must have carried into the outer office.

"Just talking to myself," Laura said.

"Oh, sorry. I thought you were talking to me."

Terri waited in Laura's door with the hint of a good-natured smirk. She had definitely heard everything.

"Go order that new fax machine," Laura ordered with exaggerated sternness. Terri left, smiling and shaking her head.

Picking at her salad, Laura felt vaguely irritated. Terri meant well, but why did people always take it upon them-

THE ETERNITY CURE • 127

selves to monitor the romantic lives of single women? So Terri knew she had a date. She wouldn't give her the satisfaction of talking about it.

Besides, it was a harmless basketball game, with her son in tow, with a man she barely knew. What could possibly come of it?

16

FRANK ERICKSON CROUCHED BEHIND A HIGH STONE FORMA-tion, trying to catch his breath. The drive up here from the camps outside Ashkabad, then the hike up the hillside, had been grueling. A typical day in Erickson's life involved drinking in the bar of a foreign hotel at which a summit or diplomatic conference was being held. Before the last round he would sift through the various disseminations and deceits of official sources, then file his story via modem.

Two days before, he had flown from Islamabad to Turkmenistan at the behest of his editor, Nick Mills. A local source had uncovered something, Mills had said—the people there said armed Americans were passing through. The foreigners were thought to be carrying something precious from the way they acted, and they had hired Iranian guides for the drive south into the mountains.

It was no problem for Mills to send Frank to this hell-hole. Nick was probably at that very moment sitting in the New York offices of *Worldweek,* drinking Irish Breakfast tea and reviewing expense accounts.

'' 'If they've left the city, you can always hire a

driver,' " Erickson said into the wind, mocking his editor's rasping voice.

Easier said than done. It had taken a lot of dollar-waving to find a driver willing to take him so close to the Iranian border. And as for the roads—to call them goat paths would be too much of a compliment to local engineering. The hired jeep had rocked and groaned through the harsh terrain, where sheer drops without guardrails appeared from out of nowhere on the far side of blind curves.

Erickson had left the driver and climbed a rocky, steep hill, from which he would have a good view of the more heavily traveled road below, the only one in the immediate vicinity that could handle truck traffic. Erickson had given the driver fifty dollars to wait for him until sunset. It would be a complete miracle if he was still down there waiting.

"You're in over your head, Frank," Erickson said. The wind whipped around the big rocks, pushing him closer to the edge of the precipice. He tried not to look down; below him was a sheer drop of a couple hundred feet onto rock and sun-hardened earth.

Erickson pressed himself against the sturdiest part of the outcropping and opened his field pack. Inside was his laptop computer, his cellular phone, his digital camera, and his binoculars. Most importantly, there was a pack of cigarettes. He took the binoculars from their hard plastic case, then found a cigarette and lit it.

This was ridiculous. He was pushing forty, he wasn't a young cowboy anymore. In fact, he had *never* been a young cowboy. Stupid risks were for stupid reporters. He preferred safety, good meals, and warm hotel rooms.

"It would help if I knew what I was looking for," he muttered, focusing the binoculars. He looked over the landscape on the far side of the road below, over the chalky dust and stone, the small batches of sere brown shrubbery.

"Holy Mother," he said.

Perched on the far side of the sloping hill across from his, Erickson saw a vulture—or was it a buzzard? Anyway, it was a big one. Its wings flapped gently as it stared at him, a picture of malevolent concentration.

He took the binoculars from his eyes and looked uneasily around. For all he knew, that bird had friends—hungry friends. That was it. He would go back down and hope like hell his driver was still there. If not, Erickson would get on the cellular and call into town. Someone would come get him for a hundred bucks. He looked through the binoculars one last time, training them on the road below.

There was a big truck down there, heading in his direction.

He would pretend he hadn't seen it. Who would know the difference? It was a good plan—stow the gear, put out the cigarette, go down the hill, get to the airport, and get the hell out of the country. That was all he had to do.

"Oh, what the hell," Erickson cursed. His instincts took over. He pulled the electronic camera out of his bag and, with a thin cable, attached it to his computer. Flipping a switch, he turned on the laptop and initialized its internal cellular modem to dial *Worldweek*'s photography department. The camera worked digitally, and attached to the laptop, it could scan a picture into its circuitry and beam the image across the world in moments. Technicians in New York could digitally enhance the photo, exposing details and nuances in the image.

"Just one picture," Erickson promised himself.

A wind gust blew up the sheer stone face as Erickson edged around the rock he had hidden behind. Panicked, he grabbed on to a bush at his feet and steadied himself. He dragged the electronic equipment closer to the edge and waited.

It was surely a routine supply run. He was probably risking a fall to his death for a picture of an old Soviet-era truck. But why would it be heading south? There were no towns or bases between there and Iran.

The truck grew closer. Erickson stood up, one hand on the rock, the other gripping the camera. He was in plain sight now, but the chance was slim that the truck's occupants would look up at just that moment. The sun was at his back. The glare might obscure him from view. He realized he was making excuses—he simply wanted this picture.

It was almost below him. Erickson took more than the one picture he had promised himself—he took two, then three. It looked like a military truck, with a canopy in the back and wide, rugged wheels. It bore no marks of state.

The laptop computer hummed and beeped as it dialed the transatlantic code. A familiar hiss emerged from its speakers as it began to transmit the data.

He was done. He could pack up and go.

The truck slowed down, then stopped. Erickson watched, realizing he was exposed to their view. His mind raced: Engine trouble? A flat tire? No, the tires looked fine.

From the rear truck came three men dressed in khaki fatigues and hats slung low over their foreheads. The driver emerged joined them.

Erickson took another picture. The computer, still working, made its inconspicuous noises of transmission. Erickson focused the camera's zoom lens as far as he could go while maintaining a relatively clear picture. He saw their faces.

They were looking up at him and pointing.

''Oh, no,'' Erickson said.

17

JEFFERSON FABER'S ESTATE WAS LOCATED IN AN EXCLUSIVE precinct of Beverly Hills north of Sunset Boulevard. In the ten years since he had bought it, he had installed a sculpture garden, complete with Roman and Greek antiquities. The place was gated and guarded, the dimensions of the house itself obscured by lush, meticulous grounds-keeping.

His life had been a long, sometimes brutal process of acquisition. He had increased his sizable inheritance ten-fold through land deals, leveraged buyouts, and an almost instinctual acumen for knowing when an opponent was at his or her weakest. Even his marriage had been a sort of business move; he had found Danielle when he was cash poor, and combined her wealth with his. When she had drowned in the Aegean Sea eight years ago, her own port-folio became his. It had been a terrible accident, but fortune continued to smile on him nonetheless.

"Jefferson. We're out of champagne. Open another bottle, baby."

Faber paused in the foyer of his first-floor living space, a room equipped with high-tech sound and video, plush sofas, a bar, diffused light from hidden sources, and a view looking out onto his sculptures.

"Don't you think you've had enough?" he asked, frowning.

The girl was young, probably barely out of her teens. She reclined on the long black leather sofa, dressed only in a sheer white nightgown, her eyes closed and her head nodding to the soft music playing from speakers arranged throughout the room. Her long black hair cascaded down onto her bare shoulders, and in her hand was an empty champagne glass, fine-cut crystal that dangled precariously from her fingertips.

"Watch that glass, Jennifer," Faber added harshly. He tightened the sash of his robe. "It's part of a set."

Jennifer set the glass down on a table, a bit too hard; Faber winced. "Come on, Jefferson. You can afford to open another bottle."

"What I can afford, or can't afford, isn't the question." Faber sat on the sofa next to Jennifer. "I simply think you've had too much to drink."

Jennifer looked up at Faber with eyes that couldn't properly focus. Faber hated this. The girl would probably pass out right there, and he would be stuck with her until she awoke.

"Now, now," he said, raising her to a sitting position. "You need to wake up. Why don't I have the cook put on some fresh coffee?"

"I don't want coffee," Jennifer whined. "Do you have anything stronger?"

"Stronger? What do you mean?"

"You know," she replied, giggling. She brought her face close to his. "Some coke, pills, something like that."

Faber gently stroked the hair that curled down around

her ear. She certainly was beautiful. "Jennifer, I don't take drugs. They're illegal."

She pressed her face against his hand. "Oh, and Jefferson would never do anything illegal."

He raised his other hand, ringing her face. "I'm glad we have an understanding."

Faber tilted his face and kissed her, his hands moving down her shoulders to her slim waist. Jennifer murmured and embraced him, her kiss sloppy from drink. He caressed the contours of her hips, her thighs.

Jennifer went stiff in his hands, but not with arousal. Faber opened his eyes and saw her face agog with astonishment. "What's the matter?" he asked.

She said nothing; she continued staring over his shoulder, as if what she saw there was beyond her power to describe, Faber turned. They weren't alone.

"Oh, damn it," he said. He turned to Jennifer with a flash of panic. "You have to go. Now. Where are your clothes?"

Something in Faber's voice had successfully communicated to Jennifer that she was in danger, because her eyes cleared instantly. "I guess they're in your bedroom," she said. "Where else would they be?"

"All right." Faber glanced over his shoulder. His new guest was working on the patio door. The lock would probably hold for another sixty seconds. "Go to my room and get dressed. Take the back staircase down to the kitchen. Whoever you find there—the cook, the maid, whoever— tell them to ring for a car. Take the back way out."

Jennifer was already halfway out of the room. "Who is that?" she asked. "Do you know her?"

"Just go," Faber barked. "I'll call you later."

Jennifer did as she was told. Faber regained some measure of dignity on the sofa, arranging his sash and arranging his robe to hide his graying chest hair. Then he waited and watched Jeanette Madison dismantle the door lock.

The lock gave way; Faber crossed his legs and waited. Her expression was cold and methodical, as it had been since she had appeared in the sculpture garden. She was dressed in military boots and a leather bomber jacket. When she reached Faber she slapped him open handed across his cheek. Though it wasn't easy, he refrained from flinching.

"It's good to see you, too, Madison," he said.

Madison dropped her canvas bag on a Persian rug. "Interesting choice of friends, Jefferson. What did you do, cruise the high school in your limo?"

Faber smiled. "If I didn't know better, I'd think you were jealous."

"You're an egomaniac," she said disdainfully. She went to the bar and took out a bottle of water. "I'm surprised to find you enjoying yourself like this in the middle of the afternoon. Weren't there any schools for the blind to foreclose on?"

"Not today," Faber said. She sat on a cushioned stool in front of the bar; he watched her hands, trying to imagine why she had arrived unannounced.

Madison took a long slug of water and looked out into the garden. "Your security is a joke," she said. "It's amazing you're alive."

"I keep good account of my enemies."

"Well, I didn't say you were stupid." Madison walked over to the sofa where Faber sat and stood over him. "Jefferson Faber, are you collaborating with local, state, or federal authorities?"

"No."

"Are you wearing a wire, or are there recording devices active in this room?"

"No."

Her posture relaxed a fraction. "When was the last time you had a countermeasures expert come in here to sweep the place for listening devices?"

"Three weeks ago, give or take a couple of days. Believe me, I attend to security. No one comes near me without my knowing everything I need to know about them."

"Well, I can see *that*." Madison bent over and picked up a small Japanese slipper that Jennifer had left behind in her haste. "Seriously, Jefferson, I thought you had better taste."

He ignored her. "Let me see where we stand. You materialized on my property without warning, interrupting a perfectly pleasant afternoon. I assume you have a good reason."

To his surprise Faber thought he saw a flicker of hurt feelings cross Madison's features. "Come on, now. You know you're always welcome in my home," he told her.

"Don't patronize me," she said. "You're aware that we have a crew of my men in the field right now?"

"Of course." Faber allowed his hand to wander up to his stinging cheek. He guessed it probably would turn discolored and bruised within the hour. "Our third transfer."

"I have my communications gear with me." Madison motioned toward her bag. "They're supposed to be in touch with me by midnight, local time."

Madison sat down on the long sofa, as far physically from Faber as she could be. "I'm concerned that we didn't alter their travel route enough. They're traveling farther east than before, but I'm still worried about satellite surveillance."

Faber ran his hand through his hair, feeling the conversation shift in his favor. "Well, Madison, we are all taking risks in this enterprise. I've done everything in my power to minimize the possibility that anything might go wrong."

She took off her coat. Faber allowed his eyes to wander over her; she wore form-fitting black pants tucked into her boots. Her sleeveless T-shirt showed off her muscular arms and dark, flawless skin. Her close-cropped hair contoured her exquisite face like a frame around a painting.

Madison looked at Faber; she could tell what he was thinking. He could see that she wanted to resist him. "I have to take you on your word that you've minimized our chances of failure, and I hate that," she said. "I don't want anyone else to be in control of something this critical."

"No one can control you," Faber said, and it was the truth. "And if you don't mind my saying so, I have more to lose than you. Do you honestly think I would carelessly risk all that I possess?"

"Of course I don't." Madison edged closer on the sofa, her eyes on his. "But you're a greedy bastard. You sell people out to cover your ass. I can imagine me and my people taking the fall, and you using your money and connections to walk away."

"But you have plenty of money now for your organization." Faber said. "And soon you're going to have even more."

"Don't talk to me like an idiot," she said angrily. "You can buy immunity. I can't. Do you want me to run down the list? I'm black. I'm a woman. I'm in a radical group. I'm a documented anarchist. My husband died in police custody—"

"You have me on your side," Faber answered gently. This, too, he meant. Though he understood in his heart that he would never sacrifice himself for her—or for anyone else—he cared about Jeanette Madison. In his mind this made her very fortunate.

"On the second mission my men spotted a military caravan twenty-five miles across from the Iranian border," Madison said, her voice cold. "They got through. But nothing like that was supposed to happen."

"I don't know what to say," Faber replied. "They made it through. They finished the delivery. Isn't that all that matters?"

Her eyes narrowed with animosity. "It's a matter of time until the FBI taps my phones and plants bugs in my compound. You read the papers. You know what's happening to groups like mine."

"Then you have to be smart," Faber said. "I'm not responsible for your political leanings. You know I don't agree with them."

"But you don't believe in anything," she said.

Without warning Madison lashed out and struck Faber again, this time on his other cheek. His tongue probed around his mouth, searching for loose teeth.

Faber smiled and tried to look relaxed, then leapt across the sofa to knock Madison to the ground. But she was quick; she grabbed him around the ribs and, using his momentum, threw him over her. He banged against the coffee table and landed on the hard carpet.

He got up, fumbling to keep his robe closed. Madison rose to her feet. Hoping to surprise her, he stepped toward her and feinted to his left, sweeping his right leg into her knee. It worked; she tumbled to the ground with a howl of anger.

Pressing his advantage, Faber slid behind her and secured her neck in the crook of his arm, pulling tight. He heard her gasp and choke for breath. A second later her elbow thudded into his ribs with such force that Faber feared he might throw up on his rugs. His hands went to his sides, his breath gone. It was over.

Madison punched Faber hard in the breastbone. With a queasy gasp he tumbled backward, falling near the patio doors. She was on him in an instant, slapping him once, then twice, on the face. He felt her free hand opening his robe, and she slid between his legs. The fabric of her shirt was rough against his chest.

"You've been practicing," she said, smiling. She kept his arms pinned beneath her. "That was a good kick, and not a bad choke hold. You have to be prepared to finish it, though. Or else you're dead."

"If you bruised my face, I *will* kill you," Faber said, laughing through the searing pain in his ribs.

"You vain man." She took his face in her hands, kissing his cheeks and neck, finally reaching his lips.

When she pulled away, just a few inches, Faber saw her looking into his face, examining him. Good, he thought, she still didn't know what to expect from him.

"Are any of your staff going to interrupt us?" she asked.

"No." He pulled at her shirt. "They only come into this part of the house with my permission."

"I'll talk to your security people later," she said, her hands moving over his body. "They need to change a few things."

"I'd like that," Faber murmured.

"Do you understand that, if anything happens to me and my people, you'll pay for it?" she asked, her eyes closed.

"We're in this together," Faber replied, distracted by the heat of her body. "There are no weak links."

Madison, like him, would always protect herself. He had always thought that she could be neutralized or discredited if she tried to implicate him. Now he fully understood why she had arrived that afternoon. It was a show of strength.

"Have I told you how pleased I am to see you today?" Faber asked. He pulled her tightly to him, and tried to quiet the spiraling anxiety that gripped him from within.

18

The Iran/Turkmenistan Border.

THE LOW GRUMBLE OF THE TRUCK'S ENGINE IDLING FILLED the stillness of the rocky gorge. The road was clear ahead; behind them the dust stirred by their passage had just begun to settle.

"What's going on?" Andy Hall asked nervously. "Why are we stopped?"

Ron Jameson held out his hand for silence. "Is he alone up there?" he asked Werner.

Werner's long hair was wrapped in a bright blue bandana. He peered through the binoculars, his mouth tight.

Jameson had to fight off the impulse to grab the glasses from Werner. But he was the group leader. He couldn't panic. "I asked you," he said slowly, "is he alone?"

"As far as I can tell," Werner said in his reedy voice.

Werner finally turned over the glasses. Jameson focused them at the top of the hillside, and saw what had compelled Werner to order an emergency stop: a man dressed in a navy-blue coat and slacks, looking down at them and hastily packing away some sort of equipment.

"Give me the rifle with the scope," Jameson ordered Hall. He took the gun and pointed it up the hillside.

* * *

FRANK ERICKSON LOST HIS FOOTING AND SMASHED HIS KNEE against the sharp stone outcropping he had been using for balance. His equilibrium left him for a nauseating instant; he flapped his arms, compelling himself not to look down.

"That's not how it's done," he whispered to himself. "You get killed *after* you're caught, not before they ever lay a hand on you."

He had packed everything away. He was positive that his photographs had made it to *Worldweek* in New York. He wished he could transport himself around the world in an instant, like those bits of electronic data. Across the street from the *Worldweek* offices was a delicatessen that served smoked salmon on bagels and piping hot coffee. Erickson ached for its safety and familiar comfort.

He dared one last look down through his binoculars. Alongside the Arab drivers were the three Americans. Erickson gasped when he saw one of them raise a rifle and point it up toward him.

"They're fucking serious," Erickson hissed. He began to scramble up the rocky slope, with only one small hill to climb before he reached cover and could scramble down the opposite side. He prayed his driver was still there waiting.

Erickson's pants caught on a prickly shrub near the top of the hill. Panicked now, he let go of his pack. It fell at his feet and slid, stopping just short of the cliff's edge. His arms afire, Erickson reached up for the edge of the hill, ignoring the pain.

He arrived at the top. He now needed only to dive forward to safety. The men below—whoever they were, he didn't care—would never be able to double back on the unmarked roads to find him. Erickson flexed his legs to jump.

Before he could, he felt a sharp impact explode in the middle of his chest. Gasping for a breath that wouldn't come, he tumbled backward, his body slamming against rock and finally coming to rest next to his pack.

"YOU GOT HIM!" WERNER EXCLAIMED. HE CLAPPED JAMEson's back. "That was a tough shot. I'm impressed."

The Arab drivers were out of the truck now, gesticulating and talking to each other in worried voices. The gunshots had agitated them, and Jameson needed no interpreter to understand that they wanted no part of what was happening.

And neither did he.

Jameson pointed the gun at the ground and flipped on the safety. "My shot hit the rocks next to that guy," he said. "I didn't shoot him."

Werner was already heading back to the truck. He stopped with one foot on the rear bumper. "What the hell did you say?"

"You heard me," Jameson said. "I'm positive I missed him."

The Iranians stopped talking, sensing a change in the mood of their passengers. All eyes were on Jameson.

Hall looked up at the inert form above them on the hillside. "Then if you didn't shoot the guy, who—"

First there was a low throb, as though from a giant insect. A moment later the sound grew to a roar, and the first rotors appeared, cruising low over the hillside.

"Choppers," Werner cried out. He dived out of the truck and took cover on its opposite side. The drivers joined him, followed by Andy Hall.

Jameson threw the rifle to the ground and placed his

hands on top of his head. Given the accuracy of the shot that had felled the stranger on the ridge, they would already be dead, if that was what the helicopter's occupants desired. They were outgunned, and there was no place to hide.

Jameson looked down the road in the direction they had been heading. There were at least a half-dozen military-style trucks heading toward them at high speed. They would reach them within a minute.

In the sky above were four helicopters, circling like predatory birds. It was over.

19

6:50 p.m., September 11. Los Angeles.

BY THE TIME THEY REACHED THE ELEVATOR LEADING UP TO the luxury boxes, Carlo had, thanks to Neil Reynolds, become the proud owner of a pennant, game program, T-shirt, and gimme cap. He sipped thirstily from a jumbo soda, wide eyed.

"I think someone's having a good time," Neil said.

"That's an understatement." Laura glanced down at her son, who was peering at a glass case containing photographs of various Hall of Fame basketball players.

The evening had passed perfectly to that point. Neil had arrived on time, and the three had eaten pizza and talked as though they had known one another for years. It had been a bit odd to see Neil dressed in a casual blazer and tasteful wool slacks; in her mind Laura had pictured him in the buttoned-up military uniform he'd worn at the San Diego conference. He had surprised her with his relaxed, easygoing manner. He wasn't like so many other men, who always seemed to have hidden agendas. He was open and engaged with her, but he was also keeping his distance and not pushing too hard. So far, Laura was giving him excellent marks.

She tapped Carlo on the shoulder. "Come on," she said. "We're heading up to our seats. You know all about those old guys, anyway."

Stepping into the elevator, she and Neil shared a smile at the boy's relentless enthusiasm, which had started with his first glimpse of the concrete arena. Since then he had kept up a running dialogue with Neil on the relative merits of Michael Jordan versus Karl Malone versus a dozen other players whose names Laura didn't recognize. Neil kept up his end of the debate—he had, he confessed to her when they were alone, done research on pro basketball in anticipation of the game—and he was an instant hit with Carlo. Laura had been on two dates since Steve; neither had led to a second date, and Carlo had been openly hostile to both men.

The crowded private elevator was full of L.A.'s elite. Amid the silk suits and minidresses Laura spotted an actor who played in one of her mother's soap operas. She looked him over, knowing her mother would want plenty of details about his appearance and who he was with.

"I hope you're having a good time," Neil said to her, gently putting his hand on her shoulder. His touch was comfortable and reassuring. "I know you're not much of a sports fan."

She smiled at him. "I'm not big on sports, but I like a good spectacle. It was sweet of you to bring us."

They trooped through the crowd to their seats, which were in the second row of a cordoned-off area affording a perfect overhead view of the court. On the floor below, the home team and the visitors took practice shots and ran choreographed drills.

Before he was in his seat Carlo grabbed at Neil's jacket, rattling on about a player on the home team who had just turned professional after a single college season. Neil took a seat between Laura and Carlo.

Laura peered at the people seated around them. From what she saw, this would be a new experience for her. The women looked as though they had stepped out of fashion magazines. It seemed that every second person was either talking on a cellular phone or holding one in anticipation of a call. She had taken Carlo to a game the year before but they had sat in the cheaper public seats, where they had a clear view of only one end of the court.

Carlo's lecture ran out of steam; he gazed at the court as though taking in every detail to share with his classmates.

"You have a very bright and charming little boy," Neil said to her. "He's inherited a lot from his mother."

Laura tugged at a curl of hair that hung down over her shoulder. "He likes you," she said, quietly enough for Carlo not to hear.

Neil looked down at the court, and she examined his profile. His nose was thin, his cheeks a bit rounded. His brown hair was receding at the temples. He was by no means an exceptionally good-looking man, but she felt an attraction to him. She sensed from him a core of rock-solid decency, as well as strength and protectiveness.

He glanced around, as though noticing his surroundings for the first time. "Quite a crowd in this section, isn't it?" he said. "Not my usual social milieu. I guess you've noticed by now that I tend to be pretty . . . conventional."

Laura sensed that his shyness and insecurity were returning. She put her hand on his. "You've been to my place now," she said. "You know I'm not a candidate for *Lifestyles of the Rich and Famous*—"

"Hey, what are you guys talking about?" Carlo interrupted. He leaned across Neil, forcing the colonel deep into his seat.

"Carlo," Laura said, "you're crushing our host."

"Sorry," Carlo said. "Can I have money for another soda? And some popcorn?"

Laura began to reach for her purse—she had already come to terms with the fact that tonight would involve indulging Carlo a bit more than usual—but Neil stopped her.

"Let me tell you a secret, Carlo," Neil said. "One of the best things about sitting in this section—and I mean something really *cool*—is that you get free drinks and food. Hot dogs, popcorn, you name it. After you receive permission from your mother, go through that door back there. That's where the chow is—all you do is show them your ticket."

Carlo looked as though Neil had just revealed a great and incredible secret. "Anything I want?" he asked.

"As long as it's all right with your mother. She's in charge here."

Laura chimed in. "One more soda, but make it last this time. And you can have one kind of snack, whatever you want."

Carlo leapt from his seat and bounded up the aisle. "Free snack food," Laura mused. "A little boy's paradise."

"I hope you don't mind," Neil said. "I should have asked whether you keep him under any dietary restrictions."

"You did good," Laura said. "You asked me first."

"That reminds me," Neil said. He turned around to see if Carlo was gone. "I should have asked him to grab something for me."

Laura laughed. "Let me guess. You're an ice-cream man."

Neil patted his slightly rounded belly. "Does it show?" he asked, his cheeks turning red.

Laura laughed even harder. "That's not what I meant," she said. "There's just something about you, something almost boyish. I can see you pigging out on junk food when you're all alone."

"Guilty as charged," Neil said.

"I'm a great judge of human character," Laura teased.

"So am I," Neil quickly answered. He paused. "I hope you know . . . I mean, I hope it's clear that I'm fond of you, Laura."

She felt slightly uncomfortable, but also flattered. "I was pretty sure that was the case."

Neil nodded with satisfaction, suddenly serious. "Good," he said. "It's just that I'm often very distracted . . . with my work. You see, I've reached a vital point in my research."

"I'd like to hear all about it," Laura said. "I'm very interested in your work. But that's not why I agreed to go out with you."

"That's nice to know," Neil said, smiling uncertainly. "I thought this game would be a good, low-pressure way for us to spend time together. I'd like to get to know you better, Laura. I would like us to have a chance to learn more about each other."

Laura laughed nervously, inwardly amazed at the giddy rush of pleasure she felt. "I'd like that," she said. "But there's not much to know about me. What you see is pretty much what you get."

"I doubt that," Neil said. "I think you're very complicated—I mean that in a good sense."

Laura didn't reply; it didn't seem necessary. They were slipping easily into the sort of intimacy that she had often thought she would never feel again. It was frightening, exciting, troubling, and hopeful—all at once.

A couple appeared and squeezed past Laura and Neil to reach their seats. Laura caught a whiff of French perfume from the impeccably dressed young blond woman, then the cologne of the man who accompanied her. Not for the first time that night she felt a bit dowdy and tame.

A question occurred to Laura that she had meant to ask at least a dozen times before but that had slipped her mind—under whose auspices were they attending the game? Neil had never identified his friend, the part owner of the team.

"By the way, Neil," she said. "I never found out—"

Laura glimpsed motion in the corner of her eye and paused. She looked up and saw people milling in the area behind the seats start to move back to allow a man and woman to pass. Laura craned her neck to see who had made such an entrance.

Neil was oblivious. "You wanted to ask me something?"

Amid the glittering and rather plastic exemplars of L.A.'s fast lane, Laura saw a face she recognized. Leaving his date—a starkly beautiful African-American woman—at the top of the stairs, Jefferson Faber scanned the crowd until he saw Neil and Laura. When he saw them, he moved quickly down the aisle, his face unsmiling.

He reached them at the moment Neil finally noticed that Laura's mood had changed. Faber arrived in the aisle next to Neil. "Dr. Antonelli," he said in a dry voice. "I'm very glad you could join us tonight. I hope you enjoy the game."

Laura was speechless. "Colonel Reynolds, I hate to be rude," Faber added, his manner surprisingly brusque, "but I need a brief word with you in private. Doctor, I hope you'll forgive me. I'll have him back to you in a few minutes."

Laura met Reynolds's eyes and saw a momentary flash of anxiety that was quickly replaced by a tight smile.

20

7:12 p.m.

NEIL REYNOLDS WAS STRUGGLING TO KEEP HIS EMOTIONS IN check. He was his own test subject—the first human to undergo cognitive enhancement through endocrine manipulation and bioelectrical implants—and he observed himself with a scientist's clinical detachment. He had been able to connect with Laura, and make his sincere feelings known to her. Faber had ruined the moment, the bastard. Reynolds feared that he would be unable to concentrate his increasingly diffused mind again on interacting with Laura.

In antiquity the characteristics of a man were classified as: intellect, will, and sensibility. He was intellectually changed forever, but his feelings and temperament remained the same. His mind was possibly now the most powerful in human history, but he was also infatuated with Laura. He knew that he might inadvertently hurt her by drawing her too near to the dangerous forces he was toying with. But he was still a man. He still craved human contact, and love.

At the moment he felt boundless anger. Jefferson Faber had sprung upon him and Laura before Reynolds could explain his connection to Faber in a way that might have been palatable to her.

"Come back to Earth, Colonel," Faber said, rudely snapping his fingers in front of Reynolds's face. He closed the door behind them.

They were alone in an unmarked room behind the arena's concessions section. It contained two sofas and a television, which now displayed the players in their colorful warm-up suits being introduced on the court downstairs.

"It was uncouth of you to pull me away like that," Reynolds said. Faber settled onto one of the sofas; Neil remained standing.

Faber took a leather case from his suit jacket pocket and pulled out a cigarette that he used to gesticulate while he spoke. "That's no way to thank me," he said. "After all, you're here tonight as my guest."

"Thank you, then," Reynolds said. He felt strangely alienated; at moments such as this he sensed how different he had become. Faber, for all his wealth, power, and cunning, seemed like a representative from a species doomed to extinction.

"That's more like it." Faber lit the cigarette and took a long drag. "I wouldn't have bothered you, but we have a hitch in our plans."

Reynolds struggled to concentrate. He suddenly felt as though his mind were threatening to come unhinged from his body and take flight. "A hitch? Is it Madison? I'm surprised you're willing to be seen with her in public. That alone could create difficulties for us."

"I've decided that's an acceptable risk. And it's not her I'm talking about," Faber said. He crossed his long legs. "I talked to Chapman today. Our latest convoy didn't arrive at the drop-off point."

Reynolds looked at Faber's face for the first time since they had come into the private room. "Good," Faber said in a droll voice. "I have your attention."

"Where is her crew?" Reynolds asked. "Could they have sold the uranium elsewhere?"

"That would be stupid," Faber said. "I don't think our soldiers of fortune are incapable of stupidity, but Madison has them under control."

"Then they were captured," Reynolds said.

"That could very well be the case." Faber paused for a moment to stare at the television monitor. He cast a proprietary gaze over the players.

"Do you think our local contact with the Iranian faction has betrayed us?" Reynolds asked.

"Who knows?" Faber said. "It's always a possibility."

"Start over," Reynolds said slowly. "Why did you have to speak with Chapman?"

"Because his Senate seat gives him access to intelligence information—the kind of information, I might add, that your State Department connections have been failing to provide lately. That's why we pay Chapman, remember?" Faber stared at the end of his cigarette. "Really, Neil, are you feeling well? You look a bit pale."

"I'm fine. Go on."

"Chapman was able to find out only rumors," Faber said. "But we obviously have to lend them credence. An attaché with the Iranian embassy hinted today that the Iranian military has encountered and captured a group of Americans in the Kopet Dagh mountains."

"Hinted?" Reynolds asked. "What does that mean?"

"None of this is official," Faber said. "But Chapman's foreign relations subcommittee seat has already become useful to us. The Iranians are avoiding official channels for the moment. God knows why."

"Obviously, they're calculating how to use this to their best advantage," Reynolds said. "This will be a colossal embarrassment to the U.S. government."

"I see," Faber said. "And that would be the same government in which you're supposed to be maintaining intelligence connections? Instead of—for example—spending your time here with Madonna and child while we still have a convoy in the field?"

"The intelligence I've obtained has been the cornerstone of our entire operation," Reynolds said. "Once the uranium is in transit there's nothing I can do."

"That's a convenient way of looking at it," Faber said. "Don't push me, Jefferson."

Faber leaned back and flicked cigarette ash on the carpet. Reynolds realized the man was enjoying this needless bickering.

"I wouldn't dream of it, Neil," Faber said. "A man has needs. Is she fulfilling yours?"

Neil grimaced with disgust. "Oh, come now, Colonel," Faber said. "I think I deserve a bit of bitterness. I made ridiculous concessions to her on your behalf—when I would have relished destroying her in court. Still, I can see why you called in a favor for her. I have to admit, I share a fondness for the dark Mediterranean type."

Reynolds ignored him. "If they were captured," he began, "it wasn't by the faction we're doing business with. And the faction haven't been able to step in, otherwise you would have been contacted by your man here in town. They must have been apprehended by the mainline army under the command of the government."

Faber tapped out another cigarette. "There's only one thing for us to do: act normally," he said. "Act as if nothing is the matter."

"We have to assume that Madison's men will talk,"

Reynolds said. "The trail will be traced back to her. That makes her our real problem."

"Which is why I have her with me," Faber said. "If she becomes unpredictable, I will have her taken care of."

Reynolds shook his head. Talking with Faber like this was like swimming in sludge. It was too slow. "Madison is intelligent," he said. "She'll realize immediately that she poses a danger to us. We should take care of her now."

Faber frowned. "Honestly, Neil, I'm surprised with you. You've never struck me as the bloodthirsty type."

"Nothing can stand in my way, not now. My research is too important."

"Well, then," Faber said, "do me the favor of remembering all I've done for you. When you became rabid about those semiconductors a year ago, I paid to have the secrets stolen."

"You also discovered a company you could acquire— one that's going to make you a fortune," Reynolds replied.

"True, but that was only a happy consequence of my generous spirit," Faber said. "And don't forget, when you wanted to get close to this Antonelli woman, I backed off from her lawsuit. I'm surprised you didn't also have me ask her out on a date for you."

"Go to hell, Jefferson," Reynolds barked.

"Perhaps," Faber replied. "In any case, let's give this situation a day or two to develop. I can see you don't have much respect for me, Neil. I'm also capable of feelings. I've grown comfortable with Madison. I don't want to lose her unless it's absolutely necessary."

"When we have to act, we'll act quickly," Neil said. The tone of his own voice surprised him. "You don't know how important this moment is."

Faber rubbed his cheek and looked warily at Reynolds. "You're sounding messianic this evening," he said.

"There are things more important than you or me, or money, or power. One day you will beg me to share the fruits of my work with you."

Reynolds regretted speaking the words as soon as they escaped his mouth. There was no need for Faber to know anything about his research or the unthinkable path he had discovered.

Faber smiled. "Keep yourself in check, Colonel," he said. "I understand the research facilities in federal prison are substandard."

The television screen went dark as the lights in the arena dimmed. Reynolds could hear the announcer's voice reverberate in the arena. "We'll talk soon," he said. "You'll be in town?"

"I'll be here," Faber said. "Nothing has changed."

Reynolds's mind processed dozens of thoughts at once; he tried to filter out the mental static. He had always known a hitch in the plan with Chapman and Faber was possible, but he had desperately needed the money the enterprise brought him to fund his private research. Now, though, he was beginning to wonder if it might be time to cut his losses.

"Enjoy the game," Faber said, smoothing his silk tie.

Reynolds opened the door; the din from outside filled the room, the cheers rising with the introduction of each player.

"And, Colonel, remember that you live in the same world as everybody else," Faber called out from behind him. "It is a world I happen to own and control. Someday we'll see who does the begging."

Reynolds closed the door, leaving Faber alone.

THE HOME TEAM TRAILED BY A POINT BUT POSSESSED THE ball with five seconds remaining in the game after a hasty time-out. Laura looked to see if Faber and his date were still present, but they had left.

"Who do you think will take the last shot?" Carlo asked Neil. The boy was up past his bedtime, but the home team's comeback from a ten-point deficit had awakened him.

"Harper," Neil answered. "Definitely Harper."

"But he's been cold all night," Carlo said. "They have to give the ball to Keats. Right, Mom?"

"Don't ask me," Laura said. "I'm just along for the ride."

She stared down at the court, aware that Neil had been watching her out of the corner of his eye. Her feelings were in flux. The surprise of learning that Neil and Faber knew each other hadn't worn off. Neil had begun to explain when he returned from his talk with Faber, but Laura had insisted they discuss it later.

"Jeez, Mom," Carlo said. "You have to have an opinion. Harper's been cold all night."

Neil gave her a sweet smile. "Yeah," he said. "Jeez, Mom."

Her first instinct had been to feel conspired against. Neil had kept the truth from her. During their conversations about her conflict with Faber's corporation, Neil had never mentioned his personal connection to Faber himself. She didn't like men who didn't tell the truth, but she was willing to hear him out. She was still attracted to Neil, and she still found him fascinating.

The crowd rose to their feet when the time-out ended. The teams took their positions.

"Harper," Neil said, good-naturedly nudging Carlo.

"Keats," Carlo said petulantly.

The ball was passed inbounds. The home player who received it pivoted on one foot, instantly surrounded by two opposing players, and lobbed it to a player waiting in a far corner of the court. Laura glanced up to the game clock and saw that only two seconds remained.

Alvin Harper leapt in the air; the ball left his outstretched fingertips an instant before the blaring buzzer sounded the end of the game. Thousands of eyes in the arena focused together as the ball took a high, looping arc into the direct center of the basket. The net shuddered as the ball passed through; the home team raised their arms in triumph.

The din within the arena was deafening. Neil gave Carlo a warm but ironic look. "Told you so," he yelled above the noise.

"You were right," Carlo shouted. "That was pretty smart."

Neil looped his arm in Laura's. "Not a bad night out," he said.

Near the exit doors Carlo announced that he needed one last trip to the rest room. Laura and Neil watched the flow of spectators heading out of the building.

"You've been quiet," Neil said. "It's about Faber."

Laura nodded. "I'm very sorry," Neil said softly. "Faber's been involved with various projects I've worked on in the past. He has a number of corporate contracts with the Department of Defense."

"That's fine," Laura said. "But it doesn't explain why you hid the fact that you know him."

"I wasn't—" Neil began. "I do know Faber, but only peripherally. I know him well enough to ask for a small favor, such as sitting in his section at this game. But he and I have never had a conversation about anything but budgets and project schedules."

"Then why were you so distracted and tense for a while after you talked to him?" she asked.

"I was? I'm sorry. Faber is abrasive and demanding. He's not pleasant to deal with."

She looked at him and saw a trace of fear in his eyes; he was afraid that she would reject him.

"During our conversation about my legal action you never said a word about Faber. The lawsuit was your idea in the first place."

"Well, it was a pretty good idea," he said. "I wanted to help. I didn't think it was relevant to mention that I've dealt with him over funding."

"Then why did he snap you up out of your chair to talk the second he got here tonight?"

"Laura, you might find this hard to believe, but I don't have an unlimited budget, not with the congressional cuts to the military budget over the last few years. I have to be political. If Faber wants to talk, I'll talk to him."

"What did he want from you?"

Neil shoved his hands in his pockets. "Well, he wanted me to be more political than I'm willing to. He wants an inside track on a new research program I've started. I told him he has to submit a bid just like everyone else. He didn't take it too well."

"That sounds like what I've seen of him," she said. "He seems completely ruthless."

"You can say that again." Neil peered through the thinning crowd, looking for Carlo. "I think I see your son."

"He really likes you, you know," Laura said.

"And what about you?" Neil asked.

Laura paused. "I like you too," she said. "But do me a favor. No more favors from creeps like Faber to impress me, okay?"

"It's a deal," he said. "You know, I have to leave for Washington in the morning," he said awkwardly.

"You told me that earlier," Laura replied.

Her retort made Neil obviously uncomfortable. In a strange way it made her feel that she could trust him.

"I don't want the evening to end here," she improvised.

Neil tugged at his blazer. "I . . . I don't either."

"But I have to keep up appearances, you know," she said. "I don't want Carlo to have any confusing ideas about things. It's been hard for him since his father died."

"I can imagine," Neil said sympathetically. "I don't want to create any problems for him."

"Here's a plan, submitted for your approval," Laura said. She felt herself slipping into unknown territory, but she liked it. It was, she realized, time to get on with her life again. "You drop us off and go back to your hotel. I'll put Carlo to bed. He's exhausted. Come by in about an hour, and we can have tea and talk."

"I would like that very much," Neil said.

Laura saw Carlo emerge from the dwindling crowd. Just before he was in earshot, she said, "Don't have any expectations. I can drive you back to your hotel late, or we can call you a cab."

"Of course," Neil said.

"You'd better not be too good to be true," she added.

Carlo joined them. His eyes were heavy with sleepiness. Unconsciously, he walked between Laura and Neil, holding both their hands. Neil clutched Carlo's armful of souvenirs in his free hand.

21

11:50 p.m.

FERRY TAFRESHI SAT IN HER KITCHEN LOOKING OUT THROUGH the skylight. As always, the stars were obscured by the misty haze of Los Angeles, leaving only murky blackness for her to contemplate.

"What are you doing?" Cyrus asked in a surly voice. He walked into the kitchen, opened the refrigerator, and peered inside. Apparently finding nothing to his liking, he closed it and began to pace.

"Just thinking," Ferry said. "Have you put the children to bed?"

"They're already asleep." Cyrus leaned on the kitchen counter, his shoulders hunched. "Davood made me read to him. But he didn't even make it to the middle of the story."

Ferry smiled. "He likes it when you read to him."

"I haven't had much time lately," Cyrus said.

The family's bankbook lay open on the breakfast table. While Cyrus had been upstairs with the children, Ferry had sat and stared at it, almost unable to comprehend the numbers listed in symmetrical columns. They were wealthy now. Then why had their life together never been more miserable?

Cyrus noticed the ledger. "Counting the money?"

Ferry struggled to decide what his tone indicated. "I was just trying to understand everything that's happened," she said.

"What's there to understand?" he asked. "Faber bought us."

She waited before responding. "So we take his money and start over," she said. "We can do even better this time. Our life here at home doesn't have to change, Cyrus. I don't want anything material. We can use all this money to fund a new company."

Cyrus didn't answer. "What's wrong with that?" Ferry asked, feeling as though she had been contradicted. "Other people have to start over. We knew the risks when we started Emergent Technologies."

"I didn't know all the risks. I never imagined what would happen." Cyrus leaned back against the counter and sighed.

"What do you mean by that, Cyrus? I've watched you walk around like a ghost for the past week. What's affecting you like this?"

She stood up but didn't approach him. "What is it, Cyrus?" she demanded. "You're frightening me."

"I don't mean to. I'm sorry," he said. "I'm not feeling well tonight. I feel like I have a fever."

"Maybe you should go to bed."

Cyrus's expression was vaguely apologetic. "I can't, there's too much on my mind. I feel as though I've backed us into a corner," he said. "Damn that Faber. He's made me feel fear, and I've never feared anything."

His confession warmed Ferry; she had hoped that the demons haunting her husband had been brought to life only by the loss of their company. What she hadn't been able to bear was her unshakable apprehension that he had hidden something more serious from her.

Ferry walked to Cyrus, cradled his head in her hands. "You have to talk to me more," she whispered. "We've always been partners in everything. Share what you're feeling with me."

Cyrus fell into her arms. Ferry held him there, feeling the collapse of his weight upon her as a surrender and the sign of a new beginning.

He was trembling; Ferry started to console him, until she felt him begin to convulse. Ferry tried to hold him up, but he collapsed heavily on the floor.

"Cyrus!" she screamed.

She dropped to her knees; Cyrus's eyes were bulging horribly. He tried to speak but couldn't. His face was mottled with red splotches.

Ferry repeated his name, holding him, knowing with terrible certainty that her husband's life was ebbing away before her eyes.

1:30 a.m., September 12.

LAURA HEARD A SOFT KNOCK AT THE DOOR. SHE PAUSED FOR a second at the mirror next to the entryway and arranged her hair. She allowed herself one more quick, shy glance before opening the door.

Neil was dressed in the same slacks and blazer he had worn to the basketball game. Laura saw the taxi pull away from the curb, its yellow light signaling that it was again available for fares.

"You're late," she said. "I wondered if you were going to show up."

"I'm sorry," Neil apologized. "I got caught up in some work I brought with me from Washington."

"Well, come in," she said. "But keep it quiet."

He brushed by her as she locked and chained shut the front door. Still fiddling with the latch, she sensed movement behind her and felt an acute, painful sting in her neck.

"Hey!" she said, moving away from Neil.

He stood in the foyer, a befuddled expression on his face. "What's the matter?" he asked.

"I felt like I was stuck with a pin."

He pulled his hands out of his jacket pockets and motioned for her to move closer to the light. "Let me take a look," he said.

She did as he asked and felt the warm proximity of his body as he touched the nape of her neck, examining closely. At one point he pressed his fingers into the flesh just below her neckline, rubbing.

"I don't see anything wrong," he said. "Maybe you have a pinched nerve. Have you had any other symptoms?"

"Oh, boy," she said, laughing. "Two doctors together. Let's not overdiagnose. It must have been a thread from my blouse or something. Don't worry about it."

She walked with him to the doorway leading to the family room, where Neil produced a bottle of wine from his jacket.

"I don't—" she said. Neil looked suddenly embarrassed. "It's really nice of you, but I can't. Sit down. We have to talk about some things."

They sat together on the couch nearest the window. Laura watched Neil look around the room, taking it all in: the functional furniture, the rows of books, the framed photograph of the Tuscan landscape, the family portraits, the aged and dusty records.

"No one is ever going to hire me to be a decorator," she said.

"I like this place," Neil said. "It feels like a home. I have boxes that I haven't unpacked since I bought my house."

Neil put the bottle of wine on the coffee table. "About that—" Laura began.

"I shouldn't have assumed you like to drink," Neil said. "I don't like it much myself."

"Don't worry, I'm Italian," Laura said. "I'm not going to be outraged by a bottle of wine. It's just that . . . well,

I used to drink a lot. Too much, and I also took pills. This was when my husband and I were having serious problems. I sort of crawled inside a bottle for a while, and I didn't take very good care of either Carlo or myself. I had to get professional help to pull myself out of it.''

Laura had kept the lights in the room dim, and she couldn't read Neil's expression. She had told few people about her substance-abuse problem, feeling it was tantamount to admitting a grave weakness. Part of her waited in terrible anticipation to see how he would react.

"Alcoholism and drugs are occupational hazards for physicians," he said. "It's a trap a lot of us fall into."

"I guess so," she said. "But I hated myself for it. Carlo needs me. My mother needs me. My patients need me. I have too much responsibility to give up like I did."

"You have a responsibility to yourself," Neil said.

"I know," she answered. "Believe me, I got a lifetime's worth of analysis in rehab. I always hated psychoanalysis, you know, I thought it was just a bunch of babble. But it taught me to look out for myself more. I think that's what it all boiled down to."

"The human mind is extraordinarily complicated," Neil said quietly. "It contains self-regulating mechanisms, but it's prone to ignore them. You're obviously a very intelligent person, but intelligence has nothing to do with emotional equilibrium."

"You sound as though you're speaking from experience," Laura said.

She sensed Neil stiffen for an instant. "In a way," he said. "I've lived for my work for a long time. It's why I never got close enough to anyone to even consider marriage. Lately . . . I feel a bit like a vessel for my work."

"A vessel?"

"Let me explain." Neil moved closer to her. "I've recently had some remarkable breakthroughs. At times it feels as though these discoveries are *using* me as a way to come into being.''

"It sounds like giving birth," Laura said.

His eyes widened. "That's a very appropriate analogy," he said. "It's a matter of bringing something new into the world."

He had avoided mentioning specifically what he was working on. She knew researchers tended to be like this, usually out of superstition that talking about a discovery would jinx its future—or out of fear that their ideas might be stolen. She decided not to press him.

"I want to be honest with you," he said. "Since we met in San Diego I can't stop thinking about you. I haven't ever paid much attention to my emotions. I wanted, if nothing else, to come here to tell you how I feel."

Neil stopped talking; they sat together in silence punctuated only by the hum of the cycling refrigerator and the sound of cars passing by outside. Neil was shy and awkward, but he had the courage to tell her how he felt, and to risk rejection.

She searched within herself for her own courage. Since her drug and alcohol dependency she had felt fragile. She had tried to avoid facing anything that might upset her equilibrium, whether it be legal combat with Faber or an emotional investment with a new man. She understood intellectually her reasons for being this way, but it was time to change, to live again, to take risks. She was strong enough to face life again.

"I didn't mean to put you on the spot," Neil said.

Laura looked up; he had been watching her while her mind spun. His eyes shone with penetrating concern. In the soft light he seemed younger than his years, with a naive vulnerability and openness.

"I'm not often guilty of coming on too strong," he continued. "But I can understand if you're in the midst of putting your life together after some setbacks. I should probably—"

"Neil," she interrupted.

Laura moved closer and put her hand up to his cheek. The tension between them had grown, and he flinched almost imperceptibly.

"You've already explained yourself," she said, smiling. "You should quit when you're ahead."

She leaned to him and pressed her lips against his. She felt his arm encircle her waist, pulling her close.

FEELING AS THOUGH SHE HAD JUST GONE TO SLEEP, LAURA awoke with her alarm clock in her hand. She grabbed it and shut it off before fully awakening. It was a habit of hers that had begun in medical school, when a full night's sleep had more resembled a normal person's catnap.

In the dark of her bed her eyes adjusted; the early-morning red sunlight peeked demurely through the drawn shades. It was five-thirty in the morning.

Laura sat up, reconstructing in her mind what had happened. Her eyes popped open with the recollection, and she felt the bed beside her. Neil was gone. In his place was a note:

Laura,

It's almost five o'clock, and I'm leaving for my hotel. I thought it would be best if I wasn't here when Carlo wakes up. I know that his adjustment to losing his father will take some time.

Writing about what we shared last night would be to cheapen it. Your presence in my life has added a fullness that I could never have foreseen. I have to return to

Washington this morning. I hope you will join me there soon, or allow me to visit you again. I hope you feel as I do—that what we've shared is just a beginning.

Yours, Neil

She reread the note, peering intently at his precise block handwriting. The events of the night before came back in a series of images: the basketball game; Neil and Carlo becoming instant friends; the awkward conversation in her living room; the slow, quiet love they had made when conversation became irrelevant.

He was the first man she had slept with since Steve. It had been easy, natural; it felt as though their being together was inevitable.

He was also leaving town, and Laura felt her defenses setting up to guard her against disappointment. Though she had never been much for playing the singles game, she knew how smooth some people were with a kiss-off. She knew how she felt. Now she would wait and see.

Though it was Saturday, Laura had surgery scheduled for eight-thirty that morning—a routine appendectomy. She rose from the bed, donned her nightgown, and padded off toward the bathroom.

Laura peeked into Carlo's room when she passed by, able to make out his sleeping form through the cracked door. She would let him sleep until it was almost time to go, then drop him off at her mother's while she worked.

The shower took a long time to warm up. While she waited, Laura felt an itchy spot on the back of her neck. Her mind flashed to the sharp stinging she had felt the night before. Neil had said he didn't see anything wrong, but it felt strange, as though a tiny insect barb had become lodged in the tissues of her neck.

She took a mirror from the medicine cabinet and tried to

find a good angle for viewing her neck. It was almost impossible—she had to hold her hair back with one hand, twist her body, and position the hand mirror while also peering into the mirror above the sink.

"Damn it," she muttered, turning off the water.

What she had thought was the sound of water tinkling in the bathtub had actually been the phone ringing in her bedroom. Laura dropped the mirror and ran down the hall. She thought it might be the hospital on the line. Her patient might have developed some sort of presurgery complication.

It was still ringing when she reached her room and dived across the bed. She picked up the receiver, dropped it, and retrieved it from the floor. By the time she said hello, she was breathless.

"Hello, Laura?" said a tiny, hushed voice. It was Ferry, Laura's eyes sought out the clock. It was almost six.

"Ferry, what is it?" Laura asked. "What are you doing up so early on a Saturday? Is everything all right?"

Silence.

"Ferry, talk to me," Laura said in a soothing voice. "Where are you?"

"St. Catherine's Hospital," Ferry said. Her voice was strange.

"What are you doing there, Ferry?"

"I came here with Cyrus, last night," Ferry said.

Laura pulled her hair away from her face. Ferry sounded extremely disoriented. "Let me talk to Cyrus," she said.

"That's impossible," Ferry said as though she were talking to a child. "You can't talk to Cyrus."

Laura took a deep breath. "Ferry, I want to help," she said. "But you have to tell me—"

"Cyrus died early this morning," Ferry said. Her voice snapped into a logical, precise tone. "We were talking in the kitchen and he collapsed. He died two hours after we reached the hospital. They . . . someone is going to look at him to find out what happened.''

''The medical examiner?'' Laura asked.

''That's right,'' Ferry said. ''They can't figure out why he died.''

PART THREE

22

LAURA NOSED HER CAR INTO THE TAFRESHIS' DRIVEWAY AND waited for a moment, steeling herself before going inside. She hadn't smoked in more than two years, but she had bought a pack at a corner market on the way from her mother's house. She ignited one with the dashboard lighter and took a long drag.

The events following Ferry's early-morning phone call had been chaotic and painful. After calling Valley Memorial to line up a replacement surgeon for the appendectomy, Laura had raced to St. Catherine's to find Ferry in a darkened lounge with her two children sleeping at her side. Ferry's features were slack and expressionless. After Laura spoke with an ER attendant, she knew why: Ferry had been in such a hysterical state that the doctors had decided she required sedation. Under the effects of the medication she barely seemed to realize where she was.

Laura had dropped Ferry off at her house and put her to bed. With Davood and Mina still in tow, she stopped by her own place to wake up Carlo, giving him a quick uncensored explanation of what happened. He showed maturity beyond his years, quickly understanding that Cyrus had died and that his young children would need emotional support in the coming hours. Her load eased by Carlo's conscientious attentiveness to the children, she had left them off at Maria's house. Laura explained to her mother what had happened, and Maria had agreed to watch the children for as long as necessary.

Leaving her mother's house, Laura had seen Davood's face appear in the window. He looked stern and serious, and he wasn't crying. It was this last sight that had made Laura stop off for cigarettes.

She got out of the car and let herself into Ferry's house. Laura had expected to find the place quiet, with Ferry sleeping off the sedatives upstairs. Instead she was met with a strong smell of spiced tea when she walked in.

Ferry was in the kitchen, standing over the stove. "Since I woke you so early, I thought you might want something caffeinated," she said.

Ferry had changed clothes, her rumpled slacks and sweater replaced by a new-looking, vibrant orange dress that clung to her trim figure. The cheerfulness of her clothes was contrasted by her haggard features. Her eyes were smudged with deep red; her lips were dry and chapped.

"You shouldn't be up," Laura said, accepting a cup of tea from her friend. "They gave you very strong drugs at the hospital."

Ferry seemed not to hear. "Let's sit down." She was unsteady on her feet as she took a chair in the breakfast nook.

Outside the sun had risen. The backyard glowed dewy and green. "I want to tell you what happened," Ferry said. "Maybe you will have some ideas. The doctors at the hospital couldn't tell me anything."

Laura looked closely at Ferry, trying to gauge her

friend's emotional state. Ferry avoided eye contact, and her voice was flat and businesslike. It was classic emotional shock. Laura needed to be sure this condition didn't lead Ferry to any desperate or dangerous behavior.

"Only if you want to," Laura replied. "Whatever makes you feel comfortable. I'm not going anywhere."

Ferry stared into space. "We were talking, right over there." She motioned toward the kitchen. "We were fighting, but we had just made up. Cyrus fell into my arms, and I thought . . . I thought it was because he was embracing me. But I think that was when it started. When I let go of him he fell down onto the floor."

Her words came out in a steady, emotionless stream, as though she were telling a story.

"How did he act?" Laura asked.

"He was hot, very hot all of a sudden." Ferry closed her eyes. "He was sweating and grabbing at his chest. He kept twitching in my arms. He couldn't keep still."

"That's when you called 911?" Laura suggested.

"Yes," Ferry began. "But I waited maybe a minute before I did. Maybe I shouldn't have, but I knew he was dying. I wanted to hold him while he was still mine."

Ferry suddenly looked into Laura's eyes. The fierceness of her gaze made Laura want to turn away. "Do you think that was wrong?" Ferry asked. "Do you think my waiting killed him?"

Laura grabbed her friend's hand and held it tight. "Don't say that, Ferry. You can't blame yourself. Thirty seconds didn't matter."

Ferry was silent. An unspoken thought passed between them: the understanding that Steve had died alone, far away. Though their marriage had ended and her love for Steve was gone, Laura had once told Ferry how much she had regretted not having the opportunity to say good-bye to the father of her only child.

"I'm so sorry, Ferry," Laura said. "I'm going to try to help. My mother can take care of Davood and Mina for a couple of days. We can stay here until you're feeling stronger."

Ferry seemed not to hear. "Jefferson Faber had something to do with this," she whispered, staring into her teacup.

"Faber?" Laura asked. "Why would you say that?"

"Cyrus was starting to open up about what had been bothering him lately," Ferry said. "It had to do with Faber. Cyrus was frightened of something."

"Cyrus was under a lot of stress because of the buyout of Emergent Technologies," Laura said. "And that stress might have contributed to his death. But there's no reason to think that Faber could possibly have—"

"He was scared," Ferry interrupted. "I had never seen Cyrus frightened of anything before. And now he's dead."

"I saw Faber last night," Laura said. "He seemed normal. He was a vulture for taking your company, but I don't see how he could have harmed Cyrus."

Ferry's cup rattled against her saucer. Laura told Ferry about seeing Faber at the basketball game and about Neil's association with the billionaire. She avoided mentioning anything about Neil spending the night or their making love.

"It doesn't matter, I suppose," Ferry finally said. "There's no way I could ever prove anything."

"There's nothing to prove," Laura said adamantly. "Cyrus was distraught over losing the business. It's not going to do anyone any good to fixate on conspiracies. You have to think of your children, Ferry."

Even as she spoke, Laura's words turned hollow in her

own ears. From all accounts Cyrus had been acting very strangely, even taking into account the considerable pressure of losing his business.

Laura willed herself to snap out of it. She knew that paranoia had a tendency to be contagious. Faber was shrewd, calculating, perhaps even utterly amoral, but he didn't have to power to snap his fingers and make a man drop dead. Cyrus's cause of death would have to be determined from an autopsy. A perfectly acceptable explanation would be found for this tragedy.

"You're right, I have to take care of Davood and Mina," Ferry said. She sounded more like herself than at any time that morning. "I let my imagination get away from me. Cyrus was worried about the future, but he would be happy to know that he provided for us. I'll be able to send them to college. He . . . he took good care of us."

Ferry's eyes filled with tears. Laura embraced her. "He was a good man, Ferry," Laura said. "That's how we should remember him." Ferry's sobs grew louder. It would be a long time before they subsided.

But Laura's eyes were open and fixed in the distance over her friend's shoulder. No matter how she tried, she couldn't shake Ferry's notion that Cyrus had been involved somehow with Faber, and that this association might have doomed him.

It was absurd, but the idea wouldn't go away. It was crazy, it was irrational. Why, then, did it sound so plausible?

23

LAURA CIRCLED THE LABYRINTH OF ONE-WAY STREETS, TRY-
ing to find an open parking place within walking distance of the county medical examiner's office. Finally she
gave up and pulled into a commercial lot—three blocks
from the drab institutional building. She handed the attendant a ten-dollar bill and waited for change. When none
was offered, she looked up at the sign painted over the
entrance. Her ten dollars had bought her three hours of
parking. Each additional hour would cost her another five.

After walking a block Laura felt a fine mist of sweat
under her collar. The temperature was about ten degrees
hotter downtown than near the water, and this sultry afternoon was uncharacteristically humid.

Once inside she paused. It had been years since she had
witnessed an autopsy, and she'd never attended an examination performed on someone she knew. She felt slightly
embarrassed—squeamishness was hard to admit for a doctor—but dead flesh was something to which she had never
been able to become inured.

The glassed-off reception desk was staffed by a young
African-American man in a short-sleeved dress shirt and

tie. He glanced up from his newspaper when Laura approached.

"Can I help you?" he asked.

Laura showed him her photo identification from Valley Memorial. "A friend of mine was brought here this morning from St. Catherine's," she began. "The cause of death was unknown, and I wanted to attend the autopsy."

The attendant folded his hands. "Ma'am, I'm sorry about your friend, but we can't let the public into the examination rooms. You can call later today for the report if you want."

"I'm not the public," Laura said. "This man was also a patient at my hospital, and there's been talk he might have had a nosocomial infection. If you keep me out of there, your name is going to come up when I have to explain why an entire ward came down with a fatal virus."

The young man examined Laura's identification anew. "All right," he said. "You don't have to strong-arm me. Take the elevators down to basement level two. There are scrubs and masks right outside the examination room."

"One more thing," Laura said. "Who's the examiner for Cyrus Tafreshi?"

The attendant sighed and grabbed a sheet of computer printouts. "Dr. Hyong Choe Kim," he said. "Your friend is first on his duty list for today."

Laura thanked the young man and made for the elevators. She didn't blame him for trying to keep her out; the medical examiner's office often dealt with delicate cases, from gunshot deaths to overdoses. The ramifications of their work were wide spreading, touching on everything from criminal charges to insurance claims to physician malpractice. It was a difficult enough job without the added pressure of spectators.

Pressing the elevator button, Laura took a deep breath.

She hadn't wanted to lie to the attendant, but it seemed her only option if she wanted access to the autopsy. Cyrus hadn't been a patient at Valley Memorial, or anywhere else that she knew of. He was stubborn about his good health, with a bravado that masked his phobia about medicine. Laura had never heard him or Ferry mention that he had ever seen a doctor for any kind of malady.

Outside the examination room Laura found a sink and washed her hands after leaving her purse in an open locker. Though she wouldn't participate in the autopsy, the examiner would expect reasonable measures to preserve a sterile working environment. She donned a thick rubber gown, along with surgical gloves and paper shoe covers and a mask.

She tried not to think about the queasy light-headedness she had experienced in medical school during anatomy lessons on cadavers. Instead she thought of Ferry, and of the strong feeling of suspicion she had felt in the Tafreshi family kitchen. For her own peace of mind she had to go through with this.

In the examination room Laura smelled disinfectant wafting in the cooled air. The facilities included two rows of stainless-steel tables lining either side of the generous work space. There were more than a half-dozen workers, all wearing gowns and masks, working alone or in pairs on bodies in various stages of autopsy.

Most of the doctors and assistants peered up when Laura entered, then returned to their work. Laura looked around until she spotted a small man whose Asian eyes gleamed above his mask.

"Are you Dr. Kim?" she asked, walking up to him.

The corpse on the table nearest the examiner was covered with a white sheet. The doctor looked up from his tray of instruments. "Yes," he said in a deep voice. "Can I help you with something?"

"My name is Dr. Laura Antonelli. I work in the surgical department at Valley Memorial," Laura said.

Kim stepped toward the corpse. "Isn't that something," he said. "It's not often we get surgeons down here."

"I came to watch your work on a friend of mine," Laura said, not sure whether his comment had been friendly or not. "His name is Cyrus Tafreshi."

"Well, this is him right here," Kim said, indicating the covered body. "You say he was your friend? Who let you in here?"

"I told the attendant upstairs he was a patient at my hospital," Laura admitted. "That was just to get me down here. The truth is, his wife is one of my closest friends. Cyrus dropped dead last night even though he was in perfect health. I came here to find some answers."

Kim listened impassively. "All right," he finally said. "It's fine with me. You didn't have to lie upstairs. You could have had me paged, and I would have allowed you down here. I don't mind having someone to talk to while I'm working."

"Thank you," Laura said. She wasn't sure she believed him, but she was glad he was allowing her to stay. Just a month before, she recalled, a minor scandal had rocked the medical examiner's office involving a double shooting that might or might not have been instigated by the police. Apparently the autopsy findings hadn't squared with the police report, which had prompted an investigation.

Kim reached for the sheet covering Cyrus. "You're sure you're here only out of personal curiosity?" he asked, perhaps mindful of his office's recent travails.

"Scout's honor," Laura said. "I'm just here to watch."

Apparently satisfied, Kim pulled away the sheet from

Cyrus's nude body. Laura's gaze wandered up to his face, which was frozen in an uncomprehending stare. The whites of his eyes were ringed with broken blood vessels. She looked down at the floor and struggled to stay steady on her feet.

"Are you all right?" Kim asked with concern.

"I'll be fine," Laura said. "It was just the initial shock."

Laura willed herself to focus on Cyrus's body, avoiding the sight of his familiar face. She focused on perceiving Ferry's husband as an academic subject, as Kim unceremoniously cut into Cyrus's skin with a blade. With experienced motions Kim made the traditional Y-shaped incision, cutting down from Cyrus's neck to his pelvis.

Kim reached for a microphone that was hanging on a track from the ceiling and drew it to his face. While Kim recited the date, the time, and other information pertinent to the examination for the permanent record, Laura peered at an open file that Kim had left on a nearby stand. She didn't want to watch as Kim sawed through Cyrus's ribs to expose the chest cavity.

According to the report from St. Catherine's, Cyrus had been barely alive when he arrived by ambulance. His breath had been spotty and labored, and he was coughing up trace amounts of blood. He was restless and feverish, with an extraordinarily accelerated heart rate. He hadn't responded to aggressive treatment, and died of cardiac arrest without ever regaining consciousness.

Laura looked back at the table when she heard Kim give out a low whistle of surprise. He had removed Cyrus's heart from the chest cavity and was slicing samples in a steel tray.

"What do you have?" Laura asked, sliding around the table.

"This heart took a lot of damage," Kim said. "He shot out a lot of blood vessels in a very short period of time."

Laura watched Kim work, and agreed with him. "Did he have a history of heart disease?" Kim asked without looking up. "I didn't get any charts from the hospital."

"Not at all," Laura said. "He was as healthy as a horse. As far as I know, he never even went to a doctor."

Kim set aside samples for lab analysis and returned to the body. He efficiently cut away the liver and dropped it on a scale. "How about smoking? Alcohol? Drugs?"

"None of the above," Laura said. She paused while Kim activated the microphone and announced that the condition of Cyrus's liver was within normal parameters. "He was a devout Muslim," she added.

Kim worked for a while in silence while Laura leaned against a steel rail that separated the table from the rest of the row. Around her the other medical examiners continued their work, speaking to one another in low voices.

"Now, this is really something," Kim said. He had begun inspecting Cyrus's lungs.

"What's that?" Laura said, moving away from the rail. Her brief respite had successfully forestalled a wave of nausea.

"Definite effusion of serous fluid into the air vesicles," Kim said. He made a deft cut. "And major effusion into interstitial tissue."

"Pulmonary edema," Laura said.

Kim concurred. "Which explains the blood in his expectoration upon presenting to the emergency room."

"You sound as though you have an idea what happened to him," Laura said.

Kim looked up from the damaged lung. "Fever, sweating, and restlessness were all present when the patient arrived," he said. "Cause of death, grossly speaking, was pulmonary edema or congestive heart failure."

"I think I see what you're getting at," Laura said glumly. As they moved closer to a cause of death, she began to feel more acutely sad that Cyrus was gone.

"Look at the eyes," Kim said. "Those blood vessels."

Laura didn't have to look; Cyrus's face in death remained indelible in her memory. "Exophthalmia," she said. "Protrusion of the eyeballs."

Together she and Kim had quickly surmised that Cyrus had died from an acute hyperfunction of his thyroid gland—a condition known as thyrotoxicosis. All the symptoms added up, pointing to a chain of reactions that had led to the expiration of his cardiopulmonary system. It was known as a "thyroid storm," and it was a very painful way to die.

"We'd better have a look in here," Kim mumbled. He began cutting at the anatomical structures around Cyrus's neck.

"It definitely looks like thyrotoxicosis," Laura said. "I'm not aware that he had any preexisting condition. It certainly wasn't a surgical emergency."

Kim sliced at the sternothyroid muscle at the base of Cyrus's neck, pulling back the tissue. "You knew him," he said as he worked. "Did he have any kind of weight fluctuation recently?"

Laura thought back to the last time she had seen Cyrus alive: in the Tafreshi home, when they had celebrated Laura's legal victory over Ellington-Faber. "Not that I noticed," she said. "He was always thin, but not unusually so."

She watched Kim clip back the thick sternothyroid muscle, exposing the thyroid cartilage and the actual thyroid gland below, which was nestled amid the larynx and upper trachea.

They both stared at the gland, which consisted of two lateral lobes connected by an isthmus. ''It's really enlarged,'' Laura said.

The two thyroid lobes looked angrily engorged; they were swollen and had turned red and blue. Laura could almost see the hot fluid hormone serum oozing from the fiery gland. She knew the T3 and T4 levels would be off the board when they came back from the lab, probably in the thousands.

''You can say that again.'' Kim flicked on a lamp to enhance the light focused on the table. ''I don't see any signs of pathology,'' he added, ''but I'll have to wait for lab results. I'm willing to bet we're going to see really high levels of thyroxine and thyrotropin.''

Laura waited for Kim to make entries into his vocal recording and to excise samples of the thyroid gland for lab testing.

''His wife told me that he was apparently healthy one moment, and that he collapsed the next,'' Laura said. ''That's what bothers me about the case. There was no warning and no previous indicators.''

Kim didn't seem to hear; instead he pulled the light down even closer, as though his eye had caught on something.

''Strange,'' he muttered.

''What's that?'' Laura asked. ''What do you have?''

When Kim didn't answer, Laura knew she would have to wait. The medical examiner struck her as thorough and competent, if not particularly gregarious. She glanced at the table nearest her, where an examiner and student were engrossed in the autopsy of an elderly woman. She couldn't imagine how they ever got used to the constant parade of the dead that passed through their doors every day.

"Got it," Kim finally proclaimed. Laura saw that he had used a long, thin pair of surgical tweezers to probe amid the upper section of Cyrus's right thyroid lobe.

"Did you find some kind of tumor mass?" Laura asked. This would be a good explanation for Cyrus's sudden death—and it would also dispel any lingering paranoia she might have felt regarding his connection to Jefferson Faber.

"This ain't no tumor," Kim said in a cartoon voice. Laura realized this was his idea of a joke. He held the tweezers up close to the light. Laura could immediately see that the object wasn't organic in nature, though it was covered with a film of blood and internal secretions.

"Do you know if your friend ever had surgery?" Kim asked, moving the object to and fro in the light. It was very tiny, perhaps only a centimeter across. Laura was impressed that Kim's eyesight was strong enough to have spotted the object.

"Not that I know of," she answered. "I'd have to ask his wife to make sure. He grew up in Iran and, as I said, he never saw doctors here."

Kim held the object up to his eye. "What a strange little bugger," he said. Laura could tell this would be a high point of his day—finding something strange and inexplicable. "It's been in there at least a month, probably more. Look."

Laura leaned closer; the object was covered with a firm brown fibrin. Cyrus's immune system had isolated and covered it, as it would any intruder.

One of the other examiners left his own table, overhearing Laura's conversation with Kim.

"Jon Baker," he said, greeting Laura. To Kim he said, "What've you got there, Doctor? A foreign object?"

"Look at this damned thing," Kim said in a collegial tone. He held out the object for Baker to examine.

"Looks like metal," Baker said, squinting. "And it's got little spiky things coming off it. Was it from prior surgery? Something that got left inside?"

"It has to be," Kim said. He looked at Laura. "This must have been something from his days in Iran, if not here."

"But there's no surgical scarring on his neck," Laura said.

"Well, that doesn't mean much," Kim said. He pointed to two faint lines on Cyrus's abdomen. "These might be surgical scars. Objects left in the body have a way of traveling. You'd be surprised what we find sometimes."

"Sure," Baker said. He, also, obviously relished the discovery of this abnormality in Cyrus. "Gauze, pieces of debris. Hell, one time I found a surgical sponge. On the other hand, maybe this guy was abducted by aliens from outer space—this could be their tracking probe, so they always know his whereabouts."

"I don't find that particularly funny," Laura snapped. "This man was a friend of mine."

Baker's face turned red above his mask. "I'm sorry," he stammered. "Sometimes we get a little cavalier down here. I didn't mean any disrespect to your friend."

"Apology accepted," Laura said. Despite what Baker and Kim said, something struck her as inexplicable about this object. She took it from Kim and scrutinized it again. It was metallic, shaped irregularly, with small jagged bits emerging from a round center. It was covered with far too much cementing fibrin to really determine what it was.

Baker quietly excused himself and returned to his work.

Kim put the object in a small plastic bag, then sealed and marked it.

"You'll have to excuse Jon," he said in a conciliatory voice. "It's the nature of the work. We crack jokes to relieve the monotony, it's pure gallows humor and not very tasteful."

"I understand," Laura said. "No offense taken."

"I've got to finish this up. I have two more to do before I can grab lunch," Kim said. "Stop off at the desk and ask for my business card, it has my phone extension on it. I'll be in tomorrow at nine, and I should have the results of the tests by then—if the lab isn't too backed up."

"Thank you," Laura said.

"Don't worry about it." Kim pulled out a motorized saw, and Laura suddenly felt relieved that she was leaving.

On her way out Laura stopped to say good-bye to Dr. Baker, and to let him know she harbored no hard feelings. He seemed genuinely relieved. As she pushed on the swinging door to leave, a voice called out from behind her.

"Dr. Antonelli," Kim said. He held the saw in one hand. "I'm very sorry about your loss."

Laura waved weakly with one hand, touched by this small show of sympathy from a total stranger.

In the dressing area Laura dropped her gown into a basket and discarded her shoe covers and mask. Her purse was where she had left it, in a nearby locker. She sat on a bench and thought about what she had just witnessed. The lab results were a foregone conclusion. Cyrus had displayed all the signs of an unusually severe thyroid storm, with no prior warning, an immediate onset of symptoms, and a particularly quick and deadly failure of his cardiopulmonary system.

Thyrotoxicosis couldn't be caused by a sliver of metal, no matter where it came from. It was an endocrine imbalance that created a severe hormonal crisis in the body—and lethal though it was, it was perfectly natural. Laura had come downtown for answers, and she had found them.

Unfortunately, she felt no better than she had before.

24

7:58 a.m., September 14. Los Angeles.

JEFFERSON FABER WAS ALONE IN HIS OFFICE. HE HAD GIVEN orders not to disturb him until further notice; he needed time to gather his thoughts.

He had deliberately decorated the room with objects designed to accomplish two ends: to intimidate and to distract visitors. The walls were lined with original oil paintings; the floors were covered with lavish Persian carpets; the shelves were filled with photographs of Faber in the company of politicians, world leaders, and celebrities. The floor-to-ceiling window behind him faced west, focusing late-afternoon sun in visitors' faces. It was a room expressly designed as a place for making deals—deals that would favor Faber's interests.

The curtains were drawn, the music shut off. Faber had the Sunday edition of the *Los Angeles Times* spread out on his desk. There was still no mention of American militia members having been captured in Iran. This was good news, but only for the time being. Faber had based his power on knowledge—knowing his opponents' weaknesses, and knowing their next move before they made it. He had no idea what was happening with his latest and most dangerous venture, and it was nearly enough to drive him mad.

Faber tapped his desk with a pencil and pulled his computer keyboard closer. With a series of practiced keystrokes he launched his communications protocol and switched on the baseball-shaped video camera bolted to the top of his monitor.

When the program was installed and the machine had run through its security measures, Faber realized he was chewing the eraser off the pencil. He tossed it into the garbage. This wouldn't do. The last thing he wanted now was to appear nervous or out of control.

A minute later his computer-monitor display split into two vertical static-ridden fields. Faber stared into the screen, composing himself; the right half of the image resolved into the image of a dark-blond, square-jawed man.

"Senator," Faber said.

"Jefferson," Chapman answered. The communications link showed the senator's face from the neck up, in a series of stop-action images that seemed disjointed at first. Faber knew that enduring the strange effect was worth the bother. He found it essential to be able to see his allies' and opponents' facial expressions.

"We don't have Neil on the line?" Chapman asked. "I wonder what's keeping him."

"We both know the answer to that," Faber said. "His laboratory. It's a wonder that he ever leaves."

Chapman smiled. "That's not entirely true," he said, his voice couched in a hiss of static. "I hear he came out to Los Angeles last Friday to see your basketball team play."

"It was for a woman," Faber said.

"A woman?" Chapman appeared genuinely surprised. "You mean our colonel has displayed actual human feelings? This must be a first. Did you get to see her?"

"Oh, I've met her once or twice," Faber said. He unconsciously reached up and smoothed back a shock of his hair.

Suddenly the image on the right side of Faber's screen blinked twice, then took shape. Neil Reynolds stared out at him, side by side with Chapman. It was quite a contrast. Chapman was handsome in a classic American sense, with blow-dried hair and an easy smile that was never far from his lips. The colonel glowered from the screen, his thick face looking a bit sallow, as though he hadn't had enough sleep.

"Congressman. Jefferson," Reynolds said. He stepped out of camera range for a moment, then returned.

"I'm so glad we could all be together, if only in spirit," Faber said. He kept his eyes focused on Reynolds's half of the screen.

"It's enough of a risk that we're doing this," Reynolds said. "Let's not waste time with chitchat."

"Agreed," Faber said. "Congressman, you go first, if you don't mind. What do you know?"

"What's coming out of Teheran indicates that their army has definitely caught some smugglers," Chapman said. "It's all unofficial. Their government hasn't even contacted our State Department. There's no sign that anyone here knows who the Iranians caught, or that the smugglers were carrying uranium."

"It's going to become public," Reynolds said. "It's inevitable."

Chapman frowned. Faber regarded the senator as an unflappably shallow man, with the politician's innate knack for treating unhappy information as the product of misguided pessimism.

Chapman continued, "What I can't find out—and what we need to know—is what faction of the military caught these men. It could still turn out to be our contacts. Maybe that's why nothing has been brought up in the international community.''

''You're not thinking it through,'' Reynolds said. He wiped his brow with a handkerchief.

''Are you all right, Neil?'' Faber asked. ''You don't look well.''

''I have the flu.'' Reynolds stared out from the screen, his expression cold. ''May I continue, Jefferson?'' he asked sardonically.

''Of course.''

''Here is the chain of facts.'' Reynolds didn't look into the screen; instead he stared down. It looked as if he were talking to himself. ''Our men were captured, but we can take measures to disassociate ourselves from them. As for the Iranian government—there are two opposing factions there. One has been buying the uranium without the other's knowledge. We have to assume that the capture of our men has made this schism apparent in the highest reaches of the power structure. What is occurring now is either political conflict or reconciliation between the two factions. They will have to reckon with each other internally before showing a face to the world.''

Chapman stared blankly.

''So, you're saying our prospects fall outside of an either/or framework,'' Faber said.

Reynolds appeared not to have heard him. ''The other factor, as far as we're concerned, is the recent death of our go-between with the Iranians,'' he continued.

''That was a shame,'' Faber said. ''Although it means I won't have to keep all the promises I made to him.''

''But the access he afforded us is gone,'' Reynolds said.

''There's been a lot of dying surrounding this enterprise,'' Faber mused aloud.

"Who are you guys talking about?" Chapman asked, sounding as though he felt left out.

"Don't bother yourself with it," Faber said to him. "It's a minor detail compared to what we're dealing with now—"

"We have to move into a new stage," Reynolds interrupted. "Complete and terminal shutdown."

"That's a curious choice of words," Faber said.

"Neil's right," Chapman chimed in. "We've got to get our asses out of this mess."

"We have to systematically eradicate anything that could tie us to Jeanette Madison and her men," Reynolds continued.

Faber glanced at a newspaper clipping on his desk, headlined, "L.A. BUSINESSMAN DIES SUDDENLY." It showed a picture of Cyrus Tafreshi. It *was* a shame. He had stolen Tafreshi's invention, robbed him of his company, and exploited his contacts in Iran. Faber had bought Tafreshi's cooperation with cash and false promises of allowing him to stay at Emergent Technologies as president. He had paid Tafreshi well, though, and had planned to continue doing so. He would miss Tafreshi, in a sense, particularly those scathing phone calls when Tafreshi's conscience got the better of him and he would berate Faber before finally acquiescing. Faber knew he was also receiving pressure from Iran to assist the uranium sales. The poor man had been caught between two nations.

"How strange that our Iranian friend would die at such a crucial moment," Faber said. Reynolds looked away. "Just like the Russian colonel, Bolkov. And old man Patterson."

"What are you saying, Jefferson?" Chapman asked in an unsteady voice.

All three sat in silence. Faber listened to the humming

fan within his computer and the faint whir of the video camera.

"Yes, Jefferson," Reynolds said, "you sound as though there's something you wish to insinuate."

"We've had our share of fortunate coincidences," Faber said. He willed himself to smile.

"We certainly have," Reynolds replied. "I don't think we could have made it this far without such luck. It's a shame it had to run out."

"We'll survive," Faber said.

Faber began to calculate. Chapman wasn't a problem; the senator couldn't be connected to Patriot's Path. And he was fiscally vulnerable—he would never turn on Faber and risk losing connections and campaign contributions. Politicians were the most predictable people to do business with.

But what about Reynolds? Neil had become an unknown variable. Everything had fallen into place so well in the beginning: Neil had his contacts in Russia, and Faber had supplied Tafreshi. They had agreed to split their profits equally. But as Faber cast his memory back, he realized that Reynolds had seemed always a step ahead, his assessments and predictions always coming true. His mind was quicker than Faber's, which made the colonel a very dangerous man.

Reynolds was motivated almost entirely by scientific inquiry curiosity—as well as his instinct for self-preservation. But to what end? He had alluded to a secret he possessed, which was infuriating. And he wasn't a materialist. He needed money, but it didn't control him.

"It's not me you should be worried about, Jefferson." Reynolds's voice crackled from the speaker, snapping Faber out of his reverie.

"What . . . I'm sorry, what did you say?" Faber asked. It was as though Reynolds had read his mind.

"I said you don't need to be concerned with me," Reynolds repeated. "We're partners. We'll look out for each other."

On the left side of Faber's screen Chapman's dumb face screwed itself into a mask of confusion. Faber reflected how—on a purely visceral level—he absolutely couldn't stand either of these men.

"Don't double-talk me, Neil," Faber snarled. "In case you've forgotten, I can buy and sell both of you. I have more to protect than either of you can imagine—so don't you dare tell me what I should be concerned about."

As soon as he'd spoken, Faber realized how he sounded: panicked and childish. His regret doubled when he saw Reynolds's condescending smile. "Far be it from me to not acknowledge your power and fortune, Jefferson. But tell me—what are you going to do about the woman?"

"The woman?" Faber asked, feeling defensive and confused. "Do you mean Madison?"

"Of course," Reynolds said. "I'm sure you've already compromised us in a number of ways through your personal association with her."

Chapman edged closer on the screen. "Neil's right," he said. "She could be a real problem for us."

Faber had dreaded this. Madison had returned to her compound after her operatives had failed to communicate with her. Faber hadn't told her what he had learned from Chapman, but she surely knew that something had gone wrong.

"She won't be a problem," Faber said. "Her integrity is beyond question. She's reliable under pressure."

"Don't be foolish," Reynolds said. "Her connection to our captured operatives will be discovered almost immediately. The federal government has compiled a partial database of all known militia-group members."

"Madison is tough—she won't cooperate with the government," Faber said. "She's not a dilettante. Is it lost on you that she's devoted her life to her political beliefs?"

"Human nature is human nature," Reynolds responded. "We can't be sure that you've earned any great degree of personal loyalty from her."

Faber was consumed with loathing for Reynolds, who had smugly hit a nerve. Faber had developed a loyalty and affection for Madison within his spirit that had surprised him. But he couldn't begin to gauge the depths of her feelings for him.

"I don't care if you love her, or if you love sleeping with her," Reynolds added. "That's beside the point."

"Don't talk about her that way," Faber said. "In fact, don't talk about her at all."

"I can see the following series of events occurring," Reynolds said. "The field operatives lead the government to Madison. She leads them to us. Another possibility: she protects you, but sells out Chapman and myself. If that occurs, I will lead them straight to you—because your stupidity will have led to my arrest."

Faber put his head in his hands. The inevitability of Reynolds's argument oppressed him.

"I hadn't felt the need for us to have a truly frank discussion before, but now I do," Reynolds declared. "Our agreement is over. I have enough money for my purposes."

"You can't just—" Faber began.

"We had two successful missions and one failure. We've stopped short of selling the Iranians enough quality uranium for them to assemble a warhead. Now we face the danger of being caught. We need to sever all connections now—even those between one another."

"You saw Madison at the basketball game," Faber said. "Why didn't you talk to her then?"

"I didn't want anyone to learn about my acquaintance with her," Reynolds said. "And I knew there was no point in trying to convince her to protect me. She's too intelligent to act against her own interests."

Chapman's face stared out from the screen with an expression of befuddlement and fear. He cleared his throat like a student who wanted to speak in class.

"What?" Faber asked harshly. "What in the world do you think you can possibly contribute to this?"

"I agree with Neil," Chapman said. "The Iranians don't have enough uranium, as I understand it, to make any trouble. We've socked aside some money and now we can call it quits. I don't know what to do about this Madison girl, but someone has to take care of her."

"Stunning," Faber said. "You never cease to impress me."

"My connections to both of you are undeniable but can be accounted for with prosaic explanations," Reynolds said. "Madison is our only problem."

"She's a human being, for God's sake," Faber said. "We can give her a chance. She knows how to disappear. I can give her money from my own pocket to protect her."

Reynolds wore a haughty, bored expression. Faber now knew who his real enemy was.

"I've tolerated your standard diatribe about your money, your power, and the indestructibility of your world," Reynolds said. "And it's all I can do not to laugh. You are like a rat in a maze, Jefferson. You have no idea how ridiculous you sound."

Faber wanted to reply, but couldn't. He was afraid fear would creep into his voice and give him away.

"I'm finished with our endeavor," Reynolds continued,

"which means both of you are as well. If you want to stay out of jail, you'll think very hard about what I've said."

"I saw you with the Antonelli woman," Faber blurted. "Don't talk to me like you live in an ivory tower."

"You will not mention her again," Reynolds responded. "You have a problem. Take care of it."

Reynolds's image disengaged; the right side of Faber's computer screen showed black undulating nothingness.

"Neil's up on his high horse, but he's right," Chapman said. "It's time to step away."

"Maybe so," Faber said, trying to betray nothing in his voice.

"It's all been out of hand for a long time." Chapman sighed. Faber watched the senator's face collapse with genuine remorse. "Maybe this is a godsend. I'm still in a position to do positive things with my life. You and I can still work together. Our needs aren't necessarily exclusive."

"We'll talk later," Faber said. He reached out and turned off his computer.

He sat alone in his office for nearly an hour, watching dust motes dancing in a band of sun that poked through the curtains.

25

2:20 p.m. Washington, D.C.

TIME WAS CLOSING IN ON COLONEL NEIL REYNOLDS.

In a sense it was to his liking that events had transpired
as they had. The endeavor with Faber and Chapman had
run its course, along with its attendant moral dilemmas and
compromises. The project had served its purpose: he had
amassed enough money to entirely fund the secret aspects
of his research.

The army and Department of Defense had also begun to
present problems for him. Reynolds had been out of the
administrative and political loop for too long. He had
missed too many briefings and meetings—meetings at
which, he had been told, his recent lack of budget account-
ability had been discussed in an unfavorable light.

Reynolds had locked himself inside his soundproof laboratory. His research staff were outside reviewing code
sequences and verifying data, the application of which was
unknown to them. He turned on his portable cassette deck;
Beethoven's second Concerto for Piano and Orchestra
filled the room with its complexity and beauty. Most importantly, it was a piece that had been successful in drown-
ing out the worsening cacophony in his mind. Reynolds

swiveled in his rolling chair and propelled himself over to a monitor and keyboard.

The first action on his part that had elicited disapproval from the army was his taking his computers off the Army Medical Research Center's network. This meant that no one could examine or review Reynolds's work without physical access to his machines. Which was incalculably unlikely—getting into the room required knowledge of the ever-changing door codes, then knowledge of the pass-words that guarded his files. Better to receive disapproval than share his discoveries.

Reynolds rubbed his eyes and hit a modular switch that lowered the lights. He was fatigued and under stress. He wasn't sure how near he might be to a complete physical and psychological collapse, given the recent strains on his neurological systems. If only there were some kind of pre-cedent, some records to draw upon for guidance.

Which reminded him that it was time to update his verbal log. He had never been able to type well; his fingers were too thick. He unlocked a small safe he had welded to the underside of his workstation and produced a microcas-sette recorder.

He started the recording: "This is United States Army Colonel Neil Reynolds, continuing the anecdotal record of my experiments. As always, I recommend cross-analyzing my verbal reports with the daily readouts of my vital signs that I have compiled on computer disk."

Reynolds paused. One day someone would play this tape. Reynolds might be dead by then—he might have moved on to something greater. He had already foreseen the possibility of outliving his identity.

He continued, "Consider how our brains work. Recent experiments have indicated that humans can, at best, learn, process, and subsequently remember about two bits of information per second.''

Reynolds made some rapid mental calculations. ''If an individual continually took in information at this rate for twelve hours a day for a century, this person would have stored in his mind approximately three billion bits of information. This is less data than we can currently store on a five-inch CD-ROM.

''The bit is a measure for expressing hard information,'' he continued. ''It is a machine term. We know that human experience, full of nuance, emotion, and interaction, is far richer and more complicated than a shelf of books about medicine or chemistry. We have four senses and our souls to contend with, which makes us greater thinkers than machines yet poorer at remembering.''

Reynolds turned off the recorder. He had to leave adequate documentation to ensure that his methods could be reproduced in the future. It would be reprehensible not to do so. Humanity deserved the opportunity to evolve into something potentially greater.

But who would listen to the tape? Reynolds knew he couldn't necessarily dictate who received it. Humanity was rife with scoundrels and fools. Years before, he would have turned everything over to the U.S. government, but he now understood that large institutions weren't trustworthy. Greed and the thirst for power would dictate their actions.

He could have sold his secrets for an unimaginable fortune, but this would have been tantamount to laughing in the face of the higher levels of being he had experienced in tantalizing glimpses. And as for power, he already possessed it.

''Laura,'' he said aloud. He pictured her beautiful face.

Reynolds was glad to be alone at the moment. Lately he had been prone to talking to himself and drifting off into contemplation—in short, to temporarily losing control. He had painstakingly detailed these episodes in his logs. It was all he could do.

He turned on the recorder. "Our brains are thought to house approximately one hundred trillion synapses. Through electrical communication our brains learn, remember, process, and make new connections. We are able to use only part of that storage capacity. Even with enhanced functioning of synaptic connections we would eventually reach a point at which we have met our inviolable physical limits.

"This is what defines our identity as a species: the limits of our intelligence, our ability to grow, the nature of our souls." Reynolds paused, looking for words. "This defines the limits of how we can affect our world, including the nature of our bodies."

Reynolds glanced up at the digital clock on the wall. It was late afternoon. He knew his staff outside would work several hours longer. They didn't know that their current assignments could well be the last they would receive from their current superior.

"As you have learned from my notes and records, I have successfully made fundamental changes in the human brain," Reynolds said. "Utilizing nanotechnology, I have created machines capable of working in the human body on a minute scale of size unprecedented in medicine."

He paused. "This was made possible by recent advances in semiconducting materials that enabled me to power these devices. The new substance is a low-voltage alloy of gallium, indium, germanium, and arsenide. This discovery was made by the late Cyrus Tafreshi, in work he spearheaded for a firm known as Emergent Technologies."

It was, after all, only proper to give credit.

"I have developed an implant that has been successful

in matching electroneural energy, and used it to stimulate previously untapped synaptic connections in my brain. Concurrent with this I have designed a technique for breaching the cell membrane in order to simulate the human endocrine system in a variety of ways. With this combination of treatments I have increased the synaptic electrical levels within my mind on an order of several hundred percent.''

Reynolds's palms were sweating; he wiped them on a handkerchief. ''I am the first case study of this process. Perhaps you will be the second. I cannot know whether you will conclude that this transformation is an experience you can endure.''

With his eyes closed he saw patterns of light. Like a beehive. His mind buzzed from within.

Reynolds switched off the recorder. He felt more than human, and at times less than human. How to explain that a minute to him now seemed like an hour, his mind making connections at a rate that bordered on hallucinatory? How to explain the discomfort as information coursed through a biological mechanism still ''wired'' for its previous existence?

He couldn't explain. He couldn't make himself understand why he had fallen in love at the precise moment he was ready to change humanity. So he wouldn't. He would let history make its judgments.

Reynolds activated his workstation and initialized a program sequence. He glanced around at the machines, quietly and steadily acquired as his needs had broadened. His ledgers would one day be checked by military personnel, questions would be asked. But by then it would be over.

Reynolds toggled through a series of menu options until his cursor rested on a batch of programs. They bore three names: his own, Laura's, and Carlo's. Above them was a heading: "The Gift."

It had been so difficult to pretend to Laura that he was still an ordinary man. But he loved her. And she would soon understand everything.

He donned his virtual-reality headpiece and waited for the initialization series that would match his senses with that of the microscopic device within him. When he opened his eyes, it was to the sprawling infinity of the human genetic code.

26

NATIONAL SECURITY AGENT JACK PARSONS LIT ANOTHER cigarette, this one off the smoldering tip of the last. He was well into his second pack of the day, and as the afternoon lapsed into evening he wondered whether he should have bought a third.

In front of him on his desk were stacks of photographs representing the past week's satellite-surveillance images from the Middle East. The technology that created them was superb, yet still the pictures required a trained eye capable of distinguishing a jeep from a shadow, a man from a stack of crates.

This wasn't how Parsons had imagined serving his country. He wasn't unrealistic—scenes of international intrigue and shoot-outs with foreign spies had been the farthest things from his mind—but he had thought, after Annapolis and a tour of duty in the Persian Gulf, that he would have been ordered to perform work more stimulating than desk duty and satellite-recon analysis.

Parsons rubbed his eyes and decided to create some order out of the mess of photos on his desk. It would have helped if he had been told what to look for. Instead he had been given typically cryptic orders to seek out any "irregularities" along the northern Iranian border from hundreds of grainy pictures.

So far Parsons had earmarked four pictures that might have shown something out of the ordinary—though they probably didn't. The first, which revealed a congregation of jeeps outside a small village, would probably turn out to be a refueling station. In two pictures he found groups of armed men setting up tents in the foothills—these were probably Iranian military platoons on routine exercises. The fourth, which Parsons had reluctantly put in the pile of anomalies, would almost surely turn out to be a shepherd and his flock.

His cigarette had nearly burned down to the filter. Parsons stubbed it out in the overflowing ashtray and looked around the room to exercise his eyes. There wasn't much to see: a shelf of manuals and regulations, a locked credenza full of files, and a little window looking over the Potomac.

"Well, this isn't going to get done by itself," Parsons said aloud. He flipped open the file containing photos taken from five days before.

He decided that he would work through this file and perhaps halfway into the next before heading home. Little awaited him there at his efficiency apartment, save for a stack of unpaid bills and some dirty dishes. He felt no particular compulsion to hurry.

When he was halfway through the first file, he lit another cigarette. Almost unconsciously, he hummed the opening melody from Thelonious Monk's *Brilliant Corners*.

Parsons saw mountains in the pictures, and little else. The rocky hills stretched out under the satellite's eye. Roads looked like riverbeds, more the product of nature than of man.

Then he saw something.

"That's strange," Parsons said. He flipped on his extra lamp to provide maximum illumination in the cramped office. With a magnifying glass he peered closely at a picture of a road passing under a rocky precipice. No clouds barred the satellite's image, so the picture was better than average.

He saw a truck, and men standing next to it. Above them on the crag was a shadowy form.

The next photograph, taken three minutes later in the satellite's routine reconnaissance, showed four helicopters landing on a flat ridge near the truck. The five men seemed to be lying down on the road. The shape atop the ridge now revealed itself as a man lying in a contorted, broken position.

Parsons picked up the phone. He had something.

27

9:05 p.m. Los Angeles.

LAURA SLOWLY WALKED UP THE STAIRS, THE WEIGHT OF THE day pressing on her. She had spent four exhausting hours that afternoon working on a difficult ulcer case that had required careful open surgery.

Following that tiring experience she had visited Ferry. Ferry had seemed calm and almost cheerful—she had been making a cake with Davood and Mina when Laura arrived—but there was a funereal air about the house. Cyrus's briefcase and jacket remained on the kitchen chair where he had left them the night he died.

Laura then found that she had problems of her own. Upon picking up Carlo at her mother's, Laura discovered that her son was feeling feverish and lethargic. She had given him a quick checkup when they got home, and found nothing particularly wrong with him. He had eaten some soup and crackers and gone to bed early—a sure sign that he wasn't exaggerating about his symptoms in a stratagem to miss his spelling test the next day.

Laura opened Carlo's door a crack and looked inside. Federico's eyes shone at her, reflecting Carlo's basketball-shaped night-light. The cat yawned and sprang from the bed, nudging past Laura and making his way down the stairs for his nighttime snack. Laura flipped on Carlo's reading lamp and took a thermometer from her shirt pocket.

"Carlo, honey, wake up," she said, nudging the boy.

"What?" he said in a dreamy voice, squinting at the light.

"We have to take your temperature again." She felt his forehead, which seemed as hot as it had earlier that evening.

Carlo started to complain; Laura used the opportunity to put the digital thermometer in his open mouth. He scowled but didn't have the energy to maintain his grumpiness.

His temperature was 101.8 degrees, two tenths of a degree greater than when she'd put him to bed.

"How are you feeling?" she asked.

"Sleepy," he mumbled.

"Well, your temperature is a little higher, but it's not high enough to really worry me." She always kept her son informed about any illness either of them suffered, in an attempt to demystify health and medicine for him.

"That's good," Carlo said.

"Hey, what's that?" Laura asked. The boy had a patch of bright-red skin just below his collarbone.

"I don't know," Carlo said. "It was itching."

Laura looked closer at the patch of skin; though she wasn't sure, there might have been a small puncture wound or abrasion at the center of the inflamed area. It could have been a bug bite.

"Stay awake for a minute," she said.

In a moment she returned with a tube of antibacterial cream. She applied it liberally to the inflamed area of Carlo's skin.

"When did you notice this?" she asked him.

"I don't remember," he replied in a dreamy voice. "The other night or something." He closed his eyes.

Before she let him alone, Laura made him chew another analgesic to control his fever, insisting he wash it down with half a glass of water. He acquiesced, then immediately fell back into a deep slumber.

Downstairs Laura rattled around the house, unable to concentrate on anything for long. It was nearly ten, so she decided she would finish tidying up the place and go to bed early. It hadn't been the kind of day she was anxious to prolong.

She ran hot water and started to rinse off the day's dishes before putting them in the dishwasher. Federico loitered around her feet, hoping for some scrap of food or attention. Laura turned on the radio and half listened to a community-affairs program on the local public-radio station. This evening's discussion was on managed care in medicine, which forced an ironic smile from her.

The heat from the water, the boring radio announcer's voice, and the overall stillness of the house put her in a meditative state. Random, unfocused thoughts passed through her mind.

First was the memory of Cyrus Tafreshi's autopsy. She couldn't stop thinking about the strange foreign object Dr. Kim had found near Cyrus's thyroid gland. Though the medical examiner had thought little of it, it seemed inexplicably odd to her. She had peered inside countless bodies in the course of her surgical career and had never seen anything like it.

"Wait, that's not true," she said to herself. There had been one time. What was the patient's name?

Laura put a stack of plates in the dishwasher. "Carlson? Coleman?" she said. Federico sprang to attention, assuming she was speaking to him.

Then she remembered. Patricia O'Connell. White female, mid-forties. It had been almost a year ago when she
came to Laura complaining of symptoms that suggested
cholecystitis. Laura had performed surgery to remove her
diseased gallbladder, in the process removing a small metal
object encased near Patricia's liver. O'Connell had died of
a pulmonary embolism days later, never making it back to
Laura's office for a follow-up examination.

She hadn't thought about the incident since. She had
sent the object to pathology for examination and never
heard back. She hadn't, she realized, because O'Connell's
unexpected death had precluded her needing a follow-up
lab result, since the cause of death had been unrelated.

Laura filled the dishwasher with detergent, closed it,
and turned it on. Federico ran from the kitchen, frightened
by the noise.

There was no point worrying about Patricia O'Connell,
or about Cyrus. Both were dead of explainable causes. This
was idle, unproductive speculation.

Laura suddenly recognized the feeling that had plagued
her all evening, a sort of vague anxiety and ennui. A year
before she would have called the sponsor assigned to her
by the rehabilitation clinic in order to talk through her
problems. But she was stronger now, more able to read
her own moods and deal with them. Part of this process
was taking an interest in her own health and well-being,
rather than worrying about everyone else at her own expense. With this in mind she found her phone index on the
dining-room table and picked up her portable phone. Then
she stopped herself.

Of course. It was after one in the morning on the East
Coast. Neil would surely be asleep.

Laura went back to the kitchen and began scrubbing the
counter. The radio announcer was taking calls; she listened

to three in a row from patients describing various unpleasant experiences with managed care. Unfortunately, two of the three seemed to blame their doctor rather than the system. She was tempted to call in herself.

Laura put down the sponge and drew a painful breath with a hard gasp. A strange ringing filled her ears. She leaned against the counter for support.

She saw an image in her mind—still and clear like a photograph—of Steve, with the infant Carlo bundled in his arms. There was blue sky, water, a crowd of tourists in San Francisco. She was remembering a weekend trip she and her husband had taken a few months after the birth of their son.

She wondered why this half-forgotten memory had appeared in her mind. The memory itself didn't strike her as strange, but the crystal-clear nature of the image did. By then the picture was gone.

Something wasn't right. Laura suddenly felt cold. She shivered in front of the stove after putting on a pot of water to boil for tea.

Looking down, Laura saw that she had turned on the wrong burner. She switched it off as a wave of nausea overtook her.

Another picture flashed through her mind; it was more than a memory, almost like reliving the experience. Her father's burly frame was next to her as they rode through the Los Angeles streets in his car on a hot summer day. She felt as though he were truly next to her, his presence palpable yet somehow escaping her.

The sensation of cold was gone, replaced by a tingling that began in her neck then worked into her lower extremities. It was neither painful nor pleasant, more a sort of energy burning inside her. She felt her knees buckle and saw her vision blur into a cascade of darkening colors until she surrendered her awareness.

When Laura awoke, she sat bolt upright. Her legs and arms were prickly from the pressure of the floor, and her back ached.

She checked her watch. It was nearly eleven-thirty. She had been unconscious for more than an hour.

Laura looked around, listening. The house was quiet and still; the dishwasher had cycled through.

She felt her face, her head, searching for some sign of injury.

"Something's wrong with me," she whispered.

28

11:50 p.m. Washington, D.C.

WITHIN THE QUIET OF NEIL REYNOLDS'S LABORATORY ob-
servers would have seen such an abundance of machinery and computer equipment that they might not notice the
standing figure perched on a rubber mat at one end of the
room, his frame bathed in reddish light. His movements
were subtle and methodical, his hands moving control
levers with delicacy and concentration. His eyes and ears
were covered by goggles and earpieces.

His staff was gone for the day, and the halls of the
military medical research complex were empty save for
guards and night staff in charge of overseeing computer
programs that processed data through the night. Behind
locked doors, Neil Reynolds explored answers to questions
never before asked.

REYNOLDS FLOATED IN A VACUUM, WITH NO SENSE OF SPACE
and time. He sensed his feet below him, the cool feel of
the controls, the rhythmic push of his lungs, but for the
moment those sensations were irrelevant. His mind was
connected to a machine that could rest with dozens of its
duplicates on the nail of his smallest finger.

He had manipulated several of these devices that night. Utilizing the world's telecommunication's network, he had directed their movements through human tissue. His vision was accustomed to the baroque radiographic representations that his devices beamed into his visor. He knew the murky undulations of blood flow, the starry masses of white blood cells, the caverns and striated structures of anatomy he had memorized in medical school.

Reynolds moved his device up from the cerebral aqueduct. He saw smooth walls to either side, and felt an eerie calm here in the brain. Within the body was a rhythmic pulse that was greatest closest to the heart and lungs. He felt this pulse influence his own—inevitably, he would begin to breathe in time with his subject.

All around him was cerebrospinal fluid, the watery cushion that protects the spine and brain from physical shock. Reynolds began his plodding climb up to the corpus callosum. It occurred to him that two lovers had never been so close to each other before.

"The subject has normal brain structures," he spoke. He had turned on his tape recorder, leaving it to run while he worked. "Lateral ventricles are healthy and well formed."

Reynolds now encountered the great branching curvature of the corpus callosum, the band connecting the two hemispheres of the brain. It looked like a marble monument.

"My methodology on this subject differs from the procedure I performed on myself," Reynolds said. "As a result of hormonal manipulation the subject should experience an increase in brain function—without the mental strain I encountered from using the bioelectrical implant."

All around him now was the gray matter of Laura's brain. He saw the gradated shades of tissue, the seemingly infinite softness of the hemispheres. Though he couldn't feel everything the robot did—just the pressure exerted by and on its mechanical arms—he sensed electricity, the power of thoughts fired from synapse to synapse.

"When my new condition made it possible for me to assimilate greater amounts of information, and to synthesize it in new ways, I moved on to the most radical stage of my experimentation," he added.

He directed his movements now toward the hypothalamus.

"I first directed my attention toward refinement of my work with the endocrine system," Reynolds said. "I examined the mechanisms that control the human cell—specifically the integrity of the cell wall and the sodium pump, a mechanism in which sodium is pumped out of the cell and potassium into it. The electropotential of this system maintains cell integrity; I found a way to manipulate it.

"From here my hormonal adjustments could become more refined. I was able to use cells as chemical factories, replicating CRH and AVP from the hypothalamus and ACTH from the pituitary gland. First I learned to flood a subject's system creating fatal cascades of these hormones. Then I refined their chemical balance, soon enhancing the cerebral process I've undergone."

He envisioned each step of discovery, including the last: when the secrets of the cell fell before his eyes.

"Once I went beyond the cell membrane, I was able to tamper with chemical products inside the cells themselves. With increasing miniaturization I have been able to work down to the microscopic level."

With this he felt a wave of power flush through him. He adjusted the vision enhancement on the robot as he activated the device's smallest titanium arm, far too minute to be seen by the unaided eye. The world before him shifted;

small objects became mountains, and new strange structures began to appear. He looked to either side until he saw what he was seeking: a single human cell, rounded and alive. Its membrane was mottled with phospholipid molecules, and branched carbohydrate chains emerged from its surface like giant leafless oaks.

Reynolds activated the microcamera installed on the tip of his grasping arm, then executed a verbal command: "Move to fingertip visual on my mark . . . now."

He simultaneously plunged the arm toward the cell and his world was shattered. First infinitesimal radar devices housed on the arm picked up howling electrical static, which was sent into his ears. He winced and braced himself as his vision flooded with strange-colored electromagnetic fields chaotically merging and undulating in space. This was the sodium-potassium membrane, which creates pressure outside the cell and keeps foreign entities from entering. But he had breached it. He felt like a space explorer who had just pierced the turbulent atmosphere of a strange, inhospitable planet.

Then he seemed to be floating in a primeval sea: here was the messenger RNA, the amino acid sequences, the cisternae, all moving like ingredients in soup. Reynolds felt his breath catch in his chest. He reflexively ducked when a giant membranous endoplasmic reticulum swept by, so close he could have touched it with his mechanical arm. He admired the fluid shape of the membrane, as it moved about sucking up amino acids and proteins and synthesizing them into polyribosomes.

It was a world of shapes and shades; here was another universe so vast and intricate that he wished he never had to leave. Here outside the cell's nucleus, in the cytoplasm, proteins were transported into mitochondria, into membranes, into the nucleus; others were designed for export from the cell. It was a living, unthinking, relentless factory.

In his body he sensed this organized motion and constant transformation, feeling the power and grace of near perfection. And now he saw a miracle: NH2 termini in sequences of fifteen to thirty. He witnessed the fruition of his work—identifying the signal sequence of the ribosomal complex making contact with the cell membrane, then transporting amino acids and proteins from the cell to the Golgi bodies, then out of the cell wall. Reynolds watched the flattened Golgi saccules, the bright combinations of the chemical stew.

"Every discovery begins with a moment of contemplation," Reynolds mused. "I began to theorize following the discovery of the 'molecular clock,' even before my mental enhancement."

He closed his eyes, trying to recall himself and the world in which he normally lived.

"This clock is called the telomere. It is a segment of human DNA that controls the process of cell division and the creation of new cells. Studies have shown that, each time a cell divides within the body, the telomere is shortened slightly. Eventually it is nearly gone, and the cell can no longer reproduce itself. This leads to cellular degeneration, disease, and death."

He plunged the arm farther, now piercing the rough, spotted surface of the nucleus. "Increase magnification," he ordered. What he saw was nearly enough to drive him mad: the vast glacial expanses of cellular clockwork, the curling helix of DNA. Here he felt stillness and shelter from the storms raging outside. He stared long enough to be satisfied that his work was progressing, then closed his eyes. It felt like peering into the face of God.

Reynolds felt a bead of sweat run down to his neck. It

startled him, and for a moment he felt frightened and disoriented. He pulled the arm back again, moving quickly now, his eyes still closed. Again he felt the roaring turbulence of the cell membrane all around him. A loud pulse of energy filled his ears, and when he opened his eyes for a second he saw the fury and capricious power of the membrane, like a thunderstorm gone mad. Then the raging chaos ended.

"Restore preset visual levels," he said. "Switch to main camera and stow cell-level manipulation arm."

Before him now was the pendulous node of Laura's hypothalamus; he reached out and touched it, feeling its contours.

"There is no absolute, inviolate rule that the body must break down, age, and eventually die. When I increased my cerebral capacity I began to envision gene therapy strategies aimed at stopping the body's tendency toward atrophy. I sought every doctor's dream: the cure for death. I sought the Holy Grail."

Reynolds paused. His eyes wide, he admired the abstract shapes all around him: Laura's flow of life and memory. He now realized that falling in love at the moment of his greatest breakthrough wasn't, as he had first thought, an unfortunate distraction. It was destiny.

"I found the grail," he said.

Finally he anchored the device where it would do no harm, against a fibrous branch of cartilage. Reynolds switched off his connection to the robot and took off his visor.

The laboratory was quiet; all around him were his computers, their screens flickering. The recorder ran out of tape and switched off with a loud click.

He took off his gloves and gently placed them on the workstation, careful not to bump the delicate sensors built into their palms and fingers. Physical awareness washed over him: his breath, the weight of his body, the hunger in his stomach, all that was human.

He felt a powerful longing to return to the machine, to don the visor and gloves, to experience the universe of the human body as the great and infinite thing that it was.

Looking up, he saw his reflection in a small mirror hung over a desk topped with files and papers.

His hair was plastered to his head with sweat; his eyes were ringed with red; his mouth hung slack and open.

Neil Reynolds didn't want to admit to himself that his reflection was that of a madman.

29

10:15 a.m., September 15. Los Angeles.

AMID THE BUSTLE OF THE POSTOPERATIVE SUITE LAURA filled out the paperwork on the operation she'd just performed. There were a half-dozen patients in the ward, including Laura's; all had just undergone surgery and were making their slow ascent from anesthetic oblivion back into consciousness.

The paperwork was tedious but essential. If her patient were to experience any postsurgical complications, her report would be scrutinized by the hospital oversight committee, which now reported directly to Ellington-Faber. After her recent entanglement with the corporation Laura felt under pressure to properly fill out the labyrinthine paperwork.

The operation had been a standard hernia repair on a forty-five-year-old man who worked at one of the oil refineries in southern Los Angeles. She had stabilized the hernia and repaired it with Prolene mesh. During the procedure there had been only one mishap: a small bleeder had emerged during dissection, which she had quickly cauterized. Laura had felt unusually sharp and alert throughout the procedure.

Laura signed the report and dropped it off at the nurses' station, saving a copy for herself. She looked back one last time at her patient, a burly man with brusque manners who now slept in a corner with a placid, almost angelic expression on his face.

Heading back to the OR to change out of her scrubs, Laura relinquished the trancelike mental focus required for performing surgery and recalled what had happened to her last night. She had passed out in the kitchen, which was alarming enough. She was fortunate she hadn't bumped her head on anything when she fell. Even more disturbing was what she'd experienced just before unconsciousness— the rush of memories and associations, almost like a fugue state.

Her first thought was that the episode might have had something to do with her consumption of pills and alcohol in the past. She lived constantly with the fact that, should she have done lasting damage to herself during that dark period, Carlo would have been left to deal with the repercussions. The thought was almost too much to bear.

But it wasn't likely. Her period of addiction had been relatively brief, not long enough to do any lasting neurological damage. More likely was the possibility that she had experienced some sort of stress reaction, her personal worries compounded by the death of Cyrus and her affair with Neil Reynolds—which, however much happiness it had brought her, represented change and added uncertainty to her future.

"Excuse me," a voice said from behind her. "I have to get through."

Laura realized that she was blocking the supply closet that served the north wing of the surgical suites. A nurse was waiting impatiently with a heavy-looking carton of gauze pads.

"I'm sorry," Laura said, moving out of the way.

The nurse, harried and too busy for niceties, dumped the carton on a shelf inside the closet and moved on without a word.

Laura knew that if one of her friends or patients had complained of symptoms such as she had experienced the night before, her reaction would have been to order him or her into neurology for a complete work-up. She didn't feel this was necessary for herself, though; in fact, since she had awoken that morning she had felt much better than usual, her thoughts clear and her mind lively and sharp. Neurology wasn't her specialty, but she felt safe in assuming that if she felt this good, there must be nothing wrong with her.

She didn't have another surgery scheduled until early afternoon, so Laura decided she would go back to her office to catch up on insurance billing and the phone messages stacked on her desk.

To reach the nurses' lounge, where she had stored her clothes in a locker, Laura had to pass through the main surgical hall. Most of the rooms were in use. She paused for a second to look in one of the glass windows, out of idle curiosity, and saw a team inside working on a patient under heavy light. She couldn't recognize the surgeon in his mask and gown, but she saw that their work was centered on the patient's knee, probably some sort of ligament repair.

At the end of the hall the double swinging doors burst open; Laura pressed against the wall to allow room for a gurney pushed by Andrew James, the surgical resident assigned to the emergency room. Accompanying him was a frantic team of nurses maintaining IV lines and a respirator over a small, obscured body.

"We're in room two," ordered James, a young man

from Oregon who was regarded as a rising star in the surgical department. "Get him prepped, stat!"

Laura saw that the patient was a little boy, about Carlo's age, his face covered with an oxygen mask. She caught up with James outside the operating room.

"What have you got?" she asked. "Do you need me to scrub in?"

James hurried to the stainless-steel sink in the hall, where he donned a paper mask and began to vigorously scrub his hands and arms. "No, thanks," he said. "We have Chaney coming in. He should be here any minute."

Laura craned her neck around the doorway and saw that the anesthesiologist was taking vital signs from the boy.

"Chaney from cardiology?" she asked. "For a little boy?"

"He came in turning blue with an irregular heartbeat after collapsing at school," James answered. His attention remained on his hands and fingers, which he continued to scrub. "We got him stabilized, but I think there's some kind of congenital defect. Chaney's going to open him up and have a look around."

Laura knew that the young resident's urgency derived from two sources: his humanitarian impulse as a doctor, and also from the opportunity to assist on a surgery with a renowned cardiologist such as Carl Chaney. She had experienced the same pressure as a resident, lobbying to scrub in to as many different surgeries as possible—all the while shoring up her resume to enhance her employability.

Laura watched from the doorway. The anesthesiologist took a seat on a rolling chair and wheeled himself over to his cart, where he started to prepare the proper chemical mixture to anesthetize the patient—which was particularly difficult in this case, Laura knew, because of the boy's age and delicate condition.

She could see the boy now, his form prone on the table. He had a skinny frame, with thick dark hair curling around his forehead. His small chest rose and fell heavily.

It was Carlo.

Laura's mind flashed on her son's illness the night before, his fever and lassitude. He had felt better in the morning and had insisted on going to school. When she had checked his temperature it was normal, so she had assented. Now—

She made a strangulated gasping noise. She would have to scrub in and assist on the operation. Where the hell was Chaney? Why was he taking so long?

From the end of the hall the double doors slammed open. Carl Chaney, slim and bearded, jogged toward the OR.

Laura turned back into the OR; the surgical team was staring at her. She felt her shoulders begin to convulse with grief and fear.

"Is there anything wrong, Dr. Antonelli?" James asked, now fully masked and gowned. Chaney was scrubbing at the sink, oblivious.

Laura looked again at the young boy and blinked. It wasn't Carlo. She stared, waiting for her eyes to trick her again. She had seen Carlo on that table, there was no doubt about it. Now she saw an unfamiliar child.

The surgical team returned to their work, save for James. Laura realized he was waiting for an answer.

"No, there's nothing wrong, thank you," she said in an unsteady voice. "Good luck in there."

She stepped aside to let Dr. Chaney into the room. The doors swung closed behind him, and Laura heard his deep voice booming out commands.

Laura leaned against the wall and tried to regain her breath. Her hallucination could have been the product of a worried mother's guilty anxiety, but it hadn't been. It was something more serious. She pulled her hair away from her face and rested her hands on her temples. Her face was burning hot.

Something was affecting her mind.

30

1:15 p.m., September 16. Southeastern Nevada.

THE AFTERNOON SUN BLASTED THE BAKED DESERT EARTH. It would be hours before it descended over the Delmar Mountains. Jeanette Madison surveyed the sere land from her headquarters, which now felt more like a bunker than a place from which to conduct her political business.

It was her own fault. She had made a devil's bargain, trading the skills of her best-trained men for enough cash to fund Patriot's Way for the next five years. She had relinquished control. She had trusted Faber's judgment and his connections.

Her men had been captured or killed in northern Iran. Otherwise they'd have contacted her. Faber hadn't called or returned her messages. She had a feeling that things were going to change very quickly.

The camp had emptied save for a couple of men who had likely stayed in their quarters from a lack of anywhere else to go. Daily exercises had been called off, as had planning and operational meetings.

The Nevada desert wasn't much of a place in which to spend idle time. But Madison, like the other stragglers, had no place to go. Faber was her only option, and she didn't know where he was. She had long ago cut off contact with her surviving family. Her thoughts returned to her late husband and his suspicious death soon after his arrest. She doubted that the times had changed.

She had finally gone too far. She had tied the noose and stuck her neck into it. She had—

She paused, hearing something. There it was again. A dog's barking, growing louder and more enraged.

"Trotsky," she said. She got up from her desk.

Madison moved through her command center into her personal living quarters. When she reached the hallway connecting her rooms with the large communal kitchen, she heard the unmistakable sound of motors and tires on gravel.

She listened. Trotsky barked even louder, trained to alert his mistress to the presence of intruders.

"This is it," she said.

There were automatic machine guns in a case next to the front door, along with a single grenade launcher. She couldn't win a battle, but she could scare them. She could say she had hostages and stall for time.

Stall for time. What a hilarious thought. No one would come to save her. She had nothing to stall for.

Madison threw open the front door. From the shaded porch she watched them coming: three unmarked brown cars with tinted windows.

Trotsky was howling in the road, ready to match his German shepherd aggression against the intruders. Madison was touched by his loyalty, and she called for him to come to her. He looked at her, then at the cars, confused. She finally succeeded in making him go into the house. After she had locked him inside she could still hear him barking through the windows.

The cars slowed as she stepped off the porch into the

bright sun. She unrolled the sleeves of her military tunic and waited. She wished she had grabbed a hat on the way out; the glare was almost blinding.

When the cars reached the wide turnaround in front of the compound they pulled off in a row, probably forming a line of defense in case shooting erupted from inside. Madison wondered where her remaining men might be. They were probably asleep. Since the place began to shut down they had spent most of their time drinking Jim Beam and arguing. It was for the best. She didn't need any help.

Madison slowly moved her hands away from her body, holding her palms up to show that she was unarmed. A man emerged from the lead car, dressed in a blue suit and dark sunglasses. He walked toward Madison, his shoes crunching on the gravel. Inside the compound Trotsky's baying grew more desperate.

"Thanks for putting the dog inside," he said.

"No problem," Madison said. "Trotsky hates strangers."

The man seemed to ponder this for a moment. He looked younger up close, his skin baby smooth and his cheeks red from shaving. Madison guessed he was barely thirty.

"Jack Parsons, State Department," he said, producing a badge from inside his jacket pocket.

"I knew that already from your shoes," Madison said. "Patent leather wing-tips. You're either here to sell me insurance, or else you're a fed."

She kept an eye on the parked cars. "Are your friends getting out?" she asked.

"I told them to wait," Parsons said. "They have a strong prejudice against militia groups that they expressed to me in great detail on the ride over."

"And you don't?" she asked.

"A lot of these organizations serve purposes they don't even understand. Anyway, I don't much care, as long as they operate within the law," he said. "I checked into Patriot's Path and looked into your background. You're not the usual militia type."

"Well, the 'usual militia type' wants to start an Aryan nation and send the blacks to Africa and the liberals to Russia," Madison said. "We put together something different out here. We're survivalists. We have libertarian political beliefs, but we're not like the others."

Parsons stuck his tongue in his cheek absentmindedly. Madison wondered where this was leading, and whether Parsons was the sort of cop who wanted to chat before making the arrest.

"So what brings you here today, Jack?" she asked in a friendly tone. "I know the law and I run a tight ship. We're not looking for any kind of confrontation."

"I should think not," Parsons said, his voice hardening. "Particularly since most of your group has abandoned camp. Even Napoleon couldn't fight without an army."

Madison got the sense that this young man was toying with her; she sensed a zealot's arrogance beneath his innocent surface, and it irritated her. "Well, then, what do you want?" she asked angrily. "Are you rounding up candidates for the gulag, or do you want to talk political theory with an ex-professor? My tutoring fees are higher than you can afford."

Parsons smiled. "I just want to ask a few questions."

"Ask them," Madison said. She allowed herself to hope that she might not be arrested.

"What's the scope of your international activities?" he asked.

Madison laughed and hoped it sounded sincere. "International? We're dedicated to social change, as well as survival after the breakdown of this society. We're not the United Nations.''

Parsons stood perfectly still and stared at her from behind his dark glasses. Each lens reflected an image of the sun.

''Has anyone associated with your group recently taken soldier-of-fortune work in other countries?''

''A lot of these guys talk—'' Madison said. She tried to construct a plausible answer. ''I discourage getting involved in other countries' internal affairs. But you know good old boys. You can't tell them anything, and I can't control what they do when they're not here.''

Madison noticed that the cars' engines were running. Parsons's associates stayed inside, probably basking in air conditioning. She felt sweat gathering around her neck.

''Have you ever been to Iran?'' Parsons asked.

Madison's insides lurched. Her worst fears were coming true. Why hadn't she been arrested? This interrogation, if that was what it was, should have been taking place in a jail cell and not in front of her residence. The only answer was that Parsons was fishing for information. He was onto something—but he probably had no idea how close he was to the truth.

''Iran?'' Madison asked. ''As in, 'I ran the zoo'?''

''Please,'' Parsons said. ''Don't try to be funny.''

''Never been there,'' Madison said. ''Don't want to go there.''

Parsons stared at her with a half smile. He had to know about her men—she wished she could ask him if they had been captured or if they were dead.

''Here's my card,'' Parsons said, handing one to her. ''I'll be in touch. I'd appreciate your telling me if you decide to leave the country anytime soon.''

"Why is that?" Madison asked. She pocketed the card. "Am I some sort of suspect? What are you investigating?"

Parsons shoved his hands in his pockets and slouched boyishly; Madison calculated that he couldn't have been more than a few years out of school. It was a good sign— the government had sent a low-level agent to scout for leads. She might yet survive.

"A number of militia and radical groups are currently under investigation," Parsons offered. "We think some cowboys might have been doing a little foreign policy."

"You might try looking in your own backyard first," Madison said. "You've got plenty of cowboys in the government who make wars no one ever hears about."

Parsons smiled, grim and tight-lipped. "You may be right," he said. "But like you said, I can't afford your tutoring fees."

He walked toward his car. When he opened his door he called out, "Stay out of trouble. I don't have to tell you we're watching."

Madison watched them drive away, grinding gravel and churning dust all the way back to the highway. Though the sun burned her neck, she waited until she was sure they were truly gone.

Walking back to the compound, she understood how close she had come to losing her freedom—forever. If she didn't do something now, someone else would.

JACK PARSONS LOOSENED HIS TIE IN THE BACKSEAT, LETTING the cool air-conditioned air waft over him. "Christ, it's hot out there," he said.

The agent who was driving glanced in the rearview mirror. "You should have arrested her," he said. "We should arrest all these damned militia freaks just on general principles."

"Well, maybe so," Parsons said laconically. "But the Bill of Rights says we can't. As long as I'm running this investigation we're not making any arrests until we have concrete grounds to make a charge."

The driver snorted. "Is that what they taught you in Annapolis?"

"Among other things. You know—" Parsons was interrupted by his cellular phone ringing. He switched it on.

"Parsons."

"Jack, it's Sam Garcia. I've got someone on the line who wants to talk to you."

Sam was back at the Agency in Washington, coordinating the field investigators who were searching for clues in the Iran case. Parsons switched the phone to his good ear and pulled out a notepad.

"Who is it?" he asked.

"It's Nick Mills at *Worldweek* in New York," Sam began. "He has his shorts tied up in a knot, says he'll only talk to you."

Parsons sighed. He had dealt with Mills a few months before, over some chemical-weapons inspections in the Persian Gulf. Mills must have heard about the cowboys caught in Iran—which was disturbing as hell. It still hadn't been made public.

"The hell with him," Parsons said. "He must think I'm his personal information source now."

"I don't know, Jack," Sam said. "He says he has information to trade. That's the reason I called to put him through to you."

"Tell him we got cut off and take his number," Parsons said. "I'll call him when I get back to town tomorrow."

Parsons clicked off the phone. He watched the barren landscape pass by outside his window. "You know," he told the driver, "this job would be a hell of a lot easier without the media interfering all the time."

"We finally agree on something," the driver said with a chuckle.

31

4:40 p.m. Washington, D.C.

SENATOR ROBERT CHAPMAN OF CALIFORNIA WAS ALONE ON a bench at the deserted end of a small park in Washington. He felt a bit ridiculous. He had eschewed his regular car and driver that day in favor of his wife's economy car, and had also worn dark glasses and a raincoat to keep from being recognized. Since he could never bear any period of idleness, he had brought along a newspaper and a sandwich to occupy himself while he waited.

Neither was much help. He didn't feel like reading the newspaper. He would panic over every article on the Middle East and Iran; every mention of the region now confirmed his apprehension that a trail of trouble was winding its way directly toward him. His emotional life had deteriorated into depths of panicked despair alternating with fragile, ephemeral optimism. Eating the turkey sandwich was out of the question. He hadn't had an appetite in days.

Through a copse of trees Chapman could see a little playground populated by young children playing on swings and rides, their mothers watching and talking. Chapman thought of his own children. He wasn't an introspective man—in fact, he knew that a reflective nature was anathema to the successful political animal. But there was no denying that he would be to blame for the ruin that probably awaited him and his family. And the source of it all had been his own damned, blind personal ambition.

NEIL REYNOLDS PARKED, SWITCHED OFF THE ENGINE, AND looked around. The park was small but scenic, with plenty of trees and a pond. There was no one around but children, their parents, a few lovers probably on their lunch breaks from work, and a few homeless people congregated under a tall elm tree.

He walked along a dirt path past the playground, deeper into the park. He zipped his windbreaker up to his neck, feeling a chill. The sky was overcast, and the wind bore with it the first hint of the long winter that lay ahead.

Chapman waited several hundred feet away, at the end of the path. The senator was dressed in a trench coat and sunglasses, like something out of a spy novel. Reynolds would have found it funny, but he was losing his sense of humor. Chapman was a man with a dull wit and simple mind who had been malleable and easily manipulated. He wasn't the sort of man with whom to cast one's lot during difficult times. He wasn't the sort of man you could rely upon.

"Senator," Reynolds said. He glanced around and, satisfied that no one was watching, settled onto the wooden bench next to Chapman.

"Colonel," Chapman said. "You're looking sporty today. Slacks and a polo shirt. I never thought I'd see the day."

"Military dress is conspicuous," Reynolds said wearily.

Reynolds felt a seemingly infinite fatigue come over

him—an almost overpowering need to sleep, to get away. Yet he had slept nearly nine hours the night before.

"You don't look so good, Neil," Chapman said. "Do you still have that cold you mentioned?"

"I'm fine," Reynolds said. *Focus,* he commanded himself. "Let's talk and then get away from here. This isn't the best time for us to be seen in public together."

"That's not a problem," Chapman said. "We're known acquaintances. I can say you were lobbying my vote on next year's defense budget on behalf of your research unit."

"You could say that, Bob," Reynolds answered. "But it's better to avoid explaining anything. I sure wouldn't want to explain why you met me dressed up like a Stasi agent about to make an arrest."

Chapman took off his sunglasses. "Sorry about that," he said. "I'm just nervous."

"It's reasonable to be nervous," Reynolds said. He stared straight ahead, avoiding Chapman's eyes. He didn't want to become caught up in the man's fearful, animallike humanity.

"That's easy for you to say, Neil," Chapman said. "We're talking about my entire political career here. I could be sent to jail."

"We all face the same risks," Reynolds said.

"I know, Neil. Christ, I'm sorry, I know we're all in this together." Chapman crossed his legs and started to wring his hands. "It's just that I never thought anything like this would happen. I thought we had everything under control."

"You thought that Jefferson and I had everything under control," Reynolds corrected.

"Damn it, that's not fair, Neil." Chapman slapped his thigh.

Reynolds sighed. In addition to his fatigue he had a dull headache, with tendrils of discomfort radiating from behind his ears to the center of his forehead. It could have been the effect of the treatments he had performed on himself. There was no way to know.

"It's *not* fair," Reynolds mocked. "You wanted to meet me, Bob. Don't waste my time with inane rhetoric. Give me information."

"What's the matter, Neil?" Chapman asked. "Haven't your State Department contacts kept you up to date? Or maybe you need me more than you're willing to admit?"

Even through his discomfort and fatigue Reynolds could see that Chapman felt slighted. The senator was rebelling against the fact that he had been manipulated. Reynolds recalled the time when he first knew Chapman; he had been impressed by the politician's decency and idealism. They were both corrupted now. Reynolds wondered who had been the corrupter and who the corrupted.

"We brought you into the enterprise for a reason," Reynolds said. "You obviously have a vital role to play. So stop grandstanding and tell me what you know."

Chapman looked out across the trees and cleared his throat, suddenly all business. "We're dealing with whispers, and that's all we'll have until the Iranian government goes public or approaches us through diplomatic channels. But our intelligence is sound. Their government is holding our crew, along with the materials they were carrying. It's delicate right now. They're having a struggle between the military and the clergy. We won't see a civil war, but there'll be a shuffling of power alignments between the government and the military."

"That's just common sense," Reynolds said.

"Common sense," Chapman repeated. He let out a short, bitter laugh. "I would never have gone along with you if I'd known we were going to do business with the Iranians.''

''You never asked,'' Reynolds said.

''For Christ's sake, Neil, you're in the military. This is treason.'' Chapman's voice rose in pitch. ''That's why you and Jefferson kept it from me until it was too late. You knew I would never have gone along with nuclear sales to Iran.''

''Maybe that's true,'' Reynolds conceded. ''We understood your innate simplemindedness. It would have been too hard to explain to you that the Iranian faction was the only group with ready cash. I showed you my calculations. We stopped long before they had enough enriched uranium to build a working weapon.''

Reynolds wished this conversation had never begun; if there were any listening devices in the vicinity, they had as good as confessed.

''We also took care to sell them materials that were developed during the Soviet Union's disintegration. I seriously doubt whether the quality is good enough to use without further enrichment—which is currently beyond their capabilities.''

''You're talking like a scientist,'' Chapman said in a pious voice. ''But you don't know for sure. They could have also been buying from other sources. I swear, it keeps me up at night. I never, ever, would have become involved if I knew—''

Reynolds felt his jaw tighten. ''I asked you not to talk nonsense,'' he snapped. ''You would have done anything for that Senate seat.''

''I *earned* my seat in the Senate,'' Chapman said. His fair skin flushed red. ''I campaigned, I worked, I served the party—''

Reynolds leaned back on the bench and laughed.

"I *did*!" Chapman barked. "I'm a member of the Federal Heritage Leadership Council! I served two years in the state party steering committee! As a state representative I embarked on three separate fact-finding international tours to secure my standing on foreign affairs, so that when I had the chance to—"

Reynolds laughed even harder. When he felt his amusement abate for a second, he looked at Chapman's serious expression. It made him crack up anew.

"Stop that!" Chapman yelled.

"You were in line for that seat," Reynolds said. "Jefferson and I knew it. We merely had to expedite the process."

Chapman stared at Reynolds. "I don't know what the hell you're talking about," he said after a long silence. "When George Patterson died I was able to assume his seat and take his place on the Foreign Affairs Committee. You can't tell me that . . ."

The senator paused.

"I told you," Reynolds said. "there's no such thing as luck. Do you remember that?"

"I—" Chapman looked away from Reynolds. Shaking his head, he got up from the bench and walked to a nearby trash bin, where he threw away his newspaper and unopened sandwich.

Reynolds closed his eyes and felt the cool breeze. He was in a strange state, somewhere between sleepiness and awareness.

"It's getting to you as much as me," Chapman said. "I can see it in your face."

Reynolds started; he hadn't realized that Chapman had returned to the bench.

"I mean it," Chapman said. "You act like you have this

all figured out, but you feel the heat. You look like shit. I must say, it doesn't do much for my confidence.''

''I don't care how confident you feel,'' Reynolds replied.

''This Cyrus Tafreshi, our contact with the Iranian faction—his death wasn't an accident, was it?''

A pair of joggers passed by, a middle-aged man and woman dressed in matching track suits. Reynolds waited until they were gone before speaking.

''Draw your own conclusions, Bob,'' he said. ''I won't explain everything to you. You're not a child.''

Chapman was silent for a long time. Reynolds savored the quiet, breathing deeply, trying to will away the pain and fuzziness in his mind.

''I wanted the power, the Senate seat,'' Chapman said in a faraway voice. He could have been talking to himself. ''I knew Jefferson could help me get it. And I'll need money for my reelection campaign in two years, then the one after that. I'll always need him.''

Reynolds didn't answer.

''Jefferson—well, he's Jefferson.'' Chapman laughed derisively. ''He put me in his pocket as part of the bargain, at least he thinks he did. I understand Jefferson very well. But you, Neil, I never figured out why you were involved in this. I don't believe this 'research' story. What are you doing, stashing it all away in Switzerland or something?''

''You made a classic mistake,'' Reynolds said. ''You thought everyone in the world shared your motives. Not everyone lives for the dollar—or for gaining power they don't know how to use.''

The sky above them had darkened; the air felt crisp and ionized, as though it could begin to rain at any second.

''Well, what is it, then?'' Chapman asked. He sounded

sincerely curious. "If nothing else you owe me that. Tell me what you wanted from this disaster."

"I don't have a blank check at my unit, Bob," Reynolds said. "The legislature allots plenty of money to the Pentagon, but that money goes into weapons systems and guns. My division has seen a loss in real-dollar funding for three consecutive years."

Chapman rubbed his cheek, listening. Reynolds knew this train of thought would calm the senator, by bringing him to his familiar world of political concerns.

"It's a changing world," Chapman said abstractedly. "America needs to be ready for overseas conflicts."

Reynolds felt laughter bubbling within him again. The absurdity of the man before him was stunning.

"I needed the money for technology," he said. "Nanotechnology is incredibly expensive. Producing the new semiconducting materials for my latest devices, adapting them to the old technology, putting together power sources and communications gear—it costs more than my budget allowed. It's as simple as that."

"I don't understand all that technical crap, but I can't believe you," Chapman said. "You ran all these risks just to fund your department? It doesn't make sense."

"Not my department, my own personal work," Reynolds said. He chewed his lip. How much should he tell this fool? His emotions felt out of control; he sensed pride welling up within him.

"I've been in an administrative black hole for the past year," Reynolds confessed. "Funding off-site work out of my pocket, adding equipment to my lab bought with dirty money, then falsifying the paperwork to make it look legitimate. My DNA research alone cost more than two hundred thousand dollars—but I had to work fast. I had others put together pieces of the smaller puzzle while I assimilated the data into a greater vision. It hasn't been easy, keeping workers on my commissioned projects from becoming suspicious.''

Chapman's mouth was agape.

''But I never expected the Holy Grail to come cheap,'' Reynolds said.

He was talking too much. ''You can't put a budget on the secrets of the human soul, or on changing the nature of our species.'' He had to stop. But he couldn't.

''Do you understand me?'' Reynolds demanded. ''You have the Senate. Jefferson has his money, his companies. It would be a sin if that was all it amounted to. In your ignorant fashion you have helped the human race crawl out of ignorance and mortality. Could you have ever guessed it?''

REYNOLDS HAD GONE COMPLETELY INSANE. BOB CHAPMAN tried to keep his face a mask of calm composure and reassurance.

''I—I can see you're on to big things, Neil,'' he said. ''I suppose you're right. I should be happy that I was able to help you.''

Chapman knew how hollow his words sounded; Reynolds flashed a look of disgust and turned away.

''But we need to stay focused on the here and now,'' Chapman added hopefully. ''I think that, even in a worst-case scenario, we can hold out for plausible denial.''

Reynolds seemed not to hear; the wind gusted and a few light drops of rain fell on the park.

''Leave it to Jefferson and me,'' Reynolds said. He shoved his hands into his windbreaker pockets, seeming to search within. ''Stay calm, Bob, and keep your ears open. Everything will be fine.''

''I suppose that's what I wanted to hear,'' Chapman

said. He felt honestly relieved. "We can get through this if we work together. That's all that I—"

"Hold still," Reynolds said. He slid across the bench. Chapman instinctively recoiled as Reynolds cupped his hand behind the senator's head. "Damned wind. Blew a bug in your ear."

Chapman felt the heat of Reynolds's body pressed uncomfortably close to his own. "What are you doing?" he asked, his voice revealing his fear.

"I got it," Reynolds said.

The senator felt a sting in his ear. Reynolds pulled away.

"Nature has its drawbacks," Reynolds said with a smile. "Never could stand it, myself. Bugs, snakes. Awful things."

Chapman stood up, unnerved by Reynolds's actions. "Well, thanks," he said. "I guess it wouldn't do to go back to the office with dead flies coming out of my ear."

"No," Reynolds said. He remained seated on the bench. "It wouldn't."

Chapman started to walk away, the breeze caressing his face; he glanced back at the bench, where Reynolds sat motionless. Bob Chapman thought he saw a flicker of anticipation pass across the colonel's features. But he couldn't be sure.

32

"I DON'T UNDERSTAND IT, MAMA. HE SEEMED BETTER THIS morning."

"He'll be fine, Laura," Maria Antonelli said. She settled into her easy chair with a loud sigh. "You're a doctor, but you can't keep your child from getting sick. It took your father years to learn that."

At times such as these Laura realized how much she still relied on her mother; when Carlo's school had called, saying the boy was ill and feverish again, Laura knew her mother would watch him until Laura could get away from the hospital. Laura wondered how other single mothers dealt with situations such as this. It must have been impossible without an extended family.

"You don't look very well yourself, *cara*," Maria said. She adjusted her bifocals and examined her daughter. "You're pale. Have you been working too hard?"

"I'm happy just to be working," Laura said, checking her watch. She had been able to schedule a neurological work-up for later that afternoon. After the episodes of that morning and the previous evening, she wanted a clean bill of health from a specialist.

Maria looked unconvinced. "Do you have to go right away?" she asked. "Let me warm you up something to eat."

"Thanks, I'll grab something at the hospital. I'm due in surgery." Laura hated to lie, but she didn't want to make her mother worry.

Maria picked up her TV remote control; Laura knew the time for her mother's afternoon soap operas was fast approaching.

"By the way, Mama," Laura said. She tapped a knuckle against the doorjamb, looking for the proper words. "I met a man recently. He's a doctor too. Well, actually, he's a medical researcher."

"Carlo told me all about him," Maria said. She folded her hands in her lap. "Carlo likes him very much. How do you feel about him?"

Laura looked at her shoes, suddenly feeling like an adolescent. "I like him very much," she said. "He's kind, and sensitive. He's also brilliant. I—"

"He's not the reason you're looking so pale, is he?" Maria asked.

Laura gave her mother a sarcastic smile. Maria's sense of humor was subtle. "I just wanted to tell you," Laura said. "I should have known you and Carlo would have already gossiped."

Maria shrugged and scooted out of her chair. "We talk," she said. "What do you think we do in the afternoons, make paper dolls?"

Laura laughed. "He's asleep right now," she said. "Would you check on him in an hour or so? He's due to take his medicine then."

"One of the blue pills," Maria recited. She subtly ushered Laura toward the front door. "You go back to work and don't worry about a thing. The boy will be fine."

Maria followed Laura to the door. "Have you talked to Ferry recently?" she asked.

"Not for a couple of days," Laura admitted. "One of her sisters is flying in from New Jersey to help out."

"It's a terrible thing, her husband passing like that," Maria said.

Laura paused. Her mother's comment carried a poignant depth. Maria had lost her husband to age, Steve had died a criminal. Now Ferry had also become a widow.

"It is," Laura said in a low voice. "But women are strong."

"*Molto forte,*" Maria said with a sad smile.

IN HER OFFICE LAURA OPENED THE BLINDS AND TRIED TO plow through the mountain of documents that Terri had left on her desk. Running a medical practice also entailed running a business, and Laura had been negligent lately. Several of the insurance forms at the bottom of the stack were more than a month old.

It was impossible to concentrate. She had left Neurology just a half hour before after enduring a monotonous checkup. The specialist, Walter Guerrero, had run a CAT scan, a brain scan, and an MRI, and had taken blood for lab work. Laura had found it embarrassing to describe her symptoms; several times she had to fight off the urge to leave. In the spirit of disclosure she had told Guerrero about her history of depression and substance abuse, which also had given her a feeling of mortification.

Guerrero had been very sympathetic. He had said he would rush the results through and call her later that afternoon or that evening. Laura felt as nervous as she had after taking her medical boards.

Terri had taken the day off for a three-day ski weekend. The office was too quiet and still, so Laura opened up the credenza between the two sofas at the other end of her office. Inside was a television, which she normally used to show procedural videos to patients. She tuned it to a local station. The afternoon news was just starting, with a fanfare of electronic music and aerial views of the city.

Laura poured a cup of stale coffee and picked up the phone. The paperwork would have to wait. She was too nervous. She dialed the number from memory.

"This is Colonel Neil Reynolds speaking." For an instant Laura thought she had reached Neil at home, but the recording continued, "I can't pick up the phone at the moment. Please leave a message."

Laura hung up. She hated answering machines. She flipped through her phone directory and dialed a second number. She was mildly surprised when someone answered.

"Colonel Reynolds's unit," a young-sounding man said in a bleary voice.

"Is Colonel Reynolds in?" Laura asked. She looked at the TV; over the anchorwoman's shoulder was a cartoonish representation of the chalk drawing made around homicide victims' bodies. It was framed with the word *Murder*.

"The colonel is gone for the day." She heard the clatter of computer keyboard keys in the background.

"I figured as much," Laura said. "I just hoped to catch him in."

"Really?" the man asked, in a tone that suggested he was amazed that his boss might have a personal life. Laura smiled involuntarily. "I mean, most days he'd still be here. Do you want to leave a message?"

"No, that's all right. I'll try to reach him at home later."

The young man mumbled good-bye and hung up.

Laura sipped her coffee. She had wanted to hear Neil's

opinion regarding her strange symptoms. She also wanted to hear the sound of his voice. She pondered how their geographical separation would affect the future of their relationship. They hadn't known each other long, but obviously things were working out between them. Somehow she couldn't see Neil living in L.A., dressed in shorts and a T-shirt, having abandoned his research position with the government. She also couldn't imagine leaving the city she had always called home. Her friends, her mother, Carlo's school—she was entrenched in L.A. She couldn't imagine that ever changing.

She was getting ahead of herself. She reached up to the crown of her head and unsnapped a barrette, releasing her dark curls.

The TV news shifted from local to international news, signaled by the appearance of a computer-animated globe rotating in space. When the anchors returned, the screen behind them displayed a bright red map of Iran.

Laura hustled across the room to turn up the sound. Ever since she had met Ferry, she had taken an interest in her friend's native country.

". . . a very unexpected turn of events in Cairo today," the newscaster intoned. "At a conference on international shipping rights, the Iranian delegation angrily denounced the United States for sending paramilitary forces across its borders."

The news footage showed a cavernous, drab conference room, with several dozen people arranged in seats facing a podium. A dark-bearded man stood at the lectern, waving and pointing at the crowd.

"The Iranian delegate to the conference claimed to speak with full government authority when he said the following: 'We have captured Americans in the process of violating international law and committing acts of aggression against our people. We demand that these crimes be condemned by the international community.' ''

The anchorman returned to the screen. ''The State Department denies these charges, saying that U.S. military forces, while on call in the Persian Gulf, have not, and do not plan to, violate the borders of Iran. In Congress the Senate majority leader called for a full investigation.''

Laura turned the sound down when the broadcast shifted to news of continuing civil unrest in Mexico.

It was almost four-thirty and Walter Guerrero still hadn't called. She decided not to disturb him; he had been kind enough to take her without an appointment.

Laura turned the TV off. There was no point staying in her office just to wait for Guerrero's call. She could take the paperwork home with her and work on it while Carlo rested in bed. She began to gather her things and stack them in her briefcase. She put on her suit jacket and closed the drapes.

There was a sound coming from the outer office. But that was impossible. No patients were scheduled for the rest of the day, and Terri was gone. There was the sound again, a scraping noise.

I'm becoming mentally strung out, Laura thought. Seeing Carlo on that table, passing out in the kitchen, obsessing like a hypochondriac over her test results—now she was hearing noises in an empty office. It was probably just someone in the hallway. There were a dozen other physician's offices in that wing of the hospital.

She heard a voice, low, deep, masculine—and definitely in the office. She listened. There was no reason for anyone to be out there. There had been things stolen from the hospital recently: office equipment, supplies, drugs. Perhaps someone had seen the lights off in the reception area and assumed that the place was empty.

Laura gently opened her door and peeked out. She could see into Terri's supply area, with the insurance forms, boxes of paper, and the fax machine. No one was there.

Finding nothing within reach to use as a weapon, she considered going all the way back into her office to call the police or hospital security. But then she would be trapped. The ground was three stories below her window. If she could make it out to the hallway, she would be safe.

She took a step. She hadn't imagined anything; she heard the man's voice around the corner, humming softly. It was as though he wanted her to know he was there.

Before she could run for the door, a figure moved around the corner and slammed into her. Laura cried out at the sight of a large man. She felt his hands reach for her as she bolted around him, making for the door. Before she could make it, she lost her balance and bumped into Terri's reception desk. Nearly falling, Laura reached out for balance and knocked a stapler and plastic can full of pens to the floor.

"Stay away from me!" Laura yelled. Her mind was a riot of fear and confusion. It was as though her brain was plugged into a light socket. It was several seconds before she was calm enough to see the tall, burly African-American man still standing in her hall, his hands held up in a gesture of surrender. He wore an expression of embarrassment as he pulled a set of portable headphones from his ears.

"I'm sorry, I'm really sorry," he stammered. He wore a tool belt, and had a skein of wire dangling from one elbow. "I didn't think anyone was in here. Someone called to say one of the electrical plugs wasn't working. I . . . I'm with maintenance. I didn't mean to—"

There was a frantic knocking on the office door. "I

apologize,'' Laura said. She wiped a film of sweat from her forehead. ''I don't know what I was thinking.''

The door opened hard, crashing into the wall. John Tomkins, the surgeon whose practice was next door to Laura's, entered with his fists clenched. ''What's going on in here?'' he asked. He glared at the maintenance man. ''I heard someone scream. Was it you, Laura?''

Laura looked at the badge sewed to the repairman's shirt and read his name. ''I'm sorry, Brady,'' she said. She put her hand on Tomkins's shoulder. ''John, there's nothing wrong. Brady and I scared each other. I thought I was in here alone, and—''

''It's my fault,'' Brady interjected. ''I'm not supposed to wear headphones on the job.''

Tomkins shook his head and grabbed his wrist, checking his own pulse. ''God, it sounded like someone was getting killed in here.''

Laura was about to apologize again when her phone rang. Scooting around the furniture, she sat in Terri's chair and pressed the button to answer the call.

''Laura Antonelli?'' the voice asked.

''Yes?'' she replied. In the reception area Brady and Tomkins were talking, both smiling and shaking their heads.

''This is Walter Guerrero.'' His voice was deep and resonant, with the trace of a Central American accent.

''Oh, Walter, thanks for getting back to me,'' Laura said. ''Sorry I'm out of breath. Everything's a mess at the moment.''

''I'm glad I caught you,'' Guerrero said. ''Your tests look pretty good. Your blood came back fine. My guess is that you've been under stress. You probably need a vacation.''

Tomkins and Brady were huddled together around the

mess of wires. Laura recalled that Tomkins was an amateur electronics buff, with a shortwave radio in his office.

"There's one thing, Laura," Guerrero added. "You didn't tell me you've had brain surgery. I need to know that sort of information when I take on a new case."

"Brain surgery?" Laura asked. "What are you talking about? I've never had any kind of surgery at all."

There was a long silence on the line. "Well, that's very strange. Your CAT scan found no kind of organic mass in your brain. But I saw something very small that I assumed was the remnant of a surgical staple. It seems to be metallic, because it gives off a glow on the scan."

Laura rotated the chair away from the men in her office and lowered her voice. "That's impossible," she said.

"Well, there must be some kind of explanation," Guerrero said, a dubious edge in his voice. "I'll review the film again. Either way the object it isn't large enough to cause you any harm, and I'm sure it has nothing to do with your recent symptoms. Like I said, take a rest. At the very least, take the weekend off."

"Thank you, Walter," Laura said. She said good-bye to Guerrero after promising to buy him lunch to return his favor.

A small metallic mass, unidentifiable. The same sort of object found in the dead body of Cyrus Tafreshi?

"Is everything all right?" John Tomkins asked. Laura spun around. He and Brady were staring at her. She had no idea how much of her conversation they had heard.

"Fine, fine," she mumbled. "I'm sorry for scaring you, Brady. Would you please lock up when you're done in here?"

"Of course," Brady said.

"If it's all right with you," Tomkins said, "I'm going to stick around for a while and watch Brady work. He thinks he can help me with my radio. I keep getting static on it.''

Laura walked out without replying. That anomalous mass had been pulled out of Cyrus after he had dropped dead. Were the two objects connected, or was she losing her mind?

Laura took the elevator downstairs. When she reached the ground floor and was halfway to the parking structure, she stopped.

Cyrus, then her. But now she remembered, there had been others.

''My God,'' she whispered. ''Cyrus wasn't the first.''

33

7:12 p.m.

LAURA CLOSED HER OFFICE DOOR AND LOCKED IT. THE HALL outside was quiet and deserted. Normally she hated the stillness of her wing of the hospital at night, but now she was grateful to have solitude. She needed to think.

She put down the tray of steamed vegetables and rice she had bought at the hospital cafeteria. There was a far more pressing matter: the files she had spent the last two hours requesting from the administrative records offices. A request after working hours was out of the ordinary, and Laura had received a chilly treatment from the night-shift clerks. Laura had tried to soften the imposition of her demands by helping to pull files from the long rows of hanging folders in the file room behind the computer station.

First things first. She dialed a familiar phone number.

"Mama, it's me," Laura said. She flipped on her desk lamp. "I'm still at work, and I'm going to be here for a while. How's Carlo?"

"He ate some food," Maria answered.

Laura knew what this implied: by her mother's standards a healthy appetite indicated good health. It actually wasn't a bad way of making a diagnosis.

"Good," Laura said. "Tell him to take it easy. He gets to stay home from school tomorrow."

"He's watching television," Maria said. "Do you want to talk to him?"

"It's not necessary," Laura said. She opened the top file on the stack. "Unless he wants to."

Laura heard her mother partially cover the receiver and ask Carlo if he wanted to talk to his mother. A moment later her mother came back on the line. "He doesn't want to miss any of his show," Maria said.

"That's fine. Mama, you might have to put Carlo to bed tonight. I might be here until fairly late."

Maria hesitated. "Is something the matter, Laura?"

"Not at all." Laura flipped through the file until she found the patient's autopsy report. "Thanks, Mama, I'll stop by later."

She hung up. In the cone of light from her lamp Laura checked the name on the file: Patricia O'Connell.

This was one of a handful of cases that haunted her. Laura had replayed every examination and every step of the surgery, trying to determine whether she had done anything wrong. Patricia O'Connell had been referred to Laura after complaining of abdominal pain. A subsequent work-up had revealed cholecystitis. Laura had performed a routine cholecystectomy—a gallbladder removal—within a couple of days. The surgery had been routine, with no complications other than the strange object Laura had found inside the patient. O'Connell was discharged the next day—but she had returned to the hospital three days later, unconscious.

Before she could be taken to surgery, Patricia O'Connell had died of a pulmonary embolism, a clot that obstructed blood flow through her pulmonary artery. Her death had been unrelated to her recent surgery, but Laura had nonetheless reviewed her former patient's autopsy reports. And now she remembered a detail.

"Here it is," Laura said.

It was a small note, part of the postmortem examination of O'Connell's heart and lungs: "Small metallic mass: found embedded in the pulmonary artery near blood clot."

Below this was the examiner's conclusion: the mass, however odd, was inconsequential and could not have contributed to the patient's death. A side note indicated that the patient had suffered from severe diabetes and had required extensive medical treatment over the past two decades. Her condition may have contributed to circulatory problems resulting in the embolism.

Laura grabbed a fork and took a couple of halfhearted bites from her dinner. Patricia O'Connell had actually been housing two mysterious objects inside her body. The O'Connell case was one of two that Jefferson Faber's lawyer had mentioned during her arbitration hearing.

She opened the second file. It, like O'Connell's, bore the word *Deceased* stamped across its index header in black ink, along with the name Francis Del Rey.

Francis, or Frank, as he preferred to be called, had been a schoolteacher from Simi Valley. Though he was only fifty-two, he had a series of medical problems that had plagued him since his mid-forties. She remembered how, in her office, he had listed them with his dark sense of humor: an ulcer, migraine headaches, and, worst of all, leukemia. His disease had twice gone into remission, but Laura had seen that it plagued him. His latest problem was a hernia which, he had said, was nothing compared to what he had dealt with in the past.

Laura recognized her own handwriting on the postoperative report. Frank Del Rey's hernia hadn't been particularly severe. The entire procedure had lasted only forty minutes and had proceeded without complication.

Ten days later Frank returned to the hospital dead on arrival from a brain aneurysm. He had passed out in his school's teachers' lounge and never regained consciousness.

The autopsy report reviewed a close dissection of Frank's brain, noting the presence of "two small, metallic, diffused masses" in his cranium. Again, these masses were regarded as anomalies unrelated to his death.

Laura took a deep breath. She now had evidence of four instances in which small unexplained metallic masses had been found in human bodies. Three of the four people, including Cyrus, had died suddenly. She was the fourth.

Laura walked to the window, opened it, and breathed in cool night air. She had dismissed and forgotten about the objects reported in these two patients' autopsies. As Dr. Kim had confirmed at Cyrus's autopsy, small anomalies—anatomical and otherwise—weren't that uncommon, and were generally ignored if they couldn't be connected to the pathology that had caused the death of the patient.

She left the window open, allowing the traffic noise to filter up from the street like a softly murmuring voice. She picked up the third file in her stack.

"Jorge Mesa," she read aloud. She had obtained this file by asking for a cross-referenced computer search of autopsy reports that mentioned anomalies in their findings. This esoteric request had earned Laura an impatient sigh from the clerk in the records department, but had yielded more than three dozen files from the last year.

She found the autopsy report in the file. The medical examiner had made a notation for a congenital deformation found in Mesa's left cardiac ventricle. This was an organic anomaly, tragic but completely within the realm of the ordinary.

Laura opened the next file. It recorded the medical history of Allison Leonard, an elderly woman with Alzheimer's disease who had died of consumptive coagulopathy following extensive treatment in Valley Memorial's neurology unit.

"There it is," Laura said. She felt triumph mixed with a stab of dread. A small metallic mass had been found in the patient's neck during a CAT scan. Strangely, the object appeared to have moved in the two weeks between this CAT scan and the next. There had been no indication whether the object was organic or inorganic. Probably due to the patient's age and medical history, the doctors and the postmortem examiner hadn't given the object a second thought.

For the next half hour Laura reviewed the remaining files. Most were ordinary: four more heart defects, one bullet lodged in a patient's back that had never been removed, one case in which surgical mesh had come loose and wandered through a patient's abdomen. In addition there were records of a series of small organic masses that had been analyzed and found to be either the beginnings of cancerous pathology or else benign cysts and other growths.

But, in all, there were four more instances in which examiners noted inorganic, unexplained masses. The names on the reports were all different, indicating that no single medical examiner had seen more than one case in which these masses were found. Laura was the first person to make this connection.

Frustratingly, none of these masses had been subjected to laboratory scrutiny, because they were inorganic, and thus didn't need to be checked for cancer. In addition, the objects couldn't be logically matched with the patients' various causes of death.

Laura stacked the innocuous cases containing organic anomalies into a pile and put them on the chair she usually reserved for guests and patients. This left her with six files, including her own two surgical cases.

She randomly flipped through the files, thinking there had to be another connection. There was nothing else to be found but a mountain of minutiae: prescriptions, admissions forms, reams of insurance requests, reviews, protocols, test results. There were tons of data but none of it seemed to form any kind of consistent pattern. Laura closed up the files one by one and took another bite of her dinner. The vegetables had grown cold, the rice clumpy and cloying.

She started to pace in a circuit from the window to her desk. The deceased patients had all carried these inorganic masses in their bodies. She discarded her shoes and paced in her stocking feet.

In none of the cases was the mass related to the cause of death. However, the masses were found *near* the parts of the patient's anatomy that had caused their deaths.

She checked her watch. It was almost ten o'clock. The parking lot below her window was quiet; only the emergency room, on the other side of the building, would see any considerable traffic at that time of night.

I have one of those masses inside of me, she thought. She willed the notion from her mind. She couldn't allow herself to become consumed with paranoia.

There was no discernible pattern in the files, just a complete mess of insurance forms, discharge papers, and test findings.

Laura slapped her forehead. "What was I thinking?" she said.

She set the files out side by side. They covered so much of her desk that she had to stand up in order to reach them all. The files were all extremely thick—each was much more extensive than the medical history of a healthy person who had died of the sudden onset of a terminal condition.

All the patients had persistent conditions, some more than one. Diabetes. Leukemia. Lymphoma. Lupus. Parkinson's disease. Chronic heart conditions. Recurrent cancer.

The patients' insurance forms were epic chronicles of years of disease—and multiple hospital visits, sometimes requiring stays of a month or more. Laura knew the Ellington-Faber bureaucracy well enough to understand that these were the sort of patients the HMOs hated—because they cost more money than they put into the system. From a business standpoint these patients were money pits, undesirable drags on the profit-and-loss ledgers.

Laura reviewed the high-level clearances all patients were required to obtain from their insurers to authorize lengthy hospital stays. In each instance their treatment had dragged on, and their cases had been sent to Ellington-Faber's corporate headquarters for evaluation. Laura's breath came in ragged gasps as she looked through file after file. The same elegant signature appeared in each.

"Jefferson Faber," she said aloud. She said his name again, then again. His signature appeared six times.

She opened the files that contained no mention of inorganic masses. Most of these patients had been healthy in life, and only a few long hospital visits were recorded in the files. None of these stays had been approved by Faber; in fact, his signature appeared nowhere but these six sets of records.

The fear she had felt since talking to Walter Guerrero overcame her. It was impossible. But she alone had made the connection. Small masses. Unexpected deaths. More profit for Faber.

She asked herself: what were these objects? How had they gotten there? During surgery, perhaps—but what of her own patients? She hadn't planted anything in those people. And how in the world had she come to possess a small mass lodged in her own head?

Laura calmly stacked the files. She was thinking clearly now, more clearly than she ever had before. She looked through the cases one by one, now concentrating on the patients' treatment during their hospital stays, down to the smallest detail of their day-to-day nursing.

When she was finished, she picked up the phone. Her hands were shaking uncontrollably.

34

BOB CHAPMAN HAD ARRIVED AT HIS OFFICE THAT MORNING early enough to watch the sun rise, spreading a fiery orange glow over the crisp lawns and gridlike streets of Washington. He wished he had done this more often. Watching the city slowly come to life, the cars' headlights switching off as the morning advanced, he felt invigorated and purposeful. It made him think of the ways in which things might have been different. The evening before, the first news reports had broken the story: Iran had captured Americans in their northern mountains. It was just a matter of time now.

Though he had only been in the Senate for a short time, he had managed to approximate the austere decor of the office he had occupied as a California legislator. The credenza was piled with bound reports, largely unread; the walls were decorated with maps of the nation and his native state. A lone spider plant sat on the window ledge.

The smell of coffee, brewed in the pot that Neil Reynolds had bought for him, filled the room. Chapman poured a cup and turned on his computer.

On his screen was a confusing list of files and folders,

most pertaining to the computer's operating system. Chapman was a resolute technophobe and had never really learned to use the thing. It was time to educate himself.

He located the file containing his correspondence—practically the only one he ever opened. This list of documents contained the letters and memos that he wrote personally instead of dictating: a couple of letters to his wife in California and his daughter in her first year of college in Massachusetts; some notes to lobbyists and campaign contributors that he preferred to keep as private as possible; and his correspondence with Neil Reynolds and Jefferson Faber.

The documents in the latter file spanned back for only a brief period of time; Chapman had meticulously erased most traces of his association with the two men when he had left California for Washington. Even in these newer files there was little incriminating evidence. They had written to one another in codes. Looking over the more recent notes, Chapman saw that much of his communication comprised guarded declarations of his anxiety and uncertainty.

"The Iranian military. Jesus," he muttered to himself as he deleted the documents one by one.

From his outer office came a familiar stir: first the sound of a heavy handbag being dropped on the reception desk, then the clunk of a lunch sack tossed into the office refrigerator. His assistant, Emily, had arrived.

She stuck her head in the door, her eyes wide with surprise. "You're certainly here early," she said. "Is there an emergency? You could have called me at home, you know."

Chapman tried to give her a reassuring smile. "I woke up early and couldn't get back to sleep. I thought I'd use the time to catch up on some work."

Emily was impeccably dressed in a modestly cut two-piece suit. Her short sandy hair flowed around her ears. "I need to print out some envelopes," she said. "Let me know if you need any help."

"Just close the door behind you," Chapman said.

When he was done, anyone reviewing his computer files would find no trace of his involvement with Neil Reynolds and Jefferson Faber. Unfortunately, he had been seen in public with both men. He had met with them for business, legitimate and otherwise. He had no doubt that, if a federal investigation reached them first, they wouldn't hesitate to bring him down along with them.

The unfortunate fact was that Senator Bob Chapman of California was deeply involved in a plan to sell nuclear materials to a splinter faction of the Iranian military. He could imagine the news reports; his mind filled with images of jail and disgrace. It made Iran-Contra look like a humanitarian intervention.

He got up and switched on the radio. He was relieved to hear a reporter talking about an early winter storm gripping the Rocky Mountain states. It enabled him to pretend for a moment that his life wasn't about to fall apart.

Chapman again looked out at the city. The sun was up, the traffic was snarled on the streets. Reynolds had been right. Everything that had happened to him had been controlled by others. Patterson's death had been an assassination—if he understood Reynolds properly—a means of putting Chapman into office so he could better serve Faber's greed and Reynolds's lust for his research.

"I was like a puppet," he said to himself. "A stupid puppet."

He looked up. Emily was standing in the doorway, watching him with puzzlement. "Excuse me?" she said.

"Nothing," Chapman barked gruffly. He sat down at

his desk and sipped his coffee, trying not to betray himself by appearing nervous. "What do you need?"

Emily cocked her head, wary. "Well, this is the time of the day when I usually read your agenda to you. Unless you don't want me to today."

"No, no, of course I do," Chapman said. "I'm sorry, I didn't sleep well. Please go ahead."

Emily said something about a ten o'clock budget meeting, information that he barely registered. It was as though there was a dull fire burning within him, a feeling of nothingness that had taken hold and would never leave him. He had been used. He had been stupid. He doubted that Faber and Reynolds had any respect for him at all. They had set up the plan before ever approaching him. Perhaps they saw him as a fail-safe, his senatorial access to privileged information a sort of redundancy built into the system. Reynolds was a scientist, he viewed the world in those terms.

Emily told him he would be picked up for lunch at twelve-thirty and driven to . . . somewhere. Reynolds had changed. Chapman had known the colonel for two years. At first Reynolds had been haughty, a little aloof, but ultimately approachable. Recently he seemed to be on another plane of reality altogether. It was chilling. And that research he was so rabid about, those miniature surgical devices—what had he discovered?

"Senator, are you listening?" Emily asked. Her face turned pale. She dropped her calendar to the floor. "Bob?"

It had started as a tiny pinprick of discomfort, then rapidly flowered into a riot of pain centered behind his sternum and spreading down his arm. Chapman choked for air.

"Bob, what's the matter?" Emily yelled. She scrambled around to his side of the desk.

It felt as though a truck were parked on his chest. Chapman felt himself sliding off his chair, his vision blurring.

Emily had her hands on him. He could see her mouth working but he couldn't hear her words. The pain had taken over; it was as though a terrible disaster had occurred in the core of his being.

He grabbed for his chest, unable to see. Reynolds, he thought. The bastard got to me before I even had a chance. Chapman's last thought was of the disgrace he would never live to endure. In a sense he was grateful.

35

8:30 a.m.

THROUGH HIS VISOR NEIL REYNOLDS WITNESSED THE END OF a man's life. Around him he saw the long tunnel of Chapman's coronary artery, the surfaces on all sides textured with tissue fiber and bits of plaque.

When Reynolds moved his head to the left, the camera mounted on his microrobot followed suit. For an instant Reynolds lost his sense of scale. It looked as though he were in a shaft that had been blocked by a boulder of some sort. The obstruction was rounded, pressed against the contours of the passage and blocking his way.

It was no boulder; rather, it was a small blob of plaque scraped from the sides of Bob Chapman's coronary artery. It had grown like a snowball as Reynolds pushed it along, until its mass was great enough to block the artery. Myocardial infarction followed instantaneously—in this case an extremely severe episode. Bob Chapman was in the throes of a fatal heart attack, his brain already dying from lack of oxygen.

Now Reynolds would hide, just as he had in the past. The robot—which he had planted on Chapman during their conversation the day before—was minute, but it might be found during an autopsy. Reynolds pushed his control lever as far forward as it would go, rotating the robot in the artery and moving away from the occlusion. When he reached the end of the artery he commanded the device to burrow. Reynolds's vision darkened as the microrobot dug its way into the soft muscle mass of Chapman's right atrium.

He felt a pang of sadness as he prepared to abandon the device. It was as though, after living through the machine, seeing what it saw, feeling pressure against its hands as it worked, he had developed an almost symbiotic attachment to it.

Reynolds executed the final command, which ordered the device to shut down. The camera blinked off. Reynolds envisioned what happened next: the robot drew its parts into itself, folding inward like a budding flower moving backward in time. It would appear to the naked eye as a tiny chunk of metal, a shard of debris, its surfaces obscured by the bits of flesh and blood cells that had covered it during its passage through the body.

It was over.

Reynolds took off his headgear and carefully replaced the hand controls in their case. He checked his reflection in the mirror, adjusted the knot on his tie, and smoothed the wrinkles on his blue military jacket.

There was no longer a need to worry about time. His work was finished, and the results of his experiments would go on, no matter what happened to him. He understood that he had become expendable. His work would live on.

But he wanted to live the rest of his life with freedom. Eliminating Chapman had been the first step. He felt blooming within him the stirrings of a powerful passion— for life, for experience. It couldn't end here. He still wanted to spend his life with Laura—whether it lasted a week or an eternity.

He also wanted to remain whole. It had become clear in the past few days that his mental state was deteriorating. He would have to be organized, efficient, and ruthless for his dreams to become reality.

Reynolds stepped out into his unit's office space, barely aware of the tension that filled the room. He walked amid the desks, where his small crew were still analyzing data that would refine his work.

"Gentlemen," he said. The clatter of fingers on keyboards came to a halt. Young eyes looked up at him warily in expectation of another impossible deadline, another hopelessly complicated assignment.

Reynolds glanced at the wall clock: it was 0830 hours. "I want everyone to take the rest of the day off," he announced. "Breathe the air. Get some sun on your face. Live."

With this he walked into his office and closed the door behind him. He left stunned astonishment in his wake.

LAURA AWOKE. SHE WASN'T SURE WHERE SHE WAS. HER mind raced as she realized she wasn't in her bed, that she was sitting up, and that she was still wearing her clothes from the night before.

The phone rang. It was on the coffee table, which meant that she was in her living room. Her awareness returned in a flash, and she understood that she must have fallen asleep on the sofa after coming home late the night before. Carlo was still at Maria's.

The phone was still ringing. Laura cleared her throat. "Hello?" she said in a weak voice. Through the crack in her curtains she saw that it was still dark outside.

"Laura? Are you awake? I know you get up early. I was hoping to catch you before you started your day."

This throaty male voice made everything come back to her. The files, the nonorganic masses. The deaths. Faber.

"Neil," she said.

"I got your message this morning before I left for work," he said. "Is everything all right? You sounded a bit upset."

"I'm fine," Laura said. She felt an invisible hand on her spine, a palpable reminder to be cautious.

"Are you sure?" Neil asked. "I would have called sooner, but I had to take care of something this morning."

"There's no problem," Laura said. She sat upright and pulled her hair away from her face, willing herself completely awake. "I was just getting up."

Silence on the line.

"How's your research going, Neil?" she asked, not sure how to choose her words.

"My research?" She thought she detected wary reserve in his voice. "Very well, but I didn't call to talk about that. I've been thinking of you. I want to see you. I sent everyone home early. I told them to enjoy life—and that's what I want to do."

Laura fought against the impulse to tell him everything she knew, or thought she knew. She wanted to hear him explain. She wanted him to tell her what he had done.

"I want to see you too," she said.

Now that it was a new day, it seemed impossible that Neil could be the monster she fell asleep suspecting he was. He was kind, his mind brilliant. She had thought she could love him.

"Good," he said, sounding pleased. "Why don't you fly out here? You can stay at my house. Bring Carlo, I'll take him to my labs and show him around."

"Why would you want to take my boy to your laboratory?" Laura asked. She winced at the faint accusation in her voice. In her mind two sides battled, emotion against logic. She wanted Neil; she cared about him. But she wondered if she should fear him.

"We don't have to do that," Neil answered quickly. "I simply thought he might be interested. He's a smart boy, I thought he might be inspired. But not if you don't think it's a good idea."

"I'll come out to see you, Neil," she said. "Without Carlo. I think that you and I should work some things out between us."

A long pause. "I'm not sure how to take that," he said. "I thought we were . . . developing a relationship."

"Don't make it sound like that," she said. "I want to see you. I think it's time we were honest with one another, that's all I mean."

"Give me a chance, Laura," Neil said. She heard him take a deep breath. "I care about you. I want to be a part of your life."

His words rang true. "You *are* a part of my life, Neil, you know that," she said.

Her strange sensation of mental clarity was returning, just like the day before. It was distracting.

"I hope so," Neil said. "I want to try to make you happy."

Laura stood up. She had to act, do something, but she didn't know what. All she knew was that she couldn't wait.

"I'll book a flight. When do you want me to come?"

"Why not spend the weekend?" he asked. "Will you be free then?"

"Yes," she replied.

"I have a few important things to wrap up before then,"

he said. "I'll clear the decks by the time you arrive. Then it will be just you and me."

"That's what I want," she said. "Just the two of us."

When they had hung up, Laura stood in the middle of the cool, quiet room. All of the familiar artifacts of her life looked unfamiliar and artificial. Everything she had thought true seemed illusory; she felt herself and her son trapped amid something deadly. And she knew that Neil Reynolds, somehow, was at the center of it all.

36

JEFFERSON FABER STARED OUT THE WINDOW OF HIS PRIVATE plane as it descended over Las Vegas. In the daylight the city looked like an overgrown desert encampment; the strip of hotels and casinos was tacky and dull under the revealing light of the sun. When the sun passed below the horizon they would come alive with neon and lasers and strobes that, it was said, could be seen even from outer space.

Faber gripped his armrest so tightly, his fingers had begun to ache. As soon as he received word of Bob Chapman's sudden death, he had immediately left his office for the airport, accompanied only by a single assistant. He had succeeded in the world by knowing when his opponents were primed to move against him.

The Iranian situation was volatile and unpredictable. The story had just become public, and the situation might change in a matter of hours. But Faber's primary concern was Neil Reynolds. Faber rubbed his eyes as the pilot gently nudged the craft down toward the runway. He had willfully ignored Reynolds's dangerous potential for too long. Now the circle was closing, and it was Reynolds's hand that had drawn it tight.

Within a half hour Faber was riding in the backseat of a hired limousine, racing into the desert. The tinted windows shielded him from the sun, which was huge and punishing. Faber watched the scrubland passing by, and wondered if he stood a chance.

The nuclear dealings had been Faber's creation, or so he had thought. Now he wasn't sure if anything had been his idea. Faber had looked into Cyrus Tafreshi's background when he first became interested in Emergent Technologies, and discovered that Tafreshi had highly placed relatives in his home country. It was simple commerce: a motivated, cash-poor seller, a buyer looking to move up in the market. Now Faber couldn't check the suspicion that Reynolds had engineered everything.

Outside Faber's window the earth turned darker, more rough and elemental. In the distance, through dust clouds raised by the breeze, he saw the low-lying buildings that comprised Madison's compound.

Faber glanced at the driver's rearview mirror, making eye contact. "That's our destination, up ahead," he said. "Slow down when we get close. We don't want to startle anyone in there."

The driver cast a wary eye back at Faber. "Whatever you say, sir."

Thinking back on it now, Faber realized what had gone essentially wrong. He had been intimidated by Reynolds. He had let himself fear the man, his single-minded self-possession, the ever-surprising power of his intellect.

"Those damned robots, I should have known it would all turn against me one day," Faber whispered.

"Excuse me, sir?" the driver said.

"Nothing," Faber replied. He hadn't realized he was speaking aloud. "Keep driving. Please."

Faber had allowed Reynolds into his business dealings, as a sort of macabre partner. What a horrible mistake. Faber had saved comparative pennies by killing off patients, while Reynolds had perfected his damnable technology. It had been stupid pride to even care about those people and how much money they cost him.

Reynolds had perfected remote-control of his devices on a scale that he hadn't revealed to Faber. Patterson. Bolkov. Now Chapman. Reynolds had been behind it all, and he had been willfully blind not to know it from the beginning.

He had to get away.

The car pulled slowly into the long, dusty drive. The compound looked empty and stagnant, like a desert ghost town.

"Pull to the edge of the cul-de-sac," Faber ordered. "I'll get out and walk up to the door myself. Wait inside the car."

The driver followed Faber's instructions, leaving the car running. Faber stepped out of the vehicle into searing heat; it had to be almost a hundred degrees.

Faber pounded on the front door for several minutes before he heard footsteps slowly approaching inside. He looked out over the flat barren land while he waited, saw the snowcapped mountains far away toward the horizon.

Madison opened the door, looking haggard in a wrinkled cotton shirt and jeans. She was still beautiful.

She looked him over. "So, I finally hear from you. You shouldn't have come," she said. "I'm being watched."

"Then let me in," he said. "Let's at least make it a bit harder for them to photograph us."

"I heard about Chapman," she said. "A heart attack."

"Let's talk about it inside," Faber said.

Madison glanced over Faber's shoulder at the limousine, then gave a little shrug. Faber followed her down the hall until they reached her office. There Faber took her in his arms. He felt the firmness of her shoulders, her flat belly pressed against his. They kissed, and Faber closed his eyes and tried to forget everything.

Madison pulled away. "Why did you wait until the shit hit the fan before coming here?" she asked.

"I was trying to figure out how to save us both."

She narrowed her eyes at him. "I'd like to believe you. You know, I thought you might have me killed. But when I saw you out there, I knew it was safe. You wouldn't have the stomach to witness it."

"Don't talk like that," Faber said.

"I'm not joking about being watched," she said. She took his hands in hers. "An NSA agent was out here a couple of days ago. I don't think he knew everything, but the investigation's started."

Faber looked around the room. The topographical maps and propaganda posters were gone from the walls. The computers were all stored away. Madison's stained oak dresser was empty, the drawers left open. Only the guns were out, along with a grenade launcher. Faber stifled a shiver at the sight of the weapons.

"It looks as though you're planning to leave," he said.

"Wouldn't you?" Madison moved away from him, leaning against her desk and looking out the window. "I didn't think I'd ever hear from you again. I've been out here by myself, realizing that I was about to disappear and no one would even care."

Faber felt a crushing impact on his spirit. Didn't she understand him at all?

"I wouldn't allow any harm to come to you," he said.

She looked up, surprised. "You know, I think I believe you. Isn't that funny. I finally find someone to believe in again, and he's a capitalist corporate raider. It proves you should never let your guard down."

"Not for a second," Faber said, smiling. "Unless you're with me."

"Enough of that shit," Madison said, her mood darkening. "I didn't say I necessarily like my feelings for you. And who cares how I feel—my feelings aren't going to keep me out of jail."

Faber suddenly felt exhausted. "I can't go to jail," Madison said. Her voice was barely louder than a whisper. "I just can't."

"No one is going to jail," Faber said. He motioned toward the TV, which was tuned to the news with the sound off. "I haven't been able to catch anything since this morning. Has the situation changed?"

"Not really," Madison said. "The U.S. and the Iranians are still blowing smoke at each other. The uranium hasn't been mentioned, at least not in public, and they haven't publicly identified any of my men."

"Good, that gives us time," Faber said.

Madison looked at him blankly. "Did it ever occur to you that my men already gave me up, and that the only reason I'm not in jail yet is because the government wants to find out who I'm conspiring with?"

"I thought of that," Faber said. "And I don't believe it's true. With all the furor over the militia groups, they wouldn't want to take a chance on you getting away. I don't think your men have talked, not yet."

Madison seemed to ponder this. "They're good men," she said. "I can't believe it's finished here."

"Everyone's gone?" Faber asked.

"Gone."

"You'll have to pursue your revolutionary politics elsewhere." It was time to leave. "Grab what you need."

"Where are we going?" Madison asked. She grabbed a single leather bag and turned off the television. Faber marveled that she was able to walk away so quickly, with so little hesitation. He wondered if she would ever understand the depth of his fascination for her.

"The Cayman Islands," Faber said. "I have forty million dollars there. We'll wait and see what happens. If they try to extradite us, we'll take the money and hide at the ends of the earth. We'll be comfortable no matter where we go."

Madison looked into his eyes as though searching for the truth. She knew that he lived to run his financial empire. She seemed to understand what this plan would cost him.

"It's not a very revolutionary solution," she said.

"Maybe you'd rather stay here and die with your guns," he said impatiently. "Or let them catch you and spend the rest of your life in a cage. Decide now."

Her expression softened. "That was my idea of a joke," she said. "Of course I'll come with you."

She started to leave; Faber blocked the doorway with his body. "There's one more thing, and we can't talk about it in front of the driver," he said. "From this moment on we have to consider Neil Reynolds a deadly enemy."

"Reynolds?" Madison asked. "Why? Is he going to turn state's evidence or something?"

"I don't think we have to worry about that," Faber said. He took a deep breath, wondering if he could convince her of the truth. "I think he might make an attempt on our lives. We have to be . . . alert."

Madison's cheek pulsed with tension. "You're not making any sense. Is he sending someone after us?"

He couldn't explain. He barely understood it himself. "We have to leave," he said. "My pilot has filed a flight plan that gets us out of the airport in fifty minutes. We'll barely make it as it is."

In the car Madison insisted on keeping her bag in the backseat with her. The driver remained silent as they raced through the desert, but Faber noticed him glancing several times into the mirror. Faber wondered if the man was a government agent. He had begun to think like a fugitive.

As they neared the airport Faber called the pilot on his cellular phone; they had minutes to reach the plane if they were to take off as scheduled. Otherwise they might have to wait an hour or more on the tarmac for clearance from the traffic-control tower.

Faber tipped the limousine driver and took Madison's hand. They had pulled into a private parking area reserved for luminaries with private airplanes—this being Las Vegas, entertainers and millionaires were typically loitering around. Faber was relieved to see that the area was empty. He and Madison broke into a sprint at the sight of Faber's private aircraft.

They ran in the sun, the heat seething off the tarmac in visible waves. As they drew closer the whine of the engines became louder. They bounded up the steps of the plane two at a time. Faber waved off an offer of assistance from an airport employee and began to close the heavy door himself.

"Just pull those stairs away," he ordered. "And hurry."

He closed the door and motioned for Madison to sit in the rear of the craft, where plush cushioned seats were arranged facing one another, more like a luxury train cabin than a typical plane's cramped quarters.

Faber pushed aside the thick drapes that cordoned off

the cockpit. Awaiting takeoff were the pilot and copilot, both full-time employees on Faber's payroll.

"Did I make it on time?" Faber asked. He realized he was beginning to hyperventilate and forced himself to breathe slower.

The captain, Randall Carver—a Navy veteran with combat experience and a taciturn, professional manner—glanced up from his instruments. "Just barely, Mr. Faber." He looked down at a clipboard nestled on his lap. "I'm running through the final preflight checklist. I'll have us up in the air in a couple of minutes."

The copilot's last name was Aguilera, Faber couldn't remember his given name. He was immersed in his own checklist and didn't look up. "Will we have to stop for refueling?" Faber asked.

"In Miami, sir," the captain said apologetically. "Maybe we could top off here and make it, but that could set us back an hour or so."

Faber felt himself totter on his feet; the cabin space seemed small and oppressive. "No, we'll leave now," he ordered. "But refuel in Miami as quickly as you can. I don't have time for any delays."

"Of course, sir," Carver said.

"And can you do something about the air circulation in here?" Faber asked. He pulled out a handkerchief and mopped his brow. "I'm burning up."

The copilot glanced up from his work. Faber recognized what he saw in the younger man's face: curiosity, and perhaps a vague suspicion that his employer might be in trouble.

"Can I help you with anything?" Faber asked him.

Carver glanced nervously at his copilot. Aguilera looked surprised. "I beg your pardon?" he said.

"Do you wish to continue working for me?" Faber asked.

"I . . . Of course I do, sir," Aguilera stammered.

Faber reflexively straightened the lapels of his jacket. He had to calm down. These men might be questioned later, asked how Faber had behaved before his disappearance. It was idiotic to leave them remembering that he seemed panicked and strange.

"Of course you do," Faber said. He smiled nervously, which seemed to utterly discombobulate Aguilera. "You men are doing a good job under trying circumstances. Thank you."

Faber retreated through the curtains; Carver shut the door between the cockpit from the cabin. No doubt they were already talking about their employer, speculating. Let them. The hell with it, he thought.

Faber stepped into the fore cabin and walked into a tall, stocky young man dressed in a suit. Faber let out a gasp of fear, then realized what had happened.

"Lanier, for God's sake," he said. "I forgot all about you."

Roland Lanier, twenty-seven, two years out of business school, was Faber's executive assistant. It was a lowly job for an MBA, but when Lanier had applied for the job Faber had seen something in him he liked: an ambition willing to subsume itself while watching and learning about the shadowy byways of material success. With his thick, dark hair and muscular build, Lanier looked more like a professional athlete than an apprentice mogul.

"I waited for you like you asked, Jefferson," Lanier said.

Faber mopped his forehead and loosened his tie. Faber had asked Lanier to come along because he hated to travel without having someone along to handle unexpected logistics and contingencies. Faber saw now that he would have to strand Lanier in Miami and send him back to Los Angeles alone. It would look suspicious.

Faber glanced over Lanier's shoulder. The aft cabin was curtained off. He couldn't see Madison through the gap.

"Yes, thank you," Faber said. "Listen to me now. There's been a change of plans."

Lanier's eyes widened a fraction.

"I'm taking a vacation," Faber said. "I need one. It's been a long time."

"I've always said you should get away," Lanier said with a smile.

"We're stopping in Miami. From there I want you to take a commercial flight back to Los Angeles. I'll be in touch in a day or so. In the meantime, see that my affairs are taken care of. I'm granting you day-to-day authority until I reach you."

Lanier didn't show it, but Faber understood the thought that raced through the younger man's mind: this was an opportunity he had waited nearly two years for. Faber knew that Lanier ached in his soul for everything Faber possessed.

"Thank you, Jefferson," Lanier said, trying not to smile.

"Start by linking up with the stock exchange on your computer. There should be action on our petrochemical holdings today. Take notes and prepare a report for me."

Faber knew how important it was that his "vacation" appear to be an innocent, spur-of-the-moment idea. "That should keep you busy on the way to Miami," he added. "Do not disturb me in the back cabin. Under any circumstances."

Lanier's grin showed a hint of lasciviousness.

"Don't smile at me that way," Faber said. "And don't

let this temporary promotion go to your head for a second. Act out of line and you're finished in the business community. Do good work and you'll be rewarded. Do you understand?''

"Completely," Lanier said, chastened.

Faber turned his back on the younger man. Even in these uncertain circumstances he hated to leave Lanier in charge of anything.

"Who the hell is that up there?" Madison asked when Faber reached her in the back of the craft. He sat close to her, near enough to feel the heat of her body.

"My assistant," Faber answered tersely. "I shouldn't have brought him, but I did. I told him to leave us alone."

"I don't like little suit-and-tie boys looking at me as if I'm a piece of meat," Madison said. She glared at the curtains segmenting the cabin. "But I don't suppose you do much to encourage a socially progressive atmosphere at that corporation of yours."

"Madison, please," Faber said. "Do you really think this is the time for us to fight over our ideological differences?"

Madison and Faber's faces were only inches apart. They stared each other down. Then she looked away, breaking into a warm laugh.

"You're something, Jefferson," she said. "You probably ruined my life. At the very least you gave me the opportunity to do it. So why can't I stay mad at you?"

He looked at her, feeling the moment as something elusive and delicate. He knew running away with him was counter to her ideals, and he had dreaded that she might say no to him.

"Because you love me," Faber said. "As I do you."

She glanced away. It was the first time he had even seen in her anything resembling shyness.

"This is plain crazy," she said, more to herself than him. "After all these years I'm going to live out my life in luxury in the tropics. I don't know about this, I really don't."

He desperately needed to change the subject; he noticed her leather valise tucked under a nearby seat. She had had trouble lifting it, but had refused Faber's offers of assistance. "What do you have in there?" he asked, flush with warmth inside. She hadn't said she didn't love him. Perhaps she did.

"Just some things," she said. "Some assistance in case we get backed into a corner."

The airplane lurched; the terminal outside the oval windows shifted past them. They were moving. "I don't even want to know what you mean by that," Faber said.

"Then don't ask."

Faber strode to the bar recessed into the rear wall of the cabin. He had to hold on to the wall as the plane curved in a lazy turn onto the runway. He fixed a gin and tonic for himself and found a chilled bottle of mineral water for Madison. By the time the plane had pulled onto the main runway, gathering speed until its wheels gently left the earth, he was buckled into the seat next to hers.

The city receded quickly under them, the monolithic hotels shrinking under the sun. Madison stared out the window.

"Can you see your compound from up here?" he asked.

"No, it's behind those hills." Madison pointed to the east. "I'm not looking back, anyway. I'm looking ahead."

Within minutes they had reached a cruising altitude. Faber closed his eyes and felt his heart beat in his chest. The race was over; he had saved Madison and would never let her go.

"Tell me about Reynolds," she said.

It all came back to him. "I think he had Chapman killed. Or, rather, I think he killed Chapman."

Madison sipped her water. "How? On TV they said it was a heart attack. Did he use some kind of poison?"

"No," Faber said. "It was something different."

She pondered this; Faber was amazed how easily she accepted the notion that Reynolds was a killer. "Maybe he's helped us all," she said. "You always told me Chapman was weak, that he would be the one most likely to give us away. It doesn't mean that Reynolds has turned against us."

"You don't know Neil like I do." Faber shook his head. "He's methodical and thorough. He'll want to be rid of everyone."

Madison listened quietly. Faber could tell that she didn't believe him; she thought he was caught up in a paranoid panic.

"Maybe you should have brought along a bodyguard instead of that little weasel out there," she said.

"A bodyguard wouldn't help me," said Faber.

"You have me for a bodyguard now," she added, "and we're safe for now. We're in the sky. No one can get at us."

Faber's hands shook, making the ice in his glass rattle. "That's my point, you see. I don't know if we're safe anywhere."

Madison cast a glance toward the front of the plane. "One of them?" she asked.

"No." He paused, then told her everything. He started with the buyout of Emergent Technologies and the new semiconducting substance that Cyrus Tafreshi had pioneered. He explained Reynolds's microtechnology and its ostensible surgical applications. Madison listened intently.

Then Faber told her what he thought had happened to Tafreshi, Bolkov, Patterson, and Chapman.

"You're saying he killed them by remote control using little devices he planted on them?" she said. Though she had been credulous throughout his explanation, he felt he was losing her trust in his judgment.

"He planted them on those men, I think, then somehow the devices got inside their bodies," Faber said. "Through their ear canals or tear ducts, for all I know. These machines work on a very small scale. They can go anywhere in the body."

Madison laughed. "That's impossible," she said. "There's no way he could control them at such distances. You sound like a complete maniac."

"It's real," Faber insisted. "Reynolds told me once that he could tap into the global cellular network to send and receive data—if only he could attain a sufficient level of miniaturization. He must have done it."

Faber refrained from telling Madison that Reynolds had begun perfecting his techniques while performing fatal experiments on Faber's HMO patients. He couldn't afford to send her into a moral outrage.

"I don't know much about that kind of science, but he must be decades ahead of everyone else," Madison said. Faber could see that she was starting to believe him.

"I didn't know his work was so advanced," Faber said. "Something's happened to him. I think he's capable of anything."

Madison's expression turned grave. "Could we be carrying these machines inside us?" she asked. Her voice was too loud; Faber feared it might carry into the fore cabin.

"I don't know," he answered.

Madison leaned back heavily in her seat, cursing under her breath. Faber felt an inward dam of despair give way.

He had secretly hoped that she might convince him that he was imagining the impossible. But she could see that he was right. They had figured out Reynolds's lethal potential, perhaps too late.

"Then what's the point of going to the Caymans?" she asked. "He must be able to track the damned things. He could find us anywhere."

Outside the window the long expanses of desolate desert unwound toward the mountainous horizon. Faber unbuckled his seat belt and stood up. He needed another drink.

He opened a fresh bottle of gin. "Reynolds will soon find out that we've left the country," he said. "Perhaps he will see we're no longer threats to him. We'll find a doctor in the Cayman Islands. We'll have tests run to see if we have those machines inside us. If we do, I'll pay to have them surgically removed."

"I feel like I'm going insane, just talking about this," she said. "If this is true, then Reynolds has invented the ultimate assassination weapon. He can sell it to the highest bidder and make millions."

"You've been around me too long," Faber said. "You're starting to sound like a capitalist."

Madison began to answer but Faber interrupted her with a piercing groan. He dropped his drink; the glass shattered on the floor, the gin spreading in a butterfly pattern on the carpet. His breathing came in hard, impossibly fast gulps for air.

"Jefferson!" Madison screamed. She grabbed Faber in time to keep him from falling over.

Faber felt a searing pain in his head; a wave of queasiness overtook his viscera. He vomited violently, covering himself and Madison.

He looked into Madison's eyes one final time. He saw her fear. In a fleeting instant he thought that he saw love.

The pain racked his head like a thunderclap. His vision and thoughts dissolved into a final crescendo of searing agony before his lifeless body slumped to the floor of the plane.

37

"SEE IT, LAURA?" WALTER GUERRERO ASKED. HE TILTED the computer screen and pointed out a spot. "Right there. At first I thought it might have been a small tumor mass, but your tests rule out cancer. All I know is that you have an anomaly in your brain tissue. It's unusual to see an object shine like this in a CAT scan."

Laura sat back in her chair. Guerrero's office displayed ample evidence of the neurologist's expertise: volumes of books and periodicals were stacked everywhere, and the walls were lined with diplomas and awards. What she hadn't noticed the day before—when she had come to him for tests—was Guerrero's human side: a row of photos depicted several generations of his family, and on his desk was a pen holder obviously fashioned by a child.

"I'm sorry to bother you, Walter," Laura said. "I'm just concerned."

Guerrero was in his late sixties, though his full head of hair and precise manner belied the fact. He took off his reading glasses and sat on the edge of his desk.

"I understand," he said in his resonant voice. "It's cause for concern. But I can't see a relationship between the symptoms you described—a fainting spell, brief disorientation—and the location of this mass. We'll keep an eye on it, of course. I'll have you come back in a month, and we'll take another look."

Laura got up. There had been two patients in the waiting room when she had arrived. "I understand that the location of this mass couldn't have caused my symptoms," she said. "But have you considered the possibility that the mass might have moved?"

Guerrero glowered with thought. He glanced back at the computer display, which showed a brightly colored representation of Laura's brain anatomy.

"Absolutely not," he said. "This isn't a blood clot. If it was, you wouldn't be standing here talking to me. There's no way a mass can travel spontaneously through brain tissue so quickly—it was only twenty-four hours between your first symptoms and your examination."

Trying to be reassuring, Guerrero laughed softly. "Unless this is a new type of benign mass, one with a motor and a navigation system."

FERRY TAFRESHI ANSWERED THE DOOR WEARING A SMART yellow dress, her lustrous hair pulled back into a twist. She looked better than she had in months. Her expression, however, was strangely without affect, and her eyes were ringed with discoloration. She obviously wasn't sleeping.

"Laura, it's good to see you," Ferry said, holding the door open. "Hello, Carlo. Why aren't you in school?"

Laura led Carlo into the living room and handed him his neon-green backpack. "He's not feeling well today."

"What's wrong?" Ferry asked.

"My throat hurts," Carlo said glumly. He fished in his bag for his handheld video game. "I have a headache."

"It's a flu," Laura said. "But I think he's getting better."

Laura could see that her friend was somewhat perplexed by this unannounced visit; though they saw one another often, they typically made it a practice to call before coming over.

"Can we talk in the kitchen?" Laura started walking toward the doorway without waiting for an answer.

"Carlo, do you want something to drink?" Ferry asked, casting a concerned look at Laura.

"Hot chocolate," he mumbled, engrossed in his game.

In the kitchen Ferry put a steel kettle on to boil. "You didn't come by just to say hello," she said matter-of-factly. She opened a cabinet and produced a box of instant cocoa.

"No, I didn't," Laura said.

"You look exhausted."

"I wouldn't talk, if I were you," Laura said, smiling. Ferry frowned. "That came out wrong. You look great. That dress really suits you."

"Thanks," Ferry said. "I'm trying. Davood and Mina are just now starting to show their sadness about losing Cyrus. And with this thing happening in Iran, I don't know. It's too much at once."

"What do you mean?" Laura asked. "Isn't that just some kind of diplomatic flap? Doesn't that kind of thing happen all the time?"

Ferry looked up from the stove. "Not like this," she said softly. "Cyrus's brother is a colonel in the Iranian army. When he didn't come to Cyrus's funeral I knew something wasn't right. Then I got a call from his wife. This thing that happened, those Americans being captured—it's more serious than anyone is saying. I think Cyrus's brother might be in trouble. I think he might have been involved in something illegal."

Laura bit her lip, thinking. It was hard to concentrate on this news, since she had come to discuss the strange deaths at Memorial Hospital—and the strange thing lodged in her head. She could see that Ferry was nearly overwhelmed with anxiety.

"Illegal?" Laura asked. "In what way?"

"I don't know," Ferry said. The kettle's spout let out a hiss to indicate the water was boiling. Ferry nervously removed it from the burner and filled a cup. "And neither does his wife. Cyrus's brother is an old-fashioned Iranian man. He keeps his problems to himself."

"Like Cyrus did, at the end," said Laura. She regretted the words as soon as they came out, fearing she might reopen recent wounds. Ferry nodded vehemently as she stirred the cocoa.

"Exactly," she said. "Now I wonder if Cyrus was involved somehow. I just got the phone bill. Right before he died he was making a lot of calls to his brother that he didn't tell me about."

"How could Cyrus be involved in the political situation in Iran? Neither of you has lived there in fifteen years."

"He and his brother were extremely close," Ferry said. "They always knew what the other was up to, whether it was Cyrus's business or his brother's military career. Things are very political in Iran, always mixed with religion now. Cyrus's brother supported the revolution, but he used to discuss his doubts with us."

Ferry excused herself to take the cocoa to Carlo. In spite of everything Laura felt a brief moment of brightness when she heard Carlo's polite thank-you.

"Is there anything you can do?" Laura asked when Ferry returned. They sat together in the breakfast nook, keeping their voices low.

Ferry shrugged. "I don't know. If he is in trouble, the whole family might have to leave the country. I can only help them if they come here."

They sat in charged silence. Ferry picked up a salt shaker from the edge of the table and tapped it absently on the table. Grains of salt spilled out.

"Cyrus's death," Laura began hesitantly. "You aren't thinking it had anything to do with this?"

Ferry looked up, surprised. "Of course not," she said. "You were at his autopsy. Why would you think that?"

"No reason," Laura said quickly. She couldn't tell Ferry about the fatalities at the hospital, about the object found in Cyrus, or the object within herself. Linking it all to Neil—an idea she struggled with moment by moment—would sound ludicrous. If there was such a thing as a high-water mark of pain, a point at which one shouldn't have to feel more hurt, Ferry had reached it.

"So, what did you want to talk to me about?" Ferry asked.

Laura tried to think of a half-truth, something that would sound acceptable given the favor she was about to ask.

"Well, it's about this man I've been seeing," she began.

Ferry smiled. "The army general," she said. "Is it going well?"

"That's kind of hard to say. We get along fine, it's just that we've reached a delicate point."

Laura knew her friend would be apoplectic if she knew the truth, but it was good to see Ferry's expressive eyes shine with contemplation of something besides her own recent misfortune. Ferry nudged forward in her seat, tacitly asking to be told more.

"Our geographic separation is a major issue," Laura added. "I want to go see him, to settle some things and see where we're headed."

"Go to see him?" Ferry shook her head. "You're going to fly to Washington to make him tell you his intentions?

You amaze me, Laura. I would never have the courage to do half the things you do."

Laura blushed at the compliment. If she could only tell Ferry, and gain the benefit of an objective opinion. In her mind were fragments she strained to piece together: Jefferson Faber, the expensive patients who had died within days after he reviewed their cases, the mysterious objects.

If she could only see one, if only one of them had been saved. If she could only open her skull and see that thing inside her.

"Laura?" Ferry said. "Did you hear me?"

"I'm sorry," Laura said. "I was thinking of something else."

"I asked whether you needed Carlo to stay with me for a day or two," Ferry said. "It would be good for Davood and Mina to have some company."

Laura sighed. "I'm so glad you said that. That was precisely the favor I wanted to ask of you. Mom had Carlo over last night, and I don't want to take advantage of her help. She'd say it was fine, but I know it saps her energy to baby-sit him."

Though it hadn't occurred to Laura before, Davood and Mina now had an unfortunate commonality with Carlo. They had lost their fathers. Perhaps they would be able to communicate to one another feelings they couldn't share with their parents.

"It will be good for them," Ferry said, contemplating the same notion. "When are you leaving?"

Another fact occurred to Laura: she had to be careful. Carlo had lost one parent already. If what she thought was true, she had never truly known Neil Reynolds or what he was capable of.

"Right away," she said.

38

IT HAD BEEN A PARTICULARLY POOR DAY FOR NEIL REYN-
olds. He had begun it by murdering two men. These
acts didn't prey upon Reynolds's conscience, but each time
he ended a life he felt a dislocation within his spirit, a sense
that a border had been crossed and a boundary shattered.
The events in Iran were taking on the shape of a scandal,
and the American press had caught the scent of blood.
Apparently a newsman had disappeared in the area at the
same time as Madison's men; the story had started to take
on unforeseen dimensions.

Reynolds didn't much care what happened. Laura was
the key for him—she was the only person or thing in the
world capable of eliciting his passion. She was his lifeline
back to what he once had been.

Something hadn't been right when he last spoke with
her. She had probably felt disorientation as a result of the
enhancement he had performed on her cognitive centers
two nights before. That might have affected her behavior.
She was coming soon, and he would be ready to show her
the existence he had created for her.

The question was what to tell her. She would never

accept the trials he had performed on patients at Faber's hospital, even though his interests had been experimental and actually killing them had been a favor to Faber. He had done the experiments in the hospital itself, in an abandoned conference room after one of Faber's employees had unknowingly introduced a microdevice to the patient through eye drops, nose drops, or IV injections. Even then, Reynolds could have controlled the device from Washington—but he hadn't wanted Faber to know it.

None of that mattered. The fact that he had caused them death—no matter how quick or painless were their last moments—was a breach he knew Laura would never forgive.

No one would ever tell her. He hadn't left a trail. Whatever fragmentary clues a lucky investigator might find would lead directly to Jefferson Faber. And he, of course, would never reveal the truth.

Reynolds pressed his thumbs against his eyes; red blotches filled his vision. The discomfort behind his temples seemed to ease for a moment. How could he describe this sensation? As a headache without pain? Or the feeling of thousands of effervescent bubbles rising in his mind, about to break in unison?

As for the Iranian matter, he had crafted a trail leading directly to Chapman and Faber. National Security investigators would be ecstatic to close the case—and to find that the chief conspirators were dead and couldn't embarrass the nation during televised trials.

He had succeeded. There was only one act left to perform before Laura arrived and he began his new life. He had to save himself.

Reynolds stood up. He felt slightly off balance, as though he were slightly drunk. He reminded himself to catalog every nuance of the condition in which he found himself: Disorientation. Degenerating motor skills. Blurred thought processes, becoming more pronounced. Dulled emotional response. Memory loss, short- and long-term.

He had to get these devices out of his head.

He had prepared his lab; when his assistants walked into his work space they would see nothing more than an impressive array of familiar equipment. He had already transferred his notes, tapes, the delicate manufacturing equipment, and the microrobots to his home. He opened his laboratory door and tried to remember how he used to behave.

His staff numbered four young men now, and they were all working at computer terminals with a purposeful air. Reynolds hesitated. It took him several moments to recall their names.

"Philip Kang," he said, suddenly remembering. "David Bailey."

Kang and Bailey, their desks nearest to where Reynolds stood, looked up in unison. Their expressions were wary but he saw that they were still eager to please him.

"Colonel Reynolds?" Kang said.

Reynolds almost panicked at his memory loss. The other two men, the ones who had worked for him less than a month, could have been strangers. He wished he could remember their names.

"Yes, Philip. I need to ask something of you," Reynolds said. Forget the others, he thought. He could do what he needed with Kang and Bailey.

Kang looked surprised. Reynolds knew that his staff was more used to demands than requests.

"Bailey, I need you too," Reynolds said. He motioned toward his laboratory. "Come in here with me, please, both of you."

Reynolds led the way into his lab, not waiting for a reaction.

He had to sit down or he might have collapsed. Reynolds dropped down on a swivel chair in front of his main computer console. He fought to compose himself while his assistants gazed furtively at his private sanctum. Both were obviously amazed to be there.

"I have something to ask of you that will require a bit of delicacy," Reynolds began, speaking slowly and clearly. "Do you understand?"

"Of course, sir," David Bailey said. He stood stiffly, as though at military attention.

"At ease," Reynolds said, trying to smile. "You're a civilian contractor, David. You don't have to watch your posture around me."

He turned his attention to Kang. "Philip, how long have you been with me in this unit?"

"About a month, sir," Kang said.

Reynolds nodded. That sounded right.

"I know I'm still in my probationary period, Colonel," Kang added. "If that's what this is about."

Reynolds ignored his comment. It seemed debatable from his tone whether the young man feared being fired or craved it.

"I need to move my essential equipment out of here for the weekend," Reynolds said to Bailey. "You'll need some muscle to load it up. I don't expect you to break your backs, we can get a few grunts in here for that. I need you to oversee things and to make sure the computers and VR gear are packed properly. It's very important that this remain a strict secret."

Reynolds waited for a response. "Sir," Bailey said hesitantly, "I haven't really studied the regulations around here, but I know we're not allowed to take anything out of here without permission.''

''And I don't have permission,'' Reynolds said plainly. Neither man flinched. ''You're both civilians. I'm sure you get tired of the military attitude around here. Am I right?''

Neither answered, as though they suspected that he was posing a trick question to entrap them.

''Here's my situation, gentlemen,'' Reynolds said. ''I haven't been feeling well this week, but I'm on the verge of assembling a surgical robotic prototype—the fruition of all our work here. I simply want to work at home through the weekend, where I can rest when I need to.''

Reynolds waited for his request to settle in. Removal of technological equipment was expressly forbidden. Reynolds had just requisitioned a van, and he knew that the loading bay was currently empty. He needed the quiet of home to regain his senses, and he desperately needed these two men to make it happen.

''Could we get in trouble for this?'' Bailey asked.

Such loyalty, Reynolds thought.

''You certainly could, if you weren't acting with my permission.'' Reynolds took out an envelope and handed it to Bailey. ''Inside is a series of directions for removing the equipment, along with my address and a key to my house. I want you to unpack and set up in my front room. I have good current in my house as well as surge protectors. If I don't arrive while you're there, drop the key through the mail slot in the front door before you go.''

Baily took the envelope and bit his lower lip. ''What if someone asks what we're doing?''

''Tell them you're working under my orders,'' Reynolds said. ''And that you're moving inessential equipment to my home for the weekend. Pack everything in cardboard boxes if you have to, just don't make it clear what you're doing.''

A look passed over their young faces that Reynolds recognized: they were uncertain whether he was telling the truth, and they felt compromised. He missed his regular military career at times such as this. A couple of gung-ho corporals would have looked upon this assignment as a challenge, a way of thumbing their noses at the constrictive authority under which they all lived.

''I'll return everything on Monday,'' Reynolds said. ''We're simply skirting a rule that doesn't make much sense.''

Bailey finally agreed, looking flattered to have been taken into Reynolds's confidence. Kang took the list of equipment and looked around the room, ready to start.

''And, gentlemen,'' Reynolds added, ''you should understand that I've taken you into my trust. If you violate that trust, it could have a seriously deleterious effect on your future employment potential.''

Reynolds hoped his exit was dramatic enough to have scared them into doing a good job. He left the building through the front entrance, scanning his key card at every locked door, walking with his eyes focused straight ahead.

His conversation with Kang and Bailey had been difficult. He'd had to struggle to remain lucid and coherent. It was becoming harder and harder to concentrate. But he had one final task, one final seed to sow before he could return to the safety of his home.

One more task. Then he would begin the fight to save his mind.

39

THE LINE AT THE AIRLINE COUNTER INCHED FORWARD; AHEAD of Laura were two families and several businessmen traveling alone. It was Friday, and the airport was packed. She tapped her foot and tried to contain her impatience.

A television broadcast continuous cable news to the captive viewers waiting their turn for tickets. The news showed footage of a meeting between American and Iranian diplomats. The reporter said that the recent crisis between the two countries had uncovered severe rifts within the Iranian government. Iran still refused to release its prisoners, and the situation was, for the moment, a standoff.

Laura couldn't imagine how Cyrus could have been connected to the crisis. In all likelihood Cyrus had been calling his brother simply to commiserate. Cyrus had lost his company, his brother seemed to be involved in some sort of wrongdoing. Ferry seemed to want to link the two and somehow draw a connection to Faber.

Before she could complete her thought, Laura reached the front of the line. The couple ahead of her had actually been waiting in the wrong queue; they shuffled off, exasperated over having to wait in another line. Laura stepped up to the counter.

"Can I help you?" a young airline employee asked. She had bright red hair, and freckles dappled across her nose.

"I need to catch the next flight to Washington, D.C.," Laura said. "It's an emergency."

"Has a family member died?" the young woman asked.

The question shocked Laura. "No," she replied. "Why would you think that?"

The clerk seemed surprised by the vehemence of Laura's reaction. "We offer discount tickets if you have to get to a funeral."

Laura realized how much she was on edge; she pictured Carlo in her mind, and felt a sharp stab of the maternal will to protect him. "No, it's nothing like that," she said.

"Well, then, one-way or round-trip?"

"I'm not sure how long I'll need to stay. You'd better make it a one-way ticket."

"Well, the best I can do is a flight leaving at eight, with one stopover. You'll get into Washington in the morning."

"I'll take whatever you have," Laura said.

The clerk glanced up from the ticketing computer, as though trying to figure out Laura's story. "All right," she said. "Will that be cash or will you use a credit card?"

6:55 p.m. Salt Lake City, Utah.

FOR THE PAST FEW HOURS JEANETTE MADISON HAD BEEN forced to endure what she dreaded most—interaction with law enforcement. Minutes after their emergency landing in Salt Lake City the cops had arrived, then the paramedics. Now she had to deal with detectives at the county hospital. The cops seemed to share a morbid fascination with the death of Jefferson Faber. Without exception they had all glanced with curiosity at Faber's body, as though needing to see for themselves that the man's money hadn't been able to save him from oblivion.

The first moments had been the worst. She had held on to Jefferson's inert body, crying for a long time before she called for Roland Lanier. Lanier had told the pilot to make an emergency landing. It had been too much to ask for them to escape together. For the past two years he had tried to chip away at her petrous exterior to the woman underneath, and she had grown fond of the game. Now it was over.

A half hour after Faber's death she had decided there was no time for grief. Her remaining life span, for all she knew, might have been measurable in minutes rather than years.

She sat alone now on a long vinyl sofa in a waiting area. At the end of the hall was the morgue, where Faber's lifeless body lay. There had been no need for efforts to revive him.

She was approached by a man in a rumpled gray suit. The antenna of a portable phone jutted from his inner pocket.

"Danny Smith, Homicide," he said. His face was squeaky clean, with no stubble, the skin under his eyes taut and spotless. "You're Ms. Jeanette Madison?"

"That's right," she said, turning away from him. "I've told the story a half-dozen times to every cop in the city. Do you really need to hear it again?"

"If you don't mind," he said.

So she told him. As she spoke, she wondered: Had the federal government found out she was in Utah? Why hadn't Reynolds killed her too?

"Were you and Mr. Faber romantically involved?" Smith asked.

She stared at him. "We were close friends."

This seemed to satisfy the detective. He took her address—actually a post-office box in Henderson, Nevada, that she used when dealing with any official agency.

"They're telling me there's no evidence of foul play," Smith said brightly. "So I guess I won't need to get involved. Do you know where you're headed now, Ms. Madison?"

She was always looking for traps, and Madison knew she hadn't stepped into one. Not yet. If the connection between her, Faber, and the Iranian smuggling operation were known, it hadn't filtered down to local law enforcement.

"I'm not sure," she said. "Would you excuse me, please?"

Smith politely stepped aside. At the end of the hall she saw Lanier, just finishing his interview with local police.

She knew suddenly what she had to do.

"What's up?" Lanier asked, leaning on the wall. He looked shocked and weary. No doubt he had seen all of his future opportunities dissolve with his employer's death.

"Are you all right?" she asked the young man. She didn't like him, but she needed him.

"I'll live," he said. He motioned ruefully toward the morgue doors and snapped his fingers. "Just like that. Incredible. Jefferson swam two hours a day, he watched his diet. He smoked and he drank sometimes, but who would have expected this?"

"I know," Madison said in a sympathetic voice.

"I mean, we had just talked about how I would run his affairs while he was on vacation with you. Can you believe it? Now I'll probably be let go. I was so close—"

Madison fought off the urge to slap him. She said, "Listen, I need to ask you for a favor."

Lanier snapped out of his reverie of self-pity. He seemed alarmed by the determination he saw in her eyes. "I need the plane," she said. "You have to take a commercial flight home."

"You need—that plane is the property of Ellington-Faber," Lanier sputtered. "Absolutely not. I can't just—"

Madison gripped the young man's elbow, glancing up the hall to see if anyone was watching. They weren't.

"Feel that?" she asked. She knew that paralyzing, white-hot pain was carving a path from Lanier's elbow to his fingertips. His face paled. "I can do worse. The plane belonged to Jefferson, and he and I were very close. I don't need it permanently, just for one flight. It's very important, and trust me—Jefferson would have wanted it.''

Beads of sweat appeared on Lanier's forehead. He stood a full foot taller than Madison, and probably outweighed her by a hundred pounds. A part of her felt gratified to demonstrate that hours spent on a weight-lifting bench didn't translate into physical supremacy.

"I'm going to Washington, D.C.," she said. "Tell the pilot to take me there then return the plane to Los Angeles."

"Jesus," Lanier said. His voice turned high and squeaky. "Stop that shit. Stop it right now."

She let go of his arm. He rubbed it up and down, trying to soothe the nerve cluster she had stimulated. It would take a while.

"It's a one-way trip," she said to him. "I don't know how long I might stay or if I'm coming back. Do you think you can arrange that?"

Lanier's face flashed with anger, then he remembered his arm. He had strength; she had will and expertise. It was no contest.

"Of course," he said quietly. "I assume that you want to leave right now."

"Right now," she agreed.

PART FOUR

40

IT HAD BEEN A WEEK OF SINGULAR STRANGENESS, AND JACK
Parsons didn't expect it to turn ordinary anytime soon.
The city had been abuzz with the news that Senator Bob
Chapman had dropped dead in his office the previous
morning. News reports had noted that his predecessor,
George Patterson, had died suddenly only months before.

Now Parsons was in the very office where Chapman had
died, trying to sort through leads in his mind. Parsons at
the moment was one of a handful of men in the National
Security Agency who knew the true story behind the recent
Iranian crisis. The American men captured in the northern
mountains had been carrying uranium. This was a Level
One crisis, and Jack was in the middle of it.

The most recent break had come courtesy of the editor
of *Worldweek*. An intern in their art department had been
sitting on a series of weird photographs sent by one of their
reporters a week ago. They only became significant when
that reporter turned up missing. The pictures showed the
men who had been captured by Iran, and as of that moment
the FBI was searching their files trying to match names to
the faces.

He had been so busy the night before that he had taken

little notice of an anonymous E-mail posted to his account. It had been security-coded with a scrambler program that Parsons didn't have in his files. He often received routine messages in such a fashion, and he had intended to send it to the computer labs for decoding when he had time.

It wasn't necessary. Two hours later a courier had delivered a thick padded envelope to him containing a single unmarked floppy disk. On it was the decoder for the E-mail message.

The message was very brief, though it took up a lot of space on Parsons's hard disk. The encryption program was incredibly complicated, possibly better than anything Parsons had previously encountered.

The message read as follows:

IRAN CRISIS = BOB CHAPMAN. JEFFERSON FABER.

And that had been it.

There was no way to trace the source of the disk. Parsons had immediately ordered the Agency's computer technicians to trace the source of the E-mail. It had been relayed through several Internet nodes. They kept working and eventually discovered that the original transmission site had been a public library in Washington—the city had installed a communal computer with Internet access there, to afford the needy with access to the technological revolution. It was a perfect place from which to send anonymous messages.

Within another hour Parsons had obtained clearance to search Chapman's office and, more importantly, his computer. Parsons was quick with technology and needed no assistance. He had ordered Chapman's staff out of the office. Parson's search would technically have never taken place—unless he found something.

Parsons sat in Chapman's chair in front of the dead man's keyboard and terminal. Parsons wondered: Was this the precise spot where the senator had died? Had his life slipped away in this very chair, or had he fallen to the floor? Were his last thoughts about a clandestine plot to sell arms to a hostile government?

Parsons got up and shut the drapes. He pulled a pair of ultrathin latex gloves out of a plastic bag in his pocket.

After turning on the computer the first thing Parsons discovered was that Chapman had been a technological dunce. The files were arranged in a weird, haphazard fashion. There were typical office utilities, most of them unused, and communications software stuck in an abandoned folder. Computers were often vital places to look for information, but Parsons wasn't encouraged by what he saw.

Parsons idly opened the senator's top desk drawer. A box of cigars. Scrambled pens and pencils, paper clips, and adhesive notes. The calendars and files had already been confiscated by other federal agencies: as usual there were too many agencies involved.

Parsons sighed. He was used to it. He opened another drawer. Empty. Then another.

"Now, what is this?" he asked himself.

It was round, with a lens on the front. It looked like a computer-compatible video camera. Chapman hadn't been completely out of it. This little esoteric gadget was for advanced users. Either Chapman had bought it as a toy, or he knew someone else who had one—someone who wanted visual contact when they talked.

Parsons went back to work on Chapman's computer. There wasn't much filed on the hard drive. There were very few letters, memos, games, or notes—all the trash people tend to store on their drives.

Which gave him an idea.

He took a floppy disk from his suit jacket and loaded it into the machine. When the computer had loaded the program, Parsons pressed a command:

RETRIEVE DELETED DATA: PREVIOUS THIRTY-SIX HOURS.

The computer hummed and started processing. The program was designed to retrieve information that had been erased from a computer's files. Though it wasn't common knowledge, ordering the "delete" command on a computer didn't ensure that the information was wiped away. The computer tended to save the old data until new data arrived to take its place.

"And there we are," Parsons said. "Looks like the senator deleted plenty of files before he bought the farm."

A long list appeared. Personal letters. Memos. Government business. E-mail files. There was plenty there, yet nothing of apparent interest. Chapman seemed to be a distinctly dull correspondent.

Parsons opened a file and read:

Dear Staff,
I would like it if we could bring our dress code up to a higher standard. Sometimes we will have important people visiting us. Heads of state, etc. We want to make a better impression than we have been making. I will truly appreciate it.

Parsons rolled his eyes and opened another file.

Dear Col. Neil Reynolds,
I would very much like to accept your offer to attend a weekend charity tennis tournament. I would also be willing to bring extra racquets for donation to chil-

dren's programs. I will send you the information you've
requested as soon as possible.

"Fascinating," Parsons mumbled.

But wait. It was so obvious.

Parsons looked through the list of recovered files, examining the record of the precise moment at which they were deleted. Chapman might have picked the day of his demise to do housecleaning on his computer. Or perhaps someone else had.

It was just as Parsons had suspected, or hoped. The majority of the files had been deleted at ten-thirty yesterday morning.

After Bob Chapman died.

The secretary had said she hadn't touched anything after Chapman's heart attack, and there were witnesses to corroborate that no one else had been in the office. Which meant that someone else had been meddling with Chapman's computer, someone who hadn't been physically present.

Parsons picked up Chapman's phone and dialed. The National Security Agency's computer laboratory picked up on the first ring.

"This is Parsons," he said. "I have an assignment for you, a little tracking. I need it done yesterday."

41

9:05 a.m. Virginia.

FINALLY, NEIL REYNOLDS THOUGHT. *HOME. SOLITUDE.*

Reynolds had always been frugal by nature, and in the years before he had begun to devote his personal income to his work, he had saved enough money to buy himself a small home. It was tucked away amid trees and hedges on its quiet residential street. It was small, only a story and a half, but Reynolds had undertaken a series of small renovation projects. The walls were pristine white, the floors finely sanded wood. The place was free of clutter or any sign of disarray.

The back of the house looked out on a yard that was sizable for the neighborhood. It had perfect southern exposure, and Reynolds had taken advantage of this by installing high windows along the length of the wall, as well as a series of elongated skylights in the roof. This, combined with the ivory paint job, gave the room a monastic quality on a sunny day.

Today the room was cluttered with machinery. Reynolds hadn't been sure Kang and Bailey would be able to move his lab out of the building, but his plan had worked. When Reynolds had arrived at home late the night before—after leaving his message with the NSA that would implicate two dead men—he had sighed with pleasure at the sight of his equipment.

Reynolds padded out of the kitchen with a glass of water, visually checking to ensure that everything was set up. The series of linked processors, multigigabyte storage disks, cellular communications equipment, and the virtual-reality workstation—it was exactly like his lab at the research facility.

He realized that he had been leaning against the doorway for support. Glancing down at his feet, Reynolds saw water pooling at his feet, soaking his socks. He hadn't been able to hold the glass upright, and he hadn't even noticed. He had already fallen asleep through the early morning hours, nodding out in a chair and losing valuable time. Reynolds knelt delicately and placed the glass on the floor. In his condition it would be foolish to take liquid anywhere near the computers.

In the living room Reynolds felt the warming sun on his forehead. It was gently reassuring. At his desk he picked up the microcassette player and pressed the "record" button.

"I am preparing to perform a final series of procedures," he began. He cleared his throat. "The last of which will be on myself. It is an inescapable conclusion that the process I began on myself almost a year ago has been detrimental to my mental and physical health."

The house was absolutely silent. Reynolds watched the steady movement of the cassette tape through the recording mechanisms.

"Maintaining continuity in my thinking has become extraordinarily difficult," he said. "I had imagined that I would adjust, but I am experiencing a profound degeneration. I am quickly reaching a point at which I might permanently lose my mind."

He took a deep breath. Perhaps he was wasting time updating the record. But if he failed that day, only the tape would be left to explain.

"My physical symptoms are numerous. I have had a headache for the past three days that seems to be worsening. It is . . . distracting, and very uncomfortable."

No, he had to be honest.

"The pain is maddening," he whispered. "The cacophony of thoughts is maddening. This feels very dangerous. I must attempt to undo it."

He looked out the window. His yard was green and spotless.

"I can only offer one hypothesis," he said. "The human brain cannot survive for long with such artificial stimulation. I have done too much, too fast. By manipulating myself in such a radical fashion I have triggered a hormonal negative-feedback mechanism. My hypothalamus is recording lower-than-normal readings of corticohormones, thyroid hormones, ACTH, TSH, GH. It's responding by ordering epinephrine, adrenaline, dopamine, and bradykinin into my system. I've wrecked my endocrine balance, and it's burning out the cells in my brain."

He almost couldn't believe that he had made such a mistake; but the evidence was there in the shattered shape of his thoughts.

"Perhaps my mind could have adjusted if the changes had been more gradual. But if I had been more prudent, I might never have found the gift I am bestowing on two selected loved ones and myself. True progress always has a cost."

HE PAUSED. "I DID WHAT I HAD TO DO."

He shut off the recorder. There was nothing more to say.

The headpiece slipped onto his eyes with comfortable

familiarity. He used the hand controls to toggle through menu options, then waited for his communications link to find the tiny machine lodged inside Laura Antonelli's head.

Reynolds hummed softly while he waited. Laura would one day realize how fortunate she had been. Reynolds had wanted to share with her the gift of an expanded mind. He had been more careful with her, performing only minor adjustments to her endocrine chemistry. But, to ensure that her mind didn't disintegrate as his had, he would reverse the entire process.

His body stiffened as the nanorobot came on-line. Around him was a view of murky dark tissue. The device had remained where he had lodged it after its last series of tasks.

"Good boy," he muttered.

The machine fed Reynolds stimulus as it moved laboriously toward a blood vessel. Reynolds worked from memory, listing off the sites he had previously visited. He would return her to complete normality within an hour. Then he would have time to inspect her at the cellular level, to see how his greater work was progressing. He would not take this second gift away from her.

Then he would work on the boy. Carlo. A shining spirit, full of life and intelligence. He wanted to be a father to the boy, to provide him with a model, with context, with an example of rightness and maturity. Because, after all, they would have a very, very long time to spend together.

After Reynolds had worked on mother and child—fulfilling his responsibilities to them—only then could he deliver himself from the hell his mind was turning into.

There was time.

There had to be.

42

10:12 a.m. Washington, D.C.

JEANETTE MADISON CLOSED THE HOTEL-ROOM DRAPES. SHE felt a tide of electric fear moving through her. She thought she hadn't seen anyone watching outside, but there was no way to be sure. She had already pulled the dresser in front of the door. If they came for her, she would need a few seconds to prepare.

She had landed at a private airfield outside Washington, raced through the terminal, and rented a car. She had expected to be arrested the instant she stepped off the plane, but she wasn't. Then she was positive she would be accosted at the rental counter, but she was able to get away. She had spent a sleepless night in this room, waiting for a knock on the door that had never come.

Where *were* they?

Action. *Action.* It was constant action that had enabled her to survive the past decade, and action would serve her now. She had to find Reynolds before he reached her. She had already discovered that he wasn't listed in anything as prosaic as the phone book.

She turned on the laptop computer that Roland Lanier had left on the plane in the chaotic aftermath of his employer's sudden death. It was Jefferson's personal machine, its case emblazoned with his initials.

It felt warm. Madison had to will away the thought that the lifeless plastic was still heated from Jefferson's touch. That was impossible.

The computer's desktop display appeared after the machine finished booting up. Madison searched the files, her hand trembling.

A personal calendar. Useless—though she should remember to erase it later, in case it contained anything that might implicate her. The same applied to the file labeled "Personal Correspondence."

Most of the machine's hard drive contained data and applications pertaining to Jefferson's business empire. There were spreadsheets, lists of investments, corporate employment structures, communications software enabling him to check the stock and bond markets at any moment in the day. None of it helped her.

She found a file marked "Private." This had to be it. She pointed and clicked, moving through files of memos and notes. These, too, would have to be deleted. Then she found what she wanted, a file marked "Telephone and Address Directory."

She clicked to open it and was dismayed when a box appeared asking for a password.

"Very smart, Jefferson," she said.

A password. Madison cradled her head in her hands and tried to think like Faber. One word, eight letters maximum.

"Faber," she typed in. The machine told her this was incorrect and returned her to the desktop.

She cursed under her breath. This meant she would have to load the program anew.

"Jeffrey," she typed. His son's name. Again she was returned to the desktop, the program automatically shutting down.

"Industry." No good.

"Capital." No good.

"Power." *No good.*

Madison closed her eyes. Think like Faber, she commanded herself. She thought about the last hour she had spent with him. A man as deliberate and careful as Jefferson Faber would regularly change his password. She tried to remember what he had said to her, what he was thinking about during his final day of life.

Then it came to her.

"Madison," she typed in.

No good.

"*Damn* it," she whispered. She thought of one final guess.

"Jeanette," she typed.

The program loaded. The password was correct. After a few seconds she was asked whether she wanted to type in a name to begin searching the database.

Her first name. He loved her, as a person and as a woman. She shook her head angrily, trying to banish the hot swell of tears that threatened to erupt from within her.

To the world Jefferson Faber had been a greedy, heartless bastard. And Jeanette Madison was a crackpot, a burnout, a political subversive who lived at the margins of society in a fantasy world of her own devising. Each knew the other better than that. Somehow they had seen what was worthy in the other, something exciting and pure.

"We could have done it," she said. "We could have had a good life together."

The sadness left her as soon as it had come, replaced by anger. In a moment of clarity she understood that her time in the desert had been a cowardly retreat from life. Her dreams of self-reliance and survivalism had been illusions. She had been seeking a way to hide.

Jefferson had represented hope for her, and she for him. Neither had fulfillment in their lives, or a sense of connection to anything genuine and good. For a brief time each had found affection and understanding in the other.

A feeling of vengeance, icy and glacial, filled her. She typed in the name "Reynolds, Neil." Two listings appeared. She found the phone on the cheap nightstand and dialed the first number.

"Army Medical Research, Colonel Reynolds's division," a voice answered after five rings.

"Colonel Reynolds, please," Madison asked in a pleasant voice.

"He's gone for the day," the man said. "Is this an emergency? I can patch you through to—"

Madison hung up and dialed the second number.

"Hello?" a mumbling, gravel-filled voice said.

Reynolds. She hung up again.

Madison scanned through the database listing and found Reynolds's home address, in nearby Virginia. She jotted it down, then produced a map from her travel bag.

She saw that his home was in a small suburban enclave; she pointed her finger at the spot on the map. Reynolds was there.

Madison wiped away the tears escaping from her eyes. She had to be strong. The bastard might have planted one of those machines within her—she didn't know how it was done, so she couldn't be sure. But if he wanted to eliminate her, she would take him with her.

Madison opened the flaps of her bag. Everything was still there, including the pound of plastic explosives and the detonator.

She opened the window in order to air out the room while she was gone. Because she had every intention of returning.

43

THE TINY ENGINE IN LAURA'S RENTED COMPACT CAR groaned as she darted across two lanes of traffic, trying to make the turnoff from the Jefferson Davis Highway. Traffic coursed on all sides. She caught glimpses of maple and oak trees passing on the gentle landscape beyond the road, but she didn't have time to savor the view.

A Honda angrily honked when she cut it off, but she had made the turnoff. She glanced at the map on her lap and allowed her foot to relax a fraction on the accelerator.

The drive here had been interminable. She had been fixated to the point of distraction by the thought of the object in her head, to the point of even worrying that it might set off the airport's metal detectors. It didn't, but during those five hours in the air she had felt odd and disjointed. The only reading material she had brought along was the stack of case files that had started her on this trail, which were less than reassuring.

Her ideas were coalescing. She was sure that Faber had killed the expensive patients—through means devised by Neil Reynolds. She reminded herself that this didn't necessarily implicate Neil—Faber might have accessed the technology without Neil's knowledge.

But would Faber have known how to use the microdevices? She could scarcely comprehend that they existed.

Cyrus hadn't suffered from any sort of terminal, costly illness, and he hadn't been an Ellington-Faber patient. But he might have been involved somehow with the Americans captured in Iran.

Americans—such as Faber? Or Neil?

Laura glanced down at the handwritten directions she had drawn on the plane after poring over a map she bought at the airport. Her next turnoff was coming up in less than a mile; it would lead her off the highway and onto the roads that snaked through Arlington. Signs indicated exits leading to the Pentagon and the Arlington National Cemetery.

She took the turn and found herself on a four-lane road that curled to the left and then righted itself. The Army's Medical Research Laboratory was just a few minutes away.

Laura gripped the steering wheel hard. Her body felt like a suspension wire holding a bridge aloft. She hadn't called Neil to warn him that she was arriving early. She would tell him everything she suspected and leave it all for him to explain.

By surprising Neil she would deny him the time to devise a lie. But she was also prepared to believe him. She wanted him to convince her that he had done nothing wrong. If his inventions had been used illegally, it must have been without his knowledge. Neil could be instrumental in stopping the travesty that had taken place at Valley Memorial Hospital. Together, they could stop Faber.

By the time Laura saw that she had reached the facility's driveway, she had almost passed it. She tapped the brake and made a sharp quick turn, then slowed as she approached the guard kiosk.

Behind the guard station she saw the facility for the first time. It was long and squat, nearly windowless on the lower floors. It was surrounded on all sides by trees, making it difficult to tell its true dimensions. A guard emerged from the kiosk, holding up his hand.

She rolled down her window. "Good afternoon," she said.

The uniformed guard was young, about twenty. His face was impassive, his eyes hidden by dark glasses. Laura's eyes drifted to the revolver he wore holstered on his hip.

"Can I help you?" he asked in a deep voice.

"I'm here to visit Colonel Neil Reynolds," she said.

The guard told Laura to wait and went into the kiosk. He emerged holding a clipboard.

"Is he expecting you?" the guard asked.

"Yes," Laura lied. She told him her name, then gave him her hospital identification card as well as her driver's license. "He's a colleague of mine," she said. "He's giving me a tour of his research lab."

"Well, your name's not on the visitors' list," he said.

"That's strange," Laura said. "I just flew all the way from Los Angeles. I drove straight here from the airport so I wouldn't be late."

"You did?" the guard asked. "That's a long flight."

"Very," Laura said.

The guard's officious demeanor waned for an instant. "Tell you what," he said. "I'm going to take down your name and ID numbers, and you can pull up to the front entrance. Go to the desk and they'll page the colonel for you. I'm sure it's a misunderstanding."

Laura waited for him to jot down her ID numbers, took back her cards, and thanked the young man. It was the second time recently that she'd lied to get past security. It amazed her how easy it was.

She parked her car under a large poplar tree in the visitors' lot and walked toward the front entrance. As she opened the tall tinted glass door sheltered by a tall white concrete arch, she now felt comforted by all the security measures. Nothing would happen to her in such a place.

The receiving area was bland and sterile. There was a desk staffed by two older women, a plastic bin for outgoing mail, and a few professional-looking men and women going in and out of the four doors that led out to different sectors. Laura noticed that before the doors would open, a key card had to be presented before a red electronic eye, and a numeric code had to be punched into a keypad. Laura looked up and saw a pair of cameras rotating slowly, scanning the area.

"Colonel Neil Reynolds, please," Laura said. She told the apple-cheeked receptionist the same skeletal story she had bluffed the guard with. The older woman dialed an extension to reach Neil's unit.

"Strange. No one's picking up," she said in a delicate, throaty voice that contrasted with her blunt features and severe haircut. She seemed annoyed to be bothered so late in the day. "I remember your name. You've called for Colonel Reynolds before, from Los Angeles."

Laura smiled. "Well, you could just issue me a visitor's pass. I could find it for myself."

The receptionist seemed to consider the appeal of this course—that of least resistance—but her better judgment won out. "I can't do that," she said. "But I'll call someone to take you down there."

While she waited, Laura wandered over to a display case. There the military's medical breakthroughs were displayed in the form of faded photographs and news clippings. There was a section on surgical advances made necessary by the galling severity of battlefield wounds; a small display on inoculation discoveries that had saved soldiers from disease in faraway combat arenas; and a final display on telepresence surgery, in which the surgeon operated through virtual reality and remote control. These advances were all the by-products of war. They were laudable, but it seemed ironic that they were associated with death and devastation.

"I'll bet you didn't know how much modern medicine was developed by the military," a voice said from behind her.

Laura turned, startled. A young woman in full army dress extended her hand.

"Corporal Jennifer Booth," she said. Her black hair was cut close over her ears. Her pale skin was free of makeup.

Laura introduced herself. "I heard Colonel Reynolds was supposed to show you around," Booth said. "I'm on the security team, but I'm starting medical school in a few weeks. I volunteered to take you because I always wanted to see the colonel's lab."

Booth escorted Laura to a clear door, where she inserted her card and entered a lengthy series of numbers. She held the door for Laura to pass through, and they made their way through a long, brightly lit hall. Most of the rooms were marked only with numbers. None indicated the nature of the work performed inside.

"You're a friend of Colonel Reynolds?" Booth asked. Her walk was speedy and lithe.

Laura said she was. She felt her pulse quicken; she would see Neil in a matter of moments.

Booth seemed oblivious to Laura's nervousness. "Well, you're lucky to get a tour," she said brightly. "Reynolds is notorious for keeping everyone out of his lab. Most people here only see what he's working on when he's good and ready. When you have a reputation like his, you can get away with bending the rules a little, I guess.''

They took a secured elevator deep into the earth. At the end of another hall they had reached a thick glass door. Booth pushed her card into another slot and entered another code. The door opened with a thick clack of metal.

''What kind of medicine are you in?'' Booth asked as the door closed behind them. ''I was told you work in L.A.''

Laura felt hot and uncomfortable under the bright hallway lights; with each security check they passed through, she felt an increasing sensation of captivity. ''Surgery. I'm a general surgeon.''

''Great,'' Booth said with enthusiasm. ''Is Los Angeles a good place to work?''

Laura was gripped with the urge to ask this young woman to shut up and lead her to Neil. Young, bright, enthusiastic—Booth reminded her of herself, fifteen years before. The young corporal had no idea of the quagmire of politics medical practice had become, and Laura didn't want to discourage her.

''It's very nice,'' she said. ''Good luck to you in medical school.''

At the end of the hall Booth stopped before a door marked only with the number 144. This door had its own security lock.

Booth glanced down at a slip of paper and punched the keypad. ''Today's code for the unit,'' she explained. ''Colonel Reynolds is very security conscious. And for good reason—his research equipment is probably the most valuable in the entire facility. And forget about his personal lab. No one knows the codes for that.''

The young woman opened the door and gestured for Laura to enter. Inside, Laura was startled.

There was nothing in the plain hall or featureless door to hint at what lay inside. It looked more like a high-tech factory than a work area. Every available surface was covered with machinery: computers, some running, some dormant; surgical simulation workstations; webs of wire and electronic hookups; a long row of high-powered microscopes; metallurgical equipment with laser cutting tools. This was only the gear Laura recognized. There were other devices, more exotic, lining the tables along all four walls.

Four empty desks were topped with papers and computers. The room was silent and still, save for an electric humming.

"Strange," Booth said. "I've heard Reynolds keeps everyone here late every day. Maybe they're on break."

Booth wandered into a row of tables piled with disassembled computers. She seemed to lose track of escorting Laura for the moment, entranced by the assortment of esoteric research implements.

Laura looked down at her chest. She could see her own heart beating through the fabric of her blouse and dark blue blazer.

"Is that Colonel Reynolds's office?" Laura asked. She pointed at an unmarked door at the rear of the lab. Its blinds were drawn.

"I didn't even notice," Booth apologized. "I've never even been in here before." Her gaze lingered on a surgical simulator, her imagination no doubt occupied with her own future in medicine.

Laura saw another door, high and windowless, with its own lock, electronic eye, and numeric punch pad. She guessed this was Neil's own laboratory.

"The lights are on inside the office," Laura said. "Maybe we should knock on the door. If he's in there, he might not have heard us."

Booth anxiously smoothed her uniform, seeming chagrined at having forgotten her duty. She walked toward the door, her bearing now serious and erect. Before she could knock, it opened of its own accord.

Laura stiffened, expecting to confront Neil. Instead, a youngish man of about thirty with thick hair and sharp, observant eyes emerged. He stared coldly at Laura and Corporal Booth, not introducing himself.

"We're here to visit Colonel Reynolds," Booth said. Her hand drifted to the wireless communicator on her belt. "Is he here?"

"No," the man said. He pulled an identification card from his jacket and showed it to her. "Jack Parsons, National Security Agency."

"Does anyone know you're here?" Booth asked.

Parsons glanced at her uniform. "They certainly do, Corporal." He turned to Laura. "Ma'am, who are you?"

"My name is Laura Antonelli," she said.

Parsons nodded. "From Los Angeles, right?" he asked.

"How did you know that?"

Parsons motioned to Booth. "I don't mean to be rude, Corporal, but I need to talk to Dr. Antonelli alone. Talk to your supervisor. He'll tell you I have clearance to be here. And don't tell anyone else that you saw me."

Laura hadn't seen Parson's identification, but Corporal Booth had been impressed by it. She quietly left the room without saying good-bye. Laura heard the lock click behind them.

"You didn't answer my question," Laura said. The room, though airy and well ventilated, felt inordinately hot.

"He called you," Parsons said. "I checked his phone records."

"I don't understand," Laura said. She felt a prickly

sensation inside her temples. "Why would you do that? Where is everyone?"

"Come inside," he said.

In the austere office were Neil's diplomas from the University of Virginia, pictures of him in Vietnam, and piles of papers and books. She glanced at a cork board behind the desk and saw a ticket stub from the basketball game they attended, along with a snapshot of her and Carlo she had sent him.

Laura sat down; her breathing felt altered somehow. It was much like the sensation she had felt two nights before, when she had hallucinated and then passed out.

"Are you feeling well?" Parsons asked.

"I'm fine," Laura replied. Her voice sounded far away.

"Hey, look," he said, his voice softening. "I didn't mean to frighten you. I'm here because I need to talk to Neil Reynolds. Everyone here seems to have left early. Do you know where Reynolds might be?"

The fluorescent bulbs above were ringed with a blue-green halo. Laura felt her entire body slowly drift to the right, as though she might float out of her chair. "I don't know," she answered. "I came here to see him. I don't know where he is."

Parsons leaned back in Neil's chair. "What's the nature of your relationship with Colonel Reynolds?" he asked.

Laura couldn't meet his eyes. Parsons was a government agent. Why was he looking for Neil?

"We're friends," she said. "What were you doing with Neil's phone records?"

"I was authorized to secure them," Parsons said.

Laura paused. The wave of disorientation seemed to break for a moment, though she felt a tinge of its presence, as though it might return at any moment. "Why are you here?" she asked.

"You could answer the same question," Parsons replied. "I must say, your timing is very interesting."

What did he mean? Laura felt humming in her ears. It was starting again. "I have to get out of here," she said.

Parsons frowned. "You don't look good. Do you have some kind of condition?"

"I'm a doctor," Laura said. Her voice sounded slurred. "I have to leave. I simply dropped in. I don't know what you want."

Parsons's eyes filled with surprise. "I'm sorry," he said. "I didn't mean to play games, but I can't tell you why I'm here. I'm convinced you have nothing to do with it, that's all I can say. You should go back to Los Angeles right away. I'll be in touch with you in a day or so."

Laura heard him but barely understood. Something about going back to L.A. She couldn't do that. She stood up, hoping she seemed normal in spite of the chaos taking hold of her mind.

"Thank you," she said, and shook his hand. "I'm going to do exactly what you told me."

She left him in Neil's office, glancing back to see if he had followed her. He hadn't; instead, she saw him switch on Neil's personal computer.

Corporal Booth was making her way down the hall when Laura stepped out of the lab. The young woman's gregarious manner had completely disappeared.

They walked in silence out of the facility and parted with a curt good-bye. When Laura got into her car she glanced up. Booth had stepped out of the building and was watching her from under the front-entrance arch.

Laura knew only one thing: She had to find Neil before they did.

44

3:39 p.m.

IT WAS HAPPENING AGAIN. LAURA FELT AS THOUGH SOME invisible force was scrambling and fragmenting her thoughts. It was terrifying; she couldn't predict whether she could even stay conscious.

She pulled out of the parking space and onto the long driveway leading out of the facility. She drove slowly and carefully, struggling to keep the car moving in a straight line.

On the passenger seat was a second set of directions, guiding her to Neil Reynolds's home in suburban Virginia. She would have to find her way to the Shirley Memorial Highway, a winding express road that would lead her to the Beltway. From there she could reach the exit leading to Neil's home. In all she would have to travel less than ten miles.

"I can do it," she said, easing the car out onto the road.

Laura stayed well under the speed limit and kept a safe distance between her and the car ahead. Her vision was clear, but she didn't know how long it would last. If she lost consciousness, she prayed she would have time to pull over to the breakdown lane.

She replayed her brief conversation with Jack Parsons. Parsons was investigating Neil, going through Neil's things and checking his phone records. Parsons was a federal agent—could he possibly have known about the deaths at Valley Memorial?

Laura suddenly realized that the cars around her had become colored blurs. She concentrated harder, focusing her eyes, and they became clear and distinct. Traffic was thickening; rush hour had begun.

It hadn't occurred to her to tell Parsons everything she knew. She could have led him to her car and shown him the files. But she needed to hear the truth from Neil. She wanted to know if her affection for him had been horribly misplaced. And what if Parsons had believed her? He might have even tried to implicate her—after all, some of the dead patients had been hers. She might lose Carlo to some social services agency—and still she would carry the little device in her head, a time bomb that might end her life at any instant.

"Concentrate on the road," she ordered herself.

Speculation wasn't going to help. She would go to Neil and tell him everything. If he was the man she thought she had begun to love, then he would be innocent.

"This isn't right," she said suddenly.

She looked down at the directions, then glanced at the open road atlas. The traffic was heavy and starting to move faster. Blinking, trying to keep her mind clear, she reached a multilane turnoff.

The car drifted as she tried to reconcile what she saw with her mental image of the map. The two didn't match. There was a plethora of roads and highways delineated by overhead signs; disoriented, she drove straight ahead.

She saw a bridge coming up. Rising above it in the near

distance was a familiar white pencil-shaped object: the Washington Monument.

She was going in the wrong direction, away from Virginia and across the Potomac—directly into the heart of the capital during rush-hour traffic. Laura cursed, but it was impossible to turn around.

Before she had crossed the bridge, her symptoms worsened. Crystalline diamond shapes played before her eyes. Memories of a childhood Sunday at the beach mingled with cadaver dissection in medical school and the sight of the monument rising through her windshield.

The traffic momentarily dropped off. She sighed with relief, not confident of her ability to drive faster than a crawl. Cars began to turn off to her left and right, the colors of the vehicles like fireworks splintering and disintegrating. She gripped the wheel with such force that the tendons in her wrist began to ache.

Keep it together, she commanded herself. She felt as though the car were driving itself. She prayed silently: that she would survive this; that she would learn the truth; that her little boy would be all right.

She remembered Carlo's flu, his strange temperature fluctuations, his lassitude. The thought fired her with anger. She pressed gently on the accelerator, daring just a bit more speed. A Mercedes with diplomatic plates veered into her lane. She slowed, almost smashing its rear bumper. It darted into the next lane, then disappeared onto an exit ramp.

She had to get off this crawling expressway. If she could reach the surface streets she could get turned around somehow. An exit ramp materialized to her right. She tried to read the sign, but it passed overhead too quickly. Deciding this was her chance, Laura jerked the wheel and found the next lane and took the ramp. She slowly wound through a long curve that seemed to lead her in the direction she had come. She couldn't be sure; her sense of direction felt unreliable.

On the surface streets traffic was both chaotic and achingly slow. Laura drove through a strange tangle of streets. Office buildings appeared to either side. *Maintain your sense of direction,* she told herself. *Turn around somehow.*

She passed a copse of trees and saw, rising in the gap between two office buildings, the high ivory dome of the Capitol. She saw no place to turn around.

The next block was virtually impassable. The sidewalks and crosswalks were strewn with pedestrians: tourists in casual wear, serious-looking men and women in business suits. To accommodate them traffic came to a halt. Laura glanced at a sign and saw this was Independence Avenue. She was but a couple of blocks from the Capitol.

Laura grabbed the map from the passenger's seat. She had the sensation that she was moving deeper and deeper into an inexorable mess. In her confusion she must have missed numerous opportunities to turn around. It was as though she was being absorbed into the human and mechanical traffic; she felt as though she were being eaten alive.

A flash went through her mind like a thunderbolt. Eaten alive. She saw grotesque mental images of bodies, autopsies, surgery, open anatomy. She was a surgeon, familiar with the human body. This wave of revulsion was inexplicable.

"Need to escape," she hissed. Her field of vision broke down into a kaleidoscope of colors and movement. Sounds were amplified and distorted. She could no longer find her place on the road or feel the car. The very foundation of her world had begun to disintegrate.

She had to get out of this place. Only Neil could make this stop.

Her vision cleared a degree and she saw an open lane straight ahead. She stamped down hard on the accelerator. The car moaned and surged forward. Even through the miasma of her disorientation, Laura recognized the sound of metal impacting upon metal and felt herself slam forward into the steering wheel. After a moment she heard yelling. A throb of deep pain radiated from her forehead and shoulder.

Laura staggered from her car, grabbing her purse as an afterthought. This wouldn't do. She might be delayed for hours.

She walked ahead, willing her eyes to stay focused. Just ahead of her was a large Cadillac, its back end folded inward. Cars pulled around on all sides to pass them. A large bearded man in a suit emerged from the Cadillac.

"I'm sorry," Laura said as he walked around to inspect the back end of his car. His face fell when he saw the damage.

"Lady, you should be more careful," he said in a mournful voice. "You look banged up. Were you wearing your seat belt?"

"I'm a doctor," Laura said. She pulled her purse onto her shoulder, ignoring pincers. "All you all right, sir? Do you have any passengers?"

The man was tall and stout, with flushed skin and small dark eyes. He surprised Laura by smiling. "Don't worry about that," he said. "I'm alone, and I'm fine. That little compact can't do much to a Caddy."

"Then I have to leave," Laura said. "I don't have time to explain, but it's crucial that I go. I'll leave my number."

"No can do," the man said, his smile vanishing. "We

THE ETERNITY CURE • 341

have to call the cops from my portable phone—I'll need to collect insurance. Are you in some kind of trouble?''

''No it's nothing like that,'' Laura began. She suddenly felt worse. The disorientation had become more intense yet sporadic.

The man sensed Laura's vacillation. ''I'm sorry you're in a hurry,'' he said. ''I really am. But we simply have to take care of this.''

Laura saw a soft kindness in this man's face, which made it all the harder to do what she had to. She stepped back, looking around for a way out.

''Hey, come on,'' the man said in a pleading voice. He reached out for her. Laura felt a surge of adrenaline and pushed him away. She sprinted away from the accident toward the sidewalk. A car honked and squealed its brakes, nearly striking her.

''Come back here, goddammit!'' the portly man called out from behind her. More horns honked; Laura glanced back and saw that he had followed her partway into the street, blocking traffic.

She was wearing flat pump shoes with her suit; she knew she could run in them without falling. At first she ran slowly, looking back every few steps, but then she found her stride and pushed hard. She felt the tendons and muscles in her legs warm up and begin to work in harmony. The top half of her body felt strange and off kilter, as though its impact against the steering wheel had knocked something out of alignment. She checked her forehead for blood and found none.

People all around her on the sidewalk passed in a blur; she collided with shoulders and elbows as she passed them by. She reached a corner and turned, daring a glance back.

No one had followed. She could tell that people were staring at her, but no one had emerged from the crowd to grab her. She had outrun the man in the Cadillac, and there were no police around.

To her left was the long grassy area of the Mall, which led toward the Washington Monument and, she remembered, the White House. The police would be thicker there.

The moment of clarity she had just experienced vanished. It was as though something was tearing away at her psyche. This episode was the worst yet, and for a second she felt her sanity slipping away.

Thousands of people streamed all around. The traffic percolated and roared. Laura knew she needed something to shock her into awareness, and the throb in her shoulder and forehead weren't enough. She raised her hand to her mouth and bit into it as hard as she could. The sudden rush of pain was almost unbearably intense; she looked down and saw tooth marks on her hand in the shape of her uneven bite, along with discrete droplets of blood.

Laura looked up. People were watching. She feared that the man in the Cadillac would have called the police by now and told them in which direction she had run. She would be arrested if she were caught. Instead of letting her thoughts drift, she concentrated on the pain her hand, feeling every throb and pulse. The discomfort enabled her to keep her senses long enough to jog quickly down another crowded block.

She realized she had doubled back onto Independence Avenue—albeit blocks farther than she had left it. She looked up at a building across the street: The Department of Housing and Urban Development. Behind it, now seen from another angle, was the Capitol dome. She was getting too close to an area where there would be senators and congressmen, where security would be heavy and the police on the alert. She looked down at her hand, which was bleeding onto the sheer fabric sleeve of her blouse. She was sure to attract attention.

As though in answer to a prayer she hadn't voiced, Laura suddenly felt her faculties slip back into complete normality. She might have expected some sort of audible click in her head, but there was nothing of the kind—just regular, unhindered ordinary consciousness.

"This is a disaster," she said. She stood there, buildings all around, traffic, people, the air cool and crisp with an early autumn breeze. She thought about all that she had just done. It was amazing she hadn't killed herself driving or, even worse, killed someone else.

But she was alive, and she was free to save herself. It was time to take advantage of the opportunity.

Laura jogged to the corner, keeping her wounded hand close to her body. The police had yet to spot her in the crush of humanity. Nearly a block away she saw the roof-top lights of a police cruiser. But its lights didn't flare, and the car pulled off in the opposite direction.

She was behaving normally now; no one was staring. A half block ahead she spotted a taxi and ran toward it. When it stopped for a red light, she opened the door and dived inside, not bothering to ask if it was free.

The driver turned angrily around. He wore a knit cap and had a wizened, leathery face. "You cannot do that," he said in a Russian accent. "I am on my way to pick up a fare. You have to get out."

Laura reached into her purse and flashed her hospital identification. "I'm a doctor," she said, glancing out the back window. "It's a medical emergency."

The driver remained turned around to face her, even when the light turned green and traffic started to course forward. His eyes were blank and weary, and he didn't seem to know what to do.

"Just go!" Laura yelled. A police car drove by, then slowed down ahead of them. "Please. Just start driving."

He gave a grunt of displeasure but put the car in gear. "Where do you need to go?" he asked, his eyes on the road. "You have blood on you. Do you need to go to a hospital?"

Laura fished through her bag until she found a slip of paper with Neil's address. "Here," she said. "Less than ten miles. I'll pay a big tip if we can get there quickly."

The driver took the paper. Laura sighed and slipped back into her seat with relief when the driver gathered speed. She nearly cried with joy when they crossed the Potomac. She had escaped, and her mind was whole again.

45

4:12 p.m.

NEIL REYNOLDS UNDERSTOOD THAT HE HAD SERIOUSLY MIS-calculated. Manipulating the nanorobots within Laura and Carlo had taken too much out of him. His mind was rapidly deteriorating, and he wasn't sure he still had time to save himself.

He had been able to terminate the intellectual manipulation he had initialized within Laura. She might have felt some slight discomfort or disorientation, but it would all be over now. The small lesions within her brain tissue would heal of their own accord, leaving no trace of his work save for the microrobot that had folded upon itself and now lay harmless and dormant.

He walked across the carpeted expanse of his living room, surrounded by the computers, processors, the communications gear. The workstation he used to manipulate the nanorobots was idle near the tall windows. He wasn't sure he could remember how to work it.

Reynolds walked past a mirror; his face was pale, his eyes ringed in violet. His shirt was wrinkled and soaked with sweat. His hair clung to his forehead. The sight of his own eyes compelled him to look away. They were cloudy and vacant, like the fog that had enveloped his thinking. They were eyes that seemed barely human.

He reeled across the room and bumped into a table housing three of his vital black-cased computer processors. They hummed on, rocking gently from the impact of his body. Each step he took felt as though it passed through thick mud. What had once been a headache was now a piercing jolt of agony throughout his entire cranium, as though numerous ice picks had been shoved inside it at random.

"Think," he whispered. He had to reverse the process. He would first sever the connections to the storage units he had implanted into his cerebellum. This would stop the overflow of data and information. He had no idea what effect this would have—it was, in effect, akin to unplugging the memory of a computer. But he was no computer, he was a man, and he now wanted only the intellectual capacity he had been born with.

He touched the control pad that would direct the actions of the robot inside him, trying to visualize his own anatomy. He had done this so many times, but now it was difficult to remember how it all worked. His consciousness was flooded with ideas that weren't solid enough to call complete thoughts—rather, they were half-understood impressions, emotions without context, images without meaning.

With a series of labored keystrokes Reynolds activated the communications sequence that would grant him access to the robot. Normally he would have performed this aspect of the procedure within virtual reality, but he had spent too much time that afternoon in the nether world of virtual space. Given his delicate condition, he needed to minimize the time he spent in that altered state.

The processor initiated the connection. Reynolds closed

his eyes, imagining the invisible link between this computer and his brain. He had invented this, how could he forget how it worked?

He heard a sound behind him but registered it as nothing more than part of the tumult overtaking him. The computer emitted an electronic pulse. The connection had been forged. There might yet be time for his salvation.

"Neil," said a voice from behind him.

LAURA HAD SPENT THE RIDE INTO THE VIRGINIA SUBURBS IN constant fear that her symptoms would return, but they didn't. She had watched the terrain passing by, and thought about what she was going to say to Neil when she found him.

No vision she might have conceived could have prepared her for what she found. Neil's house was an innocuous place on a quiet residential street, the property ringed with greenery and surrounded by a crimson-stained split-rail fence. She had rung the doorbell and there had been no answer. When she tried the door, it was unlocked. After a deep breath and a prayer, she had let herself inside.

At first she saw only his back. She could see that his shirt was soaked with sweat, even from the entryway. His living room was filled with innumerable exotic devices and computers. He seemed immobile, leaning heavily on an unidentifiable steel-and-plastic machine, talking to himself in a low, deep voice.

He turned to face her. His countenance was ghoulish; it looked as if it were composed of some synthetic substance, rather than skin

"Laura," he rasped. "Are you really here?"

She took a step toward him, then stopped. All this equipment—her suspicions must have been true. "It's me,

Neil,'' she said. "What are you doing? What's the matter with you?''

He stepped away from his equipment unsteadily. "There's so much to explain, Laura, but I have to perform a final task before we speak. You have to understand—''

Laura felt as though all the strain of the past few days—all the fear and uncertainty—had hit her at once. She felt a violent rage well up from within her.

"I *want* to understand!'' she screamed. Neil winced. "Explain to me what's happened. What have you done to me? What did you allow to happen to those patients at my hospital? What the hell have you done to my son?''

She circled him as she spoke, moving through the maze of technological equipment. It was obvious something was wrong with him, but she attributed his appearance to the fear and shame he felt at having been discovered.

"I just came from your laboratory,'' she said. "There's a federal agent there poking around your office. What horrible thing have you done, Neil? Tell me!''

She stopped her circuit and stood just feet away from him. Her breath escaped her lungs in spasmodic bursts. Neil wiped his dry mouth with the back of his hand before he spoke.

"A federal agent?'' he asked.

Laura stepped closer. "This isn't about what happens to you, Neil,'' she said. "Right now, you have to answer to me.''

Neil's head rocked back on his neck and snapped forward, as though he had almost fallen asleep. "You're absolutely right,'' he said. "It's just that the timing—you see, I have to—''

He must have seen something in her eyes; instead of continuing on his rambling path he started talking in a flat, concentrated monotone.

"Less than a year ago I developed a new way of applying principles of nanotechnology," he said. "Two things happened at once. I was able to reach a level of energy efficiency that enabled me to power devices independently for indefinite periods of time. I also developed a way to create an implant within the human brain that enhanced synaptic potential."

As he spoke, Neil sat down heavily on a sturdy wooden table replete with computer monitors. Laura listened to him closely, realizing that, in his own obscure way, he was trying to explain himself to her.

"I knew that the possibilities of this treatment were phenomenal," he said. "I theorized that I could enhance a human brain's storage capacity on a scale that could change the entire nature of our species."

Laura found herself pacing around Neil again. Suddenly she understood a small part of what had happened.

"You did this to yourself?" she asked.

"And it worked," he said. "But now—"

"You did this to me?" she asked, knowing intuitively that it was so. She felt a wave of revulsion, toward Neil, toward the monstrosity within her. "You did this to me without my knowledge? How did you even put one of those *things*—"

"I pricked your neck with an ultrafine needle the night I came to Los Angeles," he said simply. "That was how I did it."

"The night—" Laura began. "The night we made love?"

"It was a gift," Neil said. He stared down at the floor, his body gently rocking. "My gift to you."

The rage within her returned. She looked around the room. She wanted to smash all that damned equipment, destroy it all, raze this house to the ground. She slapped Neil across the face.

He straightened. "I did it because I love you," he said.

"And I thought I loved you." She laughed bitterly.

"Don't—" Neil began. His waxen face flushed; his eyes welled with tears. "You can't understand what I've been through. My entire being changed, Laura. I lived in a plane of existence I never imagined. The clarity, the breakthroughs—but it wasn't the way I thought it would be."

She turned away from him. Though she seethed with hatred toward him, the sight of his tears was nearly enough to make her cry as well.

"My life changed when I met you and Carlo," he said. "I want nothing more in the world than to be with you, to be your husband, to be a father for Carlo. I want to give you everything you deserve."

"Then why did you tamper with my mind?" she screamed, turning around and pressing her face inches from his. She could stand his tears now. "How dare you? I thought I was going mad. God knows what you've done to me—the long-term effects could be fatal!"

"No, no, I stopped it," Neil said. "It's over. The process is imperfect, so an hour ago I halted it permanently. You've returned to normal."

An hour ago? Laura paused. That awful attack, the episode near the Capitol—it had been the result of Neil's experiment.

"It was a gift," he said again. His face looked awful, streaked with tears, his eyes wandering. "A gift for all three of us."

Laura felt as though time had become suspended. The words he had spoken hung between them. Without realizing what she was doing, she grabbed the lapels of Neil's shirt and squeezed.

"Tell me what you're talking about, right now, or I swear I'll kill you," she whispered. "What did you do to my son?"

"When my mind became enhanced, doors started opening in my research in rapid succession." He looked into her eyes, imploring. "I streamlined the nanorobots. At first they were automations, but then I learned to control them through my own eyes and hands."

She tightened her hold on his neck, unsure what she might do.

"It was then that I made my ultimate breakthrough." His eyes were full of fear, but she could hear pride in his voice. "I uncovered the secrets of the cell membrane, and soon found a way to alter the telomere within DNA—and with it the genetic controllers of cellular breakdown and aging. I found a way of altering the code on a genetic level. It all happened so fast. I wasn't sure what it all meant. But I did it, Laura."

She loosened her hold on his neck. A wave of nausea enveloped her.

"The Holy Grail," he said. "Immortality."

Laura released him and stepped away. She bumped into a cart bearing a wire-laden plastic device that hummed with power. "Are you saying—"

"I did it, Laura," Neil said. His face was animated with excitement. To her he looked like a monster. "I did it for the three of us. For the family we can become. Forever."

She turned away from him, but he kept talking. "There were three variations on the essential theory. I was compelled to use a different one for each of us—as a control study—but in my estimation they should all work. All three of us will be modern Methuselahs."

Laura felt her face contort as her emotions reeled

through a series of reactions. There was no way to respond to this madness.

"Any significance to the telomere is just a theory," she said. "We don't know if it's the key to aging and death."

"I know the key," Neil said. "I found the truth."

All of her rage was spent. She could only think of her son at home, the victim of this man she had nearly brought into their family. "How dare you tamper with our lives," she said in a hollow voice.

Neil put his hand on her arm. "I just noticed—you're injured," he said, his voice slurred. "There's blood on you."

"How dare you," she repeated. "You played God with our bodies."

"I had to share it," Neil said. He put his arms around her. "My love for you is the most genuine thing I have ever felt. I did this for us, so that we could be together. Time will have no meaning for us anymore. Just think of all the things we'll see."

Laura pressed her face into his chest, trying to will it all away. She believed him. She knew that his affection for her had been real all along. But she also hated him now. He was a killer, she was sure of it. The thought rekindled her anger.

It was too much to forgive. "You've made us into monsters," she said and pulled away.

He seemed to barely register what she had said. "What in the world is wrong with you?" she shouted. She slapped him for the second time.

"Who else had to pay for your experiments?" she yelled. "Who, besides me and Carlo?"

She slapped him again. "Damn you! You murderer!"

He seemed stunned. "You can't know about—"

"You left a trail!" she screamed at him. "Those

damned robots burrowed into the patients' bodies and stayed there. They were found during autopsy.''

Neil's lips moved without sound. Finally, he said, ''But the devices undergo a terminal process when I'm done with them. They become unrecognizable.''

''I figured it out,'' she said. ''I even let myself believe that Faber stole your technology, that you didn't know about it, but I know it was you. You killed his high-cost patients for him, didn't you? He saved a few dollars, and you got a few guinea pigs. That's what happened, isn't it?''

Neil didn't reply.

''Well, why didn't you expand their intellects or cure their illnesses? Why didn't you give them eternal life, or whatever the hell is going to happen to us?''

She tried to strike him again, but her strength was gone. ''Weren't they good enough?'' she raged. ''Didn't they deserve your gift?''

''Faber and I . . .'' Neil began. He looked away, apparently ashamed. ''There were other considerations.''

''You call yourself a doctor,'' Laura said. ''You're sick! You're nothing but a megalomaniac.''

''I had to make choices.''

''Those choices aren't yours to make! You don't decide who to treat, who is worth saving and who isn't. You don't kill people because they're costing too much money or because they help your research! You bastard!''

By now her anger was spent; the crimes he had perpetrated against the patients, and against her and Carlo, were of such a scale that they numbed her. She felt an endless bitterness. It was all ruined. She had been foolish to even fantasize that Neil might have been innocent, given all she had deduced before she came there.

''I regret what I did,'' Neil said.

''What's wrong—what's happening to you?'' Laura

asked. Neil's eyes had become glassy; his gaze was locked and frozen. It looked as though he was about to go into some sort of shock.

"I tried to explain when you came in. The process that I halted in you is still active in me. I have to stop it. It's . . . it's hurting me."

"But you have all the equipment here. Why haven't you stopped it?"

Before she finished speaking, she knew the answer.

"You and Carlo will be fine," he said. In his eyes she saw love and caring. "I made sure of it. My cellular procedure has to work—the three techniques were different but similar. We will all live for a very long time. But if it doesn't work, there will be no damage. I'm sure of it."

"How can you know?" she asked. She saw his gaze locking again and snapped her fingers in front of his face. "Neil, you have to heal yourself. I can't forgive you, but I don't want you to die. Let me help."

He took her hand. "I know what I've done has been terrible," he said. "But you have to believe that I love you."

"I believe you, Neil," she said. And she did.

"This is really touching, and I hate to interrupt you two," said a voice from the doorway. "But before you save your ass you and I have to have a conversation."

Neil and Laura turned. In the doorway, holding a gun, was a muscular, intense-looking African-American woman. Her eyes were fiery with rage and terror.

46

6:03 p.m.

THE LIGHT IN NEIL REYNOLDS'S HOUSE HAD SHIFTED; EARlier the sun had streamed through the glass ceiling panes above, but now there was a smoky stillness to the place. Laura heard Neil stumble behind her; his movement made the woman in the doorway pivot to point the gun at him.

Neil had fallen back onto a chair behind his equipment. His head rolled back and his eyes closed.

"Who are you?" Laura asked the woman. She looked closer at her. "Wait—I recognize you. You were with Faber at the basketball game. What do you want with us?"

"I'm an associate of the colonel's," the woman said, keeping the gun aimed at Neil. "I was listening to what he said to you. You're not buying any of that bullshit, are you?"

Laura felt frozen at the sight of the pistol, unable to answer. The woman had materialized apparently from thin air. Laura watched her attractive features pulse with tension and her intelligent eyes darting around the room.

"My name is Laura Antonelli. Whatever's going on here, I'm sure we can—"

The woman held up her hand for silence and looked at Laura with a strangely compassionate expression. "My name is Jeanette Madison," she said. She took a step toward Neil. "The colonel and I have some business between us. I won't hurt you if you stay out of my way."

Madison stepped out of sight into the entryway. Laura knew instinctively that this was her chance to subdue this intruder. She looked around the room for something she might be able to use as a cudgel or projectile, but the place had been cleared out. All that was in her reach were pieces of heavy computer equipment.

Madison returned, toting a black leather valise. Her free hand still holding the gun, she edged around a bank of computer processors and stalked toward Neil.

Laura took advantage of Madison's diverted attention to look around the clutter of equipment on the wide metal table nearest her. There were monitors and processors, but little of use: a tape recorder, two bound volumes of printouts, a set of metal boxes with the lids clamped shut. Laura tried to calculate whether she could hit Madison if she threw one of the boxes at her—and whether she could grab the gun in the moment of distraction she would have created.

"What's wrong with you, Reynolds?" Madison asked. Neil was leaning forward in his chair, his chin nearly touching his chest. Madison gently kicked his shin. "Wake up. We need to talk."

Neil lifted his head with a groan. He looked around the room until he found Laura. His eyes seemed lost, his features sagging and depersonalized. Laura edged closer to the boxes.

"Jeanette Madison," Neil said in a thick voice, turning to face her. "I can't believe you're here."

Madison pointed the gun at Neil's face, reached into her

bag's side pocket, and produced a small plastic device. From it she pulled out a collapsible antenna with her teeth.

"You'd better believe it," she said. "You've taken out everyone else, but not me. Why? What are you waiting for?"

Neil was silent for half a minute. With an air of resignation he finally said, "I have no problem with you, Madison. Let's agree to leave each other alone."

"Don't," Madison said. "Don't even try to make a fool out of me."

Laura edged closer to the table, bumping into a stand containing a wire-riddled telecommunications box. The device rattled loudly; Madison turned around and pointed the gun at Laura.

Madison was perhaps ten feet away. Laura had heard the cliché: the barrel of a loaded gun looked like the mouth of a cannon when it was pointed at you. It was absolutely true.

"Don't mess around," Madison said. "I heard what he told you. You're one of his victims. Don't force me to hurt you."

"Listen, Jeanette," Laura said. She wasn't sure what to say; Madison looked as though she wouldn't hesitate to fire the gun. "There's no need for this. Can't you see Neil is sick? He's not dangerous to anyone anymore."

"Is that right?" Madison said mockingly. "He put an electronic bug in your head. Do you call that harmless?"

Madison waited for a reply. "No, what he did was terribly wrong," Laura said. "I hate the damned thing and I want it out of me. But it's over now, Jeanette. Neil is having complications from his procedures. He needs immediate medical assistance."

Madison frowned at Laura reproachfully. Laura edged closer to the table, trying to keep Madison's eyes locked on hers.

"He didn't tell you everything, honey," Madison said. "He didn't tell you he was trading plutonium with Iran, did he? That bug in your head was paid for with nuclear bombs. Does it make you feel any differently?"

Laura stopped moving. "Neil, what is she talking about?"

Neil covered his mouth with his hands. His eyes were half closed; Laura realized that he was slipping away.

"He's not going to answer you," Madison said. "He doesn't want you to know about how he helped create an organization with Jefferson Faber and Senator Bob Chapman to turn a profit while they gambled with the fate of the world."

"Were you involved in this too?" Laura asked Madison. Laura was close enough to the table now to rest her hand upon it.

"I was," Madison said. "For the money. But at least I wasn't wearing the uniform of a United States colonel while I was committing treason."

In an instant everything came together in Laura's mind. Cyrus had died just after the Americans were captured in Iran. Because he was involved in the plan and might have exposed Neil and the other conspirators.

"Cyrus," Laura said. "You killed Cyrus Tafreshi, didn't you? He was my friend, and you—"

Neil averted his contorted face. Laura wasn't even sure how much he had understood of what she was saying.

"You're getting the picture now," Madison said. She smiled with grim satisfaction. "I didn't know about those hospital patients until he told you just now. Jefferson was evil to be involved with that, but Reynolds is even worse. He's killed everyone who stood in his way, all for the sake of that nonsense he tried to sell you on."

"And now," Laura said, "you think he wants to get rid of you?"

"You're slow, but you catch on," Madison said.

Laura by now had her hand on one of the metal boxes. She shifted it slightly on the table, trying to gauge its weight. It was heavier than she'd thought it would be, maybe fifteen pounds.

"Reynolds, tell me," Madison said. She had to crouch to meet Neil's eyes. "Did you plant one of those things inside me?"

Neil looked up. For the moment he seemed lucid. "I have to get to my computers," he whispered. "What's happening to me will be irreversible. I'm going to lose my mind forever."

Madison pressed the gun into Neil's forehead. "You didn't answer me. Did you put one of those things in me? If you did, just let me know right now. You might even get to walk away from here."

"Please let me get to my equipment," Neil said. His jaw worked some more, but no words came from his mouth.

"Answer me!" Madison screamed. Her voice echoed on the high ceiling. "Do I have one of those fucking things inside me?"

Neil shook his head weakly. "No," he said. "No. I never had the chance. I never planted anything on you."

Madison pushed against Neil's head with the gun. "I don't believe you," she announced.

"Jeanette, he's telling the truth," Laura said. "Can't you see that? Listen to him—if you don't allow him to stop the process, he's going to be permanently brain damaged."

Madison glanced at Neil with contempt. "It's all an act."

"It isn't an act. Just look at him," Laura said. She

curled her finger around the metal box. The moment had come.

Madison took a step in the direction of the kitchen. "You see, this is the problem," she said in an analytical tone. "He says he didn't plant one of his murder machines inside me. He could be lying. Assuming he *is* lying, I need him to access the device and dismantle it—otherwise, I'll never know when he might decide to have it kill me."

"You're safe. I'm telling you, I never planted one on you," Neil said. Laura was surprised; she hadn't been sure if he was listening.

"I can't trust you," Madison said. "And if your brain turns to jelly—so what?"

Madison slapped the side of her head. "But if you're a vegetable, then you can't get this thing out of me. You might have it on a timed program, set up to kill me at some point in the future."

"There's nothing there to harm you," Neil said weakly. Tears streamed from his eyes.

"Shit," Madison said. "Stalemate."

This was it. Madison wasn't looking at Laura, and Laura was now able to grasp the metal box. She calculated the trajectory in her mind. It would have to be a perfect throw, but she could do it. *Just like little league,* she thought, *just one strike on a full count. I can do it.*

"I guess it's time to tell you about this," Madison said. She looked at the small plastic device in her hand as though she had forgotten it was there.

Laura paused, just for a second.

"This is a detonator," Madison said. "Inside that bag over there is several pounds of plastic explosives. If I press this button, we go together. I'm starting to think it's our only option."

Madison's finger rested on the detonator. Laura let go of

the box. For all she knew, this could be a bluff. But if she struck Madison, the explosives might go off. Thinking of Carlo, Laura knew now that she had only one goal: to get out of the house alive.

"Tell me I'm wrong," Madison said to Neil. "I'm looking for an option here, but I don't see one."

"You're completely safe," Neil said. He stiffened in the chair, seeming, to Laura, as though he had marshaled his will for one final stretch of lucidity.

"How can I believe you?" Madison asked. "I know all about these robots now—they're tiny, almost too small to see. How can you prove you never put one in me?"

Madison turned to Laura. "You're free to go," she said.

Laura was stunned.

"Did you hear me?" Madison said, irritated. "Get out of here. You seem like a decent woman. I don't want to see you get hurt over this asshole."

"I can't," Laura said, surprising herself.

"I heard you talking to Reynolds," Madison reminded her. "You have a son. You have something to live for. Get out now. I won't give you another chance."

Madison was right. But Neil was fading away. Perhaps it was already too late to save him, but she could never live with herself if she walked out on him.

"You must have something to live for too," Laura said.

Madison cocked her head, as though unsure she had heard Laura properly. "I did, once," she said. "But that's gone. It's all been taken away from me."

"What do you mean?" Laura asked. "A child? A husband?"

Madison blinked, just once. "Your husband?" Laura asked. "Believe me, I understand. My husband died after we were divorced. He was the father of my only child, and he was gone forever. But I learned that you have to go on, Jeanette. You have to be strong.''

Laura had no idea where she was leading with this, but for the moment her stream of consciousness was having the desired effect. Madison lowered the gun a few inches and her finger loosened on the button.

''I don't mean to be rude,'' Madison said, ''but you have no idea what you're talking about. My husband was a good man. And he was killed over politics, beaten down by the government.''

''No, I don't understand your life,'' Laura said. ''But my husband was executed overseas—over a drug crime I'm not even sure he committed. I know the helplessness and the anger.''

As Laura spoke, Madison's eyes filled with a light of recognition. Neil gripped the arms of his chair; the wood frame creaked. ''Enough,'' he cried. ''Just get out of here, Madison. Leave us both alone.''

''Wait a minute,'' Madison said. ''Your husband was executed? Where?''

''Saudi Arabia,'' Laura said. ''He was there on an international medical team and he was accused of drug possession. That's a capital offense there.''

Neil tried to stand up but his arms slipped on the chair. ''Leave us be,'' he said to Madison. ''I did nothing to you. Just get—''

Madison turned around and pointed the gun at Neil. ''Did you hear what she said?'' she asked.

Neil covered his face with both hands.

''This is too good to be a coincidence,'' Madison said to him. ''Man, I had no idea about you. You're a real killer, aren't you? What you did to this woman is the coldest thing I ever heard of in my life.''

''What does she mean?'' Laura asked. She stepped

away from the table, away from the metal boxes. Above her, through the skylight, the dimming sun passed behind a cloud.

"Your husband got in his way," Madison said. "They told me all about it. He saw something he wasn't supposed to see, then he was framed by Reynolds and Faber."

Laura felt a chill. "What is she saying, Neil?" she asked again. Neil's head was turned completely away from her.

"They had my people do it. I guess Reynolds couldn't get a robot inside the guy," Madison said. "We smuggled the stuff in from Turkey, planted it, then made a call. Maxwell was in the wrong place at the wrong time."

"Steve?" Laura said. "You had Steve killed?"

Madison looked at Laura with a strange sense of sympathy. "I'm sorry," she said. "It was just business for me. Your boyfriend here has ruined just about everything in your life. I wouldn't be surprised if he sought you out, knowing how vulnerable you would be."

Neil sprang from the chair as though he had been electrically shocked. "That's not true!" he yelled at Madison. "I didn't know. I didn't know until later, and then I wished it had never happened. Things were out of control, Laura."

Madison pointed the gun at Neil. "You see, this is our problem," she said. "This bastard. Do you think he was going to let you live, after everything he told you? He was probably going to wait a day, maybe two, maybe a year. But sooner or later he would have gotten rid of you, just like he killed everyone else who threatened him."

Laura was overcome by the certainty that everything Madison said was true. Cyrus. Steve. The patients at Valley Memorial. God knew who else.

"Jesus, Neil," Laura said in a hushed voice. "How could . . . how did you lose your humanity?"

Neil wobbled on his feet, his face contorted in a grimace of pain and remorse. "The research took over my life," he said. "But everything we shared was genuine. My love for you is real. I wanted nothing more than to share my gifts with you and Carlo."

Laura couldn't imagine the ravaging taking place in Neil's mind, but she was chilled to realize that she didn't care anymore what happened to him.

"Do you want to leave now?" Madison asked. "You can. One more chance."

Before Laura could answer, a muffled voice came through the walls of the living room. For a split second the place passed from dark, to light, then to dark again as the clouds amassed in the sky.

"A bullhorn," Madison said. Her eyes darted to the bag of explosives. "Go open the window over there, but keep the blinds closed. Don't present them with a target. Let's hear what they have to say."

47

JACK PARSONS WAS IN A BIND. A *REAL* BIND. IT WAS AMAZ-
ing how fast things could fall apart. He had received a
major pat on the back for spotting the trucks and gunmen
in the satellite photos. Then he had put forth the theory that
American paramilitary groups might have been involved.
Then he had followed up on the anonymous tip leading him
to Senator Chapman, where he was able to find a link to
Colonel Neil Reynolds. It had been top-notch investigative
work, and might have blown the lid off a scandal of incredible proportions.

Now it looked like Parsons might turn into the scape-
goat for a mess that was spinning out of control. All because he hadn't arrested Jeanette Madison. The problem,
he realized, was that he had played it by the book. A more
experienced and more cynical agent would have flown out
and arrested her late that morning, when the FBI made a
tentative ID from the missing journalist's photographs
linking her to the captured Americans. Surely there had
been minor weapons violations at that compound of hers.

Parsons leaned against his unmarked federal car. Everything was out of his hands. After word of Jefferson Faber's

death filtered back to the Agency, a check with FAA flight plans found that his private plane had flown on to Washington from Salt Lake City. But by then Madison had landed and disappeared. Her entrance into Reynolds's home had been seen only by a lone surveillance unit keeping tabs on Reynolds's place until Parsons could put together a warrant.

It hadn't taken long for the sidewalk in front of Reynolds's place to turn into a real block party—two vans full of heavily armed federal agents, half a dozen NSA agents, and Parsons's boss, Davis Stanton.

"They've been in there a long time," Stanton said to Stan Presley, the tactical officer. Presley and Stanton were both in their late forties. The tactical chief was slim and muscular; Stanton was fleshy and soft.

"Don't forget the doctor," Parsons said. "She's a civilian with no connection to any of this."

"Give me the word and we go in," Presley said. He had been dying for action ever since he had shown up.

Parsons shoved his hands in his pockets. "I've dealt with Jeanette Madison—" he began.

"We know that, Parsons," Stanton said. "We know it all too well. We wouldn't be standing out here with a potential hostage situation if you'd dealt with her the way you should have. Not to mention the fact that you let that Antonelli woman get away from Reynolds's lab this afternoon. She was so whacked out, she pulled a hit-and-run. I don't know what she's on, but witnesses said she was higher than hell."

Touché, Parsons thought. Leave it to Stanton to latch on to one mistake like a dog with a piece of meat. Throughout the entire investigation Stanton had been jockeying for position, dying to take all the credit for Parsons's work.

"Well, sir, that is probably true," Parsons said in a

measured voice. "But I know a bit about Madison, so I have something to contribute to this situation. Madison is highly intelligent, and her background indicates a paranoid distrust of the government. That being said, I have a hunch she's only violent when provoked."

"Give me a break," Presley said. "She's a nut case. She was seen going in there with a large bag. She flew on a private plane, so God knows what she brought with her from that base out in the desert."

"That doesn't mean she's going to do anything crazy," Parsons said. "We think we can link her to Reynolds. She might be a valuable witness if we handle this properly."

"I doubt it," Stanton said. He scratched his head. "Stan, get on the line and tell them we're out here, if they haven't noticed yet."

All three men stared at the innocuous suburban house with its curtains drawn. One of the agents a half block down was waving away a neighbor who had wandered out to see what was going on.

Presley dialed a number on his cellular phone, glancing down at a slip of paper to make sure it was correct. He dialed again, then hung up and collapsed the phone.

"Busy," he said.

"Then break through the line," Parsons suggested.

"Forget it," Stanton said. "Give me a bullhorn."

Presley looked at the two agents as though they were beneath his contempt, then fetched a bullhorn from one of the vans.

Stanton cleared his throat and fiddled with the speaking device until he figured out how it worked.

"Attention, Neil Reynolds, Jeanette Madison." Stanton's reedy voice echoed through the quiet street. "This is National Security Agent David Stanton. You are sur-

rounded by armed agents. Come out quietly, and turn your-
selves over to our custody immediately.''

Parsons stared at the house. No reaction. Stanton
frowned and repeated his message. This time Parsons saw
curtains stirring at the front of the house.

"WELL, IT'S FINALLY HAPPENED," MADISON SAID.

Laura waited in the kitchen doorway, her breath coming
in spasms that shook her shoulders. Neil's trail of death
was more horrific than she had even imagined, running
through the very center of her life. She understood that his
dizzying breakthroughs had driven him to commit atroci-
ties. By becoming more than human, he had become less
than human.

"Please, put down the gun and the explosives, Jeanette," Laura said. "Let's put an end to this right now."

Neil leaned heavily on a steel work table, his face turned
down toward the floor. He lurched slowly to his right, obviously losing his motor function. He seemed unaware of
what was happening around him, or unable to assign any
meaning to it.

"What about him?" Madison asked. "What about the
destruction he's responsible for?"

"Look at him," Laura said. She felt an urge to go to
Neil and help him somehow, but Madison stood in her
way. "He's already being punished. His own experiment is
destroying his mind."

Madison watched Neil for a moment, then pointed the
gun at him. "Well, let me finish the job," she said in a cold
voice.

Neil looked up at Madison with dim recognition. Laura
cried out, sure that she was about to witness Neil's murder.

Instead, Madison walked around the long bank of computers. She pointed the gun at the nearest processor and

fired. Its plastic case shattered, exposing a ruined mass of wires and parts amid a rain of sparks.

Neil flinched. "No!" he said in a throaty voice. "I . . . need that. I have to stop—"

His words were drowned out by the next shot, which shattered the thick block of communications hardware that had enabled Neil to communicate with the microrobots within his and Laura's bodies. Madison started firing faster, the automatic pistol raining destruction on the entire bank of computers and electronic links. Finally she fired several times into the VR workstation, reducing it to a ruined mess of splintered plastic parts.

Laura hadn't moved. When the firing finally stopped, she discovered that her ears were filled with a loud ringing and her nose with a thick odor of spent powder. The hulks of the machines spit out sparks as though going through death throes.

Madison stood in the center of the room, the pistol smoking. She gaped at the destruction she had caused.

Neil's eyes opened wide, as though in a final moment of comprehension he had seen his last hope vanish. "I can't—" he began, then stopped. He covered his face with his hands and let out a wail from somewhere deep in his soul.

Outside the agents tensed at the sound of the first shot. It was muffled, but the noise was unmistakable. In rapid succession came another volley, then another.

Then it was quiet.

"Oh, shit," Jack Parsons whispered.

By then the armed agents had moved in, surrounding the house from all sides. They prepared their assault.

IT WAS A STRANGE SENSATION; LAURA AND MADISON looked at each other, equally startled. First came a bump from outside the wall, then a feeling that they weren't alone, an almost animallike apprehension of being hunted.

Laura felt as though she stood at a rare nexus in her existence. Along with the computers had gone Neil's mind, and with his mind the possibility that she could reverse the processes implemented within her and Carlo. She and Neil had forever lost any hope of returning to normal, at the hands of a very frightened and cornered Jeanette Madison.

"Get out of here," Madison said to Laura. "Get out now. I won't let myself be arrested."

Laura walked in a slow semicircle around Madison, keeping her eye fixed on the explosives detonator. Madison moved her finger close to the ignition button.

"Let me take him with me," Laura said.

"No," Madison said. "You go alone. Think of your boy."

"Think of yourself," Laura said. "You have reasons to live."

"I should be the one saying that to you," Madison said. "Aren't you curious about what he did to you? Don't you want to see how long you're going to live? You'll never find out if you let yourself get blown up."

Laura and Madison looked into each other's eyes. Laura knew that, in another place and time, she and Madison might have been friends. But that place and time would never exist.

Laura slid past Madison and hurled her body into Neil's. He offered no resistance, falling to the floor with a heavy exhalation.

She had seen where Madison had placed the explosives, near the front door. That was perhaps twenty feet away, a distance bridged by chairs and heavy tables. She had no idea how powerful the explosives were. Perhaps nothing was going to save them.

In the instant this thought passed through Laura's mind, she grabbed a heavy steel table and pulled at its edge, hoping to create a shield between them and Madison. The table teetered, then rocked back to its upright position.

"Damn you, you idiot!" Madison yelled. Through her damaged ears Laura heard the sharp crack of the gun. A starburst of pain erupted in her side.

Laura pulled at the table again, this time with the strength of desperation. The table fell across Laura's line of vision, blocking out the sight of Madison pointing the pistol at her and Neil. Through the table she felt the dulled impact of another bullet.

Madison was perhaps ten feet away. She had only to walk up, lean over the table, and shoot them both. Laura braced herself, pulling Neil's head tight to her chest. He was mumbling but wasn't forming words.

Death didn't come. Laura lived through what seemed an eternity of anticipation, thinking that Madison had delayed shooting them out of some sadistic impulse. Then Laura heard the heavy thud of battering against the front door. Madison cursed, and Laura heard scuffling across the carpeted floor.

Laura grabbed Neil's face and held it up to hers. To her surprise Neil's eyes focused.

"I'm sorry for you," Laura said. "I hate everything you've done, but I'm sorry this happened. Maybe we can—"

Neil raised his finger to her lips. "It's done," he whispered. "Just remember, always, that I loved you. You have to try to understand. You helped me find what humanity I had left. I'm sorry if I hurt you. I lost my mind . . . it was terrible."

"Stop," Laura said. The sounds grew louder; Laura heard the creak of wood splintering.

"But I have bestowed my gift," Neil said, insistent. "All for you. My greatest gift."

Laura tucked herself against the table, pulling Neil close to her. Her heart beat wildly.

"To live forever," Neil said in a voice that sounded unlike his own.

Dying beams of sun shone down through the skylight, illuminating the wreckage and disarray of the room.

There was a loud smash from the front of the house, followed by men shouting. Laura heard Madison scream out someone's name—she couldn't tell who. There was a deafening noise, then a feeling of being pushed. Then there was no sound, no sight, nothing.

Epilogue

May 20, 2047. Los Angeles.

BEHIND THE GATES OF THE PINE VIEW CEMETERY, TREES undulated in the gentle afternoon breeze. Rolling lawns receded into the distance, their green hue maintained by sprinklers that could be heard gently hissing like whispered voices.

A long line of cars had passed through the cemetery gates. The mourners had ridden together from St. Peter's, where a service had been held for Dr. Laura Antonelli. More than a hundred people had come for the memorial: friends, colleagues, and former patients had all stood before the congregation and offered remembrances and anecdotes.

Laura had been preceded in death by her second husband, who had died five years before. At the head of the mourners were the man and woman Laura had adopted as children in her early forties.

The priest—a short, intense man with whom Laura had worked establishing a free medical clinic following her retirement from surgical practice—watched silently as the casket was slowly lowered into the earth.

Laura Antonelli had been an unusual woman. Her involvement with the notorious Colonel Neil Reynolds in the waning years of the previous century seemed to have affected her in ways that were difficult to understand. She was a kind woman, dedicated to her profession and her family, but she had always had the air of a woman keeping a strange secret. There had been much public speculation about Reynolds's research, and she had been the only person left in the aftermath of his scandal who could have told the truth about what he had developed.

But she never did. Any attempt to wrest these secrets from her had always been met with silence and an immediate changing of the subject. The priest knew firsthand. He had been among the curious.

Stranger still had been her relationship with Carlo, her son from her first marriage. The priest had known Carlo, briefly, when the young man had graduated from college and visited his mother before moving to Europe. He had been a strange boy, reserved and secretive, with an almost otherworldly air about him. If the priest hadn't been mistaken, it had seemed that Carlo and his mother shared some kind of accord that they never shared with anyone else; Laura seemed uncharacteristically shy and guarded around her first son.

It was disappointing, that Carlo Antonelli had chosen not to return to America for his mother's funeral. The priest had sent mail to Carlo's last-known address, a post-office box in Lyons, France, but had never received a reply. It was always a tragedy when a child and a parent were rent beyond reconciliation.

The priest began speaking, the words coming automatically.

He looked across the open grave, past Laura's adopted children, past the staff from the free clinic, past Laura's extended family and young grandchildren. There was a man in the back of the crowd, in a fine suit and wide-brimmed hat. When he saw that the priest was staring at him, he turned on his heels and began walking slowly away.

As the priest allowed a handful of earth to sift through his fingers, he realized he had recognized that face.

But it was impossible. Carlo Antonelli would be almost fifty years old by then.

The man he had seen couldn't have been a day older than twenty.

"MAN, YOU JUST CAN'T STAY OUT OF THE NEWS, CAN YOU?"

John Silver wheeled the patient to the part of the room where the sunlight was strongest. He opened the window to allow in some fresh air.

"There you are, right in the obituary: 'Dr. Antonelli was injured in the explosion that destroyed the notes and inventions of Colonel Neil Reynolds, a medical researcher who was rumored to have made significant breakthroughs in miniaturized technology. Antonelli recovered, and was subsequently cleared of all involvement in the uranium scandal that led to the 1998 Vienna treaty sharply increasing safeguards against nuclear smuggling.' "

John tapped the newspaper against his knee. "Looks like people are always going to be talking about you. Hell, that was fifty years ago."

John had been working at the Veterans Administration Hospital in Orange County, California, for nearly five years. He had a better education than many of the other nurse-technicians, and so was often assigned to the facility's most demanding patients. Neil Reynolds wasn't among them, but the colonel had been one of John's first patients years before. John continued to visit Reynolds out of nostalgia, and perhaps pity.

"Well, don't worry, Colonel, it doesn't matter what people say about you," John added. "No man can judge another man. It doesn't even matter now what you did back in the nineties. We'll take good care of you here. You can count on that."

John opened the curtains all the way; the afternoon sun streamed into the room.

"I have to be going, Colonel," he said. "You have a good day."

John closed the door behind him, leaving the colonel alone. Perhaps John continued to visit Reynolds out of a sense of guilt. The man repulsed John, and frightened him. John was dedicated to his work, and having these feelings for a helpless patient was something he had difficulty coming to terms with.

The problem wasn't that Neil Reynolds had arrived at the hospital fifty years before as a semicatatonic madman, and that by the time John had met him, he had entered into a seemingly permanent state of waking coma.

It was that the man was ninety years old, and he looked like he was forty. It was bizarre.

IN HIS PRIVATE ROOM NEIL REYNOLDS STARED OUT ONTO THE hospital grounds. The day was alive with light, with birds singing in the trees outside his window and white clouds gently moving in the sky. Reynolds stared out upon it all, his mind closed forever.